HOUSEBOAT
PAUL SHADINGER

A MATT PRESTON NOVEL

Edited by Laurainne Beattie
Formatting by Kevin G. Summers
Cover design by Kevin G. Summers
Professional Photography by: Arisa Collective

DEDICATION

I dedicate this book to my wife Sandy who saw something in my writing I never saw. Thank you for your encouragement. Without her, this book would never have seen the light of day.

I also dedicate this book to my beloved little Cocker Spaniel, Buttons. (Blackjack, BJ) I miss her and I know she is waiting for me somewhere over the rainbow. My little one left quite a hole in my life which our subsequent Cockers have tried to fill.

Paul Shadinger
North Fort Myers, Florida
(2019)

PLEASE NOTE

Houseboat is a work of fiction. This means that all names, characters, places, organizations, companies, brands, clubs, businesses, streets and incidents are the product of the author's imagination, or are used fictitiously. Because this is a work of fiction, timelines and facts do not have to add up. Since this novel comes from my imagination, any resemblance to any actual events, locals, entities, or person, living or dead, is entirely coincidental.

If you continue to have issues with this novel, I would invite you to reread the first sentence of the first paragraph. Thank you.

Matt and I would like to thank you for your interest in this novel and invite you to read about Matt's other adventures and also leave a review (see the last page for suggestions of places create a review).

This is a re-write of the original *Houseboat*. The story in this novel is the same as the original but I have tried to tweak and improve the fluidity of my prose.

Regards...
Paul Shadinger
May 2019

ALSO BY PAUL SHADINGER

Fiction

Houseboat (2016)
Code Name: Crescent (2017)
The Gypsy Queen (2018)
Quick, Quick, Slow (2018)
Snooker's Legacy (2019)

A Matt Preston Novel

TABLE OF CONTENTS

CHAPTER ONE 1

CHAPTER TWO 7

CHAPTER THREE 15

CHAPTER FOUR..19

CHAPTER FIVE 29

CHAPTER SIX..35

CHAPTER SEVEN 45

CHAPTER EIGHT 51

CHAPTER NINE..59

CHAPTER TEN..65

CHAPTER ELEVEN..69

CHAPTER TWELVE 81

CHAPTER THIRTEEN 87

CHAPTER FOURTEEN..99

CHAPTER FIFTEEN 105

CHAPTER SIXTEEN..111

CHAPTER SEVENTEEN 117

CHAPTER EIGHTEEN..125

CHAPTER NINETEEN..133

CHAPTER TWENTY..149

CHAPTER TWENTY-ONE 161

CHAPTER TWENTY-TWO..171

CHAPTER TWENTY-THREE..179

CHAPTER TWENTY-FOUR..191

CHAPTER TWENTY-FIVE 197

CHAPTER TWENTY-SIX 213

CHAPTER TWENTY-SEVEN 221

CHAPTER TWENTY-EIGHT 233

CHAPTER TWENTY-NINE 241

CHAPTER THIRTY 251

CHAPTER THIRTY-ONE 257

CHAPTER THIRTY-TWO 267

CHAPTER THIRTY-THREE 277

CHAPTER THIRTY-FOUR 287

CHAPTER THIRTY-FIVE 299

CHAPTER THIRTY-SIX 309

CHAPTER THIRTY-SEVEN 317

EPILOGUE 329

CHAPTER ONE

November: 1999

I'm not a doom and gloom person, but all I hear lately is the world is ending. The fact is, I don't believe the world will end - yet. So, come on; give me a break!

I will admit, I have purchased an extra pound of coffee just in case. Let's be realistic, I mean, you can't be too careful, right?

The reason I remember the date this story started so well was because of the clamor of the media and how they were screaming the world was facing the end of time. Or at least the end of civilization, as we had known it so far. The year was 1999 and if you listened to certain people, many of them believed all computers would die a horrible death. Therefore, causing governments to topple, the economic systems of the world to end, and humanity would be reduced to savages.

Nightly newscasters told us that after midnight on December 31, 1999, our cars would not start anymore. Planes would fall out of the sky. Elevators will plummet. ATMs would cease to spit out cash and we'd all eventually live in caves again and hunt for food with spears and bows and arrows.

And the cause for all this doom and gloom; for these dire predictions would be the failure of the world's computers. Yes! ALL of the computers in the world would quit! Why? It would happen because coders had forgotten to incorporate the proper instructions, or some such thing when programs were first written, the ones which would enable computers to recognize any date after December 31, 1999. Since discovering this glitch news people told us since computers wouldn't be able to understand the year 2000, computers would fail and thus civilization, as we knew it, would come to a smashing end.

Doomsday!

The end of civilized mankind.

WHAT?

As I recall, my feelings were, "Come on, give me a break, there has to be a fix for this glitch, and it will get done!"

The other thing I remember about the end of 1999 was the miserable Fall weather that year. Reports issued in November said 1999 had seen the coldest and wettest September and October on record since they had kept track of weather information.

This story starts on a wet, Friday mid-November night in '99 and considering what was going on outside that night, it looked like November was trying hard to beat the cold wet record of the previous two months. Because of the computer problem, many people shared that feeling of doom and gloom and sadly it seemed to spread. As for the weather, it didn't seem to help dispel the somber mood of the times. I felt that since there wasn't a lot anyone could about it, the best thing to do was plan indoor activities and that's exactly what I'd been doing.

My main problem with the evening was that there were too many people in too small a kitchen, and this made it stifling hot. In addition, my chair felt more like stone than wood, and to make matters even worse, I felt like I'd been ridden hard and put away wet. My body was sore, and I was just plain raggedy-assed exhausted! The snack I had wolfed down just after midnight had become a lump sitting in my gut, trying to decide if it would move on or stay where it was and haunt me the rest of the night.

Sitting at the table, I thought to myself, "Thank God, dawn - and relief - was just around the corner."

My eyes felt like there was an entire desert of sand and grit trapped inside of them and with every blink I was positive my lids were scratching my poor eye surfaces beyond any possible repair. And then there was my mouth. That was the worst. My Lord, what a horrible taste! I know that taste. I've tasted it before. It's like the entire 6th Army division bivouacked for a fortnight in my mouth, latrine and all.

Carefully I forced my poor eyes shut for a moment, however I dared not shake my head to clear away the cobwebs for fear one of the other players would realize just how tired I was and then decide they were not ready to fold. To be honest, I really shouldn't complain too much since I was sitting here playing poker by my own choice.

Slowly opening my eyes, the room full of poker players gradually returned to focus, and I cast my gaze directly across the table at the large, flush-faced man in his early forties who kept fidgeting with his cards. Just an idle glance at his demeanor would tell you he was not having the best evening. Beads of perspiration popped out across his forehead and his thin blond hair lay flat and damp on top of his head. Deeply recessed in his puffy face his small, bloodshot blue eyes with the laugh wrinkles around them now made him appear tired and old.

What was once a crisply laundered, expensive white shirt was now damp and yellowed under his armpits, the collar stained and wilted with the tips curling up. He'd rolled the French cuffs up and I remembered earlier I'd watched

3

when he removed and placed the large gold cuff links into a coat pocket. At the start of the evening, his tailor-made expensive suit had draped well over his stout form, but now the jacket hung shapelessly from the back of his kitchen chair. His tie hung loosely around his neck and the knot had developed a greasy shine from being repeatedly fondled and tugged.

The man's pudgy hands betrayed a slight tremor when he held up his cards in front of his face. He continued chewing on his bottom lip for a few more seconds as he stared at the cards in his right hand. Plainly written on his face was anguish, making it clear he desperately wished he could alter the spots on those cards; obviously, I wasn't watching a good poker face. In his left hand, he held two poker chips he repeatedly kept nervously turning over. I watched as he finally swallowed hard, signaling to me that his mind was made up. He sighed heavily and then pushed the rest of his money into the pot.

My best friend Scott stared at the pile of money the heavyset player had just moved to the middle of the table. Staring at the money, Scott tugged lightly at his dark blond beard. Finally, he slowly lifted his gaze from the table and peered over the tops of his glasses, looking into the other man's eyes. Scott waited for the stout player's eyes to shift away and then back down at the table. Scott's voice was soft and low as he admonished, "Wheeler, it looks like you're still light... let's say at least five grand light."

The man called Wheeler looked up quickly and searched each face around the table; hoping in vain for an ally. Several seconds passed without a word from anyone while he licked his full lips. Finally, he whined, "Yeah, yeah... I know... but... can I owe the table? Huh?" Several heads shook back and forth, even those who were no longer involved in this hand, but Wheeler continued his plea, "I got the cards this time, just let me finish. Give me the credit

4

guys, please. Come on, give me a break… you all know I'm good for it. Please…" His voice trailed off.

Everyone at the table moved their heads negatively in unison. Scott verbalized the other players' feelings, "Wheeler, please don't do this to us. You know the game is table stakes only. The rules have never changed. There are no IOUs allowed. If you have no more money, you're finished. You wouldn't let any of the rest of us owe the table," Scott paused and then continued, "Would you?"

Wheeler's gaze returned to the table in front of him and Scott waited for the man to look up. When he did, Scott added softly, "Wheel, I'm sorry, but you know the rules."

Wheeler sat quietly. Once more Scott admonished, "Wheel, if it was someone else, you know you wouldn't do it." Silence filled the room, everyone waiting for something to happen until Scott asked again, "Right?" Scott would not back down and again he asked, "Wheel?" Scott paused and asked again, "Right?"

He sheepishly raised his eyes up to look at Scott without lifting his head. The big man looked like a kid who had just been caught with his hand in a cookie jar. Once he made eye contact with Scott, he quickly looked back down. He sat for a moment and then started to work his diamond-encrusted wedding band from his finger as he explained, "Here, this ring is worth three times what I owe the pot!"

Luckily for the rest of us who were still in the hand, the player sitting to Wheeler's right reached over and lightly touched him on his right arm, preventing him from removing the ring. "Let it go, Wheeler. Tonight's not your night, and for sure, no one wants your wedding ring."

Boy, was I grateful I wasn't the one to tell him that. I didn't want the ring either. God knows, I've had two of my own wedding rings over the years and the last thing I needed was to win one in a card game. The thought gave me the shivers just to think about it. Don't get me wrong, my marriages really weren't that bad; it's just the endings weren't great.

An explanation if I may. Over time, I've understood I'm too excessively self-centered to be a good mate for anyone. I'm sure some psychologist would have a field day with my Ego and my Id and all the other stuff they examine. They'd want to examine how I felt about my mother and the other mumbo-jumbo stuff as well, but I reserve the right to keep my psychoses to myself. My feelings about my marriages are my own and I want to keep 'em that way.

Wheeler raised his head from staring down at the table and he glared at the man with his hand on his arm. The man removed his offending hand and Wheeler spread his anger around to the rest of us. He snarled, "Well, thank you! And just screw all of you! Hear me? Just screw you all!"

He pushed his chair back, stood for a moment and then snatched his coat off the chair. Stumbling unsteadily towards the kitchen door, one of the other players called after him, "Wheeler, cool off, you really don't want to go any further tonight. Okay?"

Wheeler yanked the door open, then turned back, holding onto the doorjamb. His bulk filled the opening, and he hissed at all of us, "I won't forget what you did to Ol' Wheel tonight. You wait, just you wait! You'll see."

Someone else at the table murmured, "Okay Wheel, you know where we'll be. Come back another time and try again." Wheeler slammed the door and left. Now there were just seven people at the table with only four active players, three others and me.

CHAPTER TWO

Before I continue, please allow me to explain something before you think poorly of my group of players. Let's consider the cold hard facts. I've been down on my luck a few times, just as most of the other players have, it's part of the game. But we've all played together long enough so everyone knows the rules, especially Ol' Wheeler. I'll agree we don't have them exactly written down anywhere, but whenever you play with our group, we tell you right up front what's what, and you agree to everything or you don't play in our game. The game is table stakes, unless you got a killer hand, and you put up the pink slip to your car or something that the rest of the players will accept as collateral. Well, anything except a wedding ring of course.

There are no IOUs, checks or anything like that allowed. I admit this with some level of chagrin, because I had one great '57 Chevrolet convertible I lost in a card game. So, don't go feeling too sorry for Wheeler. Remember, it's our ball, our rules, our game. You play it our way, or you don't play. Anyway, it was common knowledge that sometimes Wheel pops off, and this was not the first time he'd tried the wedding band routine.

Regarding the players in our little games; there are around eighteen to twenty of us who get together and play a few times a month at someone's house. Of course, not all the guys make each game, but seven to ten of the guys usually make it. Wheeler was one of the more regular players and usually one of the better ones. Tonight just wasn't his night.

The older gentleman who was sitting to the left of Wheeler had only played with us a few times over the past year. Randy Ralph originally brought him to our game... and yeah, you got the name right. Randy Ralph. Randy as in the English word for horny; as in very sex crazed! Allow me to explain about 'ol Ralph. The overriding characteristic of Ralph is his thing for the female gender of our species. I know most guys like women, but with Ralph... well, it's different.

If we allowed a gal to sit in on our games, he would lose every dime he had because he couldn't keep his mind on the game. He'd be trying to figure a way to get her horizontal the entire time we were playing. Most men can't multi-task anyway, and when it comes to sex, Ralph is totally single threaded.

Randy is a very skinny individual. He's a tad less than six feet tall, and he's just skin and bones. I've seen him eat at some of our poker games and I know if I ate half of what he eats, I'd end up twice the size of old Wheeler. No idea how he stays so slim unless all that sex sweats it off him, but the one thing it doesn't seem to do is slow him down with women.

Don't take my comments wrong, I like women as much as the next guy. Just to make sure I'm perfectly clear, I don't ride the other bicycle, if you know what I mean? I love women, but not like Randy. I realize I'm not being very PC, but in my declining years, I've noticed women have other attributes than their genitalia, and the secrets buried therein. I believe women are as intelligent as men and just as much fun to be with; I just don't feel you have to try and have sex with everyone you meet, but somehow Randy doesn't see it that way.

I know, I know. It's not the correct thing nowadays to refer to the fairer sex in those terms, like sex objects and all. God knows in this age of political correctness one has to talk and be so careful not to offend, but at my age, it's a bit tougher to change my views. Old dogs, new tricks, you know, like that. I don't think women are less capable than men, or that they should receive less pay for doing the same job or anything along those lines. And I sure as hell don't think they are less intelligent, as many other men do, but I'll to admit to viewing women as sex symbols. Actually, they're a lot more to them than just sex symbols, but in many men's eyes, that tends to have most everything else beat. I think women look, feel, and smell great. The sight of unfettered breasts swinging free under a sweater, or a great set of legs poking out of a skirt with a slit showing a little thigh... ah well, that's pure poetry in motion. It makes life worth living.

I honestly believe Ralph even enjoys his nickname. He seems to feel it's his badge of honor. And as long as Randy has attended our games, I have no idea what his last name is. He was already part of the group when I joined, and they introduced him as Ralph. Two weeks later Scott had called him Randy Ralph, and I almost choked on my coffee when he said it. Scott told me many of the other players had called him Randy Ralph to his face and he seemed proud of the name. Go figure.

Anyway, the older gentleman friend of Randy's that he'd brought to our games was introduced to all of us as Slim. Nothing else, just Slim. I know I'd heard no other name for him, first or last. The name fit him perfectly. Slim was perhaps 5' 5" at the most and he was slat thin. I figured him to be well into his seventies and he'd obviously spent a lot of time in the sun. His heavily seamed face with its deep wrinkles made him look like a well-polished brown walnut shell. He had pale eyes that peered out from under large, bushy, sun-bleached eyebrows.

The first time I met him the word eagle came to mind. Not to imply he looked like one, just somehow the concept of an eagle perched in a tree watching everything before him came to mind. Something about him generated a need for me to watch him. I'm uncertain whether it was the shape of his nose or the feeling he observed everything that everyone said and did around him, but he was a very curious guy. Slim reminded me a lot of that rich old man from Texas. The one with the big ears and the bad haircut who several years ago kept getting himself embroiled in and then out of politics, and who could never decide if he should run for president or not.

It was now Slim's turn to bet. I'd had a slight burst of energy during the confrontation with Wheeler, but I could feel the adrenaline fading. I sat watching Slim as he decided what he would do. I noticed him reach up with his left hand and then wipe his left eye with the back of the hand. After a few seconds, he quickly did it again.

Finally, he picked up the large stack of bills in front of him and counted them. He threw in the large pile of bills and turned to the player who had stopped Wheeler from removing his wedding ring.

"Tom," Slim drawled, aiming his comments towards the host of tonight's game, "I'm tapped out." He looked around the table at the rest of the players, nodded and continued, "I know better than to offer a check, 'specially after the scene Wheel did to y'all, however, I would like to put up my houseboat. Some of you have seen it and have been aboard. Those of you who know the houseboat, know that it's worth at least a couple hundred grand. Maybe a lot more. Right?"

Tom nodded his head and Scott piped up he had been aboard once. Slim asked, "Would you say it's worth the pot, and a bit more?" Some players nodded their heads. "Then I would like to put it up as the rest of the bet and raise the bet $25,000. OK?"

Tom, who was sitting next to Slim, said he agreed to the bet and those of us in the game agreed to his bet. Tom added most of the rest of the money he had left in front of him, covering what he was short and called.

That brought the bet to the black gentleman sitting next to me. We all call him Tubs because he plays the drums in a jazz trio. Most people know him better as Bill Tate. As in the William Tate of basketball fame. Bill played fewer poker games than anybody else in our group, however, he was an excellent player and had won some good-sized pots from all of us. Tonight had not gone well for Bill and he took just a few seconds to shake his head, throw down his cards and comment, "This is crazy," his deep voice chuckling as he continued, "This is getting way too rich for me. I'm out."

That brought the bet to me. I was close to finding myself tapped out too, however I could cover the bet. But my problem is I really don't want to take a houseboat as a bet. To tell you the truth, there was a lot of money in the pot to be fooling around with in a stupid card game. I thought about just throwing in the hand. I looked around the table at the others, wondering what to do. When I looked at Slim, he sat quietly and returned my gaze, and then reached up to wipe at this eye again.

A bolt of energy shot through me, and it was all I could do just to sit still. It was nearly impossible to not let on I'd just figured out Slim's tell. I was now positive the ol' son of a bitch was bluffing. I remembered twice before during the night, and on at least two other occasions I could recall, I'd seem the same movement with his left hand. It didn't hit me then, but every time he did that movement with his hand, he'd been bluffing. Now it seemed so obvious. The other times I'd played with him, I kept getting the feeling I was missing something, and tonight I realized just what it was.

It looked like when he had a poor hand and he was trying to bluff his left eye would water. Not much, just enough so he'd try to wipe his eye with the back of his hand to remove something he thought was there. Just for a moment, I wondered if perhaps he'd just been suckering me in to keep me betting, but now it didn't matter, I knew I had to find out. I wanted to know if I was correct. I could feel the weariness drain out of me. I was so damn sure now Ol' Slim was bluffing I just had to do it. When I glanced over at Scott, he slowly nodded his head at me to go for it, and that gave me the push I needed to continue.

I had every card in my hand memorized but I still picked them up off the table and fanned them slowly. They hadn't changed since the last time I looked; there were three ladies, with a king of clubs and the king of hearts to keep them company. A full house! And I was so positive that hand would bail me out I pitched in the money required to stay in. I called.

It stunned me. Tom should have known better than to push his pair of jacks, but lately that was his style. When Slim flipped his cards over, sure enough, I had the better hand. The old guy had been trying to buy the pot with just three tens.

When my hand hit the table, it was like someone had punched a needle into a balloon the way the air escaped from everyone. I hadn't realized it, but I'd been holding my breath, too. I sat there for a few moments and stared at the pile in the middle of the table. At that point, both Tom and Scott said they'd had enough for the night and perhaps we should all knock off. Tubs informed us he didn't care if we kept playing or not, since he had an important meeting later that day, he had to leave. Since I was the big winner, I felt that it would be best if I said nothing and waited for the others to decide if they wanted to quit.

The little ol' fellow I'd just wiped out said, "Now I'm tapped out and I have to quit anyway." He looked at me, "The houseboat is at the Westlake North Marina. It's in slip C-14. I would appreciate if you would give me," he paused and looked up at the ceiling. He looked back at me and with a crooked grin continued, "Say a few days to clean out my stuff. Today is Friday, no wait, it's now Saturday ain't it?

"How about give me till a week from Monday? You come by then around 8 AM, we'll sign the final papers, and I can show you around. You can take possession of the place then. OK?"

I was feeling bad the man would lose his home. Although I tried to tell him, I would let the entire thing drop if he thought he could come up with part of the money, he refused to listen. I continued my speech until he finally raised his hand to silence me.

At that point all I could do was wait through a long moment of silence before he started his drawl, "I'll tell ya, son. I thought I wanted to live up here for a while. I was here during the War... that's WWII. Back then, I enjoyed being here in the Puget Sound area a lot. It's been fun this time, too."

Slim nodded at the group still standing around, "All of you have been a lot of fun, but I really miss the desert and the heat. I'll tell you this, I hate rain. And it's not just a little dislike, but I hate the God Damn shit with my entire aching being. Excuse, please."

Everybody laughed. Considering what was going on outside it was small wonder he hated Puget Sound so much.

Slim continued, "Moreover, the past two months have reminded me every day why I hate it so much." Slim stepped up and looked up in my face. "Trust me son, I've had enough of Seattle. I miss New Mexico. That's where I'm from and that's where I want to return. I thought I might try to entice someone to come and pay me a visit, but it ain't gonna work out. I guess this was fate showing me a good reason to go home where I belong. Thanks for the thought son, but I really want to go home, and getting rid of that houseboat makes it a lot easier now."

"You're sure?" I asked.

"Positive! But, that's real thoughty of you son," he drawled. "I'll see you in a week and a half or so."

I explained to Slim that Scott was a real estate broker and since he knew all the ins and outs of transfers like this; I would have him take care of things and asked if Slim minded. Slim shook his head as he told me he didn't mind at all and it was nice I had a friend like Scott to help out.

With that, we shook hands and parted company

CHAPTER THREE

I got into my truck and headed home, driving very carefully. I was beat! During the drive back to my place, the question that kept going through my mind: what on earth was I going to do with a houseboat? My living conditions are such that I have what I consider the most perfect place to live anywhere. A few years back, one evening I was having a drink downtown with a fellow who turned out to be an undercover narcotics police officer. During our conversation, he mentioned his division would be seizing a house because it was a drug house.

As he described the location of the house, I thought it sounded like something I needed to check out. When I drove by and looked at the address, I knew I wanted to buy it and I set my "wolves" to do their legal tasks. They uncovered the owners behind the company shell, who specialize in these rundown places. Places that are just waiting. Pieces of property people were hanging on to just to see what profitable thing they could do with them later on. While they held on to these places, they - the unknown face of some corporation didn't care to whom they rented these dumps. They set the corporations up just so the properties would bring in a little extra bread and then take their write-offs with the taxman.

Luckily for me, it turned out my wolves were a lot better at their job than the corporate wolves. Suddenly there was an empty company shell that found they owned a house which the city had condemned and a lot of trouble with the legal system. This meant trouble for everyone involved with the entire arrangement. As if by magic, it was suddenly in the best interests of everyone to sell at once, a piece of very undesirable property. My wolves snapped it up for peanuts. Because the house was worthless, the fire department had a delightful time practicing on it and burned it to the ground for me.

The reason I was so intent on buying the old house was the lot it sat on had an extraordinary view. It sits three-quarters of the way up a hill facing the west and south, thus giving me a commanding view of downtown Seattle plus a view out over most of Lake Union. I had a fantastic multi-level complex built on my new vacant lot and I kept the top unit for myself. Since I built the units stacked on top of each other, this gives my place an even more astonishing view.

The northwest end of Lake Union leads to a ship canal, which in turn leads towards the Ballard Locks. On warm summer nights as the sun settles down in the water and shimmers down the canal, it looks like a ribbon of gold. I can sit on my balcony, drink in hand, and I think I've died and gone straight to heaven. Believe me, the last thing I felt I needed or wanted was a houseboat.

I remembered Scott telling me not too long ago that houseboats were a hot item on the real estate market, and they sold quickly. I also remembered some Hollywood types who filmed a movie some time ago. The movie was about a guy who couldn't sleep at night 'cause his wife died and he was living on a houseboat in Seattle with his kid. As it turned out, some folks back east saw the flick and came all the way out to Seattle to buy the thing. I might not have too hard a time getting my money out of the damn thing after all. I could only hope.

When I pulled up to my building, I punched the button to raise the garage door and then pulled into my stall. I took the elevator up to my floor and Blackjack, my little black cocker spaniel promptly greeted me. Her nickname is BJ, and she was pawing at my shoes to let me know she wanted to go out. Actually, all I wanted to do was eat a little breakfast and then hit the sack, but I felt guilty. Normally I take Blackjack with me everywhere, but I don't take her to my poker games. I felt I owed it to her to take her for a walk so she could at least do her business.

As always, she had to sniff every blade of grass and explore under all the bushes in the neighboring vacant lot. Every day she uses the same place to do her thing and every day she goes through the same routine, checking out the lot, a blade of grass by a blade of grass. Does she really think she will find something new today? As I stood waiting for her, I continued to inform her I would greatly appreciate a little alacrity on her part this early in the morning.

Finally, she completed her tasks, and I returned to the condo to feed and bed my poor tired body. I whipped up some eggs and added a little shredded cheese. While I was waiting for my concoction to cook, I drank a quart of orange juice right out of the bottle, just one of the benefits of living alone. I ate my meal over the sink while my mind pushed around what I would do with my new possession. When I finished, I stacked the dishes in the sink and headed off to bed, which is another benefit to living alone.

As I drifted off to sleep, I mentally counted my winnings from the evening. BJ found her spot, curled up tight against my back and I continued to drift. I pulled out and then examined the feelings I'd had when I called it right and found out Ol' Slim was bluffing. I savored how great the win had felt. The last thing I knew as I drifted off I was thinking about the houseboat again, and how I would dispose of the thing.

"A houseboat," I thought. "I don't need a houseboat."

Oh shit, what have I gotten myself into now?

CHAPTER FOUR

A little over a week had passed since the card game when an incessant knocking at my back door one morning startled me out of my slumber. Actually, it was more banging than a knock.

To make everything clear, I need to explain about the door arrangement in my apartment. My front door is actually the elevator which comes from the downstairs foyer on the ground floor. Each floor of the building is a separate condo. The elevator stops at any one of the six levels if you have the correct key. Visitors call up to the unit they wish to visit on the house phone located outside on the wall by the door, and the tenant of the unit must release the elevator to bring the guests up to their level. The elevator will not stop on any other floor unless you have the key to make it stop.

I set the apartment building into a large hill and only my floor is high enough to have a back door. This door is reachable via a short bridge which leads from the side of the vacant lot which I also own behind my condo property to my kitchen door. When the apartment building was being constructed, they had to cut into the hill behind the complex. Because of the building's height and the steep rise of the hill, my apartment is the only one that ended up with a back door.

There's a concrete retaining wall behind the entire structure which holds the back wall of dirt in place. Because of the retaining wall, all the other units only have two small windows that face out against the concrete wall. I have a steel mesh security door covering my back door. Since no one can really see very well into the lot that faces the entire back of the apartment, I feel very secure with my back door arrangement.

What pulled me out of my happy sleep was somebody banging on the steel door. The noise rebounding through my entire place was impossible to ignore. Although I glanced at the clock beside my bed, in my state of fogginess, the time didn't register. On my way to the back door, I again glanced at a clock on the wall, and this time it finally sunk in. I was operating on around four hours of sleep.

When I peered out the peephole to see who was so rudely interrupting my sleep, I saw Scott standing there. I opened the main door, keeping the steel mesh door closed and locked. At this point, I wasn't feeling very friendly. "Why aren't you asleep?" I growled through the mesh. "You know I had a date last night. As I recall, so did you!" Without letting him answer, I continued on, "So the question is, why are you out running around at this time of day, ass-hole? Did your date have a headache?"

"Asshole?" He sounded hurt. "Who are you calling an asshole? You don't know it yet, but I'm the guy who is trying to help you out. And no, my date did not have a headache. Not all of us have to sleep with every girl we date." Scott reached out and tried to open the steel door and found it locked. "Damn it, Matt, let me in! I will not stand out here and talk to you like some door-to-door salesman. Anyway, this is about your houseboat."

This was great news. Hardly a week had passed, and the paperwork still had not been completed, and already it was disturbing my sleep. So, to continue this conversation I didn't want to have, I flipped the lock and turned around to go to put on some clothes. I called back over my shoulder for Scott to make coffee.

Once inside my bedroom, I went over to my date from last night and pulled up the covers. No reason she shouldn't catch more sleep. She mumbled something incoherent and moved closer to the center of the bed. Glimpsing her naked body as I covered her up I recalled last night's passion. Erotic thoughts did little to help push me to return to Scott. Besides, somehow, I knew in the back of my mind I didn't want to hear what he had to tell me about the houseboat.

When I returned to the kitchen, the aroma of coffee filled the room. Even though the pot hadn't finished dripping, I grabbed a cup from the cupboard and poured coffee from the carafe. I needed coffee now; now. Screw waiting! As I took a sip, I could tell that Scott noticed what I'd done. By the look on his face, I could tell he was considering commenting. I gave him a dirty look, and he thought better of it.

"OK, what's so important you had to wake me at this unholy hour?" By now, Blackjack had dragged her lazy butt out of the bedroom where she'd been sleeping. When she saw Scott, she went straight to him, and begged for his attention. The two of them get along well, and when I have to leave town, I usually ask Scott to dog sit for me. He's really more of a cat person, and it has surprised me the two of them get on so well. One of the first times he'd met BJ, he told me a story about when he was a kid, and the little black cocker that a car had run over. Maybe BJ reminds him of his childhood.

Scott drew himself a cup of the finished joe and took a sip before he started in. "... took the liberty of checking on the houseboat moorage. I felt it was my duty since I more or less goaded you to take the bet. I had a courier take all the paperwork to Slim last Thursday, and I also started the paperwork you must sign. After Slim finally signs everything and... well..." his voice trailed off.

The look on Scott's face and considering my mood, I thought just saying one word was kind. "Well?" I barked.

He looked down at the floor and spoke so softly I could hardly hear him, "I thought I should research the current lease on your space in the marina. It turns out you have a houseboat all right... but as of the first of next month, you won't have a place to tie it up. You have to move it."

His comment made me take in too much hot coffee, and I burned my tongue. I shouted at him, "What? How can I have a houseboat and not have somewhere to tie the damn thing up?" I knew I needed to lower my voice, but I just couldn't.

"How can somebody just tell me I have to move? I thought there was a lease or something! And how can you move anything that large? Doesn't that thing have power, and a telephone connected to it, and... and... and like that other stuff?" By now I was waving my hands in the air, but I was too wound up to stop. "Isn't there some way we can make arrangements to keep it there? Isn't there..."

Scott held up one hand, and ducked his head in mock surrender, "Slow down, one question at a time, please." He held up one finger, "They will disconnect the power and telephone on the thirtieth of next month." Another finger popped up, "You can move the houseboat with a tugboat. If you don't have a tug there on the first of the following month to move it, they'll just cast you off, disconnect the power and stuff, and your boat will float off into the lake. At least that's what they told me."

Now he held up another finger, "As for the lease, the deal is, there are two types of houseboat moorages. The first type is you own the moorage and part of the dock. All the owners are responsible for the upkeep of the docks, piers and the grounds out front. Think of it as owning a condo with dues. The other arrangement is someone else owns the dock, and each tenant is on a month-to-month rental with some type of extended lease involved. Yours was on a lease, and Slim didn't renew the lease since he planned to move, anyway. He must have thought he had more time, and you sorta got stuck."

"I just found all of this out yesterday afternoon after I filed all the papers with the title agency. Please understand that I've tried to reach you to tell you this, but I keep missing you. I knew I could find you here this morning. I'm really sorry I told you to take the damn thing on that bet. Anyway, if they do, cut the thing loose, then the city will cite you. I'll admit I know nothing about maritime law, but my guess is it is about being a hazard to navigation or something. Anyway, the coast guard will have the boat impounded, for which they will also bill you. We need to find you a new spot and make arrangements to have a tug move the boat." After his spiel, he took a long sip of his coffee.

This guy was just a fount of happy news. I could just see how every dollar I'd won in the game, and possibly a lot more was being sucked into that hole in the water. I knew I sounded as if I was whining, which I was. "How am I going to find a new spot? You know, I will beat the shit out of that little bastard Slim. I'll bet he knew this all along. I'd go down there now and whale on him except I think he's out of town until tonight. What am I going to do, Scott?" I thought about this for a moment, and a flash of insight struck me. Scott was a Realtor, so why couldn't he find me a new spot? "Are there any spots available anywhere?"

Since Scott is in the reality business, and since he has his own company, I was confident he could come up with some ideas about where I could move. Seeing him shake his head back and forth while he told me, "I'm sorry to tell you this Matt, but there's no place in the entire city to tie up. I searched every possible lead on the computer. I have calls in to two small slips, but I don't hold out a lot of hope." This did little to improve my attitude.

"What?" I exploded again. "Once again I ask you, what am I going to do with the..." I knew the word I wanted to use, but I didn't. "'Damn' thing?"

"I'm working on it. The good thing is we have over six weeks to find a spot." Scott sounded somewhat contrite. "For what it's worth, I tried to call Slim all weekend as soon as I found out about your slip. He may be away, but he isn't answering my calls."

Seeing how badly Scott felt made me feel sheepish about how I'd treated him. I needed to make up for my nastiness. "Thanks for coming right over, Scott, I may not sound like it, but I appreciate what you're trying to do. I hope you understand how I might feel to get all this wonderful news at one time?" He smiled. "But what if we don't find a slip? What do we do next?"

He seemed to ignore the 'we' part of my last statement. It seems he can use "we," but I can't. "It's my understanding when you contact one of the tug companies to tow the houseboat, you might ask if they'll let you store it in one of their holding areas for a few weeks. I believe that Foss Towing has a very large repair area up near the locks. If you talk to them, you can probably arrange a place to store it for a while. I really don't know what else to tell you, Matt. Right now, it looks as if finding a slip will be really tough."

My cup was empty, so I wandered into the kitchen and poured myself more coffee while my mind raced. When I picked up the carton of half & half, I noticed it was empty. Great... just great, now I had to drink black coffee, which I hate. I just didn't want to have to deal with this dog's breakfast right away; what with a tight timeline to find a new slip or moorage and get it moved by the deadline date. Ha! I didn't mind that I might be out some of my winnings. I didn't want to have to deal with disposing of the thing. Too bad they didn't make it entirely of wood, I could just take it out somewhere, and let the thing sink to the bottom of the bay.

I asked Scott if there was any way the marina owner would let me stay another month, or if I could pay more rent. He shook his head, "I don't know who the owner or owners are, yet. I have a call into the woman who manages the marina, but she hasn't called me back. Her secretary told me she thought someone already spoke up for that slip, and they would move in a big concrete float and build a new home on the float."

I almost dropped my cup of coffee, "A concrete float? Come on now Scott! First off, the last time I heard, concrete doesn't float. Think about this, building anything on floating concrete doesn't seem very smart to me, how about you?" Scott smiled at me. "But hey, what do I know? I've heard something about concrete boats, which didn't sound like a good idea either. So, what's next, concrete planes? Scott, you've got to be shitting me. A concrete float? Really?" Scott nodded his head, and I shook mine.

I'd had enough of Scott and his wonderful news, and I tossed him out, telling him I needed to go catch up on some much-needed sleep. Tomorrow Scott and I planned to see Slim anyway, and I was just going to lay it at his feet. I would not assume possession of that damn houseboat. That was all there was to it. From my perspective, the little bastard still owed me on the bet.

I recalled what Scott said when he had the title transfer papers couriered over to Slim. Slim was going south for the weekend, and I remembered Slim saying he'd be back early this week. The deal was once he signed the papers, I would take actual possession of the houseboat the following day. You can bet I would see if there was any way to get my money from him instead of the boat. No way I wanted to get stuck with that headache!

With that, I headed back to the sack. I wondered if I could get back to sleep what with all the shit from the houseboat running through my head. BJ settled in at her corner on the end of the bed while I curled up next to the warm soft body snuggled down in the middle of the bed.

~ ~ ~ ~ ~

The next thing I knew I was alone in my bed, and from the high position of the light coming in from outside I guessed it was well past noon. I was thirsty, and I got up and walked out to the kitchen. As I passed the window, I looked out at a weak sun trying valiantly to break out from some clouds, but with little success. Shuffling back to the kitchen, I reflected on why all of this was happening to me.

I found a note from last night's date telling me she was sorry, but she had to run. She said she was late, and thanks for a great evening. Blackjack had gotten up and was now scratching at the back door. I pulled on some old sweats and took her out.

I'm sure it would be safe to let her out alone, but she had become such a treasured friend I didn't want some creep stealing her or something worse. There are many weirdos in the world, and I sure didn't want her to fall victim to one of them. BJ did her thing, and we both headed back inside.

For the rest of the day I tried to call Scott without success. I knew he'd be at Slim's floating nightmare at eight on Wednesday morning (I still thought of it as Slim's) so I wasn't too worried. That evening I sat on my balcony nursing a small, but nourishing Scotch with a little ice. I was contemplating what I would do with my new possession if in fact I was actually stuck with it. The lights were reflecting off the lake, and I wondered which one of those lights was the houseboat.

In the end, it came down to two reasons I really didn't want the houseboat. The first reason was obvious, I didn't need, or want, the problems that were developing over the damn thing. The other reason was much more philosophical. Up to now, I feel that I've been a very lucky man. Because of my inheritance from pop's estate and through the proceeds of careful investing, I have more than enough income to support my current lifestyle. I need no more 'things of value' to clutter my life. I earn more than enough to keep myself happy, and to take care of my various hobbies. Every morning when I wake up, I thank the universe and the divine power that created the universe in all its immaculate beauty, and that same power that provides me with the lucky life I am now living. I am grateful for what I have and want to make sure I show my gratitude. To tell you the truth, I don't need more toys or things in my life. I'm thrilled with my life just as it is.

This new screw up with the houseboat had left me feeling out of sorts. I felt sad that Slim didn't like the Puget Sound area more than he did, but I could understand his feelings about the weather. The end of the year was nearing, and with that comes four months of rain. Let's not sugarcoat it, the months of January through April usually are rather bleak around Seattle. If you were used to a very different climate, I could see why you would want to leave. But I still felt bad about the houseboat.

I decided I needed some downhearted music. I put on some Ray Charles and let him cry the blues for both of us. Finally, I decided it was time to take BJ out one more time, and then crash and burn.

HOUSEBOAT

CHAPTER FIVE

My alarm went off at 6 AM and as I padded across my bedroom, I noticed it was still dark outside. Grumpily I headed for the shower. After my shower I tried one more call to Scott, but still no luck. This didn't alarm me. Not only was he an early riser, he was also a runner. I think it's great there are people who want to run. I jokingly tell people I don't run as a courtesy to others. When folks see me run, they know if I'm running, there must be something horrific happening behind me and therefore they should turn immediately and run as well. Rather than cause a panic, as a courtesy, I don't run. By the way, you're welcome.

God knows I should do more to improve my shape, but I am also cursed with a streak of laziness. Besides, as I often point out, round is a shape. Food tastes so good, and I enjoy my small but nourishing Scotch in the evening. I keep telling myself someday… someday, I should work on making some of my rolls disappear, but I think I'm realizing certain parts of my anatomy will be with me for a while. So far, it hasn't killed all my chances with the ladies, but I'm sure I'd do a lot better without the love handles. You remember, the procreation thing we discussed?

I headed down to the garage and took my ol' truck instead of the car. I have a habit of naming cars. I think it goes back to my junior high school days when guys used to give their cars names and then paint the name on the side. At least I don't paint the names on the side. Yet!

Anyway, I have named my truck Faithful Steed, which over time I have shortened to just Faithful. Faithful is a late 80's Japanese pickup with 194,000 miles on it that still runs great. In the morning it makes a few funny noises, but I keep rationalizing with myself that, as we age, all of us make funny noises in the morning. Someday I will most likely have to do something about it, but after so many miles, we have bonded.

As I pulled Faithful out of the garage, I tried to call Scott again on the cell phone. He answered on the second ring. His greeting was nauseatingly happy. I growled a little and asked him if he would meet me at Slim's marina. He told me, as promised, he'd be there by eight, and we hung up.

I had about half an hour to kill. So instead of just sitting in Faithful, I pulled over and bought a latte from one of the many coffee stands which seem to pop out of the ground in Seattle. I swear more of them grow every time it rains. And since it rains a fair amount around here, you can only imagine the abundance of stands on the street. What the exact count is, I'm not sure, but it's close to one stand for every two people living in Seattle, (or was it two stands for every person living in Seattle?).

I took my Grande latte and stopped at a grassy area where I could turn Blackjack loose. Have I mentioned it before, that I take BJ with me everywhere I go, when I can. She seems to enjoy going with me, and she doesn't mind waiting in the truck when she has to since she doesn't have to sit alone at home. I really enjoy her company, so it works out well for both of us. My two bad my marriages weren't nearly as great as my relationship is with BJ. I wonder what dark psychological fact that tells people about me?

When I pulled into the marina around 7:55, I saw Scott's Cad coming from the other direction. Scott drives a little red Cadillac sports car which they stopped building a few years back, and I'll admit I think it's very attractive. He wheeled the car in next to mine, and we headed out to the dock to see how, and if there was some way for me to shed my new possession.

Our shoes drummed on the wooden pier while BJ ran ahead of us. About a third of the way down the pier, an older gentleman with white flowing hair stepped out from one of the other houseboats. Since this was a private dock he felt he had a right to stop us and ask what we wanted.

BJ was a rescue dog. I got her when she was around three years old and somewhere during her first three years, someone on the male side of humanity had badly abused her. It took me a long time to make friends with her, and because of her mistreatment, she barks at most men when she first meets them. If you are male, and if you ignore her, she'll eventually come to you, on her terms. In that regard, I guess animals have it easier than humans do. If someone mistreats us, the world teaches us to forgive and forget. But we allow animals to remember and we even consider it acceptable for them to show that they remember. Truth be told, I've met a few people over the years I wished I could still bark at. Anyway, true to form, BJ danced and barked at the old fella and wouldn't stop. Finally, I had to reach down and pick her up to make her stop fussing. Once she was in my arms, I explained to the old gent I was the new owner of the houseboat in slip C-14… or at least until I could put my hands on Slim.

The old man's voice trembled with anger as he spoke, "I'm telling you now," the white-haired old fella shook his finger at me, "I almost called the police last night on that damn dog of yours. Barking the entire night like that! This is a nice quiet dock and a good place to live. We will not tolerate the noise from any dog, even your dog!" His face was now a picture of total fury. "Do you understand me, young man?"

I held up one hand to quiet him down. "Hold up there, old-timer," I told him, "This is the first time Blackjack has ever been here. This is only my second visit here. If you heard a dog last night, it couldn't have been her. Okay?"

The old gentleman still had an angry look on his face as he continued to shake his finger at me. He exclaimed, "I heard a dog barking over in C-14, along with all the shouting. And buster, it sounded just like that dog in your arms. It barked exactly like your dog did just now! You might think I'm old, but my hearing is still good!" Scott, and I were trying to step backward and get away from the angry old man, but he continued to shout at us. "I'm telling you again, we don't hold with any loud noises here at the marina, especially after eleven. You keep that damn mutt quiet, and you'd better keep down your noise, too."

With that warning, the old fella turned and muttering to himself, shuffled back towards his houseboat. Scott and I looked at each other as we walked down the dock. Scott shrugged, "I wonder what that's all about? Were you over here last night?"

"Get real, I was asleep."

"I tried to call you once last night, and the phone just kept ringing. I hung up before your answering machine kicked in."

"I was out with BJ for a few minutes, maybe you called then."

We continued down dock C until we came to slip 14. I hate to admit it, but the houseboat was very attractive. I liked it more this time than the first time I'd seen it. They finished the sides of the house in small wooden shingles were painted an interesting shade of dark green. The doors and window sashes were light, clear wood, and well varnished. Any visible metal parts of the houseboat were brass, and the windows consisted of small panes set in a larger window frame. They were hinged at the top and could be opened outwards. The entire place looked clean and attractive. The front door was slightly inset from the side of the houseboat. On each side of the door, set in deep pots, there were two handsome Bonsai trees, and above those were brass ship's lanterns. If I had to have the thing torn apart, it would really be a shame.

I stepped onto the small deck in front of the door and knocked. The door swung open under my knock and I looked back at Scott in alarm. I stuck my head inside and called out Slim's name twice, but after hearing no sounds, I stepped into the front room. BJ charged on ahead of me through the open doorway and even though I called her to come back, she ignored me.

Suddenly, from the back of the house, I heard her bark wildly. I followed the noise. It concerned me because in all the time I'd had BJ; she had never barked that way before. Suddenly, she burst from the back of the place and ran straight at me leaving tracks on the carpet. Red paw prints.

I wondered if she had cut herself on something and I examined her paws. Scott went on ahead of me and as he entered the next room, I heard him mutter, "Oh shit! Oh, shit... shit... shit!" Then I heard the back door open and what sounded like someone retching. I left BJ on the floor and hurried around the corner.

The first thing that struck me as I entered the kitchen was the smell. A large amount of blood gives off a metallic smell like seared copper and there was a large amount of blood. Slim was kind of sitting at the kitchen table, tied to a chair, with his head tilted forward, his chin resting on his chest.

Between 'Nam and my years of knocking around, I hate to admit it, but I've seen a few dead people. This was without a doubt one of the worst sights I'd witnessed. Someone had slit Slim's throat from ear to ear, and from all appearances, the only reason his head remained atop his torso was his spinal column.

The cut soaked the front of his shirt with blood. On the floor there was a very large, fairly dry pool, except for a single wet spot where BJ had stepped. I thought from the color of his shirt the blood looked dry around the edges. His murder wasn't a recent happening. A fleeting feeling of déjà vu hit me. Although I didn't spend a long time looking at him, I knew it would take a long time for me to forget what I'd just seen. After just a few seconds, I needed to step outside and smell some fresh air. I would not throw up, but I was damn close to it.

As I took deep breaths, I realized somehow the problem of finding a new slip for the houseboat didn't seem so important anymore.

Actually, I found that my anger at Slim had totally dissipated.

For the time being that is…

CHAPTER SIX

Scott went out to his Cad and called the police to report our grisly discovery, and for his trouble, the police demanded we not leave the scene. Perhaps it was best Scott made the call because I'd have retorted with a smart-assed comment when the operator told us not to leave.

It's interesting how quickly the police will respond when you use the "M" word. I guess when you tell them you've found a body you believe might be a murder victim, it stirs their curiosity, or some other cop instinct. They go straight to high gear and there's an immediate rush on their part to come and check it out. Why there is such a rush I'll never know. I could assure them Slim was not leaving soon.

While Scott was making the call, I walked BJ out to the truck and when I passed the houseboat where the old man lived; he glared at me from one of his windows. I stood by my truck and petted BJ for a moment trying to settle her down. She was still shaking, and I knew exactly how she felt. I rolled the windows down part way before I put her inside so she'd have fresh air. After Scott summoned the police to investigate Slim's demise, the two of us returned to the houseboat. We moved as quickly back to the boat as possible to make sure we stopped anyone else who might accidentally come by from entering the scene.

I wondered which of Seattle's finest they would send out to take on this investigation. I rather hoped it would be a true Seattleite since there are so few of us these days, but I didn't expect it. Even though I am a WASP, (White Anglo Saxton Protestant) I also qualify as part of a minority group. I've read that fewer than 33 percent of all the people who live in the Puget Sound area were actually born here. I can say I'm part of that number. I was born, raised, and other than the time I spent in the military, I've lived my entire life in this magnificent area.

Finally, the police showed up, and I was pleased to see one of the two detectives responding to Scott's call was an old childhood friend, Jeff L. Davenport. I have no idea what the L stood for or even why the L was so important, but he had always used it in his name. Every paper he turned in was signed Jeff L. Davenport. He took a lot of kidding during junior and senior high school, but he had always stuck with the L. Jeff L. and I grew up in the same neighborhood, and we had experienced much of our school lives together.

Jeff L. still looks exactly like he did as a youth, a high school/college football star. He still keeps in shape, and his body looks toned. He wears his hair as short as a military person would, even though he was never in the service. With a ruggedly handsome face and a cleft chin, he cuts a handsome figure. For a long time, when we were kids, I called him Dudley Do-Right of the Mounties. He didn't appreciate my wit.

They call Jeff's partner Sakol. I say call because I don't know if that's his first name or last name. Everyone I know has always called him Sakol. As I recall, Jeff once told me that Sakol was of Thai extraction. I'm ashamed to admit that even though I lived in Seattle, which is such a cosmopolitan area, and even seeing Asians every day, to me most of them look somewhat alike. I know in today's world, that is not a politically correct thing to say, and I'm going to hell for saying it. However, I'm willing to bet that if Asians were honest about it, we all probably look similar to them.

Sakol is not heavy, but he has a little paunch. However, one time I playfully hit his arm, and it felt like I had hit a steel rod. His five-foot nine-inch body structure has a lot more tone than it would appear. For so many reasons, I've always really liked Sakol.

Both Jeff L. and Sakol are excellent cops. I have watched the two of them do the good cop/bad cop routine with amazing results. Jeff L. usually plays the heavy (one look at his size and you understand why) while Sakol keeps telling Jeff L. to lighten up. Sakol then questions the people in his quiet and direct way and people seem to just open up.

The other thing about Sakol is his English, it is totally fractured. I've always suspected he watched too many Charlie Chan movies as a child. (If you don't know who Charlie Chan is, you need to find one of his old movies and watch. A true classic.) Because of his broken English, when Sakol asks a question, you can see by the expression on the face of those being interrogated they are thinking this dumb policeman doesn't have a clue. I'm either talking to a stupid cop or perhaps he's just mentally slow. I've even heard people say behind his back he should work on developing better English skills. I totally disagree! Sakol will ask you a question in his broken English, and as you answer, he smiles and nods his head.

Sakol has a round moon face with small crinkly eyes. If you were to describe it, you'd say he has a happy face. After a short chat with Sakol, you always felt better; he makes people happy. When Sakol asks you a question, he nods and blinks as he stares at you with this little smile on his face. After you give him your answer, sometimes he will repeat it but with a slight mistake. The suspect will quickly correct him and then Sakol waits a long time before he asks his next question. Some people feel the need to fill this silence and they'll talk again, just babbling away - usually saying things they really hadn't planned on divulging.

Because of his broken English, many people have viewed him as being not very smart. Too few people see him as the wise old owl he really is. He continues to ask people what they consider the most stupid questions possible. Several times he will repeat the same question as if he doesn't understand what you've been telling him. However, behind that goofy smile, those blinking eyes, and the fractured English, lies a mind that remembers every word you've said. Eventually, the suspects relaxes in front of what they perceive as a stupid bumbling cop asking silly repetitive questions; a cop who probably got his job through affirmative action.

When the suspect is quite comfortable, Sakol will quietly ask, "Ah, excuse please, thought you say?" And then the suspect looks at his nodding, smiling, blinking face, and wonders what exactly their answers were. Had they told him too much? And then they wonder if perhaps they've sold him short in the smarts department. The suspect now desperately tries to remember all the half-truths and lies they thought this inept person couldn't understand. His spoken English never seems to get any better. But they soon realize his understanding of English is a lot better than they ever imagined.

Jeff L. also knows of our infamous poker games and has informed me frequently Sakol would love to sit in with us. Fat chance! I can just see him sitting there smiling and blinking, asking, "Please, sorry, again how game played?" In the meantime, he sits there stacking our chips in front of his happy, beaming face, and winning all the big hands. Talk about your poker face, this guy has the best.

Jeff L. lived a few doors down from me when we were kids. Away from school we were fairly good friends and played together often. In high school, we never ran in the same clique, since he was a super jock, and I was in band.

During our school years, since Jeff had the looks and the reputation, he also fared well with the female population. Occasionally, he would take pity on me and would send me a few of his discards. After graduation, we went off to different colleges. Although over time we had drifted apart, seeing the two of us today, you would think we were the best of friends. Since both Jeff and I were born in Seattle, I guess when two minorities meet they have to bond together.

As soon as our greetings were out of the way, Jeff L. and Sakol took me aside and asked me what I knew about Slim's death. They also wanted to know why Scott and I were the ones who made the discovery. I explained to both of them where I fit into the picture. I also made sure they were aware I had somewhat of a beef with Slim. But even though it was a fact, it didn't make me upset enough to do something like murder him.

It didn't surprise me when Jeff L. took me aside right away and talked to me first. Once before, Jeff, Sakol, and I had spent some time together on another police investigation. I'd been dating a lovely woman for a few months. When I realized she was looking for a lot more out of the relationship than I was, I called it off, and we stopped seeing each other. A few days after the breakup they found her raped and brutally murdered.

Her neighbors described me to the police, also mentioning I'd been her latest flame. Jeff L. and Sakol were the ones they sent out to interview me. That was the first time Jeff, and I'd seen each other in several years. During my questioning, I had my first opportunity to see Sakol pull his dumb routine. Lucky for me, I was both innocent, and I had an airtight alibi; in addition, all the tests they gave me proved I was telling the truth.

A few days later they brought over my friend's diary and asked me to read parts. At that point, they were at a standstill. They were wondering if I might know anyone mentioned in certain portions of the diary. I agreed to read it.

In the diary, she'd written a few times about me, and I felt bad. I hadn't realized how deeply she cared for me. Even though I knew I wasn't ready to make the lasting commitment she was looking for, I still had feelings for her, and it was painful to read. Reading the diary, I felt now I should have attempted to bridge with her and somehow spared her so much pain. No one who has a soul likes to hurt anyone needlessly. But I didn't realize what I meant to her or what my actions had done.

From time to time, she wrote about a character named Arnold. The name didn't ring a bell with me. From the tone of her writing, it was obvious she was afraid of him. I couldn't find from the diary why she felt this way, or how it was she knew him.

For some reason, I felt there was something I wasn't remembering. I racked my brain trying to remember all of our conversations, and if she had ever said anything about him. You know, the small niggling feeling you get way back in your mind? Well, I had it, and it bothered me.

A few days later I awoke in the middle of the night and knew remembered what it was I'd missed. The lady and I had once been together at a large party with a few business associates and some of my acquaintances.

I'll admit I have a checkered past. If you came across some persons I'd met in my dealings, you might leave with a sour taste in your mouth. Anyhow, some people from my past were there at the party that evening. During the evening, while we were standing together chatting with a group of people, I felt her suddenly grab my hand and squeeze it so hard her nails dug into my palms. I asked her what was wrong, but she shook her head violently no.

She kept looking over my shoulder at someone behind me. Finally, I couldn't stand it, so I turned and looked. Leaning against the wall was a very large, bald man. I couldn't tell you how old he might have been. However, I guessed he had a good four or five inches over my six feet three, and he was a good eighty to one hundred pounds over my two hundred-twenty. His suit was bespoke and was of noticeably top quality fabrics. It was also obvious whoever had made it was a craftsman who'd tailored the suit well to hide his bulk.

The giant had a great tan, and when he lifted one of his massive paws to sip his drink, you could see his fingers covered in flashy rings and his wrist encircled with a heavy gold bracelet. I turned back, asked her once again what was wrong, and what it was with the man. I believe I even asked her if he had done something to her. She whispered 'no' several times, and then shook her head, as if to shake away what was eating at her. Eventually, I forgot about it. Later, whenever I thought about it and wanted to ask her what it was about the big dude, I'd forget. However, at the time, it was plain to see the man's presence frightened her.

I called Jeff L. and Sakol the next morning and told them what I had remembered. Jeff L. asked me if I would come down and to help the sketch artist do a rendering. Once the sketch artist completed the drawing, I thought it looked remarkably like the man at my party. I went with Jeff and Sakol to those I could remember being at the party. After every interview, Jeff L. would ask me what I had observed, and what I thought. Jeff L. would then ask Sakol what he had seen and heard.

Experts say every minute of the day the average person receives over fifteen thousand bits of information. However, because of the way our minds work, it only keeps forty to fifty pieces of that information. It amazed me at what Sakol could add that we had missed. It seemed obvious he was retaining more than the forty to fifty bits I remembered. This amazing man-made Sherlock Holmes look like a piker. Because of his silly grin and funny face, people relaxed, and he could get more out of suspects than Jeff L. and I ever could. In addition, he seemed to hear what they didn't say too.

Eventually, we found someone at the party who recognized the person. However, when the police tried to arrest him, he resisted drastically. He struggled with the police who eventually shot and killed him as he tried to escape. Afterward, during a search of his condominium, the police found a lot of evidence which linked him to more than just the rape and murder of my friend.

Jeff L. and his superiors told me how pleased they were with my efforts, and I told both of them I'd enjoyed being involved. Jeff L. and Sakol were the first ones to take my statement about Slim, and then they took Scott's. I didn't see Scott for the rest of the day. My assumption was that the police didn't want the two of us to have time to compare our stories. I understood the basic reasoning behind this thinking, but on the other hand, what if something one of us said triggered a memory in the other's mind? I guess that's why I never took up police work.

Talk about a ton of questions. Scott and I must have told our story at least a dozen times. Every time a new set of detectives arrived, they would want to hear the same story we'd already told the last group.

The police went from houseboat to houseboat asking questions. During the afternoon, the old man from up the dock must have told one detective he had heard a dog barking in the middle of the night on slip fourteen. He must have also commented the barking dog sounded just like BJ. The next thing I knew, a slew of detectives was hot-footing it back asking a bunch of new questions.

"No, I didn't leave home last night."

"No, I was not on the dock last night."

"No, I have no one who can vouch for my story I was asleep all night."

"No, I've never been back to this dock after my first visit."

"No, it was not my dog making that racket during the night."

"No, I didn't kill Slim."

"No, I don't know him by any other name."

"No, we left each other on good terms after I won his houseboat."

"No, I didn't kill him after I found out I'd won a houseboat with no place to tie it up."

I saw no reason to tell them I would have liked to. If they'd asked that question, that might have been just a tiny white lie. I really was upset about the slip part. Finally, they must have been tired of hearing negative responses because they left me alone. It relieved me when they finally lightened up. I was also pleased when the police told me they would direct the managers of the marina since this was now a crime scene, neither they, nor I, could move the houseboat until they released it. I wondered how long the police would hold off before they told the marina management, they could release the houseboat. If management asked how long the police thought it might be, I knew management would become quite upset.

The police said they would tell the marina it would be at least eight to twelve weeks, and possibly more. I'll admit, it wasn't a long time, but it was a reprieve to give me more time to find a new slip. At this point, I'd take every extension I could get.

During the afternoon, I realized it was a long time since BJ had a chance to visit Mother Nature and I headed off to the truck to release her. When I was about four feet away, one officer guarding the scene put his hand on his pistol butt and told me I was not to leave.

I informed him I was just going to let my dog out of the truck for a few minutes, and then I would rejoin the rest of the party. The cop must have been kinda kinky because he wanted to watch BJ do her thing. Well, at least he wanted to watch me watch BJ do her thing. I held out a plastic bag for him to pick up her poop to see if he wanted to take part... but he passed.

Wimp!

It was late afternoon when the weather turned colder, and it started to rain. By the time the fire trucks, the police, the detectives, the coroner, the reporters, and all the noisy people were through with me, it was dark. Sure enough, the rain the weather people had promised us was falling in earnest.

Finally, I could leave the marina and go home.

But I also knew I was taking the macabre vision of what I'd found sitting in that chair home with me.

It would take a lot more than just a little rain to wash away those memories from my brain.

CHAPTER SEVEN

The drive back to my place was just plain wet and nasty, which is fairly typical for a rainy, late autumn evening in Seattle. Traffic was normal, which means bordering somewhere between awful and totally sucks. I parked my truck and found the first thing going right for me today; the elevator was waiting at the garage level.

Stepping off the elevator on my floor, I heard my answering machine calling me. Well, it was more like the machine making a noise to attract my attention, but in my imagination, I think it's talking to me. I know, I'm weird.

If people knew the truth, I hate most of the new gadgets that keep coming to market, but since I have this bad habit of never checking my answering machine, this one at least prompts me when someone has called... and I need to do something about it.

My new machine makes a tone every few seconds, and this wonderful piece of technology will keep annoying me until I listen to the messages, push a button which turns off the noise, or throw the damn thing off the balcony. I have a cell phone, but I tend to leave it in my truck or at the apartment and not carry it with me, which really seems to upset people.

The missed call was from Scott, calling from his cell phone. He was apologizing again because he'd dragged me into this mess. Now that Slim was dead, it also looked as if I now had the houseboat whether I liked it or not. He also promised me he'd secure me a slip somewhere, even if he had to go down in the middle of the night and cut some other floating home loose.

My thoughts about his offer were, Thanks, Scott! Do that and I'll need to come visit you every Thursday with cigarettes, and what's even worse, you'll end up being Bubba's love slave at the state pen.

From the cupboard, I fetched down a glass and looked over my inventory of favorite brands of single malt. Since I'd dealt with such a wonderful day, I felt I'd earned some of my rare The Balvenie Double Wood 17-year-old single malt. I knew I was committing an act of sin by adding a handful of ice to the glass and then pouring in a goodly amount of Scotch over the ice, but since that's the way I like it, and since I paid for it, I get to drink it however I want.

Once I had my drink, I wandered out to the front room and settled back in my favorite leather chair. I always enjoy the sounds of the air whooshing out of the cushion and filling the room with the smell of the expensive leather. It's a big old chair with a huge ottoman, and they sit in a corner of the front room facing one of the large windows, overlooking the lake and the channel in the distance.

When I first entered the room, I went to put on some tunes, but then decided after the day I'd just been through I'd just rather sit in dark silence and brood.

Once I curled up in my chair, BJ came and put her paws up on the ottoman. I picked her up. She turned around once before she snuggled down in my lap, and we sat together in the chair, me petting BJ with one hand, and sipping my drink with the other.

I stared off across the lake and at the canal beyond, seeing the bridges crossing over the canal as it trailed off into the distance. I wondered why anybody would be out on a night like this as I watched a pleasure boat slowly meandering up the slot, its reflected lights flickering off the water. Red lights illuminating the left side of the craft, green glimmering on the right. The lights of the craft highlighted the small waves surrounding the boat, as it splashed down the canal, and the rain falling outside seemed to fit my mood just fine.

I'd kept most of the details of the morning isolated from the center of my brain during the day, but now it was quiet, keeping those thoughts at bay had become a lot more difficult. Now I allowed the flood of thoughts to cascade out and wash through my mind.

One of my main thoughts had actually finally formed into a question. The question? That was easy. "Who could have disliked Slim so much they wanted to end his life in such a brutal manner?" With all the noises of the city surrounding the marina, a pistol wrapped in a pillow would have been difficult to hear, if not impossible. Then why use a knife? A knife is such a messy weapon.

Back in the day, when I was a lot younger and somewhat dumber, I pulled a stretch with Uncle Sam wearing his lovely shade of olive drab. At that tender age, I believed a lot of the nonsense they fed raw recruits. That was before I grew older and realized it was all just a lot of hype. Anyway, at that stage in my life, I was buying what the government was selling, and I felt it had been my duty to stop the yellow horde from sweeping down from the north and overrunning the rest of all the rice-paddy lands.

After enlisting, I ended up being selected for some extra special schooling where they taught us the many ways to end a life I secretly hoped I'd never really have to use. I don't know if I was particularly motivated, or if I was just

47

good at that kind of thing, but I excelled at their training. Several of the ways they taught us to kill people involved the use of knives. I hate to admit it, but I've had to use more of that training than I'd have liked.

Over the intervening years, I concluded I had no choice but to use this wonderful knowledge. Sometimes it was an issue of kill or someone kills you. But occasionally, the ugliness would come out in the middle of the night and oh how I'd wish things could have worked out differently. Knowing you've brought about anyone's death isn't a pleasant thing to carry around inside your head.

One fact they taught us about knives I remember most vividly. The lesson was: you have to make sure you're very close to assure total success. Throwing the knife at a person might work, but it can also easily hit a bone or something else and bounce off. To be sure, you have to feel the other person's body heat, smell their personal smells, and then use the knife. It's not like a gun where you can kill from afar. A bullet can travel for great distances and still be accurate.

On the other hand, to use a knife effectively, to know for certain you have accomplished what you wanted, you need to hold the knife in your hand and push or pull it across the victim. For that reason, I always felt that murdering with a knife was committing a very intimate act.

With that thought, I kept coming back to the one big question. Who hated Slim that much? Who wanted him dead so badly they were willing to commit such an intimate act? Who possessed that much hatred for ol' Slim?

I found my glass of Scotch had magically evaporated and needed a refill. When I tried to stand, I realized I'd finished my third substantial drink. I also realized I hadn't eaten regular food all day.

I stumbled into the kitchen, found a frozen dinner in the freezer and nuked it for the prescribed amount of time. It wasn't that the dinner was so bad; it was I really wasn't all that hungry. When I finally finished picking at it, I noticed I hadn't even finished half of the dinner. I gave BJ a few bites and then I took her out to visit Mother Nature.

The fresh air and the rain felt good against my face and I decided we should go for a walk. We ended up taking a long and wet walk, and when we returned, I was finally ready to go to bed. I dried BJ and then myself off with a towel.

Once we were both dry, we crawled into bed and I guess I'd drunk enough Scotch I fell right to sleep.

Gratefully.

HOUSEBOAT

CHAPTER EIGHT

It was Thanksgiving Day, and I considered going to a restaurant and ordering a turkey dinner. However, going out in public, and dining alone, didn't appeal to me so I decided instead to go out and find an open grocery store and purchase a frozen TV turkey dinner. Thank God for 7-11. Not the best way to celebrate the holiday, but I wasn't feeling the least bit thankful or sociable. I know I have much to be thankful for and in so many ways I really am, but I couldn't seem to put the memory of Slim away and that pulled me down. His memory was present in both my thoughts and in my dreams. I'd seen worse over the years, but I found I was having a very difficult time dealing with the memory of Slim's death.

As a feeble sun finally sank into the end of the canal on the first Monday of December, I'd been moping around for twelve long days in my apartment and I decided it was enough. I needed to do something about it. The last week had been so depressing, and I realized it was partly because one of those days had been Thanksgiving and I'd been alone. Watching the pale, wan sunset made me realize I didn't want to eat another meal alone. I wondered if Sharon was home yet.

Sharon is a big, tall, honey blond who lives in the unit under mine. In stocking feet, she can almost look me in the eye. She's in her middle thirties with the greatest gray-green eyes you've ever seen. I guess you'd consider her pretty, but I see more than that in her. Sharon might seem rather small breasted when she's dressed, and because of her size, clothes don't really show how fantastic her figure is, but in the buff she is breathtaking. As someone once said about some athlete, the more she takes off, the better it gets.

Sharon is a head ER nurse, and she works in one of the hospitals on what they call Pill Hill in Seattle. The actual name of the hill is First Hill. First at what I don't have a clue, but it's the First Hill. Several hospitals look as if they're interconnected. I'm sure all of them are separate entities, but since I have an aversion to hospitals, I really don't care which one is which.

There had been an "us" for a while but when Sharon finally moved in downstairs, we'd become just friends. One evening she showed up at my doorstep, sniffling, eyes all red, and seemed quite mad. It turned out the mad part was her anger with herself. She'd allowed herself to become too emotionally involved with a patient and the patient had died that afternoon. I held her as she cried. We then talked and laughed, and I held her again while she cried some more. When it came time for sleep, she headed to my bedroom, slipped under the covers, and was instantly out.

After I finished taking BJ for her walk, I returned to find Sharon had been up long enough to remove all of her clothing and was again asleep in my bed. I debated between the couch and the other half of my king-size bed. The bed won. After all, she'd chosen to sleep with me, and if this wasn't to her liking, we'd deal with it in the AM.

I'd met Sharon a number of years ago through a mutual friend, and after a few dates, like I said, we'd tried a brief fling at a physical relationship. We quickly found that having sex was more of a competition between us than any form of tenderness. I knew she was the only girl in a family with five older brothers. I thought maybe she developed her competitive side from growing up with her brothers and trying to pace with them, and somehow this competitive attitude slipped over into her intimate side. It seemed like she's replaced intimacy and tenderness with aggression and trying to see who was the most skillful or something. Like she was looking for a prize. Whenever I'd change positions when we were making love, she'd have to try to do me one better. When we eventually stopped, I was greatly relieved, and I felt she was of a similar mind. The best part is after we stopped, we became great friends.

Even though we'd stopped dating, we'd remained in close contact, and when one of my units came up for rent, I mentioned it to her, and she promptly moved in. I doubt if she's aware she's paying a small pittance of what the other tenants are paying, but since it's my building, I make the rules on what I charge. We keep track of each other and make sure we're both doing all right. Because of our friendship, I knew she'd still be happy to see me even if I was in a funk.

I punched her number into my cell, and she answered on the second ring. Although we were not physical any longer, I still enjoyed hearing her sexy voice. A hello from her seems to speak volumes. And what torrid volumes they are! "Hi, babe, it's me. Matt! Hungry? It's been rotten the past few days, and I really don't wanna eat alone again."

"You pick the place and give me ten minutes before you pick me up." The phone went dead in my hand.

In my closet, I found a freshly laundered shirt, and over it I slipped on a sports jacket. I ran a brush through my slightly silver locks and briefly considered a shave. I say silver because silver sounds so much better than gray. Mom and dad were gray, I prefer being silver! Gray is slowly coming; however, I choose to ignore it for now.

I stopped in the kitchen, poured another good stiff drink of Macallan 10, (which is a third the price of Macallan 25) for the trip downstairs, and headed for the elevator. Since I own the building, I have the keys for each floor, and I stopped the elevator at her floor. I stepped off and called her name. She stuck her head out of the bathroom and called to me. I wandered back through the apartment.

When she saw my drink, she motioned me over. She took the drink out of my hand and gave me a quick kiss on the lips. Afterward, she took a deep sip of my drink and then smiled at me. I couldn't help but notice she was dressed only in thong panties. Even though our relationship was supposedly past the sexual point, I'm a guy and I still enjoy looking at her. Damn, she's an excellent-looking woman.

She stole my drink and took a second sip, and her smile made me realize she would keep it. I headed off to her kitchen to make myself a new one.

She kept the door open so we could talk, and I told her about the past few days. I started with the card game, and how it came about that I'd won my floating nightmare. Once I mentioned the houseboat, she flew out of the bathroom with excitement and then I watched her excitement fade as I explained how they were evicting the thing from its moorage. She grabbed my hand and pulled me into the bathroom with her to tell her the rest of the story.

It was obvious a woman used the bathroom. Two pairs of pantyhose hung over the shower curtain rail and a bra rested on top of the toilet. Many great women smells filled the room, and I watched her do her face as I continued with my story. I glossed over the part about finding Slim a few mornings ago as best I could. She asked me if there were any leads, and I told her they told me not to leave town without asking for permission first. She looked at me in her mirror, "Why? Were you really that pissed at him?"

"No... well, yes... but no, I mean... I wouldn't do that... you know, like murder him. But it seems some other boat owners heard a dog barking in the night and the police are wondering if it wasn't BJ. In addition, when we first got there, she ran ahead and tracked through the blood. Finding her bloody footprints throughout the place didn't sit too well with the detectives. A guy I went to school with is the detective in charge and he seemed to believe my story. Anyway, thanks to BJ I have to stay put."

I continued to watch her fix her face and hair until finally I had to leave and go back into the other room. There's something very sexy, very alluring about watching a woman fix her hair. The lifting of her arms over her head so her hands can work in her hair was causing her breasts to move and sway in very suggestive ways. The more she fixed her hair the more turned on I was becoming. As I mentioned, the less clothing she wears, the more you realize how fantastic her body is. I could feel my body reacting and I started getting ideas about her we'd agreed would be best to put away.

A short time later Sharon came into the front room, still clad in just her thong, and asked if I was all right. I told her I was fine, but as much as I hated to admit it, I wasn't immune to her sensuality.

I continued telling her how for the past few days I'd been having deep thoughts which caused me to have several really crummy days. Because of the houseboat, and with Slim's death, no moorage and on and on, I was feeling vulnerable and rather lonely.

Grinning at her, I tried to explain I'm not immune when I see her half-naked. And having seen Slim's gruesome dead body made me realize what a short time we all have on this earth. I also told her I felt I didn't have a lot to show for my life. Sharon stepped over and cradled my head between her naked breasts. Finally, she kissed the top of my head and stepped back. "Would it help if we laid down for a while?"

I thanked her for the thought, but told her I really treasured our friendship, and wouldn't want to jeopardize it by doing that. She kissed me again, and then she went off to finish dressing. As she walked away, I watched her naked bottom covered with just the string of her thong separating her darling cheeks. I wondered if spending the night together wouldn't be such a bad idea after all.

I need to make another quick explanation here. Two months ago I got a call from Sharon late one night, and she asked if she might come up. At that point, several months had passed since we stopped being physical. It was well past midnight when she called, and I almost said no, but there was something in her voice telling me she really needed a friend.

As soon as she saw me at the door, she broke down and cried. As it turned out, she'd gone on a date with a co-worker, and when they returned to her place, he'd tried date rape on her. Somehow, she'd convinced him to leave. But, when she tried to go to bed, she found she was more frightened and troubled by the experience than she'd realized.

We talked for a while, and then she asked if she could spend the night. I just held her for a while, and she fell asleep in my arms. The next morning, I awoke to the feel of her hands, touching me.

"I thought we were over this, what gives?" I asked in a sleepy, dazed tone.

"Please be still, enjoy... trust me..." She continued.

After a short time, I was at a point where I asked her once again because I doubted if I could stop. I asked if she really wanted to continue and she nodded her head shyly, yes.

We made love, and I found us doing things we'd never done before. The rest is best kept between us except to say it was amazing. Afterward she lay in my arms and wept. At first, I didn't understand. I thought I'd done something wrong. I was afraid I'd really screwed up our friendship. As the tears decreased, I asked her what was going on. Had I misread something? I was sick to think I might have screwed things up. Eventually, through the hiccups and a few more bouts of tears, she explained. She felt so grateful to have these new memories of our just completed passion to replace the foul ones of the previous evening.

After a while as we talked about it, both of us got interested again. We made love one more time, and it was as perfect as it could be. Afterward, we fell asleep, bodies entwined; but when I awoke the following morning her side of the bed was empty.

I looked down next to the bed, and her clothes were gone. I went to the kitchen to make coffee and found a note under one magnet on the fridge. The note from her had just one word, Thanks! And a big happy face drawn below. Ninety-nine percent of the time, I can't stand that insipid happy face symbol. But I decided this time she was the one percent exception.

That evening she showed up with a bag of groceries and fixed me the best prawn and crab fettuccine I've ever had. She thanked me for being there and for being such a friend. I had to ask again about the bed thing.

She stood there for a long time, and I could tell she was working out her thoughts. Finally, she told me that last night she knew I wouldn't do anything unless it was mutually agreeable. I was safe. She also knew she didn't want to sleep alone. With that explanation, she reached up and pecked me on my cheek.

We've never made love since. However, because of that incident we became even better friends. I even had one lady break up with me because of our friendship. My lady friend couldn't believe Sharon and I could be so tight and not be continuously doing the big nasty. And in the end, she didn't want to share.

I'll admit, I've wondered what it would be like to make love with Sharon again. However, I have a feeling it might be a price I didn't want to pay. We've never done it again. We may joke about it occasionally, but now we are much more protective of each other.

Exactly like friends are supposed to do.

CHAPTER NINE

One of my favorite restaurants is down amid the docks on the south end of Lake Union where pleasure craft are moored. The restaurant is called Tony's Hidden Harbor and to reach Tony's it's necessary to walk down a long flight of stairs from street level until you reach a small waiting area on the docks.

Directly behind the waiting area is Tony's Bar, and it looks like a cave someone has carved out from under the street above. The bar is dark with a nautical motif and is an excellent place to hang out. The drinks are large and not very expensive. They located the dinner tables around the docks and because there are yachts tied around you, it's always a fun experience. Eating there has never failed to lift my spirits. I'm pleased to report tonight's visit was no exception.

As a youth, I spent most of my summers on Whidbey Island in Puget Sound. I've spent a good part of my life on, or around, boats as you can imagine. It's always relaxing for me sitting on the docks, eating among the boats, and watching them shift as they creak and moan in their slips from the wakes of passing boats.

Dinner, as always, was good, and as we sat and ate, we laughed a lot. I could tell Sharon was trying very hard to bring me out of the dumps. At one point, Sharon slipped her shoe off and with her foot, massaged the front of my pants under the table. I quickly reached under the table and removed her foot. It would be very embarrassing to walk out of a restaurant with a tent sticking out of the front of my trousers. She giggled.

Sharon asked me if I had any theories about who would want Slim dead. I thought for a while and then responded if he'd made a habit of giving people problems like the one he gave me, I could see why many people might want him dead. I really didn't mean it, but I was still a little upset how he had dumped his houseboat on me.

"What are you going to do about the houseboat?" Sharon asked.

"That's an excellent question, Babe. First off, I don't know exactly what proof I have it's even mine. Several days after I won the thing, Scott started the Transfer of the Title and all the rest of the related paperwork. I have no idea exactly where it stands legally. I know Scott sent Slim papers to sign and then Scott was to file them. At this point, I don't know what Slim did with his paperwork. I'm not sure if he turned in his papers to his attorney for review, or what he's done so far.

"The reason I went to the houseboat was to get the final paperwork from Slim. I guess that's what I'd need to show that the houseboat is mine."

I hung my head, shook it, and continued, "I hope I don't have to get statements from the others at the game and end up having to file a claim against his estate. That would seem rather tacky because it makes me out as some sort of a gold digger or whatever... you know.

Shrugging my shoulders, I shook my head, and continued, "I'm feeling just about ready to bag the entire thing and let his estate deal with it. About the only good thing that came out of all this, if you can call it good, was while the police are still investigating the murder, they said we couldn't move the houseboat. Period!"

Sharon smiled at me, and asked, "What does the houseboat look like?"

"It's really cute. You'd find it adorable." A thought occurred to me, "Now I think about it, it seems odd that Slim lived there." Sharon frowned and shook her head, confused. "No. Really, it's true. Let me try to explain. I realized the strange part of this thing with the houseboat is I really can't see Slim living there."

Since the thought had never occurred to me before that moment, I was treading water. I went on, "It's like he just didn't seem the type who'd live on a houseboat, especially one that looked like that. Ralph told me at one time Slim was worth a lot of money, but he didn't know how much. Also, the thing was... well, the houseboat wasn't his taste... I mean the houseboat isn't a dump by any means, but he could've afforded better, a lot nicer from what I understand. Plus, I could see him living in a log cabin before I could see him in the houseboat. Does that make sense?"

Sharon nodded.

"Anyway, after we finished the game, he mentioned he was heading back to the southwest somewhere. I believe he said New Mexico. He really looked like someone from that neck of the woods. That houseboat isn't Tex-Mex in any way, shape or form."

"Okay, I'm curious now. Can we drive by the place after dinner?"

"I guess so, but I don't know if we can walk onboard. I think the police still have the area roped off. Finish up and we'll see."

She asked me what I thought my chances were on finding a new slip to tie up the houseboat. I told her what Scott had told me that morning, and added, "It doesn't look good. Most people find a slip and then go have a contractor build their home. You don't go buy a home and then try to find a place to dock it. Or, when you sell a houseboat the slip goes with it, like a package deal."

"Well, if there's anyone creative enough to do it, I know it will be you. I'm not worried." Sharon smiled at me.

"I wish I had your confidence. The way Scott makes it sound, I might just have to tow it out to Puget Sound and let it float away. Thanks anyway for the vote of confidence."

After I paid our check, instead of heading back to our condos, I drove over to the parking lot in front of the marina where the houseboat was moored. When I pulled up, I saw a uniformed police officer standing at the front of the dock, and another officer sitting in a squad car in the far end of the parking lot. I pulled through the lot while the officer in the car stared at me. Since I didn't want to deal with them this evening, I headed for home.

I stopped the elevator on Sharon's floor to let her off. Before she left, she reached up and kissed my cheek. She didn't let go right away but kept her arms around my neck and looked into my eyes, "You still look like you need a friend. You're welcome to spend the night. Nothing expected, just someone to curl up with to ward off the night dragons." I kissed her forehead, thanked her, told her I would be just fine and then I nudged her off the elevator. The elevator took me on up to my place.

As soon as the door opened, BJ came barreling at me and pawed at my shoes. I knew what that meant. See, she has me well trained, right? I changed my jacket and shoes and then took her out for a walk. The damp night was turning cold, and after a while, I wanted to return to the warmth of the condo. I tried to encourage BJ not to turn this into a major career move but she had other ideas. Finally, in desperation, I picked her up and carried her back inside.

I locked the back door and wandered to the front room where I tried sitting in my favorite chair. I found I was still restless. I decided I wanted nothing more to drink, so I put on several different CDs to see if music would help. Eventually, I ended up just sitting in the dark staring out over the dark lake.

When I tried to go to bed, I found the images of Slim tied to the chair with his chin on his chest were waiting for me. I got up and slipped on some sweats. Twice I walked to the elevator before I eventually got on and rode down to Sharon's floor.

When I got off the elevator, I saw there was a light on in her hallway. I went to her bedroom door and gently knocked. I heard her sexy chuckle, and she told me to come in.

BJ headed straight for the big stuffed chair next to her bed, jumped up on it, turned around twice, and then settled in for the night. Sharon flipped back the covers, and I saw her flawless body between the sheets. She smiled up at me, and asked, "What took you so long to ride down here? Did ya get lost?"

I guess there's a reason everyone considers her such a damn good nurse. Sharon knows exactly what's needed. As I lay there with my head cradled in her arms and engulfed by her sweet perfume, I didn't know if the tears forming in my eyes were from gratitude I wasn't alone, or for poor Ol' Slim. I finally decided it didn't matter. At that moment lying in her arms, I felt safe, comfortable, and totally secure.

Those dragons would have to find someone else to prey on tonight.

HOUSEBOAT

CHAPTER TEN

At first, I thought it was the sun shining through the gaps between the blinds that had woken me. That is until I opened one eye and found myself face-to-muzzle with BJ. As soon as she realized I was awake, her pink tongue shot out. Zap! And before I could pull away, she zapped me a couple more times to greet me. Somehow the bed didn't feel familiar and for a moment, it disoriented me. Other than BJ, nothing seemed right. Slowly, memories of my nocturnal visit came back. I reached behind me, and to my dismay, I felt an empty bed.

Laying there, my mind continued to clear, and I noticed my surroundings. I heard a shower running, and Sharon was humming a strange tune. I thought about getting out of the bed and sneaking up to my place. Instead, I waited until she finished her shower. I wanted to thank her for putting up with me last night.

Finally, I heard the shower finish, the shower door open, and then bang shut. In a few minutes, she came striding into the bedroom with just a towel wrapped around her damp hair. Again, I was impressed gazing at her naked body. You wouldn't consider her shape to be an hour-glass, but I don't believe you'd consider her Rubenesque either.

I coughed softly so as not to startle her, and she turned. I sheepishly looked up at her, and murmured, "Good morning."

"Sorry, Matt, if I woke you up. I needed to get ready to leave," she informed me, and she sounded genuinely sorry she had to go.

"No, it wasn't you. It was my other alarm clock. BJ was my alarm." I paused a moment, looking for the right words. "Ha... look... I don't know where to start... but... well, about last night..."

She put her fists on her hips, and smiled down at me, "Stop!" She leaned over, reached forward and briefly caressed my cheek. "Look, let's say I owed you one from the time I barged in and forced myself on you. You've been in the dumps the past few days... and... actually, I was very pleased you came back, and allowed me to help." As she spoke, she pulled the towel from her head and dried the ends of her hair.

"Sharon, it was more than that. I'm not in the habit of showing my emotions like I did last night. I guess I'm a bit embarrassed, and I feel a need to explain or apologize or..."

She stopped drying her hair, turned to face me, and her fists returned to her waist. She wasn't exactly angry with me, but I could tell she wasn't pleased with me either. "Oh, bullshit Matt. Just like a man, never let 'em see you cry! Right?"

Her voice softened, and she took a step towards me, "First, you don't owe me an apology. Second, you're a real dummy! Do you have a clue how good it made me feel you'd trust me enough to come down here last night? That you'd allow me to comfort you?"

She paused, I didn't know what to say. Finally, she continued, "After what you did for me that one night, I've always felt I owed you something... ha... something I didn't know if... or even how, I could repay. Now I feel we're... well... like kinda even, or something."

She sat down beside me and put her hand back on my cheek. I turned my head and kissed her palm. I could smell the fragrance of her shampoo on her hand. Her voice became a whisper, "You know I'd have made love with you last night if you'd wanted."

I smiled and nodded, "I know! And thank you, but the last time we did that, it put a scare in me. All the times before we were together it was like... well... just sex. Not making love, it was just plain sex! That last time we did it, we really seemed to connect, and it was great... actually it went beyond that." I stopped and waited a second before I continued. "Well, I've wondered if it would be... could be... like that again and... what if it wasn't and..." She put her hand over my mouth.

Her voice had a smile in it and her words warmed me. "Yes, it was fantastic. I understand what you mean. Maybe it was too good if there is such a thing." I got a cute grin with that remark. With her hand still on my cheek, she continued, "You're a very special man. I, too, treasure our friendship, and it's even more special because you're so careful not to confuse sexual act with anything else. You're a true friend. I needed someone that night and you were there for me."

When I tried to speak, she again put her hand on my lips, and said, "Someone hurt me. I was angry and I feel you gave me everything I needed. Without question, I knew I could trust you completely. I knew you'd hold me, and I was safe with you. And then the next morning I needed something else... and... well, you helped me there, too. That was even more special.

"Last night I felt I could repay a small part of what I feel I owe you. Friends are like that. I've seen you at your worst and at your best, and still we're friends. Last night, if you had told me you wanted, or needed to make love, I'd have made love with you. Why? Because I'd have wanted to as well. Partly because you needed, or wanted to, is the same as if I wanted or needed to. You know, in many ways I can say I love you. I know I feel more for you than I ever felt for my lousy ex. Anyway, this is way too heavy a talk for this time of day. I have to run." She glanced at the clock sitting next to the bed, "Oh shit! I'm incredibly late now."

Sharon leaned forward and kissed me. I reached out and pulled her down wrapping my arms around her in a big hug. She squirmed, and I heard her murmur against my chest she needed to get going, but I held her anyway, for a long time. She stopped trying to pull away and I could feel her damp hair resting against my cheek.

The feeling of her body tight against mine woke things up and after a while, it was all I could do to push her away. I told her she had to leave, now! With a very sexy chuckle she uttered, "Boy, I was worrying I'd lost my touch."

I laughed, "Baby, either you leave now or all bets were off." That got me a big kiss, and I watched her bottom sway off to her bathroom. As she dressed, I pulled on my sweats and headed for my place to find my shoes and a coat. By now, BJ had expressed her need to tend to business. She was letting me know she was unhappy I was taking so long.

Stepping onto the elevator I heard Sharon call out, "Please call me tonight. Check-in. I'm still worried about you." I assured her I would.

CHAPTER ELEVEN

After I returned with BJ from her morning outing in the back lot, I heard my answering machine demanding my attention. When I looked at it, I saw the light on top was flashing. I checked, and it told me I had three new messages. "Gee," I mused, "I didn't think I was outside that long. I must be getting more popular in my old age!"

The first message was from Scott. He requested I call him to arrange a time to meet today. In the message, he said he wanted to talk over some things with me. The first thing that came to mind was he'd discovered a way out of my houseboat dilemma; like a new spot for me to tie it up. But I also knew better than to get my hopes up.

The second call was from Jeff L., asking me to call his office at my earliest convenience. Perhaps the word I should use is "demanded" I call his office as soon as possible. Because of the tone of his voice, I wasn't very excited to return his call promptly. I call the tone of his voice "the cop voice," and I knew I wasn't ready to deal with him so early in the day. A cup of coffee first and then I'd see how I felt.

The third message sounded the most interesting of the three. A woman's voice emanated from the machine, and from the sound of her voice, she didn't sound all that old.

The voice was low-pitched and sultry and I also thought I detected a slight accent, but since it was so subtle, I couldn't quite place it.

"Um, Good morning." I could hear she was nervous, and I could tell she didn't know exactly what to say. "My name is Jennifer Rockingham," she paused and then informed me, "I got your number from my father's attorney. I was wondering if you could please call me back. There's a… ah… a matter I need to discuss with you." She left a number where to reach her, and my machine clicked off. Short, but not informative.

As I stood there staring at the machine, I halfway expected it to explain who it was that called. I replayed the message twice more to see if I'd missed any clues, but still found I was in the dark.

"Who the hell is Jennifer Rockingham?" I wondered.

I glanced at the clock on the microwave and saw it was just past eight AM and I wanted to clean up before I returned any calls. I would take my shower first, and everything else could wait.

Standing in the shower with hot water cascading over me, I tried to recall any person named Jennifer, or any Rockingham that I might have run into during my uneven past. I remembered a Jennifer from college, but the chances she'd ever call me in this lifetime were remote, extremely remote. As I recalled, the last time I saw her was when she slapped my face for a reason that now escapes me. As sad as I am to admit this fact, she wasn't the first, or only girl to slap me.

By the time I stepped out of the shower, I still was still clueless who this person was. My curiosity pricking at me. After I dried off, I wrapped the towel around me and wandered into the front room, picked up the phone and punched in the number the woman left. Two rings later, there was an answer on the other end.

"Hello!" I immediately recognized the sexy voice from my machine.

"Hello!" I still wanted to make sure I had the right person, "May I speak to Jennifer Rockingham, please."

"This is she." No doubt about it, this woman had a beautiful speaking voice.

"Good morning. This is Matt. Ah... Matthew, Matthew Preston. You called me this morning."

"Oh yes, Mr. Preston. Good Morning. And thank you for returning my call so quickly." She sounded genuinely happy to hear from me. "The reason I was calling you was regarding my father, Elmo. Elmo Rockingham."

Complete silence on my part.

And?

So?

I waited for more.

The name she gave me meant nothing, and I waited for her to continue, but it appeared she was waiting for me to speak. The silence grew between us. I was clueless and embarrassed to respond. I couldn't help but wonder who the hell are these people who know me? I don't have a clue about their identity. First Jennifer, and now a mysterious father? What's next, the shotgun?

Finally, after a very long pause I broke the silence, "I'm sorry Miss Rockingham. I don't mean to be rude, but you seem to have me at a disadvantage. That name means nothing to me. Should it?" I tried to make my voice as charming as I could because I felt embarrassed that I couldn't be of more help.

She responded quickly, "Oh! Gosh! I'm so sorry Mr. Preston, I didn't realize you didn't know his given name. Please forgive me, I assumed you knew who he was. I believe you probably knew my father as 'Slim', 'Slim' Rockingham."

"Excuse me... ah... Miss?" I paused.

And she replied, "Miss."

"Miss Rockingham, yes, I knew your father. I'm the one who needs to apologize, I'm sorry, but until this minute, I'd never heard your father's actual name. Yes, I knew him. When I met your father, they introduced him as Slim, and that's the only name I ever heard him called." I paused for a few seconds and wondered if I should say more. Finally, I continued, "I'm so sorry about your father's death, my condolences Miss."

"Thank you, Mr. Preston." She paused, and then spoke quickly, "The reason I'm calling you is ... well ... I understand you somehow might have an interest in my father's estate. Am I correct?"

It occurred to me briefly she was coming across as one rather cold lady. A few days ago, someone had killed her dad, and here she's sounding as if she's already worried that she would not get all of her inheritance. I explained, "Well, yes, in a way I guess I do. Recently, I won your dad's houseboat in a card game. My plan was to take possession of it the other day when I went over to the marina, and... um..." For some reason, I really didn't know how to end what I started to say.

Miss Rockingham interrupted, "Ah… that explains a lot. About a week ago, father's attorney called him, and father had informed him he'd finally 'gotten rid of the damn thing', as father had put it, meaning the houseboat.

"Father's attorney also mentioned you were the new owner. After his death, father's attorney became rather curious and concerned. Even though father sent him the transfer of ownership papers, signed by both of you, and all the rest of the papers involved with the transfer, none of the paperwork offered any record of money passing hands. There were no deposit slips, promissory notes, or anything. Father's attorney handled his affairs, so he should have known what the arrangements were. Father's attorney was going to ask father before he was... well... before the other day and when the attorney said he would investigate, I told him I'd be glad to call and just ask you. I guess father was too embarrassed to tell his attorney what had happened."

I decided I wanted to rid myself of this goofball in a hurry. It certainly appeared as if she had a real concern about all the money she thought she had coming. "Look, Ms. Rockingham, I offered to let your dad keep the thing. I felt bad after the game, because I might have put him out of house and home, so to speak. I'll gladly give up any claim I have to it.

"When I offered it back to your dad, he said he was ready to move back to New Mexico, and he told me he was glad to rid himself of it as well. Miss, I'm quite happy where I'm living now, and since your dad's houseboat was winnings from a card game, I'm more than willing to let you have it back. It's up to you. Tell your attorney, or your father's attorney, or whoever, I'll sign anything they need to release any claim I might have." My feelings were to let her deal with where to tie it up, or what to do with the houseboat. This might be my way out of the damn thing.

Her response was immediate, "Oh no, Mr. Preston, you misunderstand my call. I wanted to make sure there are no problems with any part of the estate, and given our discussion, we can finish this as quickly as possible. I've never seen the houseboat thing, and I can't imagine why I'd ever want to." There was a slight pause, and I felt she was considering if she wanted to tell me more, and what that might be. I heard her take a deep breath, then let it out as a deep sigh, before she continued. "Mr. Preston, I know this is none of your business, but since you now seem somewhat involved, I feel the need to explain something."

She paused for a moment and then plunged into her explanation, "Father and I have... excuse me, had a love-hate relationship for most of our lives. He loved, and I hated. I was an accident child, and I always felt he held it against my mother and me. Shortly after I was born, he left us, although he continued to provide excellent financial support. In other areas, I received nothing. Mother had such a difficult time dealing with everything she eventually sent me away. As she became more depressed, she ended up living as sort of a recluse. I've spent most of my life abroad in private schools, paid for by my loving father." I noticed the word 'loving' dripped with sarcasm.

She continued, "For many years we didn't even correspond with each other. When I finally saw him at mother's funeral, I wanted to let him know he was probably responsible for her early death, but I decided to hold my tongue. We only spoke a few words that day, however, I felt genuine remorse on his part for everything that happened. Over the past few months, we finally wrote to each other. Our first phone conversation was about a month ago." She paused, "Well, I guess in a way, I'm sad to lose him, especially now that he was attempting to build a new relationship with me. But, Mr. Preston, we were never close."

There was a pause, and I could sense now she was feeling uncomfortable because she realized she'd shared so many intimate details of her life. When she continued, her voice was soft, and I had to strain to hear her. "Excuse me, I'm rambling. You're the first person I've spoken to about him… well, since he... ah... passed away." I felt the young lady had reached the end of her rope. She had told me a lot more than she'd planned and now was embarrassed.

After a few more seconds, she gathered her composure, and her voice became brisker as she continued, "As I said, the reason for the call was to clear up any problems with the boat thing. I don't want to have to deal with it or see it or..." her voice trailed off.

Another pause, and then she resumed, "The truth of the matter is, I want to return to Europe just as quickly as I can.

My life is over there, and there's nothing here that makes me want to stay. It was just blind luck, if that's what you can call it, I'm in the States now. Mr. Preston, have your attorney contact my father's if there is anything you can think of that requires resolution." She gave me the name and address of Slim's lawyer, the same one I already had.

As we were saying our goodbyes a question sprang to mind, and I asked, "Miss... Rockingham..."

"Yes?" she replied. "May I ask a question?"

"Yes. What is it?"

"What was your father's full name?"

There was a slight pause, "Elmo... Elmo Fester Rockingham. Why?"

"I was just curious. Since it seems I stand a good chance of ending up with his houseboat, I would at least like to know his full name. I'd planned on asking him the other day."

"OK. Thank you for asking. I think that was a very nice gesture on your part." We said our farewells and hung up.

Still wrapped in my towel, I slouched down in my favorite chair, thinking about our conversation. Her schooling seemed to shine through our conversation. She'd been exactly what one would think a person educated in Europe should sound like. Cool and very reserved.

I wondered for a moment what she looked like. Then I realized whatever she looked like answered none of the questions I still had. The main one was what's the real reason she called me? I felt what she'd said made little sense, I'd have thought Slim's attorney would have called and asked me about transferring the houseboat, not her. Since the attorney was the one who wondered why no money exchanged hands, didn't it seem he'd make the call? Why even mention it to the daughter? And why allow the daughter to call?

As I sat pondering the strange call, my phone rang again, stirring me out of my deep thoughts. It was Jeff L.

No pleasantries, just straight to the point, "Where ya been, Matt? I've been trying to find you." He was using his hard-nosed cop voice, and it pissed me off.

"Why, Jeff? Let me see. I took BJ for a walk and she peed twice, took a nice dump which I picked up and disposed of... oh yeah, then my shower where I shaved if it matters. Do you also want to know which bushes BJ smelled on our walk?"

Jeff's voice softened, "Hey, lighten up. I wasn't grilling ya."

"It sure felt like it."

"Gee, why are you so touchy this morning? Your date not in the mood last night?" Without letting me answer he continued, "Someone broke into your houseboat last night, and the Captain said to ask you if you knew anything about it. By the way, did you drive by the marina last night?"

"Yeah," my internal alarm went off in my head. "I drove by. You say someone broke in to the houseboat? And you weren't the friendliest of people when you called." I heard an affirmative grunt, and I continued, "Jeff, I know nothing about the houseboat, and just between the two of us, right about now I sorta wish I'd never heard or seen the damn thing."

I was now referring to it the same way ol' Slim had. "Anyway yes, I drove by last night, and when I saw you had officers stationed out front I left. For what it's worth, I also haven't returned once to look at the thing since the other day when ... ah... well, you know, when..." I found I was at a loss for words.

"I know, look, Matt ... I have to ask you this," after a long pause, he stumbled on, "if you had to ah... do you have an alibi for last night?"

I thought of Sharon and hoped I wouldn't have to bring her into all of this. "Yes, I have someone who can vouch for me. All night if need be... and it isn't BJ. But I'd rather

I didn't have to give out any names unless there's no other way. Okay?"

"Fine with me. Just so long as you have someone to vouch for you if push comes to shove. The Captain still remembers you, and that he liked you. So far, he's being cool about not bringing you in, but I'm getting a lot of pressure to solve this case. By the way, might I ask you, what prompted you to drive by the marina last night?"

Just like Jeff L., always the cop, "Over dinner I told my friend all about the houseboat, and how I won it, yadda yadda... she was curious to see the thing. It's really her kind of place, and I knew she'd like to see it. We drove by, and when I saw the officers, I didn't want to deal with them and the reason I wanted to see the place, so I came home. How much damage did they do to it?"

"She?" Again, the cop thing never misses a beat, "No wonder you don't want to give out any names. Well, they busted in several of the walls, they cut up all the furniture, pulled the carpet up off the floor, and it was obvious they searched the place. We have no way of telling if they found what they were looking for."

I interrupted, "Hey! If you had officers guarding the place, how did anyone get into the houseboat?"

"It looks like they came in by boat. They pulled up in the back and busted out the back door. And we found out what Slim's real name was. Care to guess?"

I couldn't resist, "Naw, don't need to. It's Rockingham. Elmo Fester Rockingham."

I could tell by the silence on the other end that ol' Jeff L was not ready for my response. Finally, he whispered into the phone, "Shit, Matt! How the hell do you know that? We didn't even have his middle name."

"I spoke with his daughter this morning on the phone. She called me about the houseboat. It seems Slim's attorney has a few questions about it, and she said she was trying to help to clear it up."

For the longest time, Jeff sputtered. "Da... Da... Daughter!" His voice finally exploded in the receiver, "Daughter, what daughter? Where the hell are you coming up with all of this? He doesn't have a daughter..."

"Jeff... Jeff..."

Jeff continued to shout into the phone, "The only relative we know about is a stepsister named Bottomsley..."

"Jeff... Jeff..." My voice was rising in volume trying to cut in.

"And a dead ex-wife." Jeff was not listening.

"Jeff!" He stopped shouting. "Chill, friend. Can I talk now?"

"So talk!" he barked back at me.

"I'm about to tell you if you can just shut up for a moment. I talked to a woman just before you called who said she was the daughter. She claims her name is Jennifer Rockingham. Just a second and let me think... um..." I closed my eyes for a moment and remembered the voice. Her words played through my head like a tape machine.

"Okay, she said she and her father never had a close relationship... she was an accident and her mom and Slim split very early in her life. Jennifer believed it was because of her birth... and... oh yeah, she mentioned she got her schooling overseas. She told me it was by pure chance she was in the States. She didn't say how she found out about Slim's death. She also has a slight, but very sexy accent, and I can't place it.

"As I said, she told me Slim's lawyer called her, and he was curious about the boat thing. He saw papers transferring title to me, but there was never any record of any money passing between us. I explained to her how I'd won it in a poker game. I even offered to give it back, and she said I could have it. She claimed she wasn't interested in it at all. I can even give you the name of the attorney if you want."

After waiting a moment for Jeff to say something, I went on, "And I have to say I'm still troubled by the phone call. I can't quite put my finger on why. Now it's your turn. You tell me about the stepsister."

Normally Jeff shouldn't give out that type of information but I hoped with all I'd just told him he might feel rattled enough to spill some of his own. As it turned out, I was in luck. "Well, the murder made the news as you're aware. The stepsister's name is Bottomsley, or something like that, and her lawyer called yesterday afternoon about having us release the remains. By the way, he's a real nasty little sucker.

"Anyway, it turns out ol' Slim was worth between eighty and a hundred million bucks, give or take a million here or there." I let out a low whistle. I doubt any of us at our games had any idea Slim was worth that kind of dough. When I thought about some pots I could have won... oh well.

"According to her lawyer, the stepsister stands to inherit the entire thing since she's the only relative. However, if what you say is true, now there might be a blood relative, like a daughter, I guess several lawyers will make a lot of money for a while fightin' this through the courts."

I had to agree. I asked Jeff L. if he knew if there was a will. He told me from the way last night's phone call with the stepsister's lawyer had gone; the assumption was one existed. However, now he thought about it, the attorney hadn't said one way or the other. Jeff admitted he really didn't know. "I'll tell you this," he spoke forcefully, "We'll for sure be checking up on it now."

I mentioned now that there was so much money involved, and if a question arose about a will, many people would start falling in line. They would be the prime suspects and have about eighty plus million reasons to break into the houseboat. Jeff L. agreed. Before we hung up, I asked him for the name and phone number of the stepsister's lawyer. By now, I'd decided I would make more of a fuss about what I was now thinking of as my houseboat. Now I knew ol' Slim wasn't as destitute as I'd first feared, and the daughter wasn't interested in it, and since I'd won the damn thing fair and square, it was mine! I was forgetting about the fact I still needed a place to tie it up.

After I hung up, I laughed. Elmo Fester! Damn almighty, no wonder he always went by Slim. If I had that moniker, I would, too. I wondered if any of the others at the poker games knew his real name. I probably would have thought of him differently, had I known he was an Elmo. But then I realized it wasn't his choice of name. However, I couldn't help but feel tickled anyone would name his or her kid Elmo, let alone Elmo Fester. I was sure it was a family name; that they named him after his great uncle Fester or something. But I still felt in some ways his parents must've hated him a bunch. Besides the fact, his grade school days must've been pure hell from all the teasing the other kids gave him over his name.

I've always wondered what some parents must be thinking when they name their kids. Do they not understand that the poor kid has to live with that name forever? Didn't the parents understand that just because you named your daughter Bambi there was nothing to prevent her from ending up looking more like a King Kong than a Bambi?

One thing I understood now, I knew why he went by "Slim".

CHAPTER TWELVE

After dressing, I punched the numbers Jeff had given me into the phone. It buzzed in my ear twice before a female voice with excellent diction and of indeterminate age answered, "Good morning. Stewart, Mitchell and Green, attorneys at law. How might I help you?"

"Good morning. May I speak to Don Green?" I responded.

"Yes, sir, whom may I say is calling, please?" I gave her my name, and she put me on hold. While waiting, I found myself forced to listen to a syrupy arrangement of some sixties tune, which for drug references in the lyrics when it was new, received play time only on various obscure FM stations. Now that the tune was so old, they added violins and were using it for elevator music. Oh crap, it's probably because I'm getting old I'm so grouchy.

Green came on the line with a high-pitched, nasally, fast-paced voice with a lot of whine in it. "Don Green here, how may I help you?" He said the entire sentence as one word.

"Good morning Mr. Green, my name is Preston, Matthew Preston. I'm calling regarding Slim Rockingham. It was my friend, and I who found Mr. Rockingham the other day at his houseboat..."

Green interrupted. "Good God man, that must've been a real shocker!"

I paused a moment, startled at his interruption. "Yes, it was... um... unexpected. Anyway, the reason I'm calling is about the houseboat..."

Again, Green interrupted me before I could finish, "I'm sorry, Mr. Reston. Until the courts have settled Mr. Rockingham's estate, we can't sell anything." He paused, and I could tell he was thinking about his next statement. Finally, he continued, "And frankly, if I might say, it seems disrespectful for you to call about it so quickly after the poor man's demise."

I took a breath to calm myself, and replied, "It's Preston, Mr. Green, not Reston, and I'm not interested in buying the houseboat. It's already mine! I won it in a poker game a couple of weeks ago. Mr. Rockingham's attorney has the title assigning all interest in the houseboat to me. The reason I was at the houseboat the other day was to take possession. I called because I understand last night, you spoke with Detective Davenport with the Seattle Police Department. He mentioned that you might have something to do with Slim's estate."

"Yes, I phoned Detective Davenport. Are you an associate of the detective?"

I was getting exasperated with this clown, "No, I'm just interested in clearing up the houseboat title, and making sure it isn't accidentally included in his estate."

"Well, sir, I'm sure you're aware I can't discuss any details of Mr. Rockingham's estate." For a moment I recalled he was not Slim's attorney. I knew who his attorney was, so what was with this client privilege shit? However, I held my tongue, and he continued, "As far as your claim regarding the houseboat," He paused as he decided on his next words,

"I have heard nothing about a change in ownership of the houseboat. I also don't believe Mr. Rockingham's stepsister, Miss Audrey Bottomsley, knows of any changes either. "Miss Bottomsley; Miss Audrey Bottomsley by the way, is, excuse me, and was his stepsister. I believe they shared the same father through his mother's first marriage. I represent Miss Bottomsley, and I'm sure Mr. Rockingham's attorney would have notified me about any change of ownership. Mr. Rockingham's attorney and I often have discussions regarding the affairs of Mr. Rockingham and Miss Bottomsley. I can't believe I wouldn't have heard anything about all of this." he spoke his last comment with a little dig which I ignored.

Knowing how attorneys bill their clients for phone calls among themselves, I could imagine they talked often, very often. This jerk was getting under my skin. And attorneys wonder why the general population has such a low opinion of them. "Sir, are you insinuating I'm not telling you the truth?" I asked.

"Oh no, Mr. Priestly. I'm only saying it's strange that until now, I have heard nothing about a transfer of ownership. I, of course, will have to examine any documents which bear on this matter to make sure they're in proper order. If they are, we'll submit them when we're settling all of Mr. Rockingham's estate. At this time, from everything you've told me, I'd have to say you have nothing I wish or need, to consider. If you have an attorney, perhaps you should have him call me. I don't suppose you have an attorney?"

I let the last question drop. If this jerk wants to play the attorney game, I'll turn my wolves loose on him. I was positive they'd have him for brunch. I tried to be as polite as I could, "First off Mr. Green, my name is Preston! Matt Preston! It's not that difficult a name to remember. And since you're not representing Slim Rockingham's estate, I fail to understand why you need to see anything between Mr. Rockingham and myself. Client privilege and all that, you know.

"But since you feel you need to know, it was my understanding all the arrangements of the transfer were done between Mr. Rockingham, his attorney, myself, and my agent. And since they completed the transfer before his demise, again, I don't understand why you need to see any documents from the transfer. I don't see why any of us need to consult with you regarding the transfer of ownership. It is in fact, a done deal.

"Secondly, when I spoke with Jennifer Rockingham this morning, she seemed to feel as soon as the police finish their investigation, there would be no problems with me taking possession of the houseboat. I'll check with my attorneys, but the impression they gave me is the houseboat is already mine. It became mine the day they filed the papers. Perhaps you're the one who needs to check it out further!"

His voice seemed to jump up an octave, and he stuttered as he tried to speak so fast. "J... J... J... Jennifer Rockingham? I'm not aware of a Jennifer Rockingham. Who is this person?"

I wondered how he could not have known about the daughter. I informed him. "She told me she was Slim's daughter." I paused a moment remembering the sound of her voice and everything she'd told me. Then I continued, "She told me shortly after she was born, Mr. Rockingham left her and her mother, and then got a divorce from Mrs. Rockingham. Jennifer Rockingham told me she'd received her schooling overseas, and until recently she didn't have much of a relationship with her father."

I paused again, and then went for a dig, "Since you seem to have such an enormous concern, I think you may want to talk with Miss Rockingham, or at least her attorney."

After my well-placed dig, I mentioned I was sure I wasn't as competent as my attorneys were, and at that point,

I dropped the name of my wolf's prestigious firm. Then I continued, saying I was under the impression Miss Rockingham had a claim on old Elmo's estate. I thought about adding that a daughter would sure ace out his client; after all, isn't a blood relationship stronger than one through marriage? But I felt I'd already done a good job screwing up his day.

I asked him if there was a will, but I never received an answer. One thing though, after the mere mention of the name of my attorney's firm, I noticed ol' Donny boy's tone with me improved a great deal. He seemed to remember my name now and there was actual respect in his voice. He told me Miss Bottomsley had told him there would be no problems since she was the only heir. Green agreed with me he needed to look into the matter more. We finished the call with him assuring me he'd call me back after he'd contacted my attorney.

Once again, I found myself hunkered down in my favorite chair staring out across the lake with BJ pestering me to pick her up. I knew of the smile on my lips. When ol' Slim had played poker with all of us, who'd have thought he had two such strange women roaming around in his life? It started me wondering how many strange people someone might find in my life.

BJ had settled in, somehow knowing I would sit in my chair for a while pondering everything going on. The more I thought about it, the odder it seemed if Slim had both a stepsister and a daughter, one of them had to have known something about the other. I could understand why the daughter might not know about the stepsister because she was estranged from her father for so long, and since she was out of the country most of the time. Nevertheless, it didn't seem logical Slim would never mention his daughter to his stepsister. If Slim was half as proud of his daughter as it would seem, I'd bet he had said something to somebody along the way. If that was the case and Bottomsley knew, that would go a long way to explain why Bottomsley wanted to wrap up this estate thing before anyone knew there might be a daughter involved. During our phone call, Ms. Rockingham mentioned she was only in the States by accident. I will make a wager Bottomsley was not aware Jennifer was currently in the States.

As I lay sprawled in my chair, I wondered what my next move should be. And along with that thought, I wondered why I even wanted to get involved. I mean, I had proof the houseboat was mine and after that, it really wasn't any of my business. But when I closed my eyes, I could hear Jennifer's voice. I am such a pig... here I was fantasizing over a woman just because of her voice. But, she really had a great voice.

From Jennifer, my mind wandered to Bottomsley. How could I go about finding information about this Bottomsley dame, and what I felt was even more important, what did that woman really know about things?

The mind boggles.

CHAPTER THIRTEEN

Whenever I have a serious decision or a difficult problem that requires time to ponder, I head off to my secret hideout. My private man cave! I felt my current problems qualified; so, a visit to my sanctum was imminent. Considering my last three phone calls, it seemed a good time to retreat. Even though the modern term for my refuge is a man cave, my place of solitude isn't a cave, so I thought I'd stick with variations of hideout instead.

I undoubtedly have a lot more weaknesses than just two, but the two I'm most aware of are my tendencies to date tall blonde-haired women and my love and fascination with automobiles. If I have to explain my feelings about tall blondes, I doubt if we have much in common, and maybe you won't find any of my musings of interest.

As far as automobiles go, I'm a car whore! Perhaps that's not the best word, but my affection for cars seems to have no bounds. I admit it; I love cars. I know better than to go to automobile auctions because I'd come home with every car I found the least bit interesting, and I'd be broke. If it has four tires and burns gasoline, I'm in love.

I was lucky enough to grow up in the days when gas was cheap and plentiful, and ten miles to the gallon was acceptable mileage. I remember one weekend during my senior year in high school and it was Friday evening. I had $1.00 in my pocket and that dollar bill bought enough gas to see me through the entire weekend. That buck bought me four gallons of gas. That was enough gas for my Friday and Saturday night dates, plus some extra to go cruising, and I still had enough for the ride to school come Monday morning.

Another thing, cars had real balls back in the day! Best of all, they looked and sounded that way. My love affair with cars began when, at the tender age of thirteen and a half, I started driving on the back county roads of Whidbey Island (which is located in the Puget Sound), during the winter months. My family had a summer home on the island and often on Friday evenings during the winter, dad and I'd go over to the cabin and return either Saturday afternoon or on Sunday. Mom did not care for the cabin!

During the wintertime, since there weren't many people on the island, dad didn't have a problem with me taking whatever vehicle we were in and driving around. Pop's company had a Jeep pickup with a three-speed stick shift on the floor and I learned to drive in that vehicle. I drove that puppy all over the south end of Whidbey and by the time I was sixteen; I was quite proficient at driving.

Over the years, I've had more than my fair share of great cars, and lately, I've been fortunate enough to buy and keep some of these works of art. I have a monthly subscription to Hemmings Motor News and I faithfully look through each issue at the different older cars up for sale.

Luckily, one property I inherited from my father was a five-story turn of the last century building. Over the years, someone had installed an old lift in the back of the building accessible only from the rear alley. The lift went from the alley to the top floor with no stops in between. I've leased out, or more correctly, Scott has leased out all the bottom floors, but I've kept the top floor serviced by the lift. This is my hideout, and where I keep my collection.

Currently, there are nine pieces of "art" stored in the old building. On rare occasions, I take out and drive some of these, but only on the very nicest of days. Two of them are Corvettes. One is a 1963 split-window coupe, and the other is a 1966 roadster with a 327 cubic-inch motor that produces 350 horsepower. I admit to being a kid at heart, and on some warm summer evenings, it's like being seventeen again when I get behind the wheel. Put the top down on the '66 and with the wind licking at your hair and only the deep rumble of the exhaust to keep you company, that must be what heaven is like. I'm not bragging about my collection. I'm just saying I've been lucky in life, and I'm happy I can purchase and preserve my various cars.

At my apartment, I keep Faithful along with an '87 El Dorado convertible. All the stock motors in the Eldorado's were pieces of shit, and somewhere around sixty thousand miles, the motor dies. When my motor died, I had a mechanic pull out the old one, and replaced it with a newer North-Star 5.2 liter motor. Of course, now I've done that, I realize I can never sell the car, because of the stupid emission laws it was illegal to switch out the motor. I know I'm probably wrong, but I still believe I can keep any car running better and cleaner with proper tune-ups, etc., than the current batch of junk with all of their emission controls and crap. I also know our government totally disagrees with my opinion.

My other vice has to do with MGB's. Over the years, I purchased a bunch of '64 through '67 MGB's in various states of disrepair when and wherever I could find one. I say a bunch, because I have many parts, and some cars I bought were rusted-out bodies or frames which I used for parts. Some I only paid a few hundred bucks for and others perhaps a little too much. I really don't know how many cars

I could assemble if you could find all the extra pieces they might need. Sad to say, only one of them is actually running.

A few years ago, a firm in England purchased the dies to stamp out extra MGB parts, and it's now possible to purchase exact parts for them, and they fit like a glove. When you need a part though, they are rather expensive.

Arthur is my main man at the garage. Actually, Art is the only person in the shop. He's a gentleman in his early seventies who supplements his income by working on my toys on a part-time basis. Someday we hope to restore more of the MGs.

Art was once a mechanic and part-time driver of various types of old racecars. He has trophies to show for his efforts and an incredible wealth of stories. But the best thing about Art is his ability to fix an automobile. He views them as I do; relics of a passing era. Each day they become more like the horse-drawn wagons they replaced. Cars now have no soul. We both feel that today's cars all resemble each other, and worst of all, they only give you a few color choices to pick from, all of them very bland.

I know, step off the soapbox. I keep telling myself someday I should grow up, and rid myself of my toys, but I'm not quite ready to grow up. Maybe when I'm a little older!

I stopped by my special garage and chatted a while with Art. We discussed Slim and the ensuing related problems. He agreed that both of Slim's females didn't sound like their toothpicks completely pierced their respective olives. Basically, they sounded pretty strange.

One of the new pieces had arrived for the MGs, and Art planned to show me how he wanted to install it. After around an hour of crawling under and around the car I heard the grinding of the inside elevator. When it came wheezing to a stop. Scott stepped off. BJ sat up, gave him a half-hearted bark, and then lay down again in Art's favorite chair.

Scott stood for a moment and said, "Thanks for returning my call this morning!"

I'd dropped the ball. "Oops! Sorry 'bout that, something came up, and it slipped my mind. What did you need to see me about?"

Scott came over and handed me a piece of paper. It looked like some official notice from the City of Seattle about an upcoming change of zoning. Nothing seemed to make sense until I reached the exact address of the change. It was the marina where the houseboat was moored.

I asked Scott what it all meant. "It means not only are they going to put you out of the marina, but they might evict every houseboat. The city has wanted to shut down all the houseboats for a long time. By the way, look at the name on the notice."

Thank God, I was still sitting on the ground. When I saw the name David Wheeler on the letter I probably would have fallen to the floor. I had no idea Wheel owned the damn marina! I looked up at Scott, and it seemed like he could read my mind. "Yes, it looks as if our ol' 'Wheel' is the owner of the marina."

"Have you tried to call him and see if he'll give me a stay of execution?"

Scott laughed, and replied, "No, I got the copy of that notice just yesterday at my office and that's why I was trying to get ahold of you. I thought you could talk to him as the new owner of the houseboat. However, this notice could mean he might be in trouble, too. Now, what was so important you couldn't call me back?"

I told Scott of the morning's happenings with Miss Rockingham and the stepsister's jerk lawyer. I ended up, "I don't know what the status is now. It looks like if there's no existing will, my guess is the daughter and step-sister will probably take the estate to court, and unless my wolves are fantastic, there could be a chance the houseboat will sink before it's all over."

Scott tugged at his beard for a moment, and then spoke, "I'm not a lawyer, but I think as long as there are legal problems, Wheel can't do a thing to have the houseboat evicted. Even better, this might cause the city to stop doing anything for a while." Scott paused again, "Oh, and as long as the police investigation is ongoing nobody can move a thing, anyway."

As far back as I can remember there have been articles in the Seattle papers about how the city wants to rid itself of the houseboats scattered around the various lakes within the city limits. It looked like the council was planning to take another run at it. I was confident when most of the residents in other marinas heard about the plight of Wheel's place there would be a major ruckus down at City Hall.

I knew back in the day houseboat owners were dumping a lot of raw sewage into the lake and, for good reason, the city had demanded they change that practice. They passed laws and rules were enforced so now they have everything plumbed, and to my knowledge, no one can put anything in the lake. No wastewater and no sewage of any sort. I was curious on what legal grounds the city thought they could now do away with houseboats. I debated in my mind if I wanted to bring in my wolves, or just let things ride for a while and see what would come out of all of this.

By now, I'd developed a headache. I felt torn between giving the place up without a fight or fighting for what I felt was mine by taking on Slim's estate. I glanced up at the windows and saw it was dark outside. The day had slipped away, and I hadn't even noticed. Automobiles will do that, you know. We all said our goodbyes, and Art told me he'd lock the place up.

The drive back to my place was a dark wet one. With the influx of drivers from southern states who don't know how to drive in the rain, driving around here is really getting difficult. Worst of all is when it gets dark everyone seems to run into each other. You can always tell an out of stater when they whine about all the rain we get around here. Actually, if you compare the amount of rain that falls in New York City, and the amount that falls in Seattle, it would surprise you. You'd be very surprised! New York City gets more rain than the Puget Sound area. I also now know Atlanta has more rain than Seattle does. My thought when I hear them whine is if you're so unhappy here, go home! It sure would make driving easier.

On the way up in the elevator at the apartment, BJ kept pawing at the doors. Usually, this is her signal to go to visit the outside. As soon as the elevator door opened, BJ took off through the kitchen toward the back door.

Suddenly I heard her barking madly. I called her twice, but when she didn't return and continued barking, that sent my internal alarm bells ringing madly.

Even with all my history, I'm still not really a big gun nut, but I've always kept a Glock 21 in a secret spot in the front room. I moved quickly, removed the Glock from its hidden location, and started down the hall. BJ had gone through the kitchen to reach the back door, and I had the hope I could enter the kitchen from the back way. BJ was still barking, and then I heard a thud and heard her yelp. Then I heard her whimpering as she ran towards the front of the house.

Now that BJ wasn't barking, I could hear someone fumbling with the back door. I moved quickly down the hallway and stepped cautiously into the kitchen. By the time I turned the corner, the back door was standing open, and I saw the steel door closing. I ran to the open door and push on the steel one. As I looked across the vacant lot behind my place, I could see a dark figure running down my walkway and onto the lot exactly where BJ does her business.

Suddenly the running figure slipped and fell. As the person hit the ground, I heard a loud snapping sound and then the person on the ground cried out.

I'd reached the end of the walkway and I'd aimed my gun at the prone figure. As the person rose, I called out to him. "I'm a fairly good shot at this distance. I'm telling you if you move, I'll shoot you. Do you understand?"

The figure was not even standing fully upright as he moved towards me. When he tried to put weight on one of his legs, he fell again, and a groan escaped when he hit the ground. "I've broken my leg," a male voice informed me.

"Lie still and I'll get help." I figured with a broken leg my visitor was not in a condition to go anywhere soon. I walked back down my pathway, and as I passed my kitchen counter, I picked up my walk-around phone. I continued to the front room looking for BJ, and I found she had curled up in my chair. As soon as she saw me, her tail wagged. From what I could tell, she seemed all right for the moment, and I'd check on her again after I called the police about my visitor with the broken leg.

When I entered the kitchen on my way to the vacant lot, I heard two gunshots. I shoved the steel door open and saw the back end of a car speeding away up the hill with no lights on.

For a moment, I considered going for a John Wayne feat to see if I could hit the departing car, but I quickly realized if I missed, I might hurt some innocent bystander. I put the phone down on the railing and moved as quickly as I could towards the prone figure lying on the ground. I reached down to feel his neck for a pulse, but I could tell from the side of his face it was a wasted effort on my part.

By now there were others standing outside their homes. One of them called out and asked what was going on. I forgot I'd brought out the phone and had left it on the railing and I yelled for someone to call 911; I needed the police.

From where I was kneeling, I could smell the strong odor of fresh dog shit. I thought I'd stepped in some until I glanced over at the feet of the figure prone in front of me, now pointed towards the street and the light overhead. Some of BJ's "gifts" covered one sole of his shoes.

Since this fellow kicked BJ, it seemed only fair that Blackjack had been the one to bring him down. However, I doubted if BJ wanted him dead, but it sure seems someone else did.

BJ? I remembered I still needed to check on her. I went back into my place and searched for her. She was still curled up in my favorite chair and I coaxed her to the floor. I carefully checked her over, and she licked my hand but whimpered when I gently pushed on one side of her ribs. Nothing seemed broken, just some bad bruises. However, she was not a happy camper. I carefully picked her up and placed her back on my favorite chair, where she licked herself.

Walking back through the kitchen, I noticed when the intruder had kicked BJ she'd left a puddle on the floor. I got a handful of paper towels and dropped them on her accident. Totally wiping up the mess at this point seemed rather anal.

By now, the first patrol car arrived. I asked if they could let Jeff L. or Sakol know about what was happening. For reasons I'd yet to figure out, my senses told me somehow tonight might tie in with Slim and his death. I had no idea at the time how true that thought turned out to be.

As I sat on the steps of my walkway, Sharon came out of my kitchen door and sat down beside me. A long time ago, I'd given her a key to my elevator stop, so she could always have free rein of my place. She leaned over and pecked me on my cheek. "You know if I was the landlord, I'd have to tell you to keep it down, or I would have to ask you to move."

I turned to her, and I guess she could tell from the look on my face I was not a happy camper. She leaned over again, kissed me a little harder and whispered in my ear, "Sorry! I was trying to make you feel better."

I kissed her back, "Thanks. I appreciate the effort."

I filled her in on what had happened, and when she heard about BJ, she immediately went off to search for her. One thing about Sharon, besides being a nurse, she also seems to feel she's the original earth mother. Whatever mishap had befallen BJ, she was in the most capable hands I knew of. Sure enough, in two or three minutes they both returned with Sharon carrying BJ cradled in her arms. BJ seemed to look up at me as if to say, "Look, dad, this is the way you're supposed to comfort me." I scratched her head, and she rewarded me with another lick on my hand.

About an hour later Sakol arrived, alone. He informed me that Jeff L. was doing family things for the evening, thus he was the only one available. I told him my story. He asked me what I'd heard when I walked into my place, and all I could tell him was nothing. The first time I realized something was wrong was when BJ wouldn't stop barking.

He walked back down the walkway, turned on his flashlight, and examined the steel door. He found a few scratches on the lock, which indicated that someone picked it. But other than that, the door seemed OK. I told Sakol I thought I'd installed a good lock. But Sakol told me that if a person was skilled enough, given enough time any lock could be picked.

Sakol petted BJ for a few moments when we were done chatting. I thought it was cool of Sakol to do that. It seemed BJ was the hero of the evening. Sakol gave permission to have the body removed, and I saw the boys from the morgue had seen my visitor's shoes and had removed them before they put him in a body bag. The shoes got their own bag. After they removed the body and Sakol was through with his questions, he allowed me to return to my place.

I made sure BJ did a final visit to the back lot and then headed towards the kitchen. I had no sooner locked the back door when I heard my elevator door open. I walked through the kitchen and found Sharon standing in my foyer. She was wearing her bathrobe, and as she walked by me, she took me by the hand and led me back to my bedroom. Once inside the room, she picked up BJ, set her on the end of the bed, and then slipped out of her robe. Underneath she had on my favorite outfit of hers, which is by coincidence nothing.

Stepping to my bed, she pulled the covers down and once nestled into the bed, she looked up, smiled and said, "Get your clothes off, I'm sleeping over tonight." I contemplated what I'd seen this evening, and I decided I really didn't want to sleep alone tonight.

Later, as she lay curled in my arms, I thought this was getting to become a habit, it could be a nice habit. Actually, it was a habit I was truly enjoying. For a few moments, I reflected on all the womanly charms coiled around my body.

However, before my body could react, my mind shut down for the night.

HOUSEBOAT

CHAPTER FOURTEEN

When I awoke the next morning, I felt a very soft and very feminine bottom nestled against me. Laying there things woke up, and it didn't surprise me. Between the physical feelings of Sharon against my body, and the images of the night before dancing in my head, even a deceased man would have had some reaction. With little luck, I tried to take my mind elsewhere. I tried the houseboat, last night's shooting, even the last time I'd seen Slim. However, the physical feeling of her resting against me was overcoming all of it. The more I tried not to think about it, the more I became aware I was losing the fight. For some unknown reason, my breath had developed a catch, and each breath was becoming more difficult than the last. At that point, before anything happened, I got out of bed. To say forcing myself to get up is an understatement, but I did. I padded off to the bathroom where I had to wait a while before I could relieve myself. Guys will understand why the wait.

On my return from the bathroom, I picked a towel off the rack and wrapped it around my middle. When I entered the bedroom, I found Sharon sitting in the center of my bed, glaring at me with the covers gathered around her waist. I glanced at her inviting upper torso and realized this wasn't helping matters either. I politely asked her to cover up. She ignored me.

She continued to glower at me, and then finally asked, "What's with you? Just what the hell is it with you, Matt?" Sharon paused, waiting for an answer, and when nothing was forthcoming, she continued. "We're all curled up like spoons, and I'm thrilled because I'm here with you. I can feel you're getting interested, and trust me, I was getting interested, too. We're snuggled here together, I hear you snort like a bull in heat, I can feel you're in the mood, and then you suddenly jump up and run away. Now you tell me to cover up. What the hell's your problem?"

"I… uh... well... I thought we'd given up on the physical thing. I don't want to confuse things. I... well... I didn't think I should start… and... well… uh…" Boy, was I glib this morning.

"Matt!" At first, her voice was hard. Sharon stopped talking for a moment, took a deep breath and then resumed in a softer voice. "Matt, listen. I know at one time we tried the physical thing and… well, to be blunt about things, it really wasn't great between us. I must admit I was glad when we quit, and after that, I was really enjoying having you for a friend. And you've become a fantastic friend!"

I tried to interrupt, but she shook her head for me to stop. "Please, let me finish. You told me the last time we made love it scared you. Well, sweetheart it scared me too. I've never had making love feel that way before. It wasn't sex, we made love." She paused and shook her head, "Never like that before! And I really enjoyed being with you our last time. I think, in my head, it's become more than you just helping me over a nasty experience. I think about it a lot, and I guess I want us to try it again." Once more, I tried to speak, and again she held up her hand to silence me.

This time she asked me with more of an edge to her voice, "Please let me finish!" I nodded my head. "The last time when things worked so well, I was in need! I thought this time since you were in need… well… it might work again. To be perfectly honest, I want to see if it could be like that for us all the time."

This really caught me by surprise. Two marriages had left an unpleasant taste in my mouth. Since then, I've worked very hard at not becoming too involved with anyone that could lead to a serious relationship. I didn't know if I was ready to go where I thought, where I believed, Sharon wanted to go with our relationship. I came and sat down in a chair across from the bed.

"Sharon, you'll never know how flattered I am. I'd be less than honest if I said you didn't turn me on, a lot! But you've become so much more than a sexual partner. You're a friend. You're one of my best friends, if not my very best friend. I talk to you about things I never would have discussed with my two exes. Shit, I talk to you about things I wouldn't even talk to Scott about. I can say any fool thing to you, without censoring my thoughts. That includes any stupid fool thing I think of, and I know it's okay with you.

"I don't think I've ever had a relationship with a woman where we were just friends. Please don't take this the wrong way, I enjoy this, and I enjoy you. I'd like to keep all of this, and if it means we don't make love to do that, then I'm willing to pay the price. No matter what, I don't want to alter our relationship, and I'm afraid if we did the horizontal two-step again, things would change.

"Besides, not to hurt your feelings, but being perfectly honest, I don't know if I'm ready to have the relationship you want. Stop me if I'm making it worse… but, in some crazy way, I have the same feelings for you. I don't want to be flip or anything, but my life the past few days has been just a little on the fast side..."

Sharon interrupted, "OK, I understand." We sat and stared at each other for a few minutes. I still wished she'd cover up. She drew her lips into an exaggerated pout, and said, "But you've left me rather horny now, what am I supposed to do?"

"Cold shower?" Right after the one I need to take, I said to myself.

Sharon snatched a pillow off the bed and threw it at me. "Drop dead!" she laughed.

This seemed like it was a good time to drop out. "I need to get going. I think I might try to see Jeff and Sakol today and for sure I will find Wheeler. I want to see what that SOB will do with the marina. I need a space for that damn houseboat."

"Well, I can see I won't be getting any action around here. I guess I'll leave too." She stood in the middle of the bed with her hands on her waist, looking down at me, as if she was daring me to take her. What an amazing sight. Her body was breathtaking. This was not fair!

I could tell from the movement under my towel that my body had a mind of its own, and it was all I could do to turn away. Why was she making it so damn tough? I really didn't want to start something which might destroy our relationship. BJ looked up from her corner of the bed. She looked up at Sharon, and then looked at me, as if to say, "Dad, if you don't do something, you're dumber than I thought!" I turned and went to the bathroom to take my shower.

Sharon's bathrobe was gone when I came out of the shower. I rummaged in my drawers until I found a clean pair of shorts and a shirt that looked reasonably good with them. When I got to the kitchen, I found a note from my nocturnal visitor on the 'fridge door.

"I'm sorry if I create problems. I also enjoy our friendship! Thanks for being smart enough to see what maybe is best for both of us. I think!"

I hated to admit it, but I still wished we'd made love. I can talk a good game, but the truth of the matter is that woman really turns me on.

Oh well, it was time to get my day started, and I called for BJ.

HOUSEBOAT

CHAPTER FIFTEEN

Today was one of the very best Seattle could offer considering it was early December. Many people think it rains all the time in Seattle, but early December can be beautiful. Cold, but beautiful. Everything that day was blue and clean. The smells permeating a salt-water city gets in the blood of anyone who lives there for long. The day, I'll say it again, was gorgeous. By the time I pulled Faithful out of the garage, I knew even though it was cool outside; the day would be nice enough to take out the Corvette. I headed for my downtown storage building and pulled out the 'Vette roadster. Once I'd put the top down, BJ and I headed down the road, BJ stood on the seat with her head hanging out her side of the car, and both of us had big grins plastered on our faces.

On the way over to Wheeler's office, I pulled up at a stoplight next to a very attractive dark-haired lady with silver streaks in her hair. Her expensive European sedan was spotless, and the woman looked exactly like the lady who should drive such a vehicle. She glanced over at us and then turned her head away. Evidently, she must've seen BJ, because immediately she looked back at us. This time with a huge smile on her face. It never fails. I have more women glance at me, and then look back a second time after they see BJ. I smiled back at her, but I doubt if she even noticed. Women's reactions aren't the reason I keep BJ, but her magnetic attraction sure helps, even when I'm ignored.

I'd never visited Wheeler's office before, even though I knew its location. The front of his office faces the street but the back end of the building looks out over Lake Union. His marina is only about a block away on the same side of the lake. When I pulled up in front, I spotted Wheeler's sleek silver Teutonic sports car squatted down in his stall

I parked and as I walked up to the front doors; I glanced up the street and noticed a Seattle undercover police vehicle parked in the fire lane. When I entered the lobby, I could see all the way back into Wheeler's office. The young lady sitting at the front desk was gorgeous and I couldn't help but notice Wheel was not skimping on his selection of a receptionist.

When this stunningly attractive lady asked me how she could help, I told her I needed to speak to Wheel when he had a few moments. I'd no sooner told her what I wanted when Sakol came out the door of Wheeler's office. We looked at each other for a moment. By the look on his face, it was obvious it surprised him to see me. Sakol muttered a pleasantry, and I returned the same. By then, Jeff L. had rounded the corner and expressed his surprise to see me. "What the hell are you doing here?" Good old Jeffers, right to the point.

"I wanted to have a chat with Wheeler. He owns the marina where the houseboat is moored my friend Scott told me yesterday."

Wheeler was now standing in the doorway, his frame filling the opening. "Morning, Matt. Yes, as I was just telling these detectives, I own the marina where Slim's houseboat was, or is tied up. I've also told them I didn't know Slim except from our card games." Both the detectives nodded their heads in agreement. Wheel continued, "If you're here to talk me into letting you stay, the city says we must have all houseboats moved out in a hundred and twenty days."

Wheel folded his arms across his chest and then glowered at me. "Besides, why should I do you any favors? You didn't do a damn thing to help me at the last game."

I would put a stop to this right now. "Bullshit Wheel, you will not put that on me. You knew no one wanted your ring! You also know about table stakes and the rules, and... anyway, it wasn't your first time at the game. Right?" I kept looking Wheeler in the eye until he finally looked down. I asked him again, "Are you really going to hang that on me?" Wheeler looked back up at me for a second, then shook his head no, and smiled sheepishly at me.

"You know I blow up... sorry about that. But I still can't help you with the houseboat mess. Honest! The city has taken it out of my hands for now."

I nodded my acceptance of his apology, thought for a moment, and then asked, "How come you never mentioned you owned a marina to anyone, especially the one Slim had his boat tied up at?"

"It never came up. Later, after the game, I'd heard you'd won the boat. I knew Slim was planning to move out, and he planned to sell the thing off and give up his space. I didn't tell you because of my leftover anger at you from the game the other night.

"My idea was to sell all the spaces off instead of leasing them. Then if there's a problem with the city, it's up to the tenants to deal with it. Besides, the taxes keep going up, and the rules keep getting stiffer and the city keeps trying to find ways to run the houseboat community off the lake. It's getting too damn expensive to run the marina. Matt, the sewer bill on those units is unbelievable. In reality, I only charge the tenants a pittance of what I could, or should. The best option is to sell the spaces off and do something else with the money."

I wondered how much Wheeler knew about Slim's net worth, "Did you ever talk to Slim about buying into your idea? How much do you think Slim knew about all of this?"

Wheeler scratched at his chin as he responded, "He'd asked Margie, that's the gal who runs the marina for me... ah... he asked her if she'd help him sell his houseboat. She told him I was thinking about selling off the slots, and that it might be difficult to sell his house without a moorage space."

"Dirty bastard," I thought. Here I was feeling sorry about taking away his home, and he knew all the time he would stick me with a worthless piece of junk.

Wheel continued, "He told her he'd consider buying a bunch of slips as an investment. It was in my court to contact him and discuss it, but after the game," Wheeler paused, "Well, I was pissed at all of you, and then by the time I got over it he was... well, you know." I noticed Wheel was red in the face now.

"All I really know is he told Margie he wanted to move back to the Southwest, and he never talked about buying anything. Actually, the only time I ever spoke to him was at the games. Like I said before, I knew him from the card games. We never talked to each other away from them."

I asked Wheeler, "Tell me about this city deal. Can they really throw everyone out? What will happen to the marina if that happens?"

"They can't exactly throw everyone out. They can rezone the land surrounding the place. The idea is to leave the marina with no place to park your car. They put out signs that there's no parking between midnight and 5 AM. If you park there, they'll tow your car.

"Think about it, if you don't have a place to park, who'd live there? You already knew that if you have a boat and live aboard that it's not okay for you to put any sewage in the water. We've had our houseboats hooked up to the sewer system for a long time, but the city is always trying to

put stiffer laws in effect about what pipe you have to use...
you know, shit like that. The idea is they're trying to make
it so expensive you can't afford to have a houseboat. They
think the rezoning idea with no parking spots will shut down
the marinas, I guess."

Somewhere back in the old grey matter I remembered
once upon a time, I'd heard of an association for houseboat
owners. "Won't the houseboat owner's association, or whatever they call themselves try to file something against the
city?"

"Oh, yeah, they already had their day, but all it does
is make sure nobody can sell their houseboat until the damn
thing gets resolved. Who knows how long that will take? I
think the city just hopes people won't want to buy anything
so volatile. What the city's doing is to create a moratorium
without having to have a real law on the books.

"I really don't know how this is gonna turn out. I
thought I had a way out of this mess, but now I see they
might stick me with the marina for a lot longer. Since Slim
was moving on, I thought if I sold his spot then other tenants
would want to purchase as well. Now..."

"As I understand it, as long as the fight with the city
is going on, the houseboat gets to stay where it is? Is that
correct?" I asked.

"Yeah, I guess so. But with the police investigation,
nothing can be done anyway." Jeff grunted agreement.
Wheeler continued, "Actually, as long as there's any legal
litigation the city can't really do much. Of course, you can't
do much either. I don't see how it will help you, though. As
I understand it, one of Slim's relatives will fight you about
the damn thing. You're all going to end up with nothing if
the city wins."

For someone he claimed he didn't know very much
about, I felt Wheeler seemed to have found out a lot about
Slim's financial situation. Wheel continued, "I'm sorry but

I need to get going, was there anything else, Matt?" I shook my head no and headed out the front door.

During our entire conversation, Jeff L. and Sakol had both stood quietly in the hall listening to Wheel and myself. Jeff smiled as I passed by and then he shook his head as he offered, "Sorry the boat thing turned out to be such a problem."

I grinned ruefully at the pair and shrugged my shoulders. "I don't know if I should just see if I can give the damn thing to charity and then walk away and bag the whole thing. Or, should I make a fight for it?" Looking at Jeff I asked, 'It ain't like I need the damn thing, do I?"

Jeff smiled. I continued, "I'll tell you one thing, that stepsister's attorney pissed me off with his shitty attitude and all. I don't know what to think about all of this. But I'm telling you this, somehow, something ain't right, and I can't figure it out. I've no idea how the houseboat thing fits in all of this." I gave them both a big smile, as I asked, "Do you guys have time for a cup of coffee? I'm buying!"

They nodded affirmatively. I considered making a smart comment about covering a doughnut too, but I didn't want to be any more of an ass than I already am.

CHAPTER SIXTEEN

The three of us followed the shoreline around to a point of land sticking a little way out into the lake. We crossed over some abandoned railroad tracks paralleling the lake which back in the day serviced many industries that at one time surrounded the entire lake. Now, most of the businesses are gone, but the tracks remain, reminding one of how industrial the lake had been, and what an important part it had played in Seattle's history. Today there are only two things left from all the bygone industry; the abandoned tracks and the poisonous lake bed due to all the contaminants dropped into the lake over the decades. The businesses are gone and now the city is stuck dealing with the lethally contaminated mud under the lake.

We continued across the street to the small greasy spoon restaurant set back on the hill on the far side of the street from the lake. It looked old, and it had been at its location for as long as I could remember.

The waitress took our orders and then left. I told both of them about my two phone calls. I talked about how weird I thought it was that the daughter would call me, and not the lawyer. I almost believed her when she said the reason she was calling was because she wanted to return to Europe as soon as possible and wanted to make sure they resolved the houseboat situation. But I wondered if her true reason was she was trying to screw the Bottomsley bitch, or exactly what?

I continued and told them how I was having a hard time believing that neither one knew about the other. It was easy enough for me to understand how the daughter might not know about the stepsister. However, I sure as hell didn't buy Bottomsley not knowing about the daughter. That just didn't fly. Sakol smiled at me and nodded, giving me his wise old owl look. I wondered what he was trying to tell me. Finally, I had to ask, "OK, what gives?"

"Finally think proper." He tapped his forehead with his finger and smiled. "Stepsister say her lawyer talk to deceased lawyer," I nodded my head. "You say Mr. Slim's estate discussed between two lawyers," I nodded again. "Logical Rockingham lawyer mention sometime payment to a Jennifer Rockingham? Everyone know wife dead. Slim never marry again? Who Jennifer Rockingham?"

We both grinned at each other. It was exactly what I'd been thinking, but up to now, I hadn't put it that logically.

"Do you think the stepsister and her lawyer are trying to pull a fast one and have the estate settled before the daughter comes forward?" I asked, totally befuddled.

Jeff commented, "It still wouldn't make sense. I'm no lawyer, but I'd think, as soon as the money stopped coming to the daughter from Slim, she'd try to find out why. Once she found out dear old dad had shuffled off the planet, I think she'd demand her share of the loot. I also think she has a good case to collect part of the dough. I don't see how the stepsister thought she could get away with it. But greed does strange things to people."

A flash hit me, "Is there any way you guys can demand to see financial records and see if Bottomsley was getting money from Slim? Maybe her lawyer had a way of getting to the money. Maybe he needed time to cover something up. I know I might be reaching, but it all seems so confusing. Besides, is this helping you catch a murderer? Speaking of that, has anyone found out who was in my pad last night?"

Jeff leaned back and crossed his arms over his chest and from the way he looked at me, I could see something wasn't right. I didn't know what he would tell me, but something told me I would not like it.

Jeff looked at Sakol, cleared his throat and spoke slowly, "That's why we wanted to have coffee with you. Matt, they found an interesting tattoo on your late night caller during the autopsy." I could feel the hair on the back of my neck stand up. Jeff continued, "I've seen the tattoo before. I believe it matches the tattoo you have on your upper arm."

My right hand jumped to my left shoulder, and I wrapped it around the place where my tattoo is as if it would somehow make the thing disappear.

Do you remember the Uncle Sam part I mentioned earlier and my involvement in the rice paddy-land wars? One night a bunch of us got rather drunk and had our special insignia tattooed on our left upper arm. Most of the guys did it, the tattoo I mean. I don't know about the drunken part. Back then, we belonged to a very elite group. Even though we weren't allowed to discuss it, several of the guys wanted to commemorate a kindred spirit with a tattoo. I've always wondered if it was because of how drunk I'd been that night, or if I wanted to belong to some special club like when we were all kids. The tattoo is rather faded, and the lines aren't very distinct, but if you look at it closely, you can still make out the design. Nowadays I usually wear a t-shirt and not a tank top, because over the years, I've become rather self-conscious about it.

What the tattoo meant was the man who'd died in the vacant lot behind my apartment had served in 'Nam. Not only that, he'd served in the same unit I'd served in, perhaps not at the same time, but nevertheless the same unit. It also meant this cat had been through the same schooling I'd been, and he could have wasted me the second I stepped off the elevator, if that's what he'd wanted to do. During our training we were taught never to run out of fear; instead, face the enemy and deal with it as efficiently as possible. That way you don't end up running through a vacant lot and slip in a pile of dog shit as someone whacks you.

But, who'd want to whack him? That thought brought me up short. I blinked and looked at the two cops sitting in front of me, "Do you think I had something to do with his death?" I exclaimed.

I was very surprised Sakol was the one to answer. He usually let Jeff do the talking and he sifted through what he heard. "No, Matt. We not believe you involved with death. We believe you walk in too soon, he scare and run."

I still wasn't buying any of the scared part. I can't describe what hell the training was like, but when I tell you they taught those who went through it not to panic out of fear, believe it. The one thing they taught us was to keep our cool. Examine your options first, make your decision and then act. Those who couldn't keep their cool washed out; quick.

No, my mysterious caller ran for other reasons than panic. I never got a good look at him. Maybe I'd known him. Long shot, but… I asked the boys if they had a good picture of the guy and they told me they'd get one. I told them what I was thinking, that I might recognize him. It was dark and because of all the excitement, I never looked at him before they put him in the wagon. Who knew? We agreed when they got back they'd provide me with a picture.

When I asked them if they'd ran his prints through the government computer banks Jeff L. politely informed me even though I might think they were bumbling clods, occasionally they did some things right. Once he spoke those words, I realized my error, and I apologized. We stood to leave, and I covered the coffee and tip, said my goodbyes and we left.

I opened the door to the 'Vette and let BJ out to take a run. I trudged along after her while I kept pushing the past few days around my head. It seemed perhaps someone had dropped in out of my past and I'd caught him prowling my place. The more I worked with that idea, the more it didn't seem to fit anywhere, either.

I remember when I was a kid I used to love working on jigsaw puzzles, however, without the cover picture, it was almost impossible to put them together. It's tough to work on a puzzle if you don't know where to start, or even worse if you don't know what the picture looks like, and let's not even consider not having any idea how many pieces make up the puzzle.

I decided it made no difference how nice the day was; I didn't feel enjoy driving the roadster anymore. My next step was to return the 'Vette to its storage place. I headed back towards my storage, pulled the car onto the lift and engaged it to move the car to the top story.

Once I'd carefully covered the car, I rode the lift back down to Faithful. After I got in, I noticed someone had tried to call me while I was out of the truck. When I'm away from my rig, if anyone calls me on the cell phone it will show "call" on the display telling me someone has called me while I was out. I checked with my voice mail and found two messages. The first was from Scott and the second was from Jennifer Rockingham.

At least there was one call I was looking forward to returning.

HOUSEBOAT

CHAPTER SEVENTEEN

I'm positive I'm not the only one who wonders what a person looks like just from hearing their voice on the phone. When you talk to a stranger on the phone, don't you form some kind of mental image of what they might look like? I remember reading once that one of the best-paid 1-900 phone sex women was actually a man. He could make his voice very sultry and sensual, and he made a lot of money fulfilling many a guy's fantasies. Even though I had only heard Jennifer Rockingham's voice, I was fairly sure Slim's daughter was not a man. However, she had one sexy voice. My mental image of her was a cross of Miss June, Miss July, and Miss August, and well, you get the idea.

The soft, gently accented voice came on the phone after the second ring, "Hello, this is Jennifer Rockingham."

I told her who I was, and she paused for a moment before answering, "Thank you for returning my call. I... ah," she laughed nervously, "have a small favor to ask. Actually, it's a rather large favor. Would it be possible to meet with you? I've something I need to discuss with you, and - uh…"

"And you'd rather not discuss it over the phone?" I interrupted, trying to help her along.

"Well, it would be a lot easier if I met you. I believe you'll understand." I agreed to meet her at a well-known watering hole that overlooks the Sound where you can watch the ferries coming and going. After I hung up, I looked at my watch and noticed I had over an hour and a half before I was to meet Ms. Rockingham.

My next call was to Scott, and I asked him what he wanted. He informed me he had an old buddy who has a good friend who is someone important down at the zoning commission. His plan was to have lunch with his friend and his friend's friend to see if he could find out why there was this sudden push to close Wheel's marina. I told him to keep the bill for lunch and I'd pay him back. Scott thanked me and told me it wasn't necessary.

He went on, "I've contacted other marinas around and I hear only Wheel's place was being looked into. His is the only marina that's getting the look over. It seems strange and I hope my lunch will give me some answers."

I told him about my upcoming meeting with the Rockingham woman. We agreed to meet later to discuss what each of us had uncovered.

After we hung up, I decided it might be a good idea to look more presentable for Miss Rockingham, and I headed off to the bathroom to clean up and pondered the wisdom of perhaps wearing a suit. I thought it might help to make a good impression, so I went to my closet and pulled out one of my custom-made jobs. I also found a nice clean freshly starched French cuff shirt. After sprucing up, I stopped in front of the mirror on the way out. When I looked at myself, I thought I didn't look so bad for a man of my advanced years. Still, need to lose a few pounds, but hey, don't most of us?

I took the Eldo convertible, and it seemed like BJ was asking what's up with the suit and fancy car. I told her to act cool, since normally when I wear a suit, she rarely goes along with me. She promptly lay down in the passenger seat and nodded off to sleep.

I arrived at the restaurant early, left my name at the reception desk, and headed back to the bar to grab a good table looking out over the water. Just two minutes past our agreed upon time, I glanced up at the entrance and saw a tall, slim, dark-haired, exceptionally attractive woman enter the place. I was pleased to note this time the voice, and the person seemed to go together. The receptionist was standing next to her, and when I waved my hand, she pointed me out to the tall woman.

Her stride was long and graceful. She was wearing an unbuttoned dark grey suit with a sheer black blouse underneath. The thin blouse revealed underneath a well filled out black bra. The skirt to the suit had a slit on one side, and when she walked, one leg would show a little. The suit was tailored to fit her perfectly. As she walked, her long brown highlighted tresses swung back and forth. A few of the other males in the room turned to glance at her as she passed. There was no denying this was one very classy, gorgeous dame. God was I glad I did the suit thing. I was standing by the time she got to the table, and I extended my hand, "Miss Rockingham?" I asked.

She reached out, took my hand, and in her soft accent said, "Yes, and I appreciate you agreed to see me." I motioned for her to take a seat, and I sat down across from her. She had a beautiful wide face with deep soft brown eyes. Her lashes were incredibly long, and when she blinked, they brushed creamy cheeks. She also had a wide and generous mouth, with straight white teeth and a great smile when she wanted to share it. I tried to see any of Slim in her, but I didn't. She was at least five-feet-nine-inches or a bit taller, contrasted with Slim who'd been a very short man. I assumed her mother, Mrs. Rockingham, had been tall. Somewhere this lovely lady had gotten great genes, and it didn't appear she'd picked up too many from her father.

We both ordered something to drink, and she turned to admire the view. There was a ferry just pulling away from the dock leaving a white wake in the blue-green water. In the distance, you could see the Olympic Mountains. The setting was perfect, and she commented on the view. When our drinks arrived, I took a sip of mine, and then leaned back in my seat, waiting for her to tell me why she wanted to see me. "Ah, Mr. Preston. I… uh…"

Chuckling, I held up one hand, "Excuse me," I interrupted. "Grandpa was ninety-five when he died, and they called him Mr. Preston. If I make ninety-five, then everyone could call me Mr. Preston. For now, how about Matt?"

Jennifer nodded, "Okay!" That great smile came and went. I waited patiently through a long pause. She continued, "Matt," followed by a little more of her great smile. Hesitantly, she started, "I asked you to meet with me to talk about, well about someone I never knew existed until quite recently."

I interrupted, "Are you referring to the Bottomsley woman?"

Her hand slipped up to her throat as her eyes widened. I hadn't seen the gesture since 1940s films. For some reason, on her it really fit. She really resembled a movie star from a long time ago.

"How did you know about her?" she asked.

"I'm friends with the detectives who are working on your father's case. They told me a lawyer by the name of Green had called them, and that he represented the stepsister. I called Mr. Green to talk to him and also to inform him I owned the houseboat, and I wanted no problems."

I waited a few seconds while she considered what I'd just told her. Hearing nothing, I continued, "I'd like to ask you a question if you don't mind. I hope you don't think this is a rude thing to ask, but," as I collected my thoughts, and she nodded her head for me to continue, "How come you didn't know your father had a stepsister?"

She paused for a second, searching for the best way to explain it. "I really know little about my father. Perhaps it sounds strange, but the subject was taboo with mother. As I told you the other day, father and I were just finally putting away what had transpired between us so long ago. We were only discussing matters related to the two of us.

"I'd never discuss mother with him, and I don't think he ever mentioned anything about any of his family. I would have asked him about my grandparents, and if I had aunts or uncles, but we never got that far. I never told him much about my life, and he never told me much about his life, except he now lived in Seattle on a houseboat. All over Europe, many people live on houseboats, but they move about. I understand his houseboat is tied up; moored?" I nodded my head. Jenifer continued, "So he couldn't move it. Is that correct?"

"Well, more or less, you can move it if you have to; however, to do it you would have to have it towed." Boy, did I know about that. "But yes, it usually stays moored in just one place. Are you sure you don't want to see it sometime?"

Jennifer shook her head, "I think not. However, might I reserve the right to change my mind?"

"Of course, any time!" I waited for a moment and then helped her get to the point. "Ah, I don't think you wanted to see me about the houseboat. Was there something else?"

She gave a short bark of a laugh, "I'd forgotten how blunt Americans can be. Yes, there's something else. It's about my, what exactly do I call this woman? Is there such a thing as a step-aunt? Or is it my half-aunt? What do I call her?" I shook my head back and forth as I grinned at her; I really didn't know either. "This has taken me so much by surprise…" I could see she was searching for the words to continue.

After a lengthy pause, I leaned forward and whispered "Go ahead. Take your time and tell me the rest."

She gave me a tiny piece of the breathtaking smile, and then continued, "I know no one here in town, so I asked one of the police detectives - the one with the funny accent - if I could trust you, and he said I could." She paused, and once she'd asked me, she blurted out, "What I want to know is, will you find out if this Bottomsley woman is really related to my father? I know you must think me terribly selfish, and not to wanting to share any of father's money with her, but it's not the case. It's more than that part of it is the way her lawyer spoke on the phone, and well, he was vulgar. Also, I have a strange feeling that not everything is... I'm uncertain how to put this, but well it doesn't seem right to me.

"Miss Rockingham, I, um..."

Now she held up her hand, "Fair is fair, you insist I call you Matt, then I insist you call me Jennifer. Just never call me Jenny. All right?"

"Okay, Jennifer!" I stressed her name, "I'm very flattered you've asked me to help. But I'm not a private investigator. Your father's demise is a matter for the police to resolve. I'd think they consider anything remotely related to it would fall under their purview. I'm friends with several members of the Seattle Police Department, but I'm sure they wouldn't appreciate me getting involved in their investigation. Also, I don't really understand what you want me to do about your, um... your... Ms. Bottomsley."

Her cheeks flushed red, and she spoke fiercely, "Please, she's not MY Ms. Bottomsley!" I quickly held up my hands palms out, with a mock ducking of my head. This at least brought a small smile to her lips.

"I'm told she wants to take this entire thing to court. That nasty solicitor of hers as much as said I was lying when I said I was Elmo's daughter. He said the estate belonged to Bottomsley, especially since she'd taken care of my father over the years. I don't know how she accomplished that, since she lives mostly in California and he lived in Seattle."

As she spoke, she'd spoke faster, and then two silver tears slipped out and slid down her cheeks. I reached inside my suit pocket and pulled out a clean handkerchief. I silently thanked my mother for being such a nag when I was young, making sure I never left the house without a clean one in my pocket. She dabbed at her eyes and then smiled her great smile at me.

"I'm sorry. I thought I had it all under better control. It's just that I never expected someone to call me a liar and then treat me so rudely on the telephone."

I explained to her how I too had been on the unpleasant end of the same jerk. I asked her if she had a local attorney. She said she didn't, and she'd planned to use her father's.

I carefully explained why it was perhaps not such a good idea. She needed someone who, so far, did not already have so much tied up in the entire case. She needed someone who'd be there to represent her interests and hers alone. When she asked me if I knew of any, I told her I'd call and set up an appointment with my wolves.

She looked at me strangely.

"Sorry, it's what I call them. I think of the legal profession as animals, and of all the animals I've read about, a wolf seems to fit them the best."

That brought a big smile to her face, and she told me she liked that name for them. I told her I'd try to arrange for her to see them in the next day or so. She requested I go with her, and even though it was not something I was wild about, I felt I could at least do that for her. We agreed once I set up an appointment, she'd see the attorneys first and then we'd discuss if I could provide any further help. In the back of my mind, I was silently hoping she'd forget about trying to get me to investigate the Bottomsley woman.

After I paid the tab, we walked out together. As we were walking out, I inquired how she'd gotten to the bar. She indicated she'd taken a cab. I asked if she wanted a ride back to her hotel, and she agreed.

When we arrived at the car, BJ wagged her tail. She was elated to see me and was even more excited to meet new company. BJ greeted Jennifer with a quick lick, and then she came over to say hello. After we all settled in, BJ curled up in Jennifer's lap and gave a happy little grunt. Jennifer was all smiles. It looked like BJ had made another conquest.

I drove Jennifer to her hotel, and when she tried to exit from the car BJ tried to settle in harder. It would appear she'd become most fond of Miss Rockingham. Jennifer leaned over and put her hand on top of mine on the steering wheel. "Thank you for helping me. I know that thank you really isn't enough. I had no one to turn to."

I was a little embarrassed now, "Let's see what I can do first. Then you can thank me. OK?"

"Call me when you hear from your - how did you put it, wolves?" She turned her great smile on me.

As I pulled away from the curb, I glanced in my rear-view mirror; Jennifer was still standing at the curb watching me drive away. I picked up my cell phone and put in a call to the wolves. The earliest I could get Jennifer in to see somebody at my lawyer's office was Monday afternoon. As I pushed the end button on the cell, I remembered it was Thursday and the weekend was just around the corner. With no special plans for the weekend, I headed back to the barn and wondered what I would do with myself. I hoped that my nightmares about Slim would be over soon.

CHAPTER EIGHTEEN

Monday morning, bright and early as the old saying goes, I headed down to the Seattle Municipal Building where Sakol and Jeff L. have their offices. While driving down to the Public Safety building, I realized today would be another gorgeous day with the mountains out in all their glory. See, contrary to popular belief, Seattle has more than one nice day in a row. I needed a nice day since my weekend had been such a bust. Try as I might, I still spent too much time brooding about Slim.

By now I was past the shock of the grisly discovery of Slim's body, and what I was working on was putting Slim's death in some kind of context. His death made no sense as far as I could see. Could it really just have been some hopped up kid stoned out of his ever-lovin' on some weird drug? I had a hard time buying that idea because of how someone killed him. I can't see any stoner cutting anybody's throat as Slim's had been slashed. I needed more information and Jeff L. and Sakol would give it to me. They just didn't know it yet.

Striding down the building's corridors, I usually I got depressed with the décor. I've decided that someplace, somewhere, there is a drab little person whose sole function in life is to design buildings for various government agencies. All these designers do is design buildings just like this ugly one, complete with their dreary little interiors, and their goal is to make municipal buildings as depressing as possible. Every time I visit Jeff L. and Sakol's office, I feel shock, dismay, and some depression at how dismal and lifeless their entire building appears. To make matters worse, Jeff and Sakol have to do their… whatever it is detectives do… in that environment. I understand it's just an office building and that the city built it to service the needs of the community. But was it really necessary to make it so depressingly ugly?

What I thought was even worse was Sakol's pathetic attempt to liven up their office with a plant. And a half dead one to boot. The poor thing consisted of one very yellow, one brown, and one pale green leaf. In reality, the plant did little to cheer up their cramped quarters. My hope is the person responsible coming up with the decor must have figured most of the occupants should be out of the office and working the streets, not luxuriating in their dinky holes. Therefore, they didn't need a nice office, or an aesthetically pleasing building, just a stone block was would suffice. Even their window, which most cubicles on the floor didn't have looked out at the brick wall directly across the alley. Woopty do!

Another thing I've noticed about police buildings is the odor. I don't know if it's the doubt, the worry, or maybe just plain fear, but if you visit enough police stations and jails, you'll soon notice the same smells. Needless to say, as much as I enjoy Sakol and Jeff L.'s company, I try to spend as little time as possible in their bleak building and I try to spend even less in their depressing cell. Excuse me, their office.

Neither one of them was at their desks when I arrived, so I hung around and waited a few moments, hoping one of them might show up. I'd asked the desk sergeant on the way in if he knew if either of them was in the building. He thought they were still somewhere on site. Sitting there waiting, I got nosy, and I noticed a folder lying on Sakol's desk marked "John Doe." Curiosity got the best of me and I picked it up and flipped it open.

My assumptions about the contents were correct. It was the autopsy of the man murdered in the vacant lot behind my place. One photo of his face was very clear. I know this sounds strange, but for a moment I thought I recognized him. But the person I thought it might be looked somewhat different. I stared at the photo for quite a while, trying to see through the memories of way too many years past. The face was so tantalizing… but it remained so elusive.

Another photo was of the victim's left upper arm. The tattoo on the arm in that photo was identical to mine. As I examined it carefully, I saw it had faded, just about as much as mine. The two tattoos seemed to be from the same time period. I looked at it in hopes it might tell me something, but no such luck. I looked over the small packet of dental x-rays, which were informative. Under remarks, I read that the coroner had noted the deceased showed signs of plastic surgery. I picked up the picture again to see if knowing about the plastic surgery might help me recognize the man. It didn't.

The coroner concluded the surgery was several years old and appeared to have been expensive since it was very well done. The last paragraph of the report stopped me cold. Whoever the John Doe was, he was already as good as dead before someone shot him in the vacant lot. The coroner's report said the deceased had cancer spread throughout his body. He estimated the John Doe had only three months to live. After reading over the report and everything wrong with the John Doe, I concluded it sounded like whoever killed Mr. Doe in my vacant lot did him a favor and had saved him a lot of pain and suffering.

I picked up the picture one more time. I still had the feeling I was missing something. The face looked so familiar, but I couldn't pinpoint his name. It frustrated me. I wondered if an old friend of mine would know who it was. My friend's name is Walter, and I knew him from the old days. I decided I'd have to get ahold of him and see if Walter could tell me if he knew whom the dead person was.

After I finished my careful scan of the contents, I tossed the folder back on the desk disappointed with what I'd found. I'd hoped to recognize who died in my backyard. Our outfit wasn't that big, and I was sure I'd know who Mr. Doe had been. Just as the folder hit the desk, both detectives came around the corner carrying Styrofoam cups of coffee in their hands, but no donuts. I considered for a moment making a cop joke but decided just to keep my smart mouth shut. I pointed to the folder and asked nobody in particular, "Any luck finding out who our John Doe was?"

Both Sakol and Jeff L. shook their heads. Jeff L. remarked from the sound of my comment I didn't seem to know who the guy was either. I explained how I felt somewhere in the back of my mind; I knew the person, but he looked different. I mentioned I'd seen that JD had plastic surgery, but it was good enough to change his features, which meant I didn't know who he was.

Jeff L. continued telling me they had submitted the prints to various Washington, D.C. organizations, and they were still waiting to hear from them. Sakol said they both thought it was strange that it was taking so long to hear on the prints. Both of them agreed it usually took less than twenty-four hours, but this was dragging on. Jeff L. opened the folder and withdrew one picture of the deceased. "Here," he said as he handed me the photo, "I had them make an extra copy for you. I thought you might want one. As I remember, you still keep in touch with some of your buddies from Nam. Pass it around."

"Thanks. If I find anything out, I'll let you know, of course."

Jeff L. paused for a second and continued, "Sakol believes this is the man who murdered Slim. However, I disagree. We both believe he was some sort of ex-special forces, and as you said yourself, it sure looked like the work of a former serviceman."

I waited for a second, held up the picture Jeff L. had handed me and then dropped my little bomb, "I doubt, however, if this was the man who did ol' Slim in."

Sakol was leaning back in his chair with his feet crossed on the edge of his desk. He had his coffee resting on his tummy, and his eyes were in their usual half-closed position. After my remark, his feet hit the floor, and he pitched forward, coffee spilling from his cup. His normally happy round face took on a dark and foreboding expression, his almond eyes turned into small slits and were dark as deep pools. "How you know?"

I held up my hand with the palms facing Sakol. "Easy Sakol. It was the dental x-rays." I paused while I fished them out and handed them to him. "The pattern shows lots of dental work, but most of the upper and lower right side of his teeth are implants with caps or denture wings. His left side also has lots of work, but not as much as the right. See?" Sakol nodded his head.

I continued, "When a person brushes their teeth, they usually start on the upper opposite side of their dominant hand and then move down. In other words, if they're right-handed, they'll start on the upper left quadrant. It's the easiest side to brush and so it gets the most attention. If they're left-handed, the upper right quadrant will be the healthiest, then the lower. If they are right-handed, the upper left quadrant is the healthiest." Both of them were nodding their head. Your John Doe was probably right-handed. If you check Slim's autopsy you'll see that the positions of the knife wounds would indicate a left-handed person probably murdered him."

I waited while Sakol pushed the new bit of information around in his brain. He leaned forward and punched in some numbers on his phone. He asked for someone I didn't know, which was not surprising. I assumed it was someone in the Coroner's Office because when he came on the phone, he asked if there was any way for them to determine if the John Doe was a left-handed or a right-handed person.

Suddenly the dark look slid off his face and he nodded at me. Whoever was on the phone had confirmed my guess. Sakol hung up the phone, picked up what was left of his cup of coffee, leaned back in his chair, and his moonface grinned up at me. "Son bitch, you clever man. How you know about teeth?"

"I have gum trouble myself. One time, I asked my hygienist if the side of the mouth is in any way correlated to which hand is the dominant hand, and she said she didn't know, but in the future, she'd watch. The next time I was in, she told me it appeared I was correct. It turns out the easiest side to brush is the opposite side of your dominant hand. The side with the most deterioration is on the other side. When I looked at the X-rays of your John Doe, I saw he has, I mean had, many problems on the right side of his mouth. I've seen a lot of dental x-rays lately with my sorry mouth. Sorry to punch a hole in your theory."

Jeff L. coughed softly and with a tight smile grumbled, "I tried to tell everyone I didn't think we had the killer, but nobody wanted to listen to ol' Jeff L.!" Jeff L. turned to Sakol and continued, "Maybe next time when I tell you, Sakol, you'll listen and believe. It was just too easy to think we had the killer. Besides, we still don't know who killed our John Doe."

Sakol nodded his head, thought for a minute, and made his comment, "Our John Doe could be killer. He do job, and people who hire him, whack him! No worry now! He no talks anyone. It good theory." Sakol turned his gaze on me and finished, "Or was 'til Matt come, let air out." I noticed Sakol's normal glint back in his eyes.

"I'm sorry if I ruined your pet theory. Any more ideas about what's going on?" I tried to console him.

Jeff L. asked, "How are you coming with the daughter? Have you found out any more about her or her goofy aunt?"

"That's one reason I came by this morning. I had a drink with Jennifer yesterday and…"

"Jennifer! Now it's Jennifer!" Jeff L. interrupted. "Yes, Jeff… it's now Jennifer! And NO, we are not an item. She asked me to help her get some information about the Bottomsley dame. I'm trying to stall her. I know Slim's death is an ongoing investigation, and the department doesn't like interference from anyone. The last thing I need is for you guys to get pissed at me for getting in your way."

I turned to Sakol and finished, "By the way, Sakol, thanks for telling her I was a nice guy and all, but all it did was convince her I was her man."

"What does she want to know about Bottomsley?" Jeff L. asked.

"Well, I get the distinct impression she feels something is wrong with the entire setup. Actually, neither of us felt very comfortable with the way things are going with Bottomsley and her attorney. Both of you have expressed the same feeling." Sakol and Jeff L. nodded their heads. "What did you tell her about me?" I directed my question at Sakol.

"She ask if you honest man, say yes. She hear what she hear." Sakol smiled his wise smile at me. "What do now?"

"First off, I thought she needed legal help, so I made a call to set her up with my attorneys. Next, I wanted to check with you guys before I did anything with this crazy mess. If I help her at all, I wanted your approval before I asked any questions."

Jeff L. and Sakol looked at each other for a moment. It was then Sakol gave a slight nod, and then he shrugged his shoulders. Jeff L. turned and replied, "You understand I can't actually give you permission to get involved with an ongoing investigation of Slim's death." I nodded my head. "But if you were to ask questions about the Bottomsley woman, I don't see how we can stop you. What I would hope is anything you find out you'd share with us. Of course, I know you would want to do that, anyway. Right?"

I was quick on the uptake, "Jeff L., you hurt my feelings. Of course, I'd share everything with you and Sakol. Why do you think I wouldn't do that?"

Sakol replied, "Matt, you too involved! Big brass not happy you find Slim, a man you mad at. Big brass not happy John Doe die in back yard. You understand, we need something? You find something you share. OK, Matt?" For Sakol, that was a major speech.

"Yes, I'll share any information I pick up with both of you. I know you guys are not wild about my involvement, but thanks for turning me loose." I motioned to the file on the desk, "Does this mean you'll tell me who this guy was when you find out?"

"Maybe trade! Go find, come back, maybe have trade." Sakol grinned up at me.

I guess that was as close as I would get to an answer.

CHAPTER NINETEEN

Leaving the detectives' depressing little hole in the wall, I returned to my apartment. Jennifer had an appointment at my lawyer's firm, and I'd promised I'd go with her. Driving home I remembered the folded picture of the John Doe inside my jacket pocket which reminded me I might have a way of getting an identity on the John Doe from the back lot. Walter. If anyone might recognize John Doe, it would be Walter.

Since his return from the war, Walter has been dealing with PTSD. Walter had found the best way for him to deal with things is to live apart from society. He now lives on the Olympic Peninsula across the Puget Sound from Seattle on some land I gifted him. He refuses to get either a landline or a cell phone. This presents a problem since the only way for me to contact Walter is by sending him a letter telling him when I'm coming over. Every couple of days he walks about five miles from his place to the little general store below his cabin. While he's there, he picks up the mail and any supplies he might need. I knew it would be a few days before I could get over and see him. When he gets a letter from me, he calls me collect from the little general store and we arrange a meeting time.

Later this afternoon was Jennifer's appointment to meet with my attorneys and I only had a few minutes before I had to pick her up at her hotel. This meant I needed to get ready, and fast. Since I didn't know how long I'd be with Jennifer, I decided it was best to leave BJ at home. When I got there, the first thing I did was take her outside for a brief run. After we returned, I put on my suit and from the look on BJ's face, I could tell she knew this time she was not going with me. She crawled up on the corner of the bed, laid down with her head between her paws. She was looking sad and trying her best to make me feel guilty. My God, she was succeeding. While I changed into my suit, I mused if Jennifer should ever see the way I usually dress, she'd be in for a real letdown.

When I think about lawyers, I always compare them to gunfighters from the old westerns. Reputations! If a gunfighter had a good reputation, sometimes he could avoid a gunfight simply because the other cowpoke had heard how fast the gunslinger was on the draw. Because of a reputation, the fellow going up against the gunslinger didn't want to take a chance of losing. Maybe the cowboy thinks he might be a little faster, but finding out the answer could also be a really tough lesson. That would be especially true if you aren't as quick as you thought, or hoped, you were. Thus, because of a reputation, people backed down.

When a lawyer has a good reputation, the question you ask is, "Do I really want to go to a courtroom and find out how good that lawyer is?" Sometimes it's in your best interest to just back down, pay out a little money, and by doing so end up winning. I've found having one of the top law firms in the state behind me has saved me from some "gunfights" I didn't want to take on. I was hoping my lawyer's reputation and his abilities would be of help to Jennifer, too. From the sounds of it on the phone, Mr. Green didn't seem like he was in the same arena as my gunfighters.

Jennifer was staying at the Sorrento Hotel. The Sorrento, in downtown Seattle, is an older, smaller, but a very plush hotel. The service is excellent, and the entire place feels like something out of a movie version of a very upscale hotel from the 1930s. I thought to myself it suited Jennifer precisely.

I went to the desk in the hotel lobby, and they called up to her room. A few minutes later, she walked off the elevator looking breathtakingly beautiful. For a moment I wished I were twenty years younger. Here was obviously a woman of class. I was sure she only saw me as some old codger just trying to help her with a problem.

I gave her my best smile. "You look wonderful. You realize every person in this lobby is staring at you?"

She was blushing a little as she glanced around the room and replied, "You're too kind, but I notice you and the desk clerk are the only ones here." She finished with a cute chuckle.

"You fill up a room all by yourself!" I had no idea what that meant, but I was so taken with her looks I was at a loss for anything intelligent to say.

We headed off to the offices of Goldstein, Bradson & Silversmith in the Columbia Tower. They occupy two complete floors near the top. To reach their offices, you must take an elevator to their lobby on one floor before they take you up to the important offices above the receptionist desk.

The receptionist told us it would be a few minutes and asked if we wanted a cup of coffee. Jennifer and I both declined. As we sat down, she turned to me and quietly remarked, "I can't get used to American coffee. It's so bland when compared to European coffees. I find it too weak for my taste."

"That's odd. With all the stands that exist in Seattle, and how famous and great our coffees are, I'd think some different blend would be like what you drink back home."

"I've tried what you call European Blend, and it doesn't compare. I don't want to hurt anyone's feelings, but the taste does leave a lot of room for improvement." She gave me a dazzling smile. "Are you as big a nut about coffee as the rest of Seattle people are?"

"I have my cup or two in the morning, and that's it for me for the day. I know it doesn't look like it, but I'm somewhat careful about what I eat and drink. People my age have to act with greater care than you youngsters."

That remark brought forth her dazzling smile and another cute chuckle. She leaned over and placed her hand on top of mine. "I'm afraid I'm older than you think. Besides, when I look at you, you're doing well against the ravages of time. It would appear the 'home' is taking great care of you!" She followed her remark with a big blast of that great smile.

"I guess I deserved that, but when I look at you it makes me feel like some dirty old Letch."

Jennifer patted my hand and replied, "And you make me feel like a schoolgirl again in her uniform," she gave me a large grin and finished, "which then makes you a dirty old man. Yes? No?"

"You win, I quit!" Again, she blessed me with that great smile.

When the receptionist called us to her desk, she told us in a clipped English accent that Mr. Silversmith would see us now. I thanked her and told her I knew the way to his office. I led Jennifer up the broad circular stairs to the office suites and Mr. Silversmith's personal secretary. When she saw me, she greeted me by name, making it obvious I'd been here before. Bob Silversmith and I have had multiple dealings with various problems over the years. Because of that, I felt that Bob was the best lawyer at the firm to help Jennifer. Bob's specialty is in business law, which is just what Jennifer needed for this situation. When the secretary led Jennifer off to the next office, I dropped back.

When Jennifer saw I was not walking with her, she turned around and with a puzzled look on her face asked, "Aren't you coming with me?"

"No, this is something you need to talk about with Mr. Silversmith first. You must tell him all the details with no second-guessing what I should or shouldn't hear. Then later you can decide what you want me to know. Trust me, you really want to do it this way. This way you can tell him everything about your situation."

As she turned to walk away, I smiled at her. Then I turned and headed off to Albert Bradson's office. Albert acts as the defense attorney at the firm. And as much as I hate to admit it, I have occasionally had to take advantage of his services too.

I've met most of the other barristers in the firm, but Albert has been of the greatest help. His "fast draw" reputation is one of the best; not just in the state but on the entire West Coast. His rep has definitely worked to my benefit. Over the years, we've found we share similar passions for automobiles, blondes, and single-malt Scotch. More than once, we've tasted some fine single-malts, while trying to unravel some of the great mysteries of the other two passions of our lives.

It's never Al, always Albert. In Albert's earlier days, he'd played semi-pro baseball. Even though he's a little younger than I am, he's still in excellent physical shape. Albert told me back in the day he had the skills to move up in the ranks of professional ball. However, because he was so young, and lacked the motivation to work hard enough to advance, he never made it to the majors.

Albert was happy to see me, and as we shook hands. I was impressed by how fit and trim he still looked. Even with the silver temples, he still looked like he could turn out for spring training tomorrow. I was jealous. For the next few minutes, we brought each other up to date on what was happening in our lives. I briefly explained my problems with the houseboat and Slim's demise. I also told him what had brought me to his offices. Previously, Albert sat in on several of our poker games, so he understood how I could win the houseboat. He'd won his share of my money.

The phone on his desk rang, and when I realized this would be a lengthy call, I motioned I was leaving. We waved goodbye at one another and with that finished; I walked down the hall to wait outside Silversmith's office. Jennifer's visit took about thirty minutes longer than I expected, but when she came out, she seemed happy with her meeting. I decided I'd wait until she was ready to tell me what had so improved her attitude.

As we rode down the elevator, she asked me if I would buy a lady a late lunch. I held back a smart-assed remark, and we agreed upon a restaurant. Since we were close to the waterfront, I decided we could just walk down to the wharves and go to a rather touristy place. It serves fantastic fish and chips, along with clam chowder, which is some of the best Seattle offers.

After we ordered, we found two seats right at the end of the building where we could look out at the boat traffic, seagulls, and mountains in the distance. I waited for Jennifer to talk first.

She seemed hungry and quickly ate her chowder, and then started in on the fish and chips. For a woman who had such a great figure, it somewhat surprised me at how much she was eating. About halfway through, she slowed down and grinned at me. "Wow, I was a lot hungrier than I thought. This is fantastic. I'd thought English fish and chips were good, but this is great."

Finally, she looked around at the scenery outside. A ferry was heading off across the sound, and two tugs were escorting a large container ship. She leaned over and put her hand on mine, "This is a very interesting place! Thanks."

She poked at her food for a moment and then looked up at me. "I need to talk to you about something."

"Shoot!"

"About my, how do I say this properly, about Bottomsley," She stopped and frowned.

I had to smile, she was still trying to get a handle on what to call her, "Go on."

"I'm at a loss to explain my feelings about her. I feel certain that something is wrong with all of... with her. I can understand why father never mentioned her but if she's who she says she is, I can't believe that she knew nothing about me."

"Why?" I had my own opinions, but I wanted to hear hers.

"If my father's lawyer actually spoke to that nasty lawyer, Mr. Green as often as Bottomsley claims," Jennifer collected her thoughts. I waited a moment, and then I nodded my head for her to continue. "Well, from the past few letters father wrote letting me know how much he wanted to see me..." She stopped talking, and there was an uncomfortable pause. I sensed she was still trying to accept the fact her father was dead. "Anyway, he told me he wanted to see me and try to begin making things right between us," there was another long pause before she continued.

"Ah... I find it very difficult to believe somebody wouldn't have mentioned me... to somebody." A slight smile came to her lips, as she continued, "You would need to read his letters... they were very warm and nostalgic." Her face had a wistful look as she continued, "He apologized for my childhood and all he had missed. He'd mentioned he was moving back to his beloved Southwest. He even told me he wanted me to visit him there. I wish I had some of his letters so you could... well... read between the lines and see what I mean. I mean, his letters seemed so open and he," she paused again, almost embarrassed to continue. "He seemed almost proud of me and wanted to make me part of his life."

I could tell she was fighting to explain her feelings. I realized she really didn't fully understand them herself. "Anyway, if father was being truthful, and I really believe he was, I can't believe he wouldn't say something about me to his attorney. Matt, each letter was an outpouring of his heart. He was truly sorry for what had happened. I know... well, I believe he was trying to begin some sort of relationship with me. If that's true, then why wouldn't he tell his only other relative?"

"That makes sense. I wondered the same thing, but came to that idea a different way."

"How so?"

"That day I spoke with Bottomsley' s lawyer he told me he and your dad's lawyer talked all the time. If that's true, I find it very unlikely your father's lawyer didn't know about you. You told me you were receiving checks from your dad..." My voice trailed off, waiting for her input.

"Well, that's not entirely true. I received checks from him directly until I was eighteen. Then I received money from a trust father had established. The trust's checks have his name with 'LLC' after the name, but actually, I didn't know how it all works. All I know is that I received money which is directly deposited each month into my banking account."

"Would I be out of line if I asked you how much you get each month?"

Jenifer sat for a moment, obviously thinking over my question. Finally, she answered, "Twenty thousand dollars, US. Why do you ask?"

"No real reason, I wondered if Bottomsley is also getting a check of some sort. Do you know how much your dad was worth?"

She shook her head. "Do you?" I nodded, and she asked, "How much?"

"I don't know the exact figure, but from what I understand, it's over eighty million bucks."

Her face turned white, and she just sat there staring at me. Finally, she shook her head and tried to speak. It took two tries before any words came out. "Are you sure?" I nodded my head. "You must be kidding. Did you say over eighty million?" I nodded my head again. "I wondered about his net worth, but it never occurred to me father was worth that kind of money. Do you think that's why Bottomsley is saying I am not his daughter?"

"Jennifer, it's a good starting reason. At the moment, there are just so many twists and turns, I don't know what to think." She nodded. "I still think everyone knew. I'm positive that your father's lawyer would have mentioned to Bottomsley's lawyer of your existence! If Slim's lawyer knew, I have to believe that Bottomsley knew!"

"I hadn't thought of that."

"Would you mind if I asked what went on at Silversmith's office?"

"No. I really wish you had stayed with me. What it comes down to, if there's a will or no will, I stand to inherit something. If a will is discovered, and it gives away a large portion of the estate, I might have to live with that. But, if I can produce the letters from my father, showing how he was trying to begin a relationship with me, I might convince the courts to set aside the will. The way he explained the trust is that my father set aside a large chunk of money which funds the trust. This is a separate thing from the rest of his estate. The trust will continue to send me monthly checks. Your question about Bottomsley makes me wonder if perhaps he created a similar trust for her?"

I saw a tear forming in her eye. As it rolled down her cheek, she swiped at it with her hand. "I can't believe I'm crying about this. I've always been so angry with him for," she thought about her words, "for deserting us... he left us!" The last words were almost a cry. I knew she was sharing something with me she'd kept deep inside of herself.

"Truthfully, I have more than enough money, so I really don't care about the inheritance. I invested some money he sent over the years. I didn't know how long I'd continue to receive money from the trust, so every month, I always made sure I invested at least half.

"Matt, I've worked so hard to put all of this away. I didn't think it would matter what happened to him. Now I have to deal with all the memories and anger, and... damn it, I find I cared a lot more than I thought. Damn, damn, damn! Matt, what's wrong with me?"

"Hey, hey." Let's face it, when a woman cries, men don't have a clue what to do. When I reached out and put my hand on top of hers, she quickly turned hers over, and grasped mine firmly.

"I can't say I understand, 'cause I really don't. I had a good relationship with both of my parents. Mom died from cancer when I was in my twenties, and dad passed away a few years later. He was a lot older than mom was, but they really seemed to love each other, and they also showered a lot of affection on me. I'm just guessing, but I'd say you were probably a lot more hurt about your dad than you care to admit."

Jennifer wanted to talk, however, I squeezed her hand and continued, "Now you were getting to know your dad, and... well, you know." It sounded lame, but I didn't know how to address her father's death. I continued, "Even though you thought you didn't care, you have been opening doors and dealing with the process of discovery. His death has taken that away from you... well before you were ready. I don't blame you for being confused, and very sad, too."

With tears in her eyes, Jenifer squeezed my hand. Her voice was soft and low, "Why does it always seem you're helping me? I hardly know you, yet I sit here pouring out my heart! I find myself in trouble with this estate thing and you help me out. You, sir, are a very nice man."

I was sure I turned red. I thought I needed to explain myself, so I said, "Trust me, I'm not an angel by any means. I'm not as nice as you might think. You know nothing of my past, and you can still think highly of me. Let's leave it at that. As far as helping you, I guess I'm a romantic. I can't ignore a beautiful lady in distress."

Her smile lit up her face, and she wiped the last tears from her eyes. She looked down at the rest of her food as if seeing it for the first time and ate again. She must have still been hungry, as she really tore into the rest of her lunch.

When her plate was clean, she looked up and grinned at me rather sheepishly. "I was starving, I guess!"

"It's always nice to see someone with an appetite." Jennifer's face and neck turned a little red from embarrassment. "I guess you should take me back to the hotel. You probably have things to do."

"I have time. Is there anything you need to do? Is there anything I can do to help you?"

"I really have nothing I need to do. Mr. Silversmith is looking at what the connection between Bottomsley and my father was. But I'd rather not have to go back to my room, that's if you don't mind."

I could see that she needed a little help, "Go on."

"Would I be in the way if I tagged along?"

"I'd like nothing better. If you're finished?"

When we left the restaurant, I explained how I really would like to change clothes. I jokingly told her that a suit was not my normal attire. She responded at least I cleaned up well. When I pulled in the garage, we rode the elevator up to my place. She voiced her pleasure with the view from the elevator as it rose to my floor.

As soon as I opened the door, BJ was there waiting for me. She was dancing on all four paws and licking her lips. I reached down, picked her up, and kissed her forehead. When Jennifer reached out to pet her, BJ promptly licked her hand.

I told Jennifer to grab a seat, and I'd be right back after BJ visited her favorite spot. She insisted she wanted to go with us. Thankfully, BJ was prompt with her little rituals, and we quickly returned to my place. I excused myself and went to my room to change. When I returned, I found Jennifer staring out my window.

As I entered the room, she turned and remarked, "What an incredible view. This is breathtaking! Please tell me how you ever found an apartment like this!"

"Actually, it's my building. I had this apartment building built and kept the top unit for myself. As you can see from the view, I really don't want to move. I think the houseboat is cute and all, but I have no desire to leave this place. There have been many days I never leave here except to take BJ for her walks."

Speaking of which, she'd climbed up in my favorite chair, and already had her eyes half closed. Dad was home, and she was content. "There's also a terrace on top of the roof. Would you like a drink or something, and then I can show you my little world?"

This was different for me. It was a bold thing for me to do, since I rarely show anyone my feeble attempt at gardening. I have several plants and shrubs with a table and chairs in the middle. The table and chairs sit on a large wooden deck along with a giant chaise lounge big enough for two. I'd arranged everything, so that there was a lot of privacy. Sharon saw it once while I was building it, but since I'd gotten it finished, I've never found the time to show her.

As Jennifer and I rode the elevator to the roof, I realized that I was feeling a little guilty. Here I was showing the finished product to someone other than Sharon first. I appeased myself with the thought Sharon would be next.

The sight totally blew Jennifer away. I led her down the pathway through the shrubs. The few trees provided shade. When we reached the raised deck, she could see the complete view. She marveled that anything could be so fantastic. As we stood there, I wondered what I should do with her. I really had no plans for the rest of the day. I knew I needed to get the photograph over to Walter. However, I also knew that I'd have to write to him first and create an appointment. That would take a few days.

As we sat sipping our drinks, I asked Jennifer, "How come you were in the States?"

She laughed, "I think it was a conspiracy. Three of my friends all were getting married at the same time and had invited me to attend the weddings. Actually, one of them asked me to attend as her maid of honor. I figured since three of them were getting married, I should come. I intended to leave just after father was… ah…"

I interrupted, "I understand. Please go on."

She smiled, "Now it appears it's a good thing I was here. I want to get everything buttoned up and get back to, well, I guess the word is home."

"Do you miss the States?"

"Not really. I started school in England when I was young and then moved to Switzerland. I have a small business there that deals with jewelry. I focus on very high-end jewelry, both new and antique. So, my life is essentially all over there."

"Is anybody waiting over there for your return?" I asked.

"If you're asking me if there's a certain somebody in my life, a significant other," she smiled and nodded her head, as she said, "I have several friends I care for deeply."

"I'm sorry if I was too forward with my questions, I was just making small talk." I had to admit, now I was embarrassed.

"Why, you're blushing! Please don't be embarrassed. I feel so pleased you thought enough to even ask."

"Well, it's none of my business. But, since you're a lovely young woman, I was just wondering if you were engaged or were with a significant other."

"Matt, I have a living arrangement with two people, a man, and a woman."

I've always felt that I was an open person, but this revelation sure set me back a step. Jennifer had appeared as being fragile. But with her revelation, I now had a much different opinion of her. There was a silence between us and finally she spoke, "Have I frightened you now? You're so still."

"No, not really. I guess I admire your openness. You seem so at ease with your, how should I put it, relationship and I'm just surprised. I guess I have a ton of questions, but I feel I need to shut up and take you back to your hotel."

"I am sorry if I've made you uncomfortable. I felt you would understand; you could handle my situation." She laughed as she said the last word. "Come, take me back to the hotel. I'm waiting to hear from Mr. Silversmith about the status of father's estate. As soon as I settle that, I plan to return home."

"I'll be sorry to see you leave. You really are a most interesting young woman."

BJ rode in Jennifer's lap back to the hotel, happy and content. When I dropped Jennifer off, I told her I'd call her the next day to see how things were going.

Driving back to the apartment, I speculated about Jennifer's living arrangement back home. She sure seemed at ease and comfortable with her situation. I wondered how Slim would have taken it if he found out his daughter lived with a man and a woman.

That would have been one of the proverbial conversations where one wished they'd been a fly on the wall.

HOUSEBOAT

CHAPTER TWENTY
AUDREY BOTTOMSLEY

I don't like to complain, well, actually I guess I am, complaining. The reason is because I'm in no mood to sit for an indeterminately long time in a lawyer's office. Although it was Wednesday morning, and it was a few days since Jennifer and I were at Silversmith's office, here I was heading back to his office; again. I felt the time span between my visits was way too short. I consider Richard an excellent friend, however spending time hanging around his offices isn't my idea of a good time. In addition, I knew I'd be there for at least the entire morning. But I'd promised Jennifer I'd go with her and I felt responsible, since I had recommended and introduced her to Richard Silversmith.

From the moment Richard phoned Jennifer on Monday afternoon and told her he'd arranged a meeting with Bottomsley and her lawyer, Jennifer's terror seemed to build. And, as he provided her with updates, her panic continued to grow all the more. She finally called me early Monday evening, panic-stricken, to let me know Bottomsley and her lawyer were demanding the meeting as soon as possible, she didn't even say hello. Instead, she started right in when I answered the phone, "Matt, I'm scared. Please help. They are demanding to see me Wednesday morning. Help me; I don't know what I will do."

I finally got her calmed down enough she could tell me in some coherent manner what was happening. She explained about Richard calling Green after we'd left and Green demanding a meeting as soon as possible. Green claimed his client was so distraught she was now under a doctor's care. Green had also insinuated there was a possible lawsuit waiting in the wings if Jennifer didn't either withdraw her claim or prove she was somehow related to Slim, which Green had said he doubted was possible since he was positive it wasn't true. Jennifer begged me to go with her to the meeting. At first, I resisted, but after I realized she was crying on the phone. DUH! Of course, I gave in.

What is it with women and tears? As if they know once the tear faucet turns on and they begin flowing, a man can never say NO! To be honest, I probably would have gone anyway, but the tears sealed my fate.

So, Jennifer and I met in Richard's office at the scheduled time. I checked to see if I would be available, making sure I could be there for her. From past experience, I knew Richard wouldn't have any problems with me bringing in BJ. However, I felt Bottomsley, and whomever she might have in her entourage, probably wouldn't understand why a dog was present at her meeting. I still maintain; love me, love my dog! But, I would forego having BJ with me today.

Once more I donned a suit and tie and when I arrived at his offices, Richards's receptionist told me I looked swell. With a big smile, she took me to a small, but luxuriously appointed room directly behind Richard's office. I was only in the room for a few moments when the receptionist brought Jennifer in. What I saw shocked and worried me. Jennifer appeared pale and wan with dark circles under her red eyes. The woman I'd dropped off last Friday, and the woman standing in front of me now looked nothing alike. From the looks of Jennifer, I could imagine how terrified she probably felt just being in this room. Meeting the now infamous Miss Audrey Bottomsley was enough to cause her great fear. If I had to be honest too, it concerned me as well. Bottomsley's reputation preceded her.

I was thankful I'd thought to call ahead and ask Richard if he could have a more private area than the front waiting room for Jennifer and me to wait. I knew what she dreaded most was having to meet Bottomsley in person and I didn't want it to be when she was alone. It was only at Silversmith's insistence she would even confront the woman. I trust Richard, but I had to admit I sure hoped he knew what he was doing. It was my belief Richard felt when Jennifer finally confronted Bottomsley, if Bottomsley wasn't on the up and up, Bottomsley would cave in, and go away. At least at the meeting, Richard could see what she was trying to pull. Once Richard understood what Bottomsley was up to, he would see if he could put a stop to it. I guess it was an okay strategy, but I knew the meeting would be hard on Jennifer.

At first, Jennifer sat with me so I could hold her hand to comfort her. After a few minutes, she stood and paced the room. She reminded me of a caged wild animal looking for a way to escape.

After around five minutes, there was a sharp rap at the door. She whirled and stared intently at the door as if it held unknown danger beyond. It turned out to be Richard who asked us to follow him.

As we walked through Richard's office to a large adjoining conference room, he told us Bottomsley and her entourage arrived and were waiting downstairs in the main waiting area. This new room had a long, expensive looking wooden table occupying the center. At the far end of the room was floor to ceiling windows with a commanding view of Puget Sound. Clearly, this was the office of a very successful firm. Several chairs sat along each side of the table, and at the far end of the table was a phone. What surprised me was the presence of a few scattered ashtrays on the tabletop.

The other three walls consisted of bookshelves stretching from floor to ceiling, each bookshelf packed with books. I wondered to myself if anyone had ever read all the books volumes crammed onto the shelves.

Richard motioned us to take a seat at one end of the table next to him with our backs to the window. Richard sat at the very end of the table, and Jennifer sat to his left. I sat to the left of her. I don't know if it was on purpose or not, but the only chairs left at the table were now on both sides of the far end. There wasn't a chair at the end of the table. It was an interesting arrangement because it did two things. The first thing was the light coming through the window was behind us which put our faces somewhat in the dark, while it would make the others at the far end have to squint. It also left Richard as the only person at an end of the table. It put him in the power position at the table.

As soon as we sat, Richard leaned over and placed a hand on top of Jennifer's. Using a soft, gentle tone of voice, Richard spoke her, "Jennifer, please don't worry." The frightened look on her face didn't waver. Richard continued, "Do you trust me?" Jennifer slightly nodded her head. "Then let me do my job. I'm here to protect you. Trust me. You will be a thrilled woman by the end of the meeting." With that, he winked, patted her hand and once more asked her, "Do you trust me?" Jennifer nodded her head harder and this time gave Richard the slightest smile.

His reassurance seemed to help, and I saw her posture relax a little and her face didn't have the "deer in the headlight" look it had before. In just a few moments there was a knock on the door. I watched as Richard pushed a button I hadn't noticed before mounted flush on the table. The door opened again and one of Richard's secretaries ushered five people into the far end of the room.

I watched as all five of them paraded single file through the doorway and into the room. The first person in line was a small man with thin pale blond hair parted exactly down the middle and a pencil-thin mustache. When I first looked at him, I thought of a tenor in a barbershop quartet. His movements were jerky and quick, and he reminded me of a small bird constantly in motion. From the way Don Green had sounded on the phone when I talked to him, I wondered if this was him.

The next person through the door was a grossly large woman who could have been anywhere from fifty to seventy-five. Since she was the only woman in the group, through the process of elimination, I assumed this was Audrey Bottomsley.

I wondered who selected the woman's outfit or where she got her sense of style. She was probably very serious about her appearance, but she had failed miserably.

The woman's hair was dyed an extremely ugly shade of blue, and yes, I said blue! Bright blue! Besides her hideous color, it was styled in a mass of tight little curls. Perched directly on top of her blue curls sat a funny little dark blue straw hat about the size of a cupcake. Sticking out of the top of the cupcake hat was a fake daisy. When she walked, the daisy swayed back and forth with her movements and when she stopped; the daisy bobbed a couple more times before it came to rest. Having witnessed this spectacle, I looked up at the ceiling for a moment, trying desperately to get a grip on my emotions. It was becoming more difficult by the second not to break into uproarious laughter.

And if anything could have been more absurd than the hat, there was Bottomsley's dress. It resembled a tent, an enormous, dark blue tent which came halfway down her calves. Her dress was huge, and her breasts were even more impressive... if that's the correct word... then the dress. Her enormous breasts were ensconced in what must be an industrially wired triple G bra.

The front of her dress appeared dangerously strained, struggling to keep within what lie beneath. It wouldn't have surprised me if the seams of her dress finally ripped open at any moment because of the mass of her corpulent body and abundant breasts. On one arm she carried what resembled a small suitcase, but I assume it was her purse. Yes, it was also blue. Her stockings were droopy, and they hung bagged around her ankles, and to top it all off, or should I say to bottom it all off, she was wearing badly scuffed blue shoes.

Her makeup would have done a clown proud. Her face was heavily powdered, and she had bright pink dots painted on her cheeks. Her lips were a dark red, and I noticed some of her face powder had spilled onto the front of her dress.

As I watched her move into the room, it reminded me of something. Suddenly it came to me, she resembled the prow of some large ocean-going container ship, which pushed the waves out of the way rather than bob up and down like a smaller vessel. My analogy spread to the four men who were around her. They made me think of four tugboats getting ready to move a large ship into a berth. As my mind raced through each of these successive thoughts, it was getting harder and harder to keep from laughing.

I tried to look at Bottomsley as objectively as I could and get a grip on my imagination. I noticed under her heavily caked makeup she had a very red face. Her face was completely round and her features were exactly centered. She had a funny little nose, with a slight upturn at the end, giving her a swine-like appearance. Bottomsley possessed several chins and nestled among the folds of fat around her neck was what looked like a pearl necklace. Besides her peculiar appearance, her face was frozen in a permanent scowl.

Someone once said there's no such thing as an ugly person. Obviously, they'd never met ol' Audrey. There are many jokes about people you wouldn't want to meet in a dark alley, and for my money, Audrey was now at the top of my list. Now I'd seen Bottomsley, I felt sorry for Jennifer and what she had gone through, and the difficult time Bottomsley caused her emotionally. This woman and I hated to use that term, was an angry, unhappy person who wanted to make life an unpleasant experience for anyone and everyone else she came in contact with.

Walking behind her was a young man who I guessed was in his early to mid-twenties. He was also grossly overweight and dressed in an all-black outfit. His ensemble consisted of a black hooded sweatshirt, a black shirt visible under that, with baggy black pants covered with lots of pockets and zippers. He wore the pants so low they looked as if they would fall off at any second. He finished his get-up with black, ratty looking tennis shoes, and grimy socks which might have been white at one time but were now just an ugly shade of gray. The punk even had his fingernails painted black and his ears had some strange hoops in the lobes. His earrings had stretched holes in the lobes to the size of a dime. In addition, he wore a large chrome ring through the base of his nose.

His face was pasty white and covered with a growth of several days' worth of old stubble, which did nothing to help hide his pimple pockmarks. His dyed black hair was arranged in a row of five spikes sticking straight up from the top of his head. I wondered who this punk was and how he fit in with the rest of the group.

Next in line was a very handsome gentleman. He was wearing an expensive looking, well-tailored three-piece suit. He was a breath of fresh air with his normal appearance. His silver hair was obviously cut at an expensive salon and his mustache was well-trimmed. He had the look of success stamped in both the way he dressed and in his manner. If I was casting a movie and needed a senator or the President of the United States, I'd have cast this man for the part. Although I didn't know who this gentleman was, I could instantly tell that he was great at whatever it was he did. He was a most impressive looking gentleman.

Last to enter was another three-piece suit. However, there was no resemblance between him and the gentleman in front of him. Where the first one looked well groomed, the second man looked like he'd slept in his suit. He was wearing pants bagged at the knees with a rumpled and stretched out coat. Both of his coat pockets bulged from constant usage, and I wondered what he was carrying in them. He was wearing a yellowed shirt with a tie that was a riot of unfortunate color. Even from the far end of the table, I could see he needed a shave. Being fair though, I'll admit he was one of those people who can shave three times a day and still look as if they needed a shave.

He was a portly man who looked as if he was of Mediterranean extraction. His face had an olive complexion, but his eyes were definitely his best feature. They were soft brown puppy dog eyes. His dark hair looked like it had been some time since it had seen a brush yet there was something about that man which made me think he was not somebody to take lightly. There was a certain look of intelligence in his eyes and I felt it would be unwise to underestimate him. I guess you could call him an intelligent-looking Teddy bear.

The man who I assumed was Green pulled out an armchair for the heavyset woman. When Bottomsley tried to sit, the arms were too close together; the chair was too narrow for her massive butt. It was obvious we needed a different chair, and it took a while to locate one. Once the chair was in place, Bottomsley again tried to sit down. When she dropped the last few inches onto the chair, I heard the air whistle out of the cushion and the chair creaked. The person who I still figured was Green waited until Audrey was sitting comfortably in her chair.

The five of them carefully camped out at the other end of the conference table away from the three of us. They stayed exactly where Richard had arranged the chairs. The punk looking kid sat at the far corner of the table next to the fat woman. The man I thought was Green sat on her other side. The other two men sat on the opposite side of the table with two chairs between them.

Richard seemed to take this all in stride. He looked at the five people seated at the far end of the table, smiled warmly, and asked, "Is this everyone, then?" The man whom I'd assumed was Green nodded his head yes.

After finally seeing how absurd Bottomsley looked, and the matter of finding her a chair to fit her massive frame seemed to have relaxed Jennifer even more than Richard's pep talk had done. Under the table, she gave my hand a soft squeeze. I turned my hand over and Jennifer quickly intertwined her fingers with mine. I was happy that she was becoming more at ease with the situation.

After a short pause, Richard started the meeting by asking if anyone wanted coffee. Everyone, except for the young man dressed in black, shook their heads negatively. The young punk asked if there was any beer, and the other three men glared at him. Bottomsley went one step further though, and after she glowered at him, she told him to shut up. The punk responded by sliding down in his chair, and he crossed his arms over his fat stomach.

Richard paused and then spoke again, "I'm Richard Silversmith, Miss Rockingham's attorney." He gestured towards the two of us and continued. "And this is Miss Jennifer Rockingham and Mr. Matt Preston." All four of the men at the end of the table stared long and hard at me.

The man I assumed was Green stood up and started the introductions at his end of the table. "I'm Don Green," and as he pointed to the woman next to him, he continued, "And I represent Miss Bottomsley." So far, I was batting a thousand. He glared at me for a few moments, and then went on, "And I don't understand why Mr. Preston is here. If he's just here to protect his so-called interest in that houseboat thing, I find it in poor taste. If he's here…"

Jennifer spoke up, cutting Green off in mid-sentence, "Mr. Preston is here at my request." Jennifer had released my hand and now she pointed at the piggy creature sitting next to Bottomsley and said, "The same as her guest sitting over there. In addition, I've reviewed all the papers pertaining to the houseboat. Regardless of what you or anyone else might think, it's his."

Green's face turned red, and he sputtered. "Young lady, you are in no position to dictate any of the final distribution from Mr. Rockingham's estate."

Richard held up his hands, smiled and spoke softly, "Please, please… hold on." He didn't raise his voice, but it cut over the din, "Hold on here, let's not lose sight of the reason for this meeting." The table grew still, "Mr. Green, Mr. Preston is here at the request of Mr. Rockingham's daughter, Miss Rockingham," Richard paused, and then added with some force in his voice, "and myself."

The woman who I'd assumed was Bottomsley piped up, "I resent that you refer to her, (Bottomsley waved one of her fat fingers at Jennifer) as my dear dead brother's daughter. You don't know her relationship to my dear brother. I'd think we should…"

Richard held up his hand, "Please, can we at least first finish the introductions?"

Green continued, "This is Miss Audrey Bottomsley, Mr. Rockingham's sister." I was still batting a thousand.

I heard Jennifer mutter under her breath, "Stepsister."

Green pointed to the well-dressed older gentleman, "This is Marvin Galante, from the law firm Galante, Galante and Epstein. Over the years Mr. Galante has done a lot of work for Mr. Rockingham, and we felt it was fitting that he was present today." I recognized the name from the papers Scott had filed for Slim and me.

He then pointed to the portly man in the rumpled suit, "And this is Julius Epstein, who also has done a lot of work for Mr. Rockingham over the years."

After a long pause, and with a disdainful look on his face, he finally pointed at the little hood all dressed in black, "And this is Dudley Bell. Mr. Bell is Miss Bottomsley's nephew, whom she helped raise after his mother and father deserted him."

I thought to myself, "Holy shit, if that kid was mine I'd have deserted him, too." The young man hadn't even acknowledged his introduction to the rest of the group. Instead, he continued to sit in his chair with his arms folded over his fat chest glaring at Jennifer. For a moment, I considered making a scene by asking why the nephew was present, but I knew Richard would feel put out with me if I did.

Richard smiled at everyone seated at the far end of the table. He reached inside a folder resting on the table and extracted three pieces of paper. He stood and moved away from his chair heading to the far end of the table. As he walked to the five persons seated there, he spoke, "I see from Mr. Green and Miss Bottomsley's comments and their questions, exactly what their basic concerns are. Let me first present these documents. I believe these papers should answer a lot of questions, and then we can go from there."

Richard walked to the end of the table and handed the papers to Green. Green's face was turning blood red and his hands had trembled. I wondered if he was having a stroke. Richard smiled and continued, "As you can see, the first piece of paper is a marriage license showing that Elmo Fester Rockingham and Alice Rose Anderson were married by a justice of the peace in Santa Fe, New Mexico.

"The second piece of paper is a birth certificate showing Mr. Rockingham and Alice Rose Rockingham had a daughter, Jennifer Rose.

"Because we expected this meeting would take place, we also carried out the liberty of performing several tests. We took DNA samples taken from Mr. Rockingham's body during his autopsy, and then from Miss Rockingham. The third page you are holding has the test results from those samples. They show beyond any shadow of a doubt that Miss Rockingham is the daughter of Elmo Fester Rockingham, also known as 'Slim' Rockingham."

I thought to myself, "Oh my God! This is not what ol' Audrey expected. I'll bet she never dreamt this would happen."

CHAPTER TWENTY-ONE

The room erupted in pandemonium. To be honest, I was as stunned as anyone. It surprised me Richard had assembled all of the documents for this meeting, and since the last two pieces of paper were ball-busters, that he had them so fast was incredible. My estimation of Richard has always been high, but it had just increased, immeasurably

This gunfighter just made a bullseye.

Four of the five people at the end of the table were all shouting, each trying to be heard over the others. The nephew just sat there with his arms folded across his fat gut. I heard Bottomsley wailing, "Ridiculous! It's obviously a fraud!" I watched as Galante reached over and tried to grab the birth certificate out of Green's hand. However, since Green still had a firm hold on it, the paper ripped in half.

Richard wasn't worried. He had several more copies of the birth certificate, and the test results if anyone wanted them. Nobody heard a word over the ruckus at the other end of the room.

Finally, Bottomsley raised her voice loud enough that everyone heard her. She screamed, "Shut up. Goddamn it! Will all of you just shut the fuck up!" And she slapped the table several times with her open hand. Somehow her language didn't surprise me much. When I first saw her, I thought she was a vulgar woman and her speech only proved it. "What does this shit mean, Green?" she screamed at the poor little man. He cringed under her onslaught.

Before any of the others could speak, Richard smiled and replied, "May I have your attention? Quiet, please!" The din faded and Richard continued, "What it means Miss Bottomsley, is that Miss Rockingham is definitely the daughter of Elmo "Slim" Rockingham. And, as his closest relative, his only living relative, she will inherit his estate. Unless a will is found that dictates the distribution of the estate. Such an instrument has yet to be produced."

The nephew stood, looked at his aunt, and spoke, "Fuck this shit. I'm outta here. I'll see you around."

Bottomsley told him to sit down, but the kid ignored her and made a movement to leave the room. Green surprised all of us when he looked up at the fat twerp, and told him, "If you know what's good for you, you'll sit down. Now." The porky brat scowled at Green and then waddled back to his seat and slumped down again.

Chaos reigned. Jennifer and I sat quietly, but Richard remained standing. I don't remember when it happened, but I noticed that Jennifer's hand had found mine again, and she was now holding on tight.

Finally, Richard rapped his knuckles on the table. "Please, quiet down!" He repeated himself several times. Finally, in the most commanding voice I'd ever heard him use, he shouted, "Be still... all of you... now!"

The room quieted down, and Richard spoke again. "If everyone continues to talk at the same time, we will get nowhere. Mr. Green, since you called for this meeting, why don't you go first?"

Green had a smirk on his face as he asked, "What proof do you have that this birth certificate is real?"

Richard glowered. This was not the first time I'd seen him angry. To date, I'd never been on the receiving end of his anger, and I wanted to keep it that way. The room was silent as he stood there glaring down at Green. He leaned forward and when he finally spoke, his voice was cold, low and menacing. "Are you suggesting that I'd bring in a counterfeit birth certificate? Are you implying that I'd cook up a false DNA report? Are you calling me a crook? Mr. Green, if your comment means what I think it means, I'd suggest you tread carefully. Very Carefully! Because, if you don't, you might find yourself facing the biggest lawsuit for defamation you've ever seen, and it will be against you!"

Richard continued to glare at the diminutive lawyer and when he continued his words were clipped and tinged with anger, "As you can plainly see, there's an official seal from the city of Santa Fe, New Mexico. Are you accusing me of faking that? If you'd like, I'll be happy to give you the name of the person I dealt with and the phone number of the City Registrar's Office." Richard's voice had never risen in volume during his whole tirade, but the effect was the same as if he'd screamed at Green.

Green held up both hands as if to ward off Richard's comments. He seemed to shrink in his chair as he tried to apologize. "Mr. Silversmith, I apologize if you thought I was impugning your honesty. Perhaps I misspoke. We weren't aware of this certificate and it's a total surprise to us. I, no, that's wrong. What I meant to say is that we, Miss Bottomsley, and I, didn't know her brother had a daughter until a few days ago. To my knowledge, he'd never mentioned it to her."

Green glanced over at an extremely red-faced woman who vigorously shook her head negatively. The daisy on her hat bobbed as she shook her head. Every time she moved her head, I still wanted to laugh.

Green looked at the two other men with them, "Were either of you aware that Mr. Rockingham had a daughter?"

As he spoke, Galante shook his head. His voice was one of total disdain, "Of course not. Don, you know that."

For a moment, Epstein sat quietly and then cleared his throat. "Well, ah... I... well, um..."

Galante turned on his partner, and in a disbelieving voice asked, "Julius, do you know something about this?"

For a moment, Epstein fidgeted in his chair and then replied, "Well, a few years ago, when Slim and I were chatting, he mentioned it was the anniversary of his wife's death. I asked him what happened, and he told me she'd passed away a few years before, and every year he tried to visit her gravesite but this year he could not do that."

Epstein was now wringing his hands as he tried to explain. "I asked Slim if they had any children, and he said he had a daughter, but they hadn't spoken in some time. He said for several years he'd had no communications with her, and he believed she lived in Europe. Slim's comments as far as it concerned his daughter, was she was just as dead as her mother."

"And you waited 'til now to bring this up?" Galante growled.

Epstein became angry and retorted, "You said this whole thing was just a hoax. You said there was no way he could have a daughter without you knowing about it." Epstein paused, as he recalled the specific incident with Slim. "Slim only mentioned it once, and if I recall the time it happened, well we were having dinner and there had been a lot of drinking and I... well, I kinda forgot about the discussion. Besides, what was I to think, you seemed so positive."

As I looked at Galante, I felt concern because his face became very dark. He was so upset when he spoke spittle sprayed from his mouth. "Damn it, Epstein, you should have told me about this before now!"

I watched as Galante visibly pulled himself together. He looked at Epstein a few moments more, and then muttered, "This isn't over by a long shot. We WILL discuss this further. Later!"

Green looked helplessly between his client and Galante. I brought up a question which had bothered me since the first time I talked to Jennifer. "Excuse me, but I'd like to ask a question." I'd aimed the question at Galante. He nodded his head, and he seemed somewhat grateful for the break in the tension.

"Jennifer told me that each month she receives checks from her father, and she also said your firm handled all of his affairs." I paused, waiting for Galante to agree or disagree.

Finally, he spoke, "Well, most of his affairs, but not necessarily all of them."

I continued, "If that's the case, why is it that your firm didn't realize he was making regular payments to her? If you handled most of his affairs, should you not have known? Wouldn't you know your firm was sending checks to Jennifer Rockingham?"

Galante tented his fingers in front of his face. He seemed to stare into the void between his palms. When he spoke, it was slow and very deliberate. "Slim was a very private man and there were several areas of his life he chose not to share with us. We were aware he had several bank accounts. He had several trust funds and some other holdings which he chose not to share with us. I know frequently both Mr. Epstein and I tried to convince Mr. Rockingham to put all of his affairs with us. We requested he do it for the ease of handling and all.

"I know this sounds very self-serving, but if we'd been privy to all his affairs, this unfortunate situation would never have happened." Galante pulled his fingers apart and motioned with open hands toward the people sitting around him at his end of the table. He continued

"We'd have known about Miss Rockingham. In a way, I understand why Epstein might not have thought it important to mention this to me. When I think about all the dinners Slim and I had together, and he never mentioned having a daughter once. There was nothing, not a thing about any children." I thought Galante and Slim's relationship had been close, and perhaps this disclosure was both surprising and troubling to him. After a few moments, he took a deep breath, and spoke, "Well, where do we go from here?"

Bottomsley piped up, her voice whining, as she asked. "What's to become of me? All these years I've watched over my dear brother. I'd always thought he'd take care of me in my declining years. He always told me he'd make sure I'd have no worries about my future. What will I do?" She turned to Green, "Does this mean I'll not be getting any more checks?"

Richard and Galante spoke in unison, "What checks?" Again, I watched, as Green seemed to shrink in his chair. He motioned for Bottomsley to lean over, and he whispered something in her ear. She pulled back and glared at him. Between clenched teeth, she hissed back at him, "Tell them if you must."

Green nodded his head at Galante, "You mentioned you were aware Mr. Rockingham had several trusts and accounts you were not privy to. Well, I'm afraid this is another one. When Slim started in business, he set up a small trust fund to provide an income to Audrey. She was the closest thing he had to family. As his companies grew, the size of her checks grew. Many years ago, she came to me when she found out he was getting married.

She, Miss Bottomsley, wanted to have something in writing to ensure that she'd continue to receive support from her brother, but she felt uncomfortable speaking with him directly about the matter. So, Mr. Rockingham arranged a trust fund, which he funded and the two of us administered. This provides Miss Bottomsley with an income to cover her monthly living expenses and a little extra. Since he started this trust outside of his estate, I can't see a reason why it should be part of it or have to go through probate."

It surprised me when out of nowhere, Dudley piped up, "How much more will we be getting then?"

Richard answered, "Unless Miss Rockingham wishes to provide a portion of the estate to your aunt, only the money from the existing trust that your aunt receives will continue."

Dudley looked at his aunt, "You told me when the old fart croaked we'd be rich. You told me I could buy a new car, and we'd have a huge mansion to live in. How come? What happened, you lied to me."

Bottomsley turned beet red, and she tried to reach over to pinch the young man on the arm to make him stop talking. As she reached out, he pulled back obviously, this was something she'd done before.

"Shut up!" she commanded him. "We'll discuss this at home."

"I won't shut up." Dudley turned to Green and asked, "Is it because of that bitch," and he pointed at Jennifer, "that auntie has to wait for her money?"

Green replied, "Dudley, listen to your aunt, you need to keep still now."

"I will not, and you can't make me."

"Dudley, shut up now! Shut up now or else." I wondered what Green had over the kid, but at least Dudley shut his mouth and slid down further in his seat. As he slid down, he pulled the hood of his sweatshirt over his head, crushing the hair spikes. This kid may have been in his twenties, but he acted like he was a toddler.

Richard looked around the room, and asked, "Is there anything else?" It was obvious from the looks on all five of their faces that the meeting hadn't gone as they had expected. When no one spoke up, Richard smiled and said, "Good, then it looks as if this meeting is over."

Bottomsley reached over, grabbed Dudley by his hood, and yanked him to his feet. "Come!" she commanded.

As they left the room, I heard Dudley say, "You had better find some money real soon. I already ordered the new car, and it will be here next week."

All four of the adults spoke at the same time, "Shut up, Dudley."

As the door closed, Jennifer laughed. Suddenly the three of us couldn't hold it in any longer, and we all erupted in peals of laughter. Richard had tears running down his face from laughing so hard, and I did, too. Jennifer looked very relieved now that the meeting was over.

When Richard finally had a grip on his laughter, he spoke directly to Jennifer. "Please understand I'm not trying to tell you what you should do with your money." Jennifer nodded her head, and he continued, "But, if I were you," Jennifer nodded her head again for him to continue, "I'd suggest that you look over your situation and make an offer to give her a small... a tiny portion of the estate."

He paused waiting for a reply that didn't come, so he continued, "I doubt if they can win this in court, but on the off chance if you can make it large enough, I'm sure she'll take the money and run. This way she can save face, and maybe even buy little Dudley his car."

With the mere mention of Dudley's name, I couldn't resist any longer, "What an obnoxious little shit. He looked like he was in his twenties, but he acted like he was six or seven. I cannot believe I'm saying this, but I really feel sorry for poor Bottomsley."

Richard smiled, "I'll admit, his toothpick didn't go through the olive."

With that comment, Jennifer started in once more in gales of laughter. When she finally could speak, she said, "I'd never heard that one before. He seemed almost retard-ed."

Looking at Richard, she continued, "I can see why Matt has such high regard for you. Why don't you come up with a number you think would satisfy both Green and that woman? I hate to call her a woman and then realize she and I are the same sex. What a mean vile person."

Richard looked at Jennifer and smiled, "This afternoon, I'll have papers drawn up for you and delivered so you can examine them first thing tomorrow morning. If you approve, sign them and call me and I'll have them couriered over to Green's office by noon. That should more than likely remove any obstacles which might hinder us from settling the estate. Without the offer, all I can see Green doing is delaying the inevitable. However, this way it should go with no problems."

"How long will I have to stay in America?"

Richard glanced at the calendar on his desk for a moment, "I think we can have this done in two or three weeks." Looking back at Jennifer, Richard continued, "If it takes longer, you can go back home, and when it's finally resolved, I'll come to you with the papers for you to sign." With a big shit-eating grin, Richard winked at her and said, "I never turn down a chance to visit Europe and I'm sure you know a lot of interesting places you can show me."

She smiled at both of us. "Actually, I'd love to see both of you. You know, if I wasn't engaged to be married, I'd think one of you would be an excellent choice." Her comment stunned me. I knew she lived with a couple, but this was the first time she mentioned she was considering marriage. I never had even thought to ask her if one of her lovers was her significant other. My only hope was whichever of the two she planned to marry was worthy of her. I asked her if she needed a ride back to her hotel and she told me she'd appreciate it.

On the way back to her hotel, she seemed at ease with the situation, but I still had a feeling something was eating at her. Finally, I asked, "Why do I get this feeling there's still something?" I paused, "Care to talk about it?"

Jenifer continued to stare out the front window of the car as she took a deep sigh. "Well, yes, there's one small item. I can't help but wonder who killed my father and why."

I snorted and responded, "You aren't the only one. A lot of us are wondering what happened. At the moment it stymies the police, but if I ever find out, I'll tell you the whole story."

She smiled at me. "I know this is off the subject, but I'd love for you to come and visit me in Europe. Would you come?"

I thought about the three of them for a moment, it would be interesting to observe firsthand. "Yes. I think I'd like that."

"Then, it's a date." And Jennifer leaned over and kissed my cheek.

I found I rather enjoyed that.

I dropped Jennifer in front of her hotel and then headed home. My suit was becoming rather confining, and I knew BJ would be ready to visit the back lot when I got home.

CHAPTER TWENTY-TWO

Even though it was a cloudy Thursday morning, I was still in a great mood because of the way the meeting between Richard and Bottomsley's people had turned out. In addition, every time I thought of that funny little blue hat perched on top of Audrey's blue curls, and the fake daisy swinging back and forth as she moved, I actually would break out laughing. Considering how frightened Jennifer had been about the meeting beforehand, and how well things turned out, it had been a great day.

Thankfully, when I took BJ out for her morning walk, she did her things quickly. It wasn't raining yet, but I could tell it wasn't far off. After we returned, I poured a cup of coffee, and then I called Jeff L. It had been few days since we talked, and I wondered if they had gotten any word back on the identity of the John Doe who was killed in the back lot. Jeff L. caught the phone on the first ring. Once he knew who was on the phone, the tone of voice turned cold and demanding, there were no pleasant greetings. "Matt, glad you called. I was just getting ready to call you. We'd like you to come down to the station. Right now, if you will!"

I was thinking he needed to lighten up a little but said nothing. This was not the way to convince me to come down and see him. "Why, good morning to you too Jeff L.." I paused and got no response. I continued, "Okay, why? Why do I need to come down to the station right now? And what is this 'we' thing?"

There was a pause, and his voice softened a little, "Matt... ah... as an old friend, I'm asking you to come here on your own. Please don't make this difficult."

I couldn't help it because I felt he was badgering me and my voice took an edge, "Jeff L, if you're playing the old friend card, remember, this is me, Matt! I'm playing the same card ol' buddy, what the hell is going on?"

Now there was no masking the authoritative tone in his voice, "Matt, you have a choice, come here on your own, or I'll send out a car to bring you in."

Now I was pissed and did not try to keep my voice from showing it. "Oh, really! So, are you telling me I'm under arrest?"

The voice of authority was still there, "Not exactly. What I'm saying is we have questions we want to ask you." There was a slight pause and when he continued, I thought his voice was a bit softer. "If it were up to others here at the station, this whole thing would be a lot different if you catch my drift."

I would not back down, "And I still want to know Jeff L., who are 'we'? If you want me to come in so bad, why won't you tell me what's going on?"

Jeff L.'s voice now sounded as if he was almost begging and was now softer than it had been during our entire phone call. "Matt, please do both of us a big favor, and get your ass down here. Now! I'm begging you and this is my last request!"

I'd had enough of this bull; it was time to end this phone call. I popped off, "I'll think it over ol' buddy! Ciao."

As I slapped the phone down, I could hear Jeff L.'s voice shouting over the phone, "Matt, do not hang up!"

I wondered what the hell was going on. This was the first time I'd ever had Jeff L. pull the cop routine on me. This made me feel concerned, and I decided it was time to call Albert Bradson. Since I didn't understand what was going on, I felt like I needed legal counsel in my corner.

I called Albert's number, and I'd lucked out and found him at his office. I gave him a quick rundown of my conversation with Jeff and I mentioned when I asked Jeff L. if I was under arrest; he avoided the question. I ended up with how Jeff had threatened to send out a squad car to bring me in and I asked Albert if he thought I might need representation.

Albert asked me if I'd told him everything and after a moment's thought, I said I couldn't think of anything more. He told me he'd meet me at the station in an hour. Albert ended our phone call with a word of caution, "I'd make myself scarce until we meet downtown. I don't know what's going on, but you don't want the police to pick you up and bring you in. You realize they could take their time letting me in to see you, and we don't want that. Okay?"

"Thanks, Albert. Thank you for everything."

"Don't thank me yet, Matt. We still don't really know what's going on down there and what's caused this sudden change in attitude. See you in an hour."

I called Jeff L. back. When I told him who it was, and he started in, "Don't you ever hang…"

I interrupted him, "Jeff, shut up. I'll be at your office in an hour. Goodbye." I quickly hung up again before he said anything else.

Next, I pushed and held down the end button again on my cell and turned it off. The next time I spoke with Jeff L. and company, I wanted legal counsel sitting next to me. The rapid change in attitude down at the station had alarmed me.

Exactly one hour later Albert met me in the parking lot in front of the Seattle Public Safety Building. We checked in with the desk sergeant and then found ourselves escorted to a small room with two ancient metal chairs and a badly scarred ancient wooden desk. They told us to wait in the room for Jeff L. and whoever else "we" were.

Finally, Jeff L. came to get us and escorted us to a larger room where Sakol and Frank, the Captain of Detectives, were waiting for us. When we entered, Frank glanced at Albert, pointed at him, and asked me, "Who's that?"

Frank is an African–American man who joined the force after two years of community college. He worked his way up through the ranks and took night classes at the University in law enforcement. I knew Frank, and we had always got on well. This was the first time I was on his 'bad' side. I didn't like it.

Albert answered his question as he handed him his card, "I'm Albert Bradson, Mr. Preston's attorney."

Frank seemed to know who Albert was, but he looked very unhappy about my companion. His voice was a growl, "I know who you are," Frank then turned and looked at me, and asked, "What I want to know is who told you, you needed a lawyer? All we have are a few questions to ask you."

I paused for a moment, and then carefully worded my response. "Mr. Bradson is here because of the way Detective Davenport made his... ah... request on the phone for me to come and visit you folks. It alarmed me and when he told me the police required me to come down straightaway, and if I didn't come here immediately, he insinuated a squad car would be dispatched posthaste to pick me up and bring me in. Overall, that didn't sound good for me. Those words indicated you've discovered something you feel you can arrest me for, which sounds as if I need representation. Looking around the room now, at three against one, it seems like it was a good idea I invited Mr. Bradson. Doesn't it?"

Frank shrugged his shoulders, "Whatever!" But he still looked pissed off about something. "I want answers from you, and I want them now." He had papers lying on the table which he now picked up and reviewed. His hand shook the papers a little, as he explained, "A few hours ago we heard from the military, and that has turned into a rather ugly situation, a hideous situation for us. With no warning, several federal agents swooped in here with all sorts of federal warrants."

At this point, Frank shook the papers in his hand again, then continued, "They confiscated every scrap of evidence we had on our John Doe down in the morgue, and the body. Before they left, two agents took the three of us aside," Frank indicated Jeff L., Sakol and himself, "And told us we are not to discuss this matter ever again; with anybody. And then finished by telling us if we didn't cease and desist, we'd find our asses in a federal penitentiary for a very long time."

Frank threw the papers from his hand back on the table. Leaning towards me, he snarled, "Now, I want to know just what the hell you did in the service, and by what authority those clowns had to come rolling in here on us like that?"

I looked at Albert, and with just a subtle nod, he shook his head negatively. Cautiously, I started in, "My first reaction is to mention I thought you just told me they demanded you not to discuss any of this with anybody. Asking me what's going on is not obeying that directive, is it?" I could see all three men were not happy at my comment.

I continued anyway, "I'd like to know why you're asking me these questions? What makes you think I'd know how the government works? You should have asked them by what authority they came and confiscate John Doe, because I wasn't here to ask them.

"And, as far as what I did in the service, as much as I'd like to answer the question, I'm still not at liberty to tell you a thing. Just as you have received orders not to discuss anything about your John Doe, I also have my orders. They are extremely specific. I'm not to discuss the places I saw or any of the things I did in those places. I can't answer your questions."

Frank's entire body trembled as he screamed at the top of his lungs, "Bullshit! That was years ago. I want to know what you did over there that's so important it allows people in my town to murder people in vacant lots, and then I'm told to just leave it alone. I want answers God Damn it, and I want them now. Talk!"

I shrugged my shoulders, "I'm just doing what they told me. I'm not supposed to discuss what I did in the service. Unless you can provide me with a document which changes that, I've nothing more to add."

I turned to Albert, "If this is all they have, can I leave?" Albert looked at the three of them. Frank shouted a few swear words, turned and then stormed out of the room.

Since I did not see where I'd done anything wrong, I looked at Sakol and Jeff L., and then smiled at them. "Bye guys, I'm outta here!" I glanced at the lawyer, and I made a 'let's move' motion with my head.

As we walked out of the little room, Sakol and Jeff L. glared at us. Looking at them, I had to admit; I didn't care how upset they were. I felt I had nothing to hide and had done nothing wrong.

I walked Albert to his car, and as he opened the door, I asked him if he thought I'd done anything wrong. He shook his head. We continued our conversation. He thought, as I did, something else was going on of which we weren't aware. I was sure having the feds come storming into his jurisdiction and shutting him down probably had something to do with how upset Frank had been, but that was just my guess. I thought they had overreacted. I thanked Albert for coming down, and he told me he'd send his bill. After a few seconds, he chuckled, and we both realized he was poking fun at me. We shook hands and parted ways. Since I'd left BJ at home, I decided that it was time to rescue her.

Pulling into my condo parking slot, the door to the garage went up behind me and Sharon drove in. I waited until she'd gathered her stuff from her car, and we rode up in the elevator together. She made mention we hadn't seen a lot of each other the past few days. I apologized and asked her if she had plans for dinner. When she told me she didn't, I corrected her and told her she did now. We agreed she'd shower first, change, and then come up.

When the elevator door opened, BJ came barreling out of her hiding place. She pawed at my legs, her way of showing I should pick her up and give her some love. I held her in my arms as I walked through the kitchen and didn't put her down until we'd reached the vacant lot.

She explored the entire lot just to make sure nothing new had transpired since her last visit. Once satisfied her inspection was complete, she found the correct spot, squatted down, and did her business. There was a pale, sickly sun and even as feeble as it was, it felt good as I sat on the back stair waiting for BJ. Finally, she walked over, sat down beside me, and banged her nose against the bottom of my elbow to signal me I needed to pet her.

That's how Sharon found the two of us when she finally showed up. I was happily soaking up what little there was of the rays, and BJ was happily soaking up the lovin' I was giving her. Sharon walked down the bridge and nudged me to move over so she could sit next to me. BJ lay across our laps, and we both petted her as I told her about the past few days' strange events.

After I finished, she looked at me and commented, "I see no reason for everyone to get so upset today. I agree everybody was not really happy to have the feds come storming in and take their case away, but I agree with you, they're overreacting. Are you sure you told me everything?"

I shrugged my shoulders, "That's what Albert asked me. I think I have, at least everything I can remember... why?"

Sharon shook her head, "There's something else going on something you know nothing about."

I nodded my head, "That's what Albert and I think. But what?" Again, all I seemed to come up with were more questions. Questions without answers. I don't like questions without an answer.

I wasn't a happy camper.

CHAPTER TWENTY-THREE

It was Friday morning, and I'd no idea why I was heading back downtown to visit Jeff L. and Sakol's office again. Yesterday's visit with them hadn't turned out well and when I left, I knew they were rather upset with me. Even though I had nothing new to tell them, I still wanted to see if I could patch up our disagreement. We had all been friends for a long time and the last thing I wanted to do was harm our friendship beyond repair.

The same facts were still there: I didn't know what I was looking for, I knew the unanswered questions I still had frustrated me. All I was coming up with were loose ends, lots of loose ends and a ton of questions with no answers. I hoped if I kept pulling on the various ends, or kept looking for more ends, maybe I'd find one of them attached to something important. There was a slight possibility that just maybe, something would make sense. And having the two of them upset with me would not help provide me with any answers from them.

When I checked at Jeff L. and Sakol's office, I discovered I'd struck out as they were out of the office on a call. On a whim, I wandered over to check out Slim's car in the impound lot. A few days before, Sakol had given me a special permit which allowed me access into the yard. My thought was if Sakol or Jeff L. didn't want me to go snooping in the yard, why did he give me the pass? At least, that's the logic I was using.

Since I did not know where the stored the car might be in the huge yard, I decided the best plan was to check in at the operations shack by the front gate and ask. A tall chain-link fence surrounded the shack with lethal-looking barbed wire circling the top and from somewhere in the back of the structure I could hear the deep baying of what sounded like large dogs.

The ramshackle shed was a sad-looking affair, with a roof listing a little to one side and several cracked or missing panes in the front main window. Someone replaced the missing glass with raw plywood which was now silvered, delaminating and checked from age and weather. The little shanty presented a sad sight indeed.

I pushed open a filthy gray door, which someone had painted white, but now covered with so much grime and grit I didn't think it would be possible for paint to stick to the door ever again.

When I opened the door, I could see the floor was grubby and covered with dust and dried mud. I spotted dust bunnies lurking in the corners of the little room among the thick coating of mud. The heavily gouged old counter was even worse than the floor, if that was possible. I stood there being very careful not to touch anything.

Covering one complete wall were pictures from old calendars and magazines. Pictures of nudes and semi-nude women; most of the ladies of improbable sizes and caught in impossible poses.

One thing I've noticed of late is how many of the young lasses who grace the pages on gentlemen's magazines are now young enough to qualify for the role of my daughter. I'm sorry, but I find it difficult for children to stimulate me. If something lucky should befall me, and I was to end up with one of these lovelies in my bed, what would we talk about afterward? Let's face facts, at my age, IT only happens when IT wants. Which seems to equal around one time per occurrence. After that, all that's left is talk! Now, what common interests would a lassie barely out of her teens have with an old fart like me? Do you see my point?

There was a bell on the desk with a hand-printed sign, "Ring bell for Servus." I banged on the bell chuckling about the misspelled sign. After a long wait, the impound yard caretaker came out of the back room and waddled up to the counter.

His overalls stretched tautly across his massive girth and he looked as filthy as the room. The custodian's fat un-washed hands had ragged fingernails, with grease packed cuticles. His head resembled a large round ball balanced on top of a grimy, porky neck with all of his features centered in a tight cluster on his face. His eyes were watery, and when he opened his mouth, I noticed several teeth were missing and the remaining teeth were just yellowed stubs. It took me a moment before I realized who this guy reminded me of; he looked like a filthy version of Audrey Bottomsley. I wondered if there was some family relationship between the two of them.

The grey stubble on the custodian's face looked as if it was several days old, however because of his grimy condition, it was difficult to tell the difference between where the dirt ended, and the whiskers began. Even from across the counter I could smell the odor of alcohol on his breath along with several other pungent aromas.

He belched before he addressed me, "Watcha' want?"

"I'd like to look at a vehicle you have locked up in your yard." I tried being as friendly as possible.

"You can't go back there, too dangerous." He snarled.

"But I have permission. I have a pass." I countered.

He continued to snarl at me, "Not from me."

"Yes sir, I know," I thought perhaps a little respect might help "One detective in homicide gave me a pass which they told me would allow me to go out in the yard to look at a vehicle. I'm sorry if I should have first checked this out with you. Perhaps the detectives didn't understand how your process works." I was trying as hard as I could to be as respectful as possible.

"Let me see that pass," he said suspiciously.

I handed him the piece of paper Sakol had given me. The contrast between the piece of white paper and his hand made it fairly gleam. I knew what Sakol had written on the note and it appalled me how long he took to read it. I watched his mouth move as he read each word and when he finished, he looked up at me and asked, "So, what's this for?"

I had to explain several times more before he understood exactly what I was after. He still would not let me in his yard even with the pass from Sakol, but I kept badgering him until he changed his mind.

Finally, he turned and stared at a blackboard hanging on the wall behind him. I tried to make some sense of the board, but it looked like some form of Asian writing to me.

He gazed intently at the board for a very long time as he whistled through his yellowed teeth. Finally, he grunted, reached out, and tapped the board, without turning around he mumbled, "Next ta last row, seven cars in da middle." And with that, he made a long, wet fart, grunted again, and shuffled to the back of the shack where he came from, slamming the door behind him. I decided I'd just met the grossest person of my life.

It took a while, but I finally located Slim's car in the next-to-last row, with Rockingham written in some white paint on the windshield. I could see the car was covered in dust and one tire was going soft. The chrome wire-wheels had a lot of dust and mud on them. The entire car showed it had been there for some time now. I'd never given it much thought, but somehow the thought Slim would be a Jaguar sports car kind of guy had never crossed my mind. But then, the more I thought about it, there have been many surprises about Slim.

The Jag XKR was far from stock material. It had a custom paint job, a beautiful shade of a metallic brown, and even thru the dust, you could see the flecks of gold in the paint. The car had a light tan convertible top with very tasteful tan pinstriping on the doors, front hood, and rear deck cover which matched the tan color of the top. Opening the door, the smell of expensive leather filled my nostrils, and even though it was very dusty, the wood dash gleamed back at me in the light.

Since there were still smudges of white dust all over the car from the technicians hunting for fingerprints, I realized the lab boys had carefully looked the car over. I really didn't expect to find anything. I guess you could say I was just wasting my time, but I still wanted to look at the car, anyway.

When I reached up to the visor over both the drivers' side and the passenger's side and pulled them down, nothing but dust fell off. I opened the glove box and noticed a key sitting in the bottom. I picked the key up and tried putting it into the ignition. It slid right in. I didn't plan to start the car, just turn the key. When the key turned, the cellular phone between the seats powered up, and attracted my attention when it chimed.

I know with my cell phone in my rig there's a way you can recall the last phone number called. Looking at Slim's phone, I wondered if his phone worked the same way. When I pushed the menu button, I looked under call history, and then pushed the outgoing calls button. His phone had the same features, allowing me to see the number of the last caller and then I could hit the redial if I wanted to reach that number again.

I pushed the buttons and then jotted down the number displayed on the screen. Afterward, just for "why not," I pushed the SEND button. One ring, two rings. A male voice answered, and I could feel the fear in the man's voice, "Wheeler here."

When I heard the voice, I quickly pushed the END key. I was so stunned to hear Wheeler answer the phone my hands shook as I tried to return the phone to the cradle. I turned off the key and threw it in the glove box and shut it. My thoughts raced. I tried to recall what if any, links I knew of between ol' Wheel and Slim. I knew Slim had mentioned his interest in possibly buying a slip for his houseboat, but I didn't recall hearing if Wheel had said if either of them had followed up on it.

Even if Slim were planning to buy a slip, I'd think his calls should go through the front office. This was not making any sense.

Why would Slim have Wheeler's private number programmed in his cell phone?

Why was Wheeler's the last number he'd called?

What time had Slim called Wheeler?

Why had Wheeler's voice sounded so frightened?

Had Wheel recognized the number and been scared seeing it appear on his Caller ID?

The few times I'd called Wheeler to set up one of our poker games I called his office, and this was not a number I recognized. I realized the number hadn't even gone through Wheeler's front office.

The first thing I wanted to know was when he'd made this last call to Wheeler. I wondered if Jeff or Sakol would let me look over Slim's cellular phone bill. I also wondered if anybody had even checked it out.

Slim's cell service was the same one I used, so I had an idea on how to check his number out. I've been with my cell service for a long time, and from the beginning, I've had just one cell number with them. It rather feels like it must've been one of the first numbers ever issued. I got my first cell phone in late 1986, and every time I call the company to check on something about my bill, they kid me about how long I've had my number. What I've found is over the years this longevity usually gets me fairly good service. After all, in this era, how many people have had the same landline phone number for such a long time, let alone a cellular one?

I recalled that the last time I had a problem with my cell phone bill I'd received excellent help from a very pleasant gal at the home office. I decided it was a good idea to return to my place and see if I could find where I'd jotted down her name and extension.

In this era of diminishing service, I find it's a good idea always to ask for the name of anyone who's helping you, and to make sure they know you're writing it down. The next time you have to call and do more work on a problem, you're at least a step ahead if you have the name of the last person you talked with. Or, as in this case, if you have found the one in a million who cares, and will help, you want to know who to call again.

Returning home, luck was with me, and I found her name and number. I called, and since she was out, I left a short voice mail message leaving my name and telephone number, and that I'd like her to return my call.

~ ~ ~ ~ ~

Since I didn't want to go too far and interfere with Jeff and Sakol's investigation, and more importantly since it was not really my business, I didn't want to upset Jeff and his office. I still hadn't been able to repair the broken bridges from my last meeting with the two of them.

I called Jeff. "Sergeant Jeff L. Davenport. May I help you?"

"Jeffers, Matt here."

"Hello Matt," I felt good since his voice sounded like he was happy to hear from me.

"Jeff, I'm sorry the way our last meeting went. It was not how I would have wanted things to happen. Forgive me?"

"Yeah. We were all a little pissed about the Feds coming in here like they did. It's okay." He paused for a moment and then continued, "Hey, you, I hear you were over at the impound lookin' over Slim's car. Find anything?" I knew that Jeff knew of my car collection.

"Yeah, a big case of envy. Nice ride."

"Agreed. Not really my style, but it is a beautiful car. But that's not why you called, is it?"

I laughed. Good ol' Jeff L., right to the point, "Yes, Jeff. That's not why I called. Have you guys checked Slim's last cell bill?"

There was a brief moment of silence, and then Jeff's voice asked coldly, "Cell bill? No. Why would we want to see that?"

"Just an idea. I was wondering who he called the last day he… well… his last day."

His voice still didn't warm much, "Not a bad idea, actually. Who was his service with?"

I told him and mentioned I knew somebody who worked there, and I was trying to get a copy myself. Suddenly his voice got freezing, "Why?"

"I told you, I was just wondering who Slim talked to that last day."

"Why?" Again, more of the cold tone.

"Jeff, mellow out. All we have are quite a few open questions. I'm just looking for the beginning of an answer.

Jennifer keeps asking me if we've learned anything new, and I have to keep telling her we have nothing. I thought this might lead somewhere."

Jeff's voice still was cold, "I'll put in a request for the bill."

"Can I see it when you get it?"

"Maybe." His voice was still cold. "Let me get the bill, and I'll see what I can do. OK?" There was frost coming through to my end of the phone by now. Hey, what was I gonna do at this point? I said goodbye and hung up.

BJ was pawing at my leg to let her out, so I got up and grabbed a leash to take her for a walk. Actually, I was the one who needed the walk, but it would be to her benefit, too. When I got back to the apartment, I glanced at the clock on the stove and realized I'd been gone for over an hour. When I walked into the front room, my answering machine was demanding my attention. There had been two calls during my absence. The first was from my friend at the cellular phone company returning my call, and the other was from Jeff. His message was short, terse and not terribly enlightening. "Matt, call me at once! I need to talk to you."

I called my friend at the cell company first. I lucked out and reached Marsha, the gal with the cell phone service, right away. I figured that if I tried to play it cute I might get nowhere, so I told her flat out I was wondering if there was any way I could look at someone's cell bill. She said unless I had some legal jurisdiction, I really didn't have much of a chance. I asked her if she'd tell me just one thing.

"You know, I shouldn't. I can get in a lot of trouble."

"Let me ask you two or three yes or no questions. OK?"

"Ask one and I'll see."

I gave her Slim's number and asked her if she would pull it up on her computer screen. She told me when she had it in front of her.

"On the last day that there were any phone calls made from that number, was there more than one call made to the same number as the very last call?" I gave her Wheeler's number.

"Yes. There were six calls that day."

My pulse quickened, and I wondered what was going on. "Thank you very much, Marsha. Oh, and the last call, what time was that made?"

"Looks like it was around 10 PM."

"That's all I need to know. I really appreciate this, and I won't tell anyone you helped me. OK?"

"That's it? Gee, I thought it would be tougher," She giggled, and we rang off.

I called Jeff L. next. He must have had his hand resting on the receiver since he caught it before the first ring stopped. There were no pleasant greetings, and I was tired of never knowing if I would speak to my old buddy Jeff L. or Jeff L. the cop. As soon as he knew who was on the phone, his tone was angry and demanding. "Matt, get down to the station. Right now!"

"What's wrong now? Why do I need to come to the station again," I paused and tried to imitate his voice when I said, "Right now?"

The authoritative tone in his voice came through loud and clear, "Matt, you have a choice, come right now on your own, or I'll have you picked up."

"I'll think it over baby doll!"

As I hung up the phone, I knew it was time to call Albert again. I called and could not believe my luck; he was still in his office. Albert gave me a hard time, "What is it with you? Can't you leave them alone? Do you lay awake at night just trying to come up with ways to piss them off?" Even though he was laughing, I could tell there was also a serious tone to his voice.

"Albert, all I did was go look at Slim's car. I originally went down to try to make peace with them, but they weren't there. I had permission to look at the car. Next thing I know is I'm being summoned again to the station."

"Okay Matt, meet me there in half an hour. And I have the same advice I gave you the other day; make yourself scarce until we meet at the parking lot downtown."

"Thanks, Albert."

"This time it's gonna cost you, guy. See you in half an hour."

I noticed there was no goodbye. I think Albert was a little pissed at me!

I called Jeff L. back, told him I'd be at his office in half an hour, and then hung up.

Just like the other day, I turned my cell phone off.

HOUSEBOAT

CHAPTER TWENTY-FOUR

This was getting to be monotonous; same tune, just a different day. I got there a little early and exactly half an hour after my phone call, Albert pulled into the parking lot. We checked in with the same desk sergeant as last time and surprise, surprise; we found ourselves escorted to the same dumpy little room. This time when the sergeant left us, nobody told us to wait. I figured they thought we knew the drill by now. When Jeff L. opened the door to get us, there was no greeting. Just, "Come!"

He led us to a different room than last time. Sakol and Frank were waiting for us and when we entered, Jeff pointed to a chair and told me to sit down. Albert ignored the extra chair and leaned against the wall. From the moment we entered the room, Frank glared at Albert. Finally pointed at him, "What are you doing here again?" Frank turned and sneered, "Is this your buddy? Afraid to go anywhere without him?"

Albert answered his question, "Remember, I'm Mr. Preston's attorney. He has the right to have me here."

Frank's snarled, "I know all about you," Frank turned and scowled at me. His voice growled as he asked, "Why do you always feel you need a lawyer? We have a few questions to ask you, that's all."

I did not appreciate Frank's mood at all. I snapped back, "Same reason as last time, the way Davenport demanded my presence here," I stressed the next word, "Immediately! Or he would send a squad car to bring me in. It alarmed me. Anyway, I thought we were done with this crap the other day. Not that I don't like to see you guys, but you know, this is really getting old."

Frank lowered his voice a little, "That's not why I wanted to see you today."

I feigned indifference, "Sorry, I thought that was the reason. So, what's today's reason?" I asked.

Frank stood there glaring at me and then bent down to look me in the face as he came to the point. "Just what were you doing out in the impound yard? You had no business being out there."

I glanced over at Bradson, and he nodded for me to answer. "I asked Jeff L. and Sakol if I could look at Slim's car. Sakol gave me permission." Frank glared at Sakol and Sakol nodded his head yes.

Frank stayed in my face as he snapped at me, "Our lab people went over the entire car, carefully I might add. Why the hell do you think you know more than my lab people do? As far as I'm concerned, you've no business here or there. Neither Davenport nor Sakol has done shit to convince me you aren't interfering in things that are none of your business. I was all in favor of putting your fat old butt in jail the other day. Convince me I should let you walk out of here!" His dark face was getting darker, and I could tell from the tone of his voice he was growing even more upset with me.

I realized I needed to defuse the situation a little, and my voice took on a softer, less confrontational tone. I held up my hands and Frank pulled back a little. "Look, I don't want to end up in a pissing contest here, I wanted to see the car. I came here to make amends with Sakol and Jeff L. but they weren't around. I was bored and since the two of them had given me permission, I went out to look at the car. And, actually I didn't expect to find a thing," I couldn't help it, but there was still a silent "but" at the end of my sentence.

"And did you?" Frank snapped.

"Well, kinda."

"What does 'kinda' mean?" Frank exploded.

Again, I looked at Albert and he gave an affirmative nod. "I looked in the glove box and found the valet key. You know when you park in a parking lot, it's for the attendant. It starts the car and..."

"I know what a fucking valet key does," Frank shouted, "Get to the point."

I really had so many things I wanted to say, but I also realized being a smartass right now was not a wise idea. Quickly I continued, "When I turned the key, the cell phone powered up and made a noise, and I picked up the handset. I have the same model in one of my cars and I know the phone has a feature which shows both outgoing and incoming calls. I pushed the menu button and looked at the displayed numbers for both." I sat there wondering if I should tell them about the call I made and who answered the phone, or if I should let them find out for themselves.

When Frank realized I wouldn't tell them anymore, he leaned forward again and hissed at me. "Preston, if you want to walk out of here today, you had better tell me what you found and the number you reached."

I didn't even look over at Albert, I ain't gonna cover for anyone. "Wheeler!"

Frank turned to Jeff and barked, "Who or what's a Wheeler?"

Jeff jumped in, "David Wheeler. He owns the marina where Rockingham had his houseboat moored. We talked to him, and he said he barely knew Rockingham."

I decided I might as well let the cat out of the bag, "Actually, Slim and Wheeler called each other six times the last day he was alive. All the calls either went to or came from Wheeler's private number. And he made the last call around 10 PM the night he was killed."

And with that, the whole room exploded into angry shouts. Finally, Frank got the room under control and turned to me. "How the hell do you know all of this?"

"I have a friend at the cell phone company. She looked up Slim's account and told me the two of them had called one another six times on that day alone. I've called Wheel several times to set up card games, so I know what his business number is. The number displayed on Slim's phone was not one I recognized and I'm just assuming it was his private number."

"What's the person's name at the phone company you talked to?" Frank growled at me.

"I don't remember the name." I lied.

"Bullshit. I want that name… now."

"I don't recall the name. Besides, I'm sure you have your ways to get even more information than I can." I countered.

Frank's dark face darkened, and I was afraid he might have a heart attack. "I don't need for you to tell me how to do my business. What I need is the name of the person you spoke to at the phone company."

"I don't remember." I repeated.

"If you have any hope of walking out of here today Preston, you had better tell me right now." By now, Frank was screaming at me.

Even though Bradson's voice was soft and low, his tone got everyone's attention, "If Mr. Preston says he doesn't remember, I don't see how your constant screaming and threatening him will improve his memory."

Frank spun around and opened his mouth to say something to the lawyer. I noticed Frank's fists were balled up. Albert is just as tall as I am but in much better physical shape. He continued to lean against the wall calmly with his arms folded across his chest and stared at Frank. After a few seconds, Frank thought better of saying anything more to the barrister and instead whirled and unleashed his fury on his two subordinates.

He exploded at Jeff and Sakol. "Listen, you two clowns. I want a copy of that cell bill on my desk within an hour. Not only that, I want to know the name and address of every person who belongs to every number on that bill. And if you don't have it on my desk in an hour, you both will walk a beat tomorrow morning. Do I make myself clear?"

Without waiting for an answer, Frank spun around and unleashed some of his venom on me. "And as for you, as of this moment, you are to stay away! Do you hear me? Stay away! That means stay away from this office, stay away from these two detectives, and stay away from anything remotely connected to this entire case! Just stay the fuck away from everything! Do I make myself clear?" I nodded. I wanted to ask him if I didn't comply, would I be walking a beat tomorrow, but once again I realized my best play was to keep my mouth shut. Frank stared at me for a moment and then stormed out of the room slamming the door behind him.

Jeff looked over at me and muttered, "Thanks, we needed for him to get pissed like that at us. Really nice job, Matt."

Again, I did not see I'd done anything wrong; I looked at Sakol and Jeff and then smiled at them. "Have a nice day."

I glanced at Albert and nodded. It was time to leave.

I walked Albert to his car, and as he opened the door, I asked him if he thought I'd done anything wrong. He mentioned perhaps I should have gone straight to Sakol with the Wheeler information, and I interrupted, "Albert, I'd just found out when Jeff demanded I come down to the station at once. I think they're somewhat pissed and a little embarrassed I discovered the cell phone thing, and of course losing the body, but does that explain what's happening?"

We continued our conversation and Albert didn't see a good enough excuse for them to have blown up as they did. He felt as I did, there were things going on we weren't privy to. We were positive having the Federals come storming into Frank's jurisdiction and shutting him down had something to do with how upset Frank was, but it was still just a guess. I thanked Albert for coming down, and he told me he'd send his bill. We shook hands and parted ways. This time I was sure I'd be seeing a bill for services rendered.

Mentally I thanked Jeff, Sakol and Frank for how they were saddling me with problems that were not of my making. I discovered I was thinking of the three of them as The Three Stooges.

Bad Matt!

When I got home, Sharon was just getting on the elevator. I told her to come up when she could. I'd like to see her. I was standing in the vacant lot with BJ when she came out to find me.

Sharon asked me what I had planned for the weekend and I told her I had no actual plans other than to send a note to Walter letting him know I had to see him ASAP. However, whatever else the weekend plans might turn out to be, I sure hoped they somehow involved her.

She smiled at me, gave me a wink with a come hither grin and replied, "Gee, I think that can be arranged. Bring BJ and let's get started."

And that is exactly what I did.

CHAPTER TWENTY-FIVE

Standing on the top deck of the ferry, I watched the dock slipping away as the propellers churned a trail of white water and the ferry headed out across Puget Sound. Leaning on the ferry's wet railing I watched Seattle fade into the misty distance on a cold foggy Monday morning. Within a few minutes I decided it was too cold to stand on the windswept deck any longer and I headed to the restaurant part of the ship, hoping to find something to warm me up.

Once I had my extra-large cup of coffee, (with a lot of half & half, thank you) I headed back down to the truck where BJ looked overjoyed to see me. Of course, I had to go through the argument with her to move over to her side of the vehicle. She seems to think the entire truck is hers and I have difficulty getting her to understand that I am the one who needs to drive.

Sitting in my truck while sipping my coffee, I reflected on today's mission. I was off to visit Walter. During my time in SE Asia, we had a guy in our outfit who really seemed to enjoy what he was doing. His name was Walter McLaughlin.

When I arrived in my unit Walter was already there, and he was still in Nam when they flew me to Hawaii to start my recovery. Telling it precisely, it's not that he liked what he was doing, what he loved was the solitude of the patrols. His specialty was two to five man patrols, the smaller the better. There were many reasons Walter didn't seem to do well with civilization. I never spoke with him about it, but I always wondered about the conditions he grew up with and what caused his antisocial attitudes about life.

From my point of view, the best thing about Walter was on one occasion he'd saved my life. The mission we were on had gone wrong from the start. We had bad information, there was bad timing, bad equipment; just bad everything. During the mission, I also ended up receiving several serious wounds. At the time, Walter could have just left me where I was, and nobody would have known the difference. Why? Because I was almost dead and there was no way I would make it back without help. But I'd always been straight with Walter, a respected team player and I guess it was enough for him to return and rescue me. He came back and removed me from a terrible situation which definitely would have ended my life. Even though I thanked him many times for what he'd done, I always felt I owed him more than just a thank you.

Some years back, I was reading the cover page of the second section in our local newspaper and I came across a large picture of Walter. The picture showed him on the ground, cuffed with a large police dog standing guard over him. He was involved in a disagreement in what's called The International District of Seattle. When I was a kid, we knew it as Chinatown. The area used to back up against what was the black area of Seattle. In those days, that area was referred to as The Colored Section. But over time the actual population of Chinese living there became a minority and the district moniker reflects the new varied population. In today's world, both of the old terms are considered politically incorrect references.

Historically, time had altered all of this. As Chinatown grew because of the rapid influx of displaced SE Asians who moved into the Black area of town. This caused many of the Blacks to move out of their district. The International District moved deeply into what the blacks considered their part of town, and as the Asian population grew, the Blacks fled to other adjoining districts. At first, there was friction between the Blacks and the Asian population, but finally the conflict died down as Blacks moved on to other parts of town.

During one of the more violent altercations between the various factions, Walter, who'd been living in the I.D., somehow became involved. This resulted in his arrest by the police. When I saw his picture, I became concerned for him as I remembered his inability to deal well with conventional living, and I felt obligated to help him because of what he had done for me in Nam.

When I visited him in jail, I found Walter had no legal representation. I called Albert Bradson to help him and I told Albert I was footing the bill and for Albert to do what he does. Bradson performed his usual magic and before long, Walter was released. Once the affair got settled and the police and the court system were satisfied, Walter decided, with some encouragement from me, perhaps it would be best if he lived in a less populated area. The problem was Walter had no place to move.

At one time I'd purchased a logging contract on a large section of land on a remote portion of the Olympic Peninsula. The contract had gone sour, and I ended up being stuck with a very large amount of acreage. At the time, I had no use for the land and over the years I tried several times to sell the parcel, but with no luck. The more I thought about it the more I felt it would be a perfect place for Walter, and if he was interested, we could work something out so the land would somehow be his.

Walter agreed to go over to the peninsula and look at the property. I took him over and showed him the land. I offered him part or all of it, as a final payment, 'for him saving my sorry ass', as I put it. I remembered he asked me to wait an hour, and he left me sitting in my truck at the end of a deserted logging road out in the middle of nowhere. When Walter returned, he told me he liked what he'd seen so far. He then asked me to leave him and come back in five days to the same place I dropped him off. He told me he'd be able to give me his final answer when I picked him up. I argued with him, because all he had with him was a small backpack, until he reminded me of his duties and his survival skills back in Nam. We finally agreed upon a time for me to return and as I drove away, I left him standing in the clearing waving at me.

When I came back five days later, Walter was just sitting on a stump at the end of the road, waiting patiently for my return. He informed me he'd found a site on top of one of the larger hills facing west, and he wondered if I'd mind if he built himself a cabin. He told me he wanted to stay. He enjoyed living out in the woods. I told him he was more than welcome to build a cabin or anything else he needed.

Because of his war injuries, Walter drew a full medical pension from the military. That, besides his social security, was enough income for him, so money was not a real problem. I gave him my address and phone number telling him if anyone questioned his ownership of the property; he was to contact me. Once again, I left him standing in the clearing at the end of the dirt road, which stopped at the edge of what I now thought of as "our property".

A few months later I received a terse letter from him, giving me a post office box number in a village not too far from the property, and he thanked me for my help. At the bottom of the letter was a PS where he invited me to visit any time I wanted. His only request was I write to him at the post office box and let him know when I was coming over.

He'd then meet me at the end of the road where I'd left him the last time I'd seen him.

It was over a year before I had time to visit Walter. I sent him a letter telling him what day and time I'd be at the clearing. When I pulled up to the end of the dirt road, I stopped my truck and there he was; sitting on the same stump as the last time I'd seen him. It surprised and amazed me how well he looked. He had cut his hair short and his beard was neatly trimmed. His clothing was clean, and he looked better than in all the time I'd known him. I grabbed my pack out of the back of the truck and we headed off through the woods.

BJ was having the time of her life. At first, I was afraid that she might take off and get lost, but she stayed close to us. Sometimes she'd run off into the underbrush chasing something, but she'd return shortly afterward. After a few minutes, the trail became very difficult to decipher, and I realized I'd never have been able to follow it had Walter not been there me to guide me.

After around fifteen minutes of difficult hiking, the trail became slightly better marked, and we could move more quickly. I knew I was out of shape, but the last climb up the final hill to his cabin left me gasping for breath. All the way up Walter kept chiding me because I let myself go and was now in such poor condition. Finally, I told him to just shut up and lead the way. I already felt guilty about my physical condition. The last thing I needed was his lecture.

Without warning, we came around from behind a large outcropping of rock and we crested the top of one of the highest hills on the property. The beauty of the view overwhelmed me. It was a clear day, and in the distance, I could even see the Pacific Ocean. His cabin faced due west, with a massive porch extending across the entire front. Smoke curled lazily out of a beautifully made stone chimney, which he told me he'd built from river rock he'd brought up from the river. The front of the cabin was primarily windows with a carved door of stunning beauty. I'd always imagined Walter living in some a lean-to, or at best, a primitive log cabin. But this was a very handsome cabin with lots of character. I complimented him on how great the cabin looked and on the beauty of the setting. I noticed he seemed very proud of his accomplishment and wanted to share all the amenities the cabin offered.

As I stood there taking in the cabin's beauty and the surroundings, a very attractive young Asian woman stepped out of the door and onto the porch. I didn't know Walter had anyone there besides himself. Walter introduced us and told me this was his wife, Thien. When he'd been stationed in SE Asia, Walter had known her and her family. She was just a young girl at that time. At the end of the war, Walter had smuggled the entire family out and brought them stateside.

Thien had always been in love with Walter. However, as much as he cared for Thien, he didn't feel comfortable with the vast difference in their ages. After Walter made the final decision to live on "our" property, he went back to collect his belongings. As he was preparing to move, Thien saw him. She told him she was going with him; they argued; obviously, she'd won.

Dinner that evening had also been something unexpected. Thien had cooked several delicacies from home, and, for me, it was a touch of nostalgia from my days in the service. After dinner, we sat on the front deck and drank, smoked some excellent weed Walter grew in his backyard, and we reminisced about the old days. During the evening, Thien took me aside and kissed me on the cheek. When I asked her what it was for, she replied, "Walter was dying back in Seattle. You gave him a new life. For that I thank you."

"No… Walter saved my life back in Nam and I owed him for that. He didn't need to come back and rescue me, but he did, and now I feel my debt is partially repaid," I told her.

"No, you've paid the debt, and then some. You saved his life, and you've made me a very happy woman. Thank you."

She smiled her lovely smile at me, and I was finally at peace with the debt of honor I owed Walter.

The next day, as I left him standing there in the gravel parking spot, I couldn't help but wonder who between the two of us had the better deal in life. I had my toys, and I had to admit, I felt overall, I had a great life, but his was so simple, and it finally seemed he was at peace with the world. It made me wonder all the way back to Seattle.

Enough of my reminiscing. Today when I pulled up to the end of the road, I saw Walter sitting on the same stump, waiting. If anything, he looked in better health then he had last time I'd seen him. After we exchanged greetings, we headed off to the cabin. Since BJ seemed to remember the way, she strayed from us more this time than last.

When we arrived at the cabin, I was even more out of breath than last time, and Walter started chided me even more. When I looked up, I could see BJ on one end of the deck already curled up and resting, and Thien sitting in a rocking chair beside her. As she got up from the rocker to come over and say hello, I noticed she was about six months pregnant. I looked back at Walter and grinned. When he realized what I was grinning about he actually blushed.

Walter brought out two cold beers, explaining how he'd diverted part of a stream that was snow runoff, and how it kept things cold. I was more amazed with this visit than the last. After we settled in on the porch he asked, "So, Matt, what brings you up here? Are you finally ready to ask me to build you a cabin so you can move up here too?"

"There are days when that offer is the most tempting thing I've ever heard." I told Walter and Thien about my winning the houseboat, and the rest of my story. I finally reached the point of the story that covered the reason I made the trip to see him. "I have something I'd like you to look at..." I reached inside of my shirt pocket and handed him the photo of the man who we'd found murdered in the vacant lot behind my apartment.

Walter's hands trembled as he held the photo and his face turned visibly white. He continued staring at the photo as if he was seeing a ghost. I was positive I heard a tremor in his voice, "Matt, where did this picture come from?"

"That's a police photo taken at the morgue. He broke into my place and when he fell in the vacant lot behind my apartment, he broke his leg. I went back into the apartment to get a phone to call for help. I heard several shots and when I came back out, I found him shot and killed in the lot." I paused a moment as I noticed the fear registered on his face.

"Why? What's the big deal with this guy?"

For the first time since I'd known Walter, there was a trace of fear in his voice when he answered me. "Matt, when I knew him, this was a terrible dude. He may have worn the same uniform as you and me, but he was not on our side; he was on his side."

A long silence ensued, and I wondered if Walter was off on another of his flashbacks. Finally, I heard him mutter, "I could swear I saw him die in 'Nam. Well, actually, it was more like maybe Laos, but the borders were kinda vague back then." He stared at the picture again, and then turned to me, "Matt, why does he look kinda different? What's changed about him?"

I explained, "The autopsy showed he had plastic surgery, and they feel it was a number of years ago. The police haven't come up with a name. When the police ran his prints through the government computers, all hell broke loose, and Federal officers came down hard on the Seattle police. They swooped in, grabbed his body, all the records, and if they had known about this photo, they'd have taken it too. My friends at the station are very unhappy with me about the entire affair. In fact, I'm not even supposed to talk to you about this." I waited for a second, and then asked, "Walter, who is this dude?"

Walter continued to stare at the photo, finally, he turned it over, wiped his face with both of his hands and when he talked, his voice sounded very far away. "Shit, Matt... to be honest, you really should forget all about this cat. He was one of the two most frightening people I've ever known, and you know I know a lot of frightening people." We both chuckled, remembering the men we'd served with over there.

Walter continued, "Considering some of the shit he did, it's no wonder the military came in and told your police friends to forget the whole thing and took his body with them. When I knew him, he called himself Price, Denny Price. He was a sadistic wacko, and his way of getting information out of prisoners was truly warped. He always seemed to get a real kick out of it.

"Price was from the Deep South when the Army drafted him. A sergeant in our outfit had been in the same basic training company at Fort Knox as Price and sorta knew him. According to this sergeant, Price was amazing with a rifle. Back home, when Price went off to school, his daddy would give him one bullet. On the way back from school it was Price's job to shoot something for dinner. If he missed, the family went hungry. Because of this, Price got extremely good at shooting.

"Anyway, back in basic training the first day they had to qualify with their rifles, Price had the highest score anybody ever achieved, and I mean ever! The cat had a perfect score." I looked over at Walter, half-expecting he was pulling my leg, but the look on his face showed me he was serious. "Really!" He kept nodding his head.

Finally, he continued his story, "The next day there was a bunch of high-ranking officers and two dudes in suits. Price scored perfect that day too. The next morning Price was gone! The Sargent said someone asked him to call the company together, and a one-star general addressed them. The general said everybody in the company was to forget they ever met Price. From that point on, he didn't exist. In addition, if anybody discussed Price, they'd find themselves brought up on charges and end up in a military prison. When Sarge saw Price in Nam, he was going to say hello, but then he remembered the general and the warning, so Sarge decided he didn't want to say anything." Walter sat for a while looking off into the distance. I could tell he still had more to say, I needed to wait him out.

"Price was also gay. Back then we called them faggots, or whatever, but I guess he'd be bisexual nowadays. I knew he had a girlfriend in a village a few clicks away, and he'd go visit her off and on. When I saw her the first time, I noticed that she was tiny. In fact, I thought she looked like a boy. Anyway, another dude showed up in the unit, and they seemed to hit it off big time; We called them "butt buddies." Price didn't go as often to the village to see his girlfriend after that. The new guy's name was Heyward Hollis. Hollis would be the other man I'd consider as frightening.

"If Price was weird, you'd call Hollis certifiable. Like I said, they met in Nam, and they became very tight if you know what I mean. They didn't care who knew about it." I nodded my head. Walter continued, "They made sure they went on as many missions together as they could. Because they kept bugging the powers above us to give them more missions together, they gave them the nastiest, the ugliest missions, and those guys loved it.

"The last time I saw them, Hollis was holding Price in his arms, and I'd have sworn Price was as good as dead. We were shutting down an outpost, and everybody was busy. Both of them had just returned from a mission. We noticed that Price was not his normal self. His head wasn't on straight. The deal was, as soon as we finished with our job cleaning up what they told us to take care of we were to grab the next chopper out. So, I never knew if Hollis got Price on a medevac chopper out of there. From the looks of the photo here, I'd say they got back to somewhere."

Walter sat there, staring off into space; I could tell he was trying to remember something. After a long wait, he stirred in his chair and spoke, "I thought I heard once some things about Hollis, and from those comments, I thought he found a way back home." Walter shrugged his shoulders and chuckled, "One thing, I thought I heard once was he was a 'mechanic'. Back in my drinking and druggin' days, when I was at the VA hospital, I ran in to one guy from the old days. He informed me that, or at least I think he did." Walter held his hands up looked at me, and muttered, "Shit, Matt, you know how things were for me back then. Some things I think I remember, and I wonder if they're true, some things I hope ain't true. I'm sorry, I ain't being much of a help."

"What do you mean, 'a mechanic'? You mean he worked on cars?" I asked Walter.

Walter laughed, "No dope. He was for hire, a hit man. I can't remember who even told me that, like I said. Hells bells, maybe I dreamt it. When I think about him becoming one, it was not something which would have surprised me. If one of them became a hit-man then both of them would have gone the same way, if you catch my drift?"

I remembered when Walter lived back in the I.D. it was not a good place. He'd been drinking very hard, and I knew he'd take any kind of drug just to take the edge off things. The abuse continued over a long time. Sometimes when the two of us reminisced about the old days, I'm surprised he remembers as much as he does.

The silence grew between us again. Suddenly, I felt Walter was back in the jungle again. From time to time, it happens to all of us, and I knew it was best to let him come back on his own. We both had experienced combat in the jungles, and both of us knew the confusion and horrors. We'd both been wounded, and we both were physically and mentally scarred. It was at least half an hour before he grunted and looked over at me. "You know you once saw the two of them?"

"What!" his comment startled me.

"When I found you all messed up and brought you back, you and I were waiting on a chopper to come in and take you out..."

I interrupted, "I don't remember too much from that day. I'd had several pain shots by then."

Walter chuckled, "Yeah, you were very out of it. As they were carrying you to the chopper, a brand new guy arrived at the unit, and the other one had just returned from the field. The major ordered them to come up and help put guys in the first chopper out, and then they helped me pick you up, do you remember?"

"I remember being carried to the chopper, and that you were beside me, so there must have been others carrying me..."

"Two of those guys were Price and Hollis."

"No shit?"

"No shit. That was the day when they met each other."

"But I don't remember a thing about what they looked like."

"When they put you in the chopper, one of them accidentally banged your leg against the side of the door, and you hollered, 'Watch it faggot, that hurts.' Later, when I found out about them and their preference for each other, I cracked up laughing thinking about what you'd said. You had no way of knowing, of course, but it was funny."

I sat there, again trying to remember. I had very disjointed memories from that day. They came in bits and pieces rather than the whole. That day seemed as if it was a series of snapshots. The main thing I could recall was thinking I would die, then out of nowhere Walter showed up, and packed me back to the evacuation zone. And there was the pain; that blurred everything else that day. Eventually, I felt those wonderful injections and I recall hearing the chopper coming in to take me out of that hellhole and then being carried up to the landing site. Honestly, I didn't remember saying anything to anyone. If I said what Walter said I said, I sure didn't remember. Moreover, as to the faggot remark, we said those things all the time. We meant nothing by them.

The conversation had now sent both of us back into our memories, and I found myself immersed in old remembrances. Suddenly Walter's chair came crashing to the deck, and he exclaimed, "What the hell was Price doing in your backyard?" Walter was back

"I came home and found him in my apartment."

Walters turned in his chair, and he looked over at me, "You don't say? What happened?"

"I came in, BJ barked, and I guess he kicked her. I heard her squeal, so I ran to the back of the apartment. When I arrived, he was running across the vacant lot where he slipped and broke his leg. I went back to find a phone, and I heard shots, and by the time I got back to the lot, Price was dead, and a car was speeding up the hill."

"Wait a minute, you came home and Price ran after he heard you?"

"Yeah."

"Bullshit!"

"What?"

"Bullshit! You know he'd never run. Something ain't right."

"You know, that was my first thought. I'd never run, and I thought it would be the same for him. But times change, things change, yeah?"

Walter looked at me, "Matt, look at it this way, if things were reversed and Price came home and caught you, would you split like that?"

I sat for a long time with my feet up on the railing. A lot of time has passed since the old days and honestly, I don't know what I'd have done. If I got in a nasty situation, I'd like to think the old training is still there and would keep me alive, but I really didn't have a good answer to give Walter.

Eventually, I answered, "Walter, honestly, it's been so long, I really don't know what I'd do. Maybe he felt it was better to leave than have to deal with me. You said you heard Hollis was for hire. What about Price?"

"Like I said, if they asked one to do something, then both were up for doing it. But, yeah. Why?"

Walter looked over at me. I asked him, "Did you ever do any missions with them? I never knew them, of course. What were they like in the field?"

"Yeah. We had a couple of missions together. Both of them cats were like cold. Really cold. And Price was something else with a knife."

My blood turned frosty, and I stared at Walter. I asked, "Like how?"

"One time we got trapped by some VC Slopes while we were out on patrol. I saw Price stab one in the chest with the knife in his right hand, rip the knife out, then flip the knife to his left, and catch another dude just as he lunged at him. Then he pulled out the knife and threw it at a third dude as he was trying to run away. Nailed the sucker square between the shoulders, and the knife went in about halfway."

Walter shook his head back and forth, "Damn it was impressive. Weird, but so impressive! I doubt if he could have done the same thing with a gun." Walter turned to face me, "Price told me one time he loved to stick people, said it was 'cause he could let out all the hate and rage he had trapped inside of his head. I asked him why he had so much hate and he told me to mind my fucking business."

Walter turned to face front and was quiet again, as he relived the moments over in his head. He grunted and then turned back "I mean, I knew they were a couple; buddies, you know?" I nodded my head, "But when they were on a mission, they were all business. You'd never know they were lovers. I always wondered how they kept that part of their lives so isolated in their heads.

"One thing I know. One night I heard one of them make the other one promise if it became necessary to leave him behind, he wouldn't leave him alive. Then they both swore to that pact. Under no condition would either of them leave the other behind, alive."

Suddenly it hit me. My chair crashed down on the deck, and I exclaimed, "That's it!"

"You okay, man?" Walter asked.

"Yes... don't you see... it makes sense now? Hollis was the one who put the hit on Price that night. Hollis knew Price was dying from cancer. It was like the old days; they were on a mission. Price was down, and there was no way that Hollis could get him away from the back lot. So, in the end, Hollis finished the job he'd promised years before. He snuffed Price."

Walter stared at me wide-eyed, "You said nothing about cancer. Price had cancer?"

I nodded my head, "The autopsy said he had maybe two or three months at the best to live. From what I've learned, by ending his life Hollis actually did Price a favor. All that Price had to look forward to was a shitload of pain."

It was growing dark now, and when I looked over at Walter, I could see him staring off into space. His silhouette was just a relief in the receding dusk. "Damn..." he muttered, "Damn, he fulfilled his promise. Now Hollis has taken on the hit, Hollis will keep on until you put him down, or he finishes the hit. I wonder who was the target? And most of all, who hired him?"

"I have an idea, a pretty good idea." I responded. I told Walter it was time to move on, that I needed to return to Seattle, but he wouldn't hear of it. He didn't think it was wise of me to wander back to the parking spot in the dark. Walter told me he had a great spare bedroom, and the decision was final, I would spend the night.

Walter's wife chimed in I would not head off in the dark. I would spend the night.

So, BJ and I spent the night.

CHAPTER TWENTY-SIX

The morning mist was clearing, and I could see sections of the ocean. Even at the distance we were from the water, the sounds of the surf were a constant presence. When Walter asked me to stay for another day, I could see no reason to say no. I was happy, and content and I wanted to stay the extra day. Thien was so sweet and when I said I'd stay, the joy on her face made me happy I could do something to bring out that great smile. The three of us had an excellent time and for a whole day I hardly gave a thought to the houseboat, or Slim, or Price or Hollis. I had a one day vacation, and it was terrific.

It was Wednesday morning, and I was sitting on Walter's front deck with my feet up reflecting how well he had done for himself. I thought about his magnificent cabin in the woods and his sweet wife when Thien brought me a cup of coffee. I beamed at her thoughtfulness. "May I sit?" she asked as she smiled down at me.

"Of course, and thanks for the coffee."

Her smile warmed me as much as the cup of coffee. It was easy to see why Walter was so in love with this delightful woman. "May I speak freely?" Thien asked.

"You're silly, you know you don't have to ask."

"I've thanked you in the past, for what you did for Walter, and for me. I really don't think it's an exaggeration to say you saved his life," I started to speak, but she raised her hand, "Hush. Please let me finish. Yes, I know he saved you back in the jungle and you feel a sense of obligation. Nevertheless, what he did was just part of what he viewed as his job; it was part of being a soldier. What you did for him was out of love and concern. You're a good man, Matt Preston, and that's why I want to talk to you. I see the sorrow in your eyes. You need a person in your life. I feel you have somebody, but you're afraid to let her become a larger part of your life. True?"

I thought of Sharon and the changing relationship we were going through. I nodded my head affirmatively. She continued, "Do you love her?" I nodded. "Then why are you afraid of her? Why do you not let her into your life more?"

This was becoming a difficult conversation. "Thien, I've had two previous marriages." I paused, "And they didn't go well... either time. You don't know this, but I'm a selfish man, and I've become set in my ways over the years. I live my life the way I want to, and I don't want to change. I don't think a lot of women out there would put up with me."

"Do you feel you're more difficult to live with than Walter?"

I thought about her question. Walter had come a long way because of Thien, perhaps she was even more instrumental in saving his life than I'd been. Perhaps it was a tossup. But, could Sharon put up with me? Could Sharon accept me the way I am, or could I change enough to make things work with her? I've been alone for too long; I have my ways, and do I really even want to change?

It was a long time before I tried to give Thien an answer. "I don't know if we could make it work. At her job, she's usually the one in charge, and I don't know if she can put that aside when we're together. I've been alone for so long it would be difficult to share with her what I'm doing in my life. I know I care more for Sharon than any other woman I've known. However, I don't know if I could change enough to make a marriage work with her."

"That you'd even consider changing for her is a step in the right direction. In the past would you consider changing for a woman?" I looked down at the deck as I shook my head no. "Then there's hope," and she laughed.

Walter stepped out on the deck and asked if I was ready to head back. I said yes, but before we left, I gave Thien a hug. With her arms still around me, she leaned back, "Please bring your friend here. I want to meet her."

"I'll ask her."

Thien put a slender finger on my lips to silence me as she shook her head. She then repeated herself, "Please! Bring your friend here. Please?" She was not going to be denied. I nodded my head and smiled down at her lovely face. "Promise?" I nodded my head again. She mouthed the words "Thank you," and then responded by giving me a strong hug.

Walter and I headed off in the morning dew, returning to the parking place where I'd left my truck. Our pace back was a lot faster than when we'd hiked up to the cabin. In a way, I was now in a hurry. I had more information than before I came over to visit Walter, and because of that, I now had many things to do. I finally was getting a handle on things. my hope was the handle didn't fall off too quickly.

I'd been around Walter enough so I could read his moods. When we got to the parking place, I could sense that something was troubling him. I knew there was no point in asking him, he would bring it up when he was ready and not before. After I put my stuff in the truck and collared BJ, I said I needed to go, and even though I knew better, I asked him if there was a problem. As usual, Walter was quiet for a spell as he gathered his thoughts.

"Matt, I don't have a good feeling about any of this. Over the past two days I've told you how I feel. You know I want you to drop this whole business, but I can see you won't listen to me." Walter took a deep breath and slowly let it out. "I think... no, let me change that, I'm positive Hollis is crazy and extremely dangerous. If you doubt my words, look at what he did to Price." I started to say something, and Walter held up his hand. "I know it was all part of an agreement they had, but face it, you have to be a little crazy to blow away your lover, regardless of what the two of you had planned, or promised to each other."

Walter looked up into the sky as he spoke, "I'll be the first to admit I had..." He stopped and looked at me as he chuckled, "Well, I still have some problems, but Matt, Hollis should not be walking around in society. Please be careful. I might not show it very well, but I consider you a good friend and I don't have many." Another long pause, and I could see Water was embarrassed by his revelation.

It took a few moments before he continued, "In North Seattle there's a strip club called Robby's," I nodded my head to show him I knew about the men's club. "I know a woman who used to dance there, and she knew Hollis and Price back in the old days. Well, I know her mother knew them, and I think she did too. If she's still dancing, look for a woman who's half Vietnamese and half white. I think her name is Lan. Sorry, I can't remember her stripper name for sure, but maybe she could tell you where to look for Hollis."

Again, there was a long pause, as Walter continued to gather his thoughts. "I think she prefers dancing during the daytime. Anyway, please be careful." Walter was now speaking to the ground. I knew he was nervous about his disclosure about his feelings. Other than some therapy Walter might have received back at the VA hospital, this was as close as he ever got to talking about his intimate feelings about the things that had happened back in the jungle. His concern touched me, and I smiled warmly at him.

"Thanks, and I'll be very careful. I promise. You go back and look after Thien. You're a very lucky man. I envy you."

His went beet red and his smile lit up his face. "I know, I'm lucky to have both of you in my life." He surprised me by extending his arms and I gave him a big hug. It was the first time I'd ever hugged him and the first time he'd showed me so much of his emotions. It would seem that Thien was good for him.

As I released Walter from our hug, I had to turn away quickly so he didn't see the tears in my eyes. The more I got to know him, the more I realized how special he was.

~ ~ ~ ~ ~

The ride back to the ferry was both quiet and reflective. I thought about turning on some tunes, but once the radio was on the noise impeded my thoughts, I quickly turned it off. I needed the silence to help or try to make sense of all the information I'd gotten from Walter.

Normally I don't let BJ sit in my lap when I drive, but somehow she seemed to know I'd allow her to sit in my lap this time. As I drove, my mind kept jumping between two things. First, what Thien had said about Sharon, secondly what I'd learned from Walter about Price and Hollis.

As I drove, I remembered the morning we'd found Slim dead at the houseboat. I'd wondered how or why someone had hated Slim so much the person had killed him with a knife. At the time, the murder had seemed so brutal... so personal... so rife with hate. Now I think I understood why Price had used a knife. His hatred was not at Slim, but at the entire world. Price was dying of cancer, and he wanted to lash out and hurt others. The fact that someone had paid him to kill Slim was probably secondary. I wondered if he needed to kill because it was a way to divest himself of some of his hate and anger. Chances are that something he'd picked up in SE Asia was the likely cause of his cancer, which naturally had fueled his rage.

By the time I got to the ferry dock, it was raining lightly, and the slow slap of the windshield wipers was keeping us company on our way. Because of my visit and all the information I'd learned from Walter, I'd totally forgotten I'd promised I would call Jeff L. and Sakol. Sitting at the ferry dock waiting for the next boat, I remembered I needed to call. I punched in Jeff L's number. He picked it up after the second ring.

"Homicide, Detective Davenport speaking, "

"Jeff, it's Matt. Good morning."

"Good Morning. What's up? By the way, I tried to call you several times the past couple of days but there was no answer." After a slight pause, his voice seemed to mellow a little, "I didn't like the way things turned out the other day when you were here. I'll admit I was a little upset with you, but you didn't deserve that. Sorry. Anyway, since I couldn't find you, I figured you were out, or at Sharon's."

If I was going to tell him what I'd learned, I had to tell him where I'd been. "I've been over on the peninsula. I wanted to see an old army buddy."

His voice started to take on a sharp tone, "Matt, you aren't doing anything about the John Doe case are you? Frank will have your ass for breakfast if he finds out you're still poking around."

"Jeff L., why would you ask that?" I asked in mock surprise. "You know I always do what I'm told."

He snorted as he replied, "Yeah, right! I know you and the…" there was a pause and then he barked into the phone,

"Hey! I remembered you still have the photograph of the John Doe. I want it returned, now."

"I thought I gave that back to you."

His voice was getting frosty, "No Matt, you didn't. Now, no bullshit, I want it back. I want it back today. Understood?"

I ignored his command, "Well, I'm calling because I promised to tell you if I ever discovered any information."

Jeff's voice was so loud BJ lifted her head up and looked at me. "God Damn it, Matt, we told you to stay away from the whole case. I can't help you if Frank tells me to pick you up. Please tell me you're not getting more involved in this, tell me you ain't that stupid."

"Yeah, well, I guess I'm stupid." I rushed on so I could tell Jeff L. what I wanted before he interrupted. "I found out who the John Doe was you had in the morgue," I paused, and Jeff remained silent, "His name was Dennis Price, and I believe his killer is a guy named Hayward Hollis. They served together in Nam, in the same group as I did. I didn't know them over there, but my friend told me he knew them both and had been with them on a couple of missions to places our government still says we never entered. The two of them were very close friends. My friend believes he overheard somewhere along the line that Hollis was now a mechanic. That's a gun for hire,"

Jeff interrupted, "I know what a mechanic is." His voice was now cold and tinged with a surly edge. "Why did this Hollis guy kill Price if they were friends?"

"My friend overheard a pact the two of them made out in the jungle one night. They were lovers, and they promised each other neither one would ever leave the other behind if one of them was so wounded they couldn't go on. They agreed to kill the other person if that person was ever in a bad situation.

"Jeff, you saw the autopsy. You know Price was so sick he was almost dead anyway. When he went down in the vacant lot, he wasn't able to move, so Hollis went through with their pact and killed him. Price was the one with the contract, and I believe Hollis may now have taken over the mechanic's role."

Jeff was silent, for a moment, and then asked, "What's the name of your buddy? I want to talk to him."

"Sorry, Jeff... I don't remember. Besides, he doesn't want to get involved."

"He's already involved. What's his name?" Now Jeff's voice was rising in volume.

"Sorry, Jeff, I didn't catch his name."

His voice exploded in my ear, "Listen, Buster, if you think you're going to..." I pushed the end button on the phone and as quickly as I could, I pushed the end button again and held it down, turning off my cell phone. I wouldn't rat Walter out. Besides, I doubted if he would give Jeff any more information than he'd given me. I realize it's not my place to make that decision, but I also served with Walter, and I could see no reason to subject Walter to any form of interrogation from either Jeff L. or Sakol. If Jeff L. had been a bit more civil, I'd have told him about the strip club. But in my head, I justified the club was a long shot, and I really wasn't keeping all that much from them.

I thought about the strip club and decided I didn't want to go there by myself. Since that was the case, I chose to give Scott a call and see if he wanted to go strip club hopping with me. I knew my request would make his day. Talk about your decadent activity, visiting a strip club in the middle of the day. I couldn't help it, I was embarrassed.

But I made the call, anyway.

CHAPTER TWENTY-SEVEN

Leaving Scott a message asking if he could meet me at the club, I was sure I could hear his first comment, "Why the hell are we going to a strip bar in the middle of the day?" And then he'd want to know why I even wanted to meet him at a strip bar. Of all the places in Seattle to meet somebody, why a strip bar? Starbucks, yes. Strip clubs, no! I don't know if it was a good thing or not, but he hadn't answered his phone and I didn't have to explain my reasons for a meeting there. I left him a message telling him I had some very important information to share, and I needed for him to call me as soon as possible.

I debated going to the strip club without him, but as silly as this sounds, I wanted somebody with me. I hadn't even gotten out of downtown when my cell phone rang. It was Scott. He apologized, but there was no way he could meet me today, but he was free tomorrow afternoon. He did me a favor and didn't grill me why I wanted to meet him in a strip club in the middle of the day. I gave him a time to meet me at Robby's and he agreed. I probably should hate to admit this, but I know exactly where Robby's located. I go there about once every couple of years. Being honest, I like to look at the various men who go to those places as much as I enjoy watching the girls. Don't worry, people. I go there mainly for the women, but there's no question it's a great place to watch the watchers.

In the past, I've always attended in the evenings, but since Walter said the woman usually worked only days, I thought Scott and I should meet there around two in the afternoon. I always wondered what kind of perverts hung out at a strip club on a bright sunny day, and it looked like I would have the chance to find out.

The next afternoon when I opened the front door of the club it was like walking into a dark cave, and the volume of the music hit me like a wall. The music was so loud it literally felt like someone was pushing against my chest. Once I was inside, I waited behind a velvet-covered chain and I stood there watching and waiting.

Eventually, a burly man in a rolled up short-sleeve shirt with huge exposed biceps, many tattoos, and half-unbuttoned to show off his many gold necklaces, barreled his way to where I was waiting. There's something about the way men who lift heavy weights walk. Their arms don't hang at their sides, they make semi-circles. It's as if they're bow-legged, except I'm talking about their arms and not their legs. Is there such a word as bow-armed?

The bouncer took my money and then unhooked the chain blocking my way. Because of the darkness of the room, it took several seconds for my eyes to become accustomed. I spotted a seat against a wall, and I waited for my eyes to become better adjusted before making my way towards it.

An attractive scantily clad young woman with an excessive amount of makeup came to my table and took my drink order. The state of Washington has several antiquated or just stupid laws about alcohol and sexual matters. One such law is you can't have alcohol and nudity in the same area. Since the girls were nude when they're on stage, the only beverages they allow to serve are non-alcoholic. Even so, the price they charged would make the average person think they were drinking top brand single malt Scotch instead of watered down Coca-Cola.

Finally, my eyes became acclimated to the room, and I looked around. It surprised me how many men were there. It was quite a good crowd. Since I was a tad bit early, I didn't expect Scott to be there yet.

I spotted an older Asian man sitting in the front row directly in front of the main stage. His chair was less than three feet from the stage, and he was leaning forward from the waist, his elbows resting on his thighs. Whenever some of the dancers were nude, they would expose their private parts to his gaze and he continued to move his head and body to see the exposed parts better. When they finished, he clapped his hands, applauding wildly as he nodded his head.

The Asian fellow took off his glasses, removed a handkerchief from his back pocket, wiped his face and then his glasses. By the time the next dancer was ready to go, he had his handkerchief back in his pocket, his glasses on his nose and he was ready to go again. I couldn't help it; I felt the grin spread across my face.

I was sitting at my table for about ten minutes when a man entered, and as he walked past me, I noticed that both his front and his backside were flat. His face was flat, and he had no buttocks sticking out behind him. When you viewed his body from the front or the rear, he looked fairly normal, but when viewed from the side, it was as if he was made like a rubber eraser.

Still looking around the room, I noticed some women were exposing their breasts to their customers when they danced directly in front of them at the private tables. This was unusual; in the past when I saw them dance directly in front of a patron, they did not expose themselves during a lap dance. Also, they would never let the men touch them so openly. Today, I watched as the girls allowed the men to suck their nipples and fondle them under their panties. Occasionally, a girl would actually grasp the front of the man's pants, fondling him. I realized there was a big difference between attending this strip club at night or during the day.

Since this was the first time I'd ever been in a strip club during the day, I was surprised at the variety of women who were dancing. The last time I'd been at the club was late at night, and as I remembered there were mainly white girls with perhaps a token black and an oriental thrown in. Today there were several black and Asian dancers. I only saw two white women dancing.

When I looked up at the stage again, there was a new gal just getting ready to dance. This was one of the two white women and at first glance, I thought she seemed a little heavy for a dancer, but then I realized what I was thinking was unfair. I've read somewhere overweight people are the most oppressed minority group. Many people think of overweight people as slow-witted. Few men seem to think of them as sexy. This stripper was tall, maybe 5' 10", and large. My guess was she was a good 35 to 45 pounds overweight. I was just really surprised to see someone her size dancing. Perhaps Rubenesque was more appropriate than heavy.

The other thing I noticed about the lady was the way she stood. I've noticed so many heavy women seem to stand slumped, round-shouldered, with their shoulders hunched forward. This woman stood with her shoulders back and the look on her face seemed to tell the world she was large and in charge. After watching her for a while, I thought her attitude was actually very sexy, and I found her to be extremely sensual. Her face was beautiful.

Now that it was her turn on stage, she seductively exposed her ample breasts one at a time, but kept her lower front covered. I thought she had a sexy bottom, and the thread of her thong disappearing between full cheeks added to the allure. I had to admit her dance was sexy, and she tried hard at being provocative. She was successful. Of all the women I'd seen dancing so far this day, she was by far the best dancer. She was actually erotic. It also appeared that she was popular since when she was not on stage, many of the men were asking her to perform lap dances.

One lady came by and sat next to me for a moment. She smelled just as exotic as she looked. She told me her name, but the music was so loud I couldn't understand her. I spoke directly in her ear and asked her what her ethnic background was. She told me she was half Vietnamese and half white. She was stunningly beautiful. Her breasts were small when compared to several of the other dancers, and some would consider her a bit heavy in the hips, but her face was magnificent. Just as she asked me if I wanted a lap dance, I saw Scott arrive. I smiled at her and asked her to come by a little later.

As she walked away, Scott slid in next to me. When he leaned over, I had to shout in his ear as I told him I needed to talk to him. I could see by the look on his face he wondered how we would chat since it was so loud in the room. I motioned for him to follow me. When I stopped at the velvet chain, I asked the bouncer if we could come back in again, and he nodded his head.

Once we were outside, I explained to Scott everything I'd learned during my visit with Walter. He got a big kick out of it when I told him about shouting the word faggot at Price and Hollis as they were putting me in the chopper. I told him about Lan, and how I believed the woman who just walked away when he arrived was the stripper I was looking for. Scott asked me why, so I explained that when she asked me if I wanted a dance, I had asked her about her ethnic background, and she'd told me she was half Vietnamese and half white.

I told Scott I believed she knew where Hollis was. In addition, she might even know where he was staying. Since

I'd nothing else to share, we went back in to see if I could get a chance to speak with Lan.

Once we both sat down, I spotted her and then watched as she walked around the room trying to solicit a dance. After she'd struck out with everybody she asked, she headed to an area directly behind us. As she passed by, I reached out, and motioned for her to come and sit next to me. She asked me if I was ready for a dance and I shook my head negatively, but I asked her to sit for a while. I'd previously placed a fifty-dollar bill on the table, but I had left my hand covering all of it except the one corner with the domination showing. It was obvious she was aware of the bill, and she smiled as she sat next to me. When she sat, I told her how great her perfume smelled, and as she beamed, I couldn't help but notice her stunning face. She leaned close and spoke in my ear telling me her name was Suzi. Once she said her name, I was positive it was just her stage name, and I was sure this was the woman with whom I wanted to talk.

Suzi continued talking directly into my ear as she explained she needed to have a drink in front of her if we sat together, and I told her to order. Her drink and another watered down coke came to twenty bucks even, and I knew her drink was just apple juice.

I was tempted to ask her what she was doing working in a place like this, but I realized that's not a fair question to ask anybody. If she wanted to make a living dancing, it was not my place to put my values on anyone's life. The thing I needed to do was keep my mouth shut. I'm sure women who dance for a living have just as interesting lives as anyone else.

When the song ended, and it was a little quieter, I moved the bill over to her and lifted my hand. As she picked it up, I leaned closer to her and asked if her real name was Lan. She pulled back quickly but snatched up the bill. I could see she was afraid, and her eyes were wide as she stared at me. I asked her again. I wanted to make sure I was not making any mistakes. This time she nodded her head once. I leaned close to her and spoke into her ear. My follow up question was if she knew Hayward Hollis. She pulled back, and I watched a look of terror flickering across her face. She visibly pulled herself together. Finally, she got a grip, and she looked at me with mistrusting eyes and said, "No, I don't know name."

I was positive she was not telling me the truth. "Why are you lying?"

"Please, you not understand. I not know him."

I needed to talk to her more. "Can I meet you anywhere else, so we can talk about this?"

"Please, mister, leave me alone. I don't know him."

I pushed up my shirtsleeve on my left arm and showed her my tattoo. Since one of her parents was from Nam, I wondered if she might recognize the sign, or maybe she'd seen it on either Price or Hollis. When she saw the tattoo, she pulled back, her face now a mask of terror. "Go away!" she whispered. "Go away now! Please. Now!"

When I took her hand, I palmed her one of my business cards, and told her I needed to talk to her more. The card quickly disappeared. She stood up and fled behind some curtains, but I was pleased to see she took my card and hadn't left it on the table. I felt that was a good sign. Her interesting perfume still lingered even though she left.

When I mentioned Hollis, I'd been surprised at the amount of fear I'd seen in her eyes. I wondered if perhaps she knew where he was, or if she knew anything about him. The fear I'd seen on her face was real and I figured she had to know something. I wondered if I'd ever hear from her, but I thought my best hope might come from her desire to have Hollis out of her life. I prayed that was greater than her fear of what Hollis might do to her if he found out she'd talked to me.

I motioned to Scott it was time to leave, and we both stood. I took two steps towards the exit and the burly man who'd taken my money at the front door now stood in front of me blocking my way. As I stepped to the side, he reached out and grabbed my arm. I was in no mood for this bozo to manhandle me. I casually moved a little, so I could grasp the hand which was holding my arm. With a quick motion I remembered from my days with Uncle Sam, I had his elbow tight against my chest with his wrist bent in a very painful position. I pulled back on the hand until he was on his tiptoes, and I told him we were all leaving.

As we moved to the front door, I noticed two men moving out of the shadows towards us. I tightened my grip on the bouncer, bringing him once more onto his tiptoes. I told him to tell his friends to back off. I didn't see him do anything, but the two men stopped and then quickly stepped back into the shadows.

Scott unhooked the chain and the three of us stepped outside. The bright light was painful after coming from the dark club, and it took a moment for my eyes to adjust. I kept the bodyguard in my hand lock until we were by my truck, but before I released him, I asked him if he would make any problems. He shook his head no, and when I released him, he immediately massaged his wrist.

"What's your problem?" I asked.

He snarled. "How come you're bothering my girls?"

"I only spoke with one girl. Like I said, what's your problem?"

His voice was still menacing, but he seemed to be ready to talk about what happened. "Suzi ran to the dressing room in tears. What d'ya do to her?"

"Nothing, I asked her a couple of questions."

"And what kinda questions would lead my gals to tears?"

"I was asking her if we had friends in common."

The bouncer stood glaring at both of us for a few seconds, then barked at us, "I'm telling both of you not to come back here. I don't care what you think you were doing, but you will not spoil things for my girls. Get in your car and go. Now!"

Scott headed towards his car, and I trailed behind him. When we got to his car, he turned and asked me why I was following him. I told him to open up the car so I could enter on the passenger side. I slid in and told him to start the car and drive off. When we were a block away, I asked him to pull over. Once we'd come to a stop, he turned and asked, "What the hell was that all about?"

"I'm positive she knows something about Hollis, and I aim to find out what it is. In about an hour, I will sneak back to my truck. I'm wondering when she gets off. Anyway, I will see if I can follow her."

Scott tugged at his beard, "I don't think that's the best idea I've heard, but I can't stop you. What are you going to do for the next hour?"

"You're going to buy me a cup of coffee, and I'll tell you how come I knew the young lady knew Hollis."

Scott agreed grudgingly.

~ ~ ~ ~ ~

After I retrieved my truck from the strip club parking lot, I drove it across the street and parked directly across from the club. I lucked out, and I found a large bush to park behind which hid most of my truck. It turned out even better because there was a thin patch of leaves in the middle of the bush where I could look through and see right across the street. From my vantage point, I could watch anybody who came or went into the club.

Dusk was settling in when I saw a cab pull up and after Lan chatted with the bouncer for a moment, she climbed in the back of the cab. When it pulled out into traffic, I let three cars pass and then dropped in behind them. We continued for a couple of miles down the street, and the cab signaled a right turn and pulled into a large parking lot. The cab drove to the end of the parking lot and pulled up behind a car. When I reached the edge of the parking lot, I pulled into a parking stall and stopped. I watched as Lan paid the cabbie and then got in the car next to the cab.

I understand most of the girls park their cars away from the club and when they finish their shift, take a cab to their cars rather than have their car sit at the club's parking lot. This would prevent any of the patrons of the club seeing the girls leaving in their own cars and perhaps follow them and do who knows what.

Once the cab drove away, I saw her start her car and exit the parking lot. I let her move out onto the street before I pulled across the lot and then in behind her. We traveled a few blocks before she pulled in to a grocery store parking lot. I parked my truck at the back of the lot, and I walked up to the front of the store. I waited until she came out and then walked up behind her.

I spoke to her in the gentlest tone of voice I could, "Lan, I need to talk to you. Please, talk to me?"

She spun around, dropping her groceries. Her face was a mask of fear and I felt bad that I was causing her such terror. She stuttered slightly as she asked, "How you find me?"

I stooped and picked up her bag, and I explained, "I followed your cab. I really need to talk to you. Please talk to me for a minute."

She seemed to shrink before my eyes, "No. Go away."

"Lan, do you know where Heyward Hollis is?"

"You stupid man. He kill us both if he know you talk to me." I thought I could see her body trembling with fear.

"Then you know where he is?"

The fear in her eyes made me sad. I wished I knew the right words to comfort her, "No. Please go away. I know he kill Denny, and now he kill me if he know I talk at you."

"I can help you. I can protect you," I tried to reassure her.

"You stupid man. I know who you are, and you are dead man. You are dead man. You not protect anything or anybody. Heyward hates you. He kill you. Now, go away."

Lan turned, put her groceries in her car, and then started it. She pulled forward a few feet, then stopped, put down the driver's window, and looked up at me, "Stay away from me. He mad Denny dead. He blame you and he get even. He crazy now. He kill you, maybe he kill me. He wants to hurt. Hurt everybody. You not safe. Just stay away from me." Her car lurched forward, and she drove away. I considered following her again, but then decided that was not a wise idea.

If I had to, I knew where I could find her again. In a way, I hoped I wouldn't have to. Nobody likes to frighten people. And I'd seen the terror in Lan's eyes when she looked at me. That look would take a while for me to forget.

HOUSEBOAT

CHAPTER TWENTY-EIGHT

I know I shouldn't admit to this but driving back from the strip club to my apartment, my mind was in such turmoil I wasn't paying the least bit of attention to my driving. I had the confirmation that Hollis and Price not only were responsible for Slim's demise, but Hollis was the person we were all looking for now. I also hoped maybe I'd discovered a lead on how to go about finding Hollis. I knew I should probably call Jeff L. and tell him about Lan, but I wasn't ready to talk to him yet. And, now that I was headed home, I found my mind was more consumed with Sharon and how I would resolve a relationship with her without damaging our friendship.

Pulling into the garage, I was amazed to find I was already home. I didn't remember a thing about the drive from the strip club. I found that troubling. Was this God's way of trying to tell me I shouldn't be driving? Glancing over at Sharon's parking spot and I noticed her car sitting there. I hoped that meant she was home.

Since leaving Walter and Thien, my thoughts kept wandering to Sharon. The other night with her had been like no other I've ever had with a woman. The one night we'd been together was what poets write about, why there are love songs; the stuff of dreams. I'll admit if this is what true love is all about, I'm hooked.

I took the elevator to my floor. Once I reached my place, I headed towards the back door to let BJ outside do her thing. I walked with BJ to the end of the walkway and while I was standing at the end; I heard the steel mesh door open and then clang shut. I turned. I watched as Sharon came towards me and at that moment; I thought she was the most beautiful woman in the world. She slipped her arms around my waist and said, "I've missed you. You were gone for so long." Her voice was a whisper.

"I'm sorry. Walter and his wife asked me to stay for an extra night and I did. I would have called, but he's so far out in the boonies, there isn't any cell phone service." Then I said something I'd thought I'd never say to a woman again, "I missed you, too. And you know something else, I love you." Her eyes were big and round, her lips in a little grin,

"Really?"

"Really, really. We need to talk."

Sharon frowned, "Oh shit, is this a good 'we need to talk' or do I need to have a drink first?" Sharon winked at me, so I knew she was kidding. "You're not telling me you love me to appease the part of you that feels bad, because of the other night?"

"NO! That's not it at all. I've discovered I do love you, and yeah, we do need to talk."

Sharon's smile would have melted an ice cube, "Last time with you frightened me."

My voice went up an octave, "You! I'm the one they call Mr. Cool and all I can think about is you."

Sharon kissed my cheek and told me, "When BJ finishes, I'll be in the front room. It's cold out here."

After Sharon left, I kept encouraging BJ to finish her business, and as always, she had to fool around sniffing all the foliage in the lot. Finally, she finished, and we headed back down the walkway. The weather was cold enough that the moisture on the walkway was icy and I had to move carefully in order not to slip.

When I got to my front room, Sharon was sitting on the couch with a drink in her hand, looking off towards the canal. There was another glass on the table in front of her for me. I sat down beside her, and with her snuggled next to me, we watched the movement on the canal for a while. We saw a couple of small boats braving the cold evening as they moved up and down the canal, their lights reflecting off the water. We sipped our drinks, looking at the waves making patterns on the water. I can't really describe it completely, but at that moment, I was at peace with the world. I knew Hollis was somewhere out there and I hoped the police were looking for him. I knew there were still problems with the houseboat I needed to resolve, but just sitting with Sharon on the couch stilled my soul.

I turned my head to look at her, "I talked about you with somebody the last couple of days."

"Who?" Surprise in her voice. "Did I ever tell you about Walter?"

"The dude who saved your life in Nam and then you took him over to the peninsula somewhere?"

"Very good, one and the same."

"Why are you asking me about Walter?"

"Well, he built a cabin on that piece of land I own over there and I gave part of the land to him." I chuckled and revised my statement, "Perhaps cabin isn't really the best word to use. This place is perhaps the most unusual structure you have ever seen. It is a cabin of sorts, but more than like it's a work of art. Walter has done the most spectacular job you could ever imagine. He used stuff he found over there scattered around the forest: fallen trees he bucked up and then split, burned logs which had the burls exposed which he turned into tables, coffee table and end tables.

"Then there's the river rock fireplace. He packed up the mountain the stones from the stream and made this amazing fireplace. Sharon, the whole place really is a work of art." I paused as I reflected over what he had created just out of materials that were lying about.

"Anyway, after I took him over there and he stayed and lived up in the mountains, he came back to retrieve his stuff from down in Chinatown. Back in Viet Nam, Walter befriended a family, and he helped to get them out of the country when things fell apart in '75. The family he saved has a daughter, Thien, who was, or should I say is madly in love with Walter. She's much younger than Walter and at first, he didn't want to take her with him. She insisted, and now they live together in his cabin. Actually, she's pregnant.

"Thien and I discussed you. From the way I talked about you, and something about the look on my face as I talked about that night we spent together, and how special it was to me, she could sense I was trying to deal with how intense my feelings were, and my emotions regarding you. Just from the way I talked about you, she told me a few things which pointed out how special I thought you are. She seems to possess an ability to see inside the soul. She helped me a little to understand just how special you are. By the way, she also wants me to bring you over so she can meet you. She believes you must have some special magic to tame someone like me." Sharon laughed.

I continued, "The other night when we made love was really special. I decided, if you want, it's something I want more of too."

Sharon started to talk, but I put my finger to her lips. "Please, let me finish. I want us together, but not like married, at least not yet. I want you with me, because I want us together, not because we have some piece of paper saying we're together. I realize it's important we're together, because I want to wake up next to you, to share my life with you, and not because somebody grumbled words over us. I want us together because that's what we both want, not because the law says we are married. And the really amazing thing is I'm even telling you all of this."

I stopped and took a breath, "My turn?" Sharon asked. I smiled, and she returned the smile. "Okay! I would like us to be together the same as you. The other day when I was in so much pain because my patient died, and when you took me in your arms, the pain went away. When you made love it was... well, like magic. I know that sounds so stupid, but I lack the words to properly describe it.

"You know, my body has wanted you so much for the last couple of days, a want that borders on hunger. When I think about the other night, I become excited and wanting you. Matt, that doesn't happen to me. In the beginning, when we had sex it was more combat than making love," I nodded my head. I understood exactly what she meant. "Now, it just seems to get better and better. I crave you; I need you. I agree I like the idea of being together and not just because we have a license. I totally understand. I love you too."

I slipped my arm around her again and pulled her against me. We continued to sit there on the couch with our feet up on the ottoman. I don't know how long we sat there watching the night settle in and the slow activity of the boats on the lake in front of us. I was hungry, but the moment was so special I didn't want to break the mood. It was completely dark outside when I finally heard Sharon give a deep sigh, and I looked over at her. "What?" I asked.

"Darling, I need you to take me to bed. I want you to love me like we did last time. Take BJ out for her final outing and then come to bed. I'll be waiting." I stood and called to BJ. She jumped down and we went back outside. The walkway was now hard ice, and I had to walk carefully to keep from falling.

Standing, freezing my butt off in the field, my thoughts were back in the apartment, more precisely, in the bedroom. I was pleased Sharon felt the same way I did about things. I had no idea where this would lead, but I was ready to find out.

The night was cold, and the puffs of my breath hung in the crisp air. BJ, as always, wanted to explore the entire vacant lot and smell every frozen blade of grass. Since it doesn't get that cold very often in Seattle, she was not used to the grass being frozen under her feet, and from time to time she'd stop and sort of shake one of her paws, wondering why the grass felt the way it did.

Finally, I'd enough of the cold, and I wanted to return to the apartment. "Let's go!" I called to her, and she took off down the walkway, waiting for me at the door to let her in the house. By the time I was at the bedroom door, BJ had found her spot and was lying in her chair all curled up.

Sharon had candles burning, and the light flickered off the walls. I quickly undressed and pulled the cover back. Her beautiful body was displayed before me and for a moment it was difficult for me to breathe. "You're lovely. I really do love you," I told her.

She patted the bed beside her. "Come join me, please."

Time stood still. We could have been together for a few minutes, or a few hours. I won't bore you with details, but suffice it to say, it was magnificent.

Afterward, as she lay there up in my arms, with her head rested on my shoulder. "Thank you," she murmured.

"What for?"

"For making me the happiest woman in the world." Sharon kissed my chest and hugged me.

I don't remember when we parted in the night, but as the first rays of light crept in the bedroom, I found Sharon was beside me, sound asleep. Looking at her, I could see her tousled hair and a very contented look on her face, and the beauty of it was she was asleep. My problem was I had to relieve myself and really didn't want to move, but Mother Nature told me I had no choice.

Awake now, I reflected on the new day's activities, and I wondered about the wisdom of trying to see Jeff L. I realized I needed to talk to him about Hollis and I didn't think Jeff L. realized just how dangerous Hollis could be. I had firsthand knowledge of the things Hollis could do and somehow; I needed to find a way to make Jeff L. understand. For sure, I felt it was time to end Mr. Hollis' activities.

~ ~ ~ ~ ~

That afternoon and the next day I spent working on the MG collection with my mind split between two things. Half of my mind worked on trying to figure out two relationships. The first was how things would work out between Sharon and me, and the other half was working on my deteriorating relationship with the police and how I would talk to Jeff L. and let him know how dangerous Hollis was. I'll admit I was confused and concerned.

When I woke up Friday morning, I had formed the beginnings of a plan. I'd hoped that Jeff L. would consider our longtime friendship and change his mind. I needed for him to see his way clear to let me in on what was going on, or at least let me explain how important it was he located Hollis. Let's be honest, I'd already shared my information about who Hollis and Price were, so was I out of line to expect him to give me something in return? I'll admit I felt a bit guilty I hadn't shared the information about Lan, but in my defense, I really didn't know how much she knew about things and I didn't want to get her involved unless there was no other choice. As the saying goes, "no good deed goes unpunished" and as things turned out, I wish I'd made a different choice.

My mind continued to run through the same maze, and due to what happened with Captain Frank, I could understand a sudden change in my relationship with Sakol, and perhaps even a little with Jeff L. But, because of how far back Jeff L. and I went, I felt we should be able to move past what happened down at the station. I understood in a way why he refused to speak to me at the station, but I was hoping he'd consider talking away from work.

I kind of had a plan and I figured I'd let my plan marinate over the weekend. Besides spending time with Sharon seemed to addle my brain. When I was away from her, all I wanted was to see her and when we were together no matter how hard I tried, I couldn't keep my hands off her. Okay, I'll admit, I didn't try too hard.

And the best part was we had a weekend in front of us to spend together.

I know, bad Matt!

Tough!

CHAPTER TWENTY-NINE

It was late Saturday morning and Sharon and I were just finishing up our morning coffee when the phone rang. Sharon picked it up, listened for a moment and then asked them to please hold. As she extended the phone to me, Sharon said, "It's a woman. And she sounds really sexy." Thankfully, Sharon winked at me.

I was curious now. What sexy woman was calling me on a Saturday morning? "Good morning, this is Matt."

A familiar sultry voice greeted me, "Hi Matt, this is Jennifer. Is this a bad time?"

"Well, gee whiz, we were just having sex and…" Sharon's hand slapping me on my back stopped my comment.

"She just hit you, didn't she?" Jennifer was laughing as she asked.

"Yeah."

"You had it coming."

"Yeah. Thanks Jennifer, what can I do for you this morning?"

"I would like for you and Sharon to come to dinner this evening. Can you make it?" I told Jennifer to wait a moment, and I asked Sharon if we had plans for the evening. When she asked me what was going on, I explained about the invitation to dinner. Sharon grinned at me and said, "Go for it. Ask what time and what should I wear?" Just like a woman, wondering what to wear.

"We would love to. I need to know what time and where? Oh, and Sharon wants to know what to wear."

I heard Jennifer laugh again as she responded, "A limo will pick you up at your place at seven. As for what to wear, you look great in a suit. Tell Sharon to wear whatever looks good when you wear a suit. See you tonight." And she hung up.

"Well?" Sharon asked. "What did she say?"

"She told me I looked great in a suit and for you to try to look half that nice." Damn it, she slapped me again. "Really, she said for me to wear a suit and for you to dress accordingly."

"That is not what you said first!" I thought, picky, picky, picky!

I took BJ out to do her business around 6:30 that evening and then I started my transformation. I pulled out my best suit and my favorite cufflink sleeved shirt. I noticed I had ten minutes to go, and I could go out to the kitchen and pour myself a small Scotch. Just as Sharon entered the kitchen, the phone from the lobby rang. Our limo had arrived.

On the way down in the elevator, I complimented Sharon on just how nice she looked. Her dress was kind of clingy and it showed a nice amount of cleavage. She smiled at me and asked, "Do I look half as nice as you?"

My hand strayed down to her shapely bottom and as I caressed her, I responded, "Yes dear, you look marvelous!" Sharon whispered in my ear, "Garter belt. No panties. Just for you. Think about it all during dinner." And she kissed my cheek.

Oh damn! Things started to wake up I wanted to stay asleep.

The limo was two zip codes long, and the driver was standing by the open back door. As Sharon entered, the driver smiled at me, "Good evening Mr. Preston." I nodded. After the driver slipped behind the wheel, I called out, "Where are we going?"

"Miss Rockingham has asked me to keep that a secret." I leaned back and shut my mouth. Sharon and I sat in the back, holding hands, watching the passing view and my little brain kept returning to her last comment regarding her lack of undergarment.

Finally, we pulled up in front of a large, expensive looking home. The driver asked us to wait in the car. He went to the front door and Richard Silversmith opened it. I'd met his wife once, and the driver escorted them to the limo. There were two seats facing us and Richard and his wife took those. We all exchanged greetings and Richard's wife reached over and extended her hand to Sharon. "Sandy Silversmith."

"Sharon Crowell. Nice to meet you." She turned to Richard and asked, "You must be Richard? Thanks for keeping Matt out of jail for so long."

We all laughed, and Richard said, "It hasn't been easy." He then turned "I like her. Above your pay grade, but I do like her."

"Thanks, Richard. Do you have any idea what this is all about tonight?"

"No, I was hoping you knew." Richard responded. "I asked the driver, but he said it was a surprise."

Richard turned and called out to the driver, "How long to where we're going?"

"Just a few minutes, sir. There is a small fridge between you and your wife. There are cocktails in there for the four of you."

Richard opened the small cooler and sure enough, there were four covered glasses containing some reddish looking liquid. Richard passed out the drinks, and we took a sip. I have no idea what it was, but it was splendid. There was a definite berry flavor to it, but you could also feel the drink had a fair amount of alcohol in it. All four of us enjoyed our drinks, and they seemed to go down way too easy.

We pulled up in front of the tallest building in Seattle and the driver stopped. The doorman stepped forward and opened the limo door. After the four of us were out of the limo, the doorman invited us to follow him.

Sharon leaned close and whispered, "I've heard rumors about a very exclusive club-restaurant on the top two floors of this building. Have you ever been there?" I shook my head. I'd heard rumors about it too. The doorman showed us to an open elevator, reached in and pushed the only button on the panel. He nodded his head and as the door closed, he said, "Have a nice evening folks."

Richard spoke with some excitement in his voice, "I've heard about this place. You have to be nominated to join and then be voted in. It's very expensive to join and there are monthly dues, which I understand are rather stiff. The food and service are supposedly exactly what you would expect from a place like this."

When the elevator door opened, a wall of glass showcasing the Sound and the Olympic Mountains in the distance greeted us. The view was stunning. A lovely Asian woman in some regional dress stepped towards us. "Mr. and Mrs. Silversmith?" she asked, and Richard raised his hand. The exquisite lady turned to me and asked, "Mr. Preston?" I nodded my head, and she turned to Sharon. "You must be Miss Crowell?" Sharon nodded her head. "Miss Crowell, your dress is stunning." Sharon glowed. "Please follow me."

We walked down a hallway and then stepped into a small private dining room set for seven people. No sooner had the lovely hostess left the room when Jennifer entered followed by Scott and a woman I had never met. Scott has nice taste in women, but this was way beyond any woman I'd ever seen him with. The woman was almost as tall as I am and the word that came to mind was voluptuous. Her dress looked to have been spray painted on her and her long black hair swirled around her face. She was stunning. She looked familiar but I couldn't place her.

Jennifer smiled at all of us. "I want to thank you for coming this evening. I wanted to show you my appreciation for all you've done for me. Shall we take our seats?"

Sharon was on my left and Scott's date was on my right. I turned to the young woman, extend my hand and said, "My name is Matt Preston."

She smiled at me. "So, you're Matt Preston? I've heard so much about you." I sat there like a bump on a log. She continued to smile at me. "My name is Anne Small."

Sharon had been listening in and she leaned across me. "Why you're Anne Small, the actress." The light bulb went on in my head. That was why she looked familiar.

"Guilty. But please, call me Anne. And let's forget about the actress thing. Please." The woman was warm and genuine. She asked, "Isn't this the loveliest view?"

Two people entered the room, one male and one female. The female introduced herself as Betsy. She then introduced the man as Bill. Both of them made a small bow and explained they would be taking care of us this evening. Betsy asked us if we would like a drink and Sandy Silversmith asked if it was possible to get another drink like we had in the limo. They told her she could and then Sharon and Anne said they wanted another one as well. I thought the drink had been okay, but I prefer Scotch. Scott, Richard and I all ordered a Scotch. As Betsy listed the available Scotch on hand, she mentioned one I had never heard of, but she said it was thirty years old. All three of us wanted to taste that one. I learned that evening I could get used to thirty-year-old Scotch. I also learned that our food was a true culinary masterpiece. They served us a tiny cup of lukewarm soup. Normally I like my soup hot, but the flavors were easy to distinguish. Next came a small salad with the most remarkable dressing. Dinner was salmon prepared as I'd never had it before. The side dishes consisted of green beans and a potato dish full of little chunks of bacon and other things.

They served each person at the same time by seven waiters directed by Betsy and Bill. As they brought out each new dish, the waiters would all come into the room in single file. They would circle the table until there was a waiter standing behind each of our left shoulders. I never saw the signal, but the waiters would uncover the dish and then at the same time, set it down in front of us. Once we were served, the waiters would then parade around the table and leave the room. Betsy and Bill never left the room except to fulfill our requests. It was fun, but a bit overwhelming.

Finally, the meal was over, and everyone was chatting about the quality and flavors of dinner. I stepped over to the window enjoying my Scotch while looking out over Puget Sound from seventy-two stories up. It was unbelievable, like a picture postcard. Scott came over and stood next to me. As we stood there looking out, Scott said "I have good news buddy."

"Oh. Please don't make me wait."

He chuckled. "Do you remember I told you about having lunch with a friend and so forth who had some pull down at city hall?" I told him I remembered the conversation. "The city will back off its stand and they've informed Wheeler he can sell the spaces if he wants and in addition, the city will not close off the parking in front of the marina."

"No shit?"

"No shit. And it gets better."

I was ready for some good news about the houseboat. Finally. "Wheel called me this afternoon and the space where the houseboat is moored is now yours. I have to pick up the papers on Monday and you'll need to sign them." I stood there with my mouth open. "Close your mouth. You look like you rode the little bus when you were in school when you stand there like that." I closed my mouth.

"Is there anything else I need to do?" I asked.

"Well, yes, there is one small thing. There's the small matter of a check." I asked him how much the slip would cost, and I almost passed out when he told me the figure. When I protested, he reminded me my other choice was to move the houseboat. The number didn't seem so bad when I looked at it from that viewpoint.

Betsy and Bill had excused themselves. They returned pushing a cart which had a box sitting on top. The box resembled a large cake box except it was about three feet tall. Everyone at the table grew quiet. Betsy and Bill took positions alongside the cart and each took a grip at the bottom of the box. With a nod of Betsy's head, the box was lifted.

Under the box was a cake.

A cake shaped like a blue hat... a blue hat shaped exactly like the one Audrey Bottomsley had worn. And sticking out of the top to the cake was a large daisy that wiggled back and forth on a long stem. Richard and I almost peed our pants we laughed so hard. Try as we might, the two of us could not stop laughing. Finally, Jennifer had to explain to the rest of the group what the significance was of this blue hat cake. Sharon had heard about the hat, so she at least had a clue.

Jennifer held up her hands, signaling for us to be quiet. "I wanted to show Matt and Richard how much I appreciated what they did for me. Richard already knows Audrey has accepted my settlement offer and everything is now in the process of being finalized. I'm headed back home in a week and I didn't want to leave until I'd thanked all of you for your help. I wanted to do something special. Especially something that would be meaningful to Matt and Richard.

"The first time I saw Audrey Bottomsley she was wearing a hat like this." She pointed at the cake. "I was so frightened, and Matt was so sweet to be there with me. When that woman came into the room with her hat on, I thought there would be no way for me not to die laughing. When I looked at Matt and saw he was biting his cheek and staring at the ceiling to keep from laughing, I knew at that moment, things would work out. I had no idea how things would turn out; I just knew things would be okay. The most difficult thing that day was not to laugh out loud. Between her fat little nephew and her God awful outfit, I prayed I could get through the meeting without disgracing myself by dissolving into fits of laughter."

She turned to Richard, "Matt said you were the best. He was correct. You really are amazing." I watched as Richard turned beet red and looked down at the table. I could tell how embarrassed he was.

Jennifer turned to me. "Matt. You didn't have to help me. I was a stranger, and you treated me like I was the best friend you ever had."

She looked at Sharon, "Sharon, if you ever tire of him, please send him my way. You have a keeper." Now it was my turn to turn red and stare at the table. "If any of you ever come to Europe and don't come and visit me, I will be hurt and furious. I have a large villa over there looking out over the Mediterranean Sea and there's plenty of room. All of you must come and visit."

Jennifer turned to Betsy and Bill and told them they could now serve the cake. I don't remember much about the flavor, but I'll never forget the sight as they lifted the lid, and the daisy flopped back and forth.

The four of us were back in the limo and headed back to drop Richard and his wife off. Richard remarked how Jennifer had been one of the most interesting clients he'd ever had. I asked him if he was aware she was getting married when she got back home. He hadn't known. I told him about her living arrangement and how she was going to actually marry two people, a man and a woman. Sandy piped up and looked at Richard, "That's not a bad idea. I would have a friend to talk to and if I wasn't in the mood, there would be somebody else to take care of you."

Sharon and I cracked up. Finally, Sharon stopped laughing, "You know, that isn't a bad idea. Should I give up Matt and move in with you or do you want to give up Richard and move in with us?" I'll be eternally grateful at that moment we pulled up in front of Silversmith's home and I didn't have to hear the answer. We all bid each other a good evening and the driver took us home.

During our ride up in the elevator, Sharon asked me, "So, do you want to have two wives?"

Even though I'd had a lot to drink, I was still aware the wrong answer could be dangerous to my health. "Darling, you are all the woman I could ever need, or ever want."

Sharon took my face between her hands and kissed me. "Good answer, boy. Good answer." I thought to myself I'd dodged a bullet. BJ greeted us and I excused myself to take her for her outing.

Sharon stepped back onto the elevator and smiled, "Take care of BJ. Let me change and I'll be back… if that's okay with you?"

"I thought you'd never ask! Hurry back. Oh…"

"Yes?"

"Leave the garter belt on please."

See, sometimes I actually know the right thing to say at the right time.

Kind of scary, huh?

HOUSEBOAT

CHAPTER THIRTY

Pop told me once the most difficult thing to do is usually the correct thing to do. Going to see Jeff L. was a very difficult thing to do. I knew where he lived since I'd visited his home several times before. It was late Wednesday afternoon, and I'd put off going to see him for long enough. I decided it was time to drive over to his neighborhood and park at the corner where I knew he'd have to turn to drive up into his cul-de-sac. I didn't want to do this, but I also knew I had to force the issue and see Jeff L. about Hollis and Price. I timed it just right, and I didn't have to wait long before I saw his unmarked police car coming down the street. When he got close enough, I stepped out of my truck and stood by the side of the road where I knew he'd see me.

At first, he looked at me and scowled as he drove on past. Suddenly the brake lights came on and he came to an abrupt stop. He paused a few moments, then I saw the reverse lights come on as he backed up. He stopped next to me and shifted the car into neutral. He put down his window. Glowering at me he barked, "Wrong area for you, ain't it? Visiting the slums today?"

I'll admit I was a little hurt by his attitude. I tried to use the most peaceful tone of voice I could. "Jeff L., it's me, childhood friend Matt. What's goin' on?"

I could see Jeff L. was working on getting his emotions under control. He growled at me as he shook his finger in my direction, "By the numbers Buster, don't you ever hang up on me again, especially when it's about a case. Do you understand?" I ignored him and when he saw I would not respond, he continued. "Secondly, didn't the Captain tell you to stay away from the case? And, didn't he tell you to stay away from me?" Without waiting for my reply, he barked at me, "What are you doing here? What part of what Frank told you didn't you get?" There was a long pause before he continued, "Matt, I don't understand your question: 'what's goin' on'? We've already told you what's going on is none of your damn business. So, I don't see where I owe you any explanations, do you?"

I almost screamed at him as I leaned towards his window. "Bullshit! Look, I know some things have changed down at the station, none of which, might I add, were of my doing. But why won't you talk to me?" I pointed my finger at him to drive my point home.

Jeff sat for a moment in thought, "OK, Matt, you wanna know what the problem is? One more time, listen to me really good. The report from the army comes back on you telling us we are to leave you alone, ask no questions and that you are none of our business.

"Plus, we had a John Doe who was lying in the morgue," Jeff paused and glared at me, "Please note the key word in that sentence. He was in the morgue, Matt, was! He was in the morgue until the Feds waltzed in, took the body and all the files, and then they tell us to forget all about him." He paused, looked out the front window and then turned back, "Oh, and while they were giving out orders, they included you as well! Which, by the way, reminds me, where's the picture we gave you of the John Doe?" Again, I stood there and stared at him without responding. He asked again, "Where is it?"

I gave him the best response I could on such short notice, "I lost it."

"Bullshit!" He frowned at me and I kept still. Finally, Jeff continued, "Matt, all we know is what you tell us. You said you were in some secret hush-hush group in Nam as was the John Doe."

I interrupted, "Why do you continue to call him John Doe? I told you his name, and I told you who I believe killed him. Jeff, I did exactly what I told you I'd do if I got any information. Maybe not as quickly as I should have, but I called you. So, what's your problem, Bunky?"

"My problem is still you. That report came back you're still part of the service, and that they can still recall you at any time." I didn't believe that. "Other than that, everything about you is top secret." He paused, waiting for my response. Since I had nothing to say, I gave none. He continued, "Do you know how pissed Frank is right now? You got a tiny taste of it the other day. Things are still ugly at work. Frank knows we're friends, and now, because of our friendship, he doesn't trust me. Since he doesn't trust me, he doesn't trust Sakol either. Shit, Matt, Frank even wanted to lock the two of us up for a while just for good measure."

Jeff sat for a moment, staring again straight ahead through his windshield. Without looking at me, he started again, "And then to top it all off, you call me and give me names. You give me names on a case you were told to leave alone. Names there is no way I could ever know!" He turned to face me, "Please tell me how the hell I tell Frank I got those names?" I continued to stare at him. "Huh? Come on, Einstein. What do I tell Frank? What do I tell Frank and keep your ass out of jail and Sakol and me still employed?"

I was such a talkative thing. I had no answer to his questions, and I figured the best plan was to keep my mouth shut. He looked back out his front windshield and growled, "That's what I thought. You got nothing. Do you see what a wonderful situation you've put me in? Damn it, Matt, every time I turn around, you're getting deeper and deeper in this case." He smacked the steering wheel with his open hand and barked, "You asked if you could poke around, not start some major bloodbath..."

"Stop!" I cut him off. I had enough. "First off, I don't consider the events which have taken place can be called a bloodbath. And you make it sound like this was something I wanted to have happen.

"Second, I told you a long time ago I did some very secret things in the military. Jeff, have I ever lied to you?" I waited, and when he didn't respond, I asked him again. Finally, he shook his head.

I continued, "Next, before the military takes me back in, they'll first be accepting widows and the handicapped, so the crap about me going back in the service is just that; crap!

"Somehow, you've forgotten I'm in this so deep because of Jennifer. Remember Jennifer, the young girl you sent to me! Not because I wanted it this way."

"Biggest mistake I ever made," he groused.

"Yeah Tootsie Bell, too late now! Besides, you've known about the tattoo for a long time. You also know why I hate it. So, once again, I'm asking you, why are you so pissed at me? I called you right away about Price and Hollis. And there's still something you haven't told me."

Jeff L. sat in his car staring straight ahead for the longest time. I wondered if he'd fallen asleep. Finally, he looked up at me. "Matt, I will give you some fantastic advice. You heard Frank, now you're hearing it from me. Listen, Matt. Stay away from anything connected with Slim or Jennifer or the houseboat or either of the two names you gave me. Stay away from the station, and most of all, stay away from Sakol and me. Do you understand?"

His voice was now almost a scream. I noticed a few of the houses in the neighborhood had people peeking out of their windows to see what the ruckus was.

"No! Why are you telling me this now? What's changed? I'm giving you information, as soon as I receive it."

"Don't you get it? This is none of your business. Leave it alone! I've said all I'm going to say. Stay the fuck out of this! I mean it, Matt. Friends or not, I'll put your sorry ass in jail if I find you in my way! Believe it!" He banged his car into gear, and hit the gas pedal as hard as he could; so hard that as he drove off, the tires chirped.

Instead of getting any good answers, now I found I had even more questions than before. I was sure Frank had chewed Sakol and Jeff L. out for letting me become so involved. I guess the thing that bothered me the most was I had a difficult time believing Jeff L. would talk like he just did because his Captain chewed him out. Jeff L. is open-minded enough he could see I wasn't responsible for things happening the way he had just insinuated.

No! There was no doubt in my mind something more was going on behind all of this.

But what? That was the big question, and I wanted answers.

HOUSEBOAT

CHAPTER THIRTY-ONE

I returned to my truck, opened the door and then I had to shoo BJ over to her side so I could get in. I started the motor but instead of moving on; I sat there and mulled over my chat with Jeff L. It disturbed me to have him so angry with me. Our friendship went back a long way, and I'd hate to lose it. As I sat there, BJ climbed into my lap and I sat there stroking her, brooding over everything that had transpired so far. Finally, I picked BJ up and moved her over to the other seat and drove off.

What I should have done was gone home. Just driven home, gone upstairs and poured me a small, but nourishing Scotch, and maybe even visited Sharon. Or, I could have curled up in my favorite chair and sipped my drink while I listened to some music because I have many excellent CDs which don't get enough play. Yes, there were a lot of things I should have done, but I didn't.

Instead, I drove down two blocks and pulled into a strip mall parking lot. One side of the lot provided an excellent view of the only street Jeff L. could use to leave his home.

As I sat waiting, BJ again climbed back in my lap and settled in. It was peaceful as I sat there waiting. What I was waiting for? I had no idea, but if he had plans to go out again,

I was curious to see where he would go. Perhaps it was because he kept looking at his watch while we were talking, but I had the feeling he was going out again tonight and I wanted to follow. I know it was not the best idea I've ever had, but give me a break, I was frustrated. I wanted to sort out this mess.

Time pushed on and I was bored out of my skull. However, I refused to leave yet. I was positive Jeff would come by. After I'd sat there for over two-and-a-half hours, I saw Jeff's squad car pulling up to the stop sign. I ducked down behind my steering wheel. Even this was a risk because I knew he might recognize my truck, but it was getting dark and I felt I had a good chance of following him without being observed. In addition, my hope was Jeff L. wouldn't dream that I'd dare to follow him. I waited for him to drive on past me and allowed a few cars to get between the two of us before I pulled out behind him.

I did well following him, even though I almost lost him at a red light. When I saw there was no traffic coming from either side, I ran the red light and caught up to him in just a few blocks. When he drove close to the freeway, I thought he would head north towards town and his office, instead he turned south. I wondered where the hell he was going.

Again, I waited for a few cars to get between us and then tried my best to keep up with his breakneck speed. Since Jeff had a badge, he didn't have to pay any attention to mundane things like speed limits. As we barreled down the freeway for about ten minutes, I prayed no police constable would stop me for speeding. If I got pulled over and told an officer I was following a cop because I wanted to see where he was going. I knew I'd be in trouble. I was very grateful when Jeff L. signaled he was about to pull off. Exiting the freeway, I realized there were very few cars in front of me and when we got to the stop sign, I'd end up directly behind him with no one between us. Even as dark as it was, I was afraid he would glance in his rearview mirror and see me. With that fear in mind, I pulled to the side of the off-ramp and waited until he cleared the intersection.

I'd seen his signal at the intersection for a right turn, but when I got to the street, I didn't see his car. We were now in an industrial park with several rows of warehouses, and for the lateness of the hour, everything was deserted. Even though it was dark, I kept my lights turned off, looking for lights from another vehicle. I wandered up and down each street, looking between and behind buildings for Jeff L.'s car. As I rolled past one large warehouse, I finally spotted the back end of his car sticking out from behind a dumpster. Quickly I pulled my truck to the curb and turned off the motor. Leaning over, I patted BJ on her head and told her to stay put. I rolled the windows down a few inches so she had air and then locked the door before I carefully headed towards Jeff's car.

A quick inspection showed me there was no one in his car and I continued walking to the end of the alley between the two buildings. Turning the corner, I noticed at the rear of the building on the left someone had jammed a door open with a piece of wood. Carefully I pushed the door open and peeked inside. At first glance, it looked strange. Ahead of me was nothing but a long hallway. It looked like there was no way out of the hallway except the doorway I was standing in and that made little sense.

I didn't know which way to go, so I took a chance and stepped into the hallway. As I started down the hallway, I finally noticed at the far end another door exactly the same color as the walls. There was no doorjamb or any architectural details around the door, it was just set flush to the wall with nothing but a small knob sticking out. This was weird.

I moved quickly down the hall and flattened myself against the wall next to the door. When I pulled the knob, I was in luck because someone had left this door unlatched from the other side. I peeked through the doorway and around the corner. The door opened into a huge warehouse. The warehouse was dark except for lights from the outside coming through windows located high on the walls. Because of the poor lighting, everything was just dark shadows.

I could hear voices somewhere in the warehouse, but because of the immense size, voices were barely an echo. Sounds bounced around the room and off the tall ceiling making it difficult for me to determine exactly where the voices came from. Slowly I slipped into the warehouse a few feet and then stopped. I hid behind a bunch of boxes stacked on pallets until I could get my bearings.

Several lights, apparently on timers, turned on. The lights were high in the rafters and widely scattered throughout the large structure. They did little to illuminate anything, but they were slightly helpful.

Now that I could kind of see, I carefully made my way in the direction of where I thought the voices were coming from. I made sure I stayed hidden as I slipped around the scattered pallets, and as I drew closer to where the voices were located, I could tell one voice sounded angry. There was shouting, but the sounds were echoing so badly it was impossible for me to make out the words. One time thought I did hear, "Listen pig, I am telling you to stay away... You have..." and the voice fell away.

As I continued to listen, I heard someone swearing, and then a loud shout. When I heard two gunshots, my heart stood still. I slowly moved towards the sound of gunfire. At the same time, I heard the sound of somebody running and then a door slamming. I picked up my pace to where I thought the gunfire had come from and as I rounded the end of a stack of pallets, with the help of the feeble overhead lighting, I found Jeff L. slumped over some boxes, a dark stain spreading across the right side of his chest.

I reached over and snatched Jeff's cell phone from its holster and punched in 911. A female voice came on and asked me what I was reporting. I told her I was calling from a Seattle Police officer's cell phone and there was an officer down. The voice on the cell phone immediately came back and asked me who I was. I knew I was in deep water. I also knew I didn't want to get in any deeper after what Jeff had told me earlier this evening.

I ignored the 911 operator's question and informed the person on the phone who Jeff L. was, and in addition, I mentioned he was the head of Seattle detectives. I told the voice I'd heard two shots, but the only visible wound I could see was to his chest. When the voice asked me where I was, I realized I had no idea of our exact location. I didn't want to leave him, but I had to give the operator an address. I asked her to hold on for a moment while I checked.

As I looked around the large room, I noticed a door on the far wall with a lit EXIT sign above it. Running over to the door I told the operator to please continue to wait and I would see if I could find an address. I knew the name of the industrial park and I gave her that information. I pushed the door open and found it led directly outside. I stepped out and when I turned around; I found numbers on the building above my head. I read them off to the operator. When she asked more questions, I interrupted her and told her I was really busy. I stressed I needed a medic, immediately, then I hung up.

I turned around, looking for something to prop open the door. I slipped off a shoe and wedged it in place so the door wouldn't close. Since I didn't want to be without my shoe, I continued looking for something more permanent which would prop the door open. I wanted the emergency workers to know where to enter the building.

Behind a dumpster, I found a busted piece of wood from an old pallet and I grabbed it. Returning to the door to prop it open, I saw a lone car sitting in a parking lot across the street. I could hear the motor and noticed smoke coming from the exhaust. The car sat there just waiting with the lights off. The car looked like an old Washington State Patrol vehicle, a Ford Crown Vic, but because it was dark, I couldn't decide if the color was dark blue or black. Due to the tinted windows, I couldn't see inside the car, but I noticed the driver's window was down a few inches.

I realized I was standing directly under a light above the door. I watched the car, and I saw what looked like a flash of metal slip through the open driver's side window and I immediately dropped to the ground. As I hit the ground, I heard the roar of a gun and the sound of something hitting the door above my head a split second apart. All of this followed up by the squeal of tires as the car sped off into the night. When I jumped up, the car was sliding around the corner still without its lights on. There was no way I could read the license plate. I remembered Jeff L. was still back in the warehouse and I finished propping open the door and headed back to see what I could do for him.

When I found Jeff L. I was shocked at the amount of blood pooling around him. To help staunch the flow, I removed my shirt and T-shirt. I folded up the T-shirt making the best square pad I could create. Then I unbuttoned his shirt and placed the T-shirt tightly against his oozing wound, using my other shirt to secure the T-shirt as best I could.

I sat there shivering in the cold warehouse and I held Jeff's hand as I spoke to him. I have no idea if he heard me or not. I think it was as much for me as it was for him. While I was talking to Jeff, his cell phone rang. I answered it and it was the 911 operator. She rudely informed me I'd hung up on her. "What is your name?" I asked.

"Nancy, why?"

"Because if this officer dies, I want them to know who held up the aide vehicle." I was going to tell her I would hang up again, and I also wanted to add if Jeff died it would be on her head for not sending out immediate help. Thinking about those comments, I decided not to hang up. I knew she would just continue to call me back, and by keeping the line open, I also could continue to harass her about why nobody had shown up yet. Instead of ending the call, I laid the phone beside Jeff's head as I continued talking to him. I told him that everything would work out, all he had to do was just hold on. I talked to him as I sat there for what seemed like an eternity, but I'm sure was actually only a few minutes. Finally, I heard the sound of sirens arriving.

The sirens stopped and in a few seconds, I heard a voice shouting, "Hello! Anyone in here?"

When I heard the shout, I called back to them, telling them where we were, and shortly there were two medics helping me try to stem the flow of blood from Jeff L.'s wound.

I stepped back and allowed them to do their job. When I heard more voices calling out, I picked up the cell and told the woman on the phone the local police had just arrived. As I closed the phone, I could hear her telling me not to hang up, asking me who I was. I hung up anyway and called out to the two new voices telling them where we were.

In a few minutes, two uniformed police officers from the local town came forward and asked questions. At that point, I reached down and removed Jeff L.'s badge from his belt. I thought this would explain who was on the floor. I told them about the dark-colored Crown Vic and why I had no more information on the vehicle. I showed them one of Jeff L.'s business cards and suggested they needed to call his office and tell them what happened. I avoided telling the police I'd been following him and instead gave them the impression I was just driving by and heard the shots. I told them I stopped to investigate; I found Jeff and saw the car drive away.

When the two officers asked me more questions, I suggested they first needed to call the numbers on the business card I'd given them. I pointed to my naked chest and mentioned how cold I was. I pointed to where my shirts were wrapped around Jeff's chest. I asked the officers if I could return to my truck and find a fresh shirt

They could see my bloody shirt wrapped around Jeff and why my shirts were saturated with blood and also the reason, I would have to discard them. They gave me permission.

While they made their calls, I went out to my truck. Once I reached it, I got in, shooing BJ over to her side, and then took off for my apartment as fast as possible. I didn't need the stress of being caught up in the aftermath of anyone's wrath; be it Frank's or Sakol's, or even worse, both of them.

Driving back to town, I wondered if Hollis played into Jeff L. being shot, but I was at a loss to figure out how it could have happened. Had Jeff L. taken my information about Price and Hollis and perhaps been working on it? I sure wished there was a way to ask Sakol what Jeff L. had been up to.

Even after I'd returned with BJ from her trip to the vacant lot, I was restless. When I heard my elevator door open and saw Sharon enter the room, I'm sure there were tears of gratitude in my eyes. She knew instantly something was wrong and asked me what was going on. I explained where I'd been and what had happened. She asked me for my cell phone and made a call. When she finished her call, she told me Jeff L. was in the ER and was being examined. Other than that, nobody had any more information.

Sharon sat wrapped in my arms for a long time on the couch while we looked out over the lake. I must have dozed off because the next thing I knew Sharon was tugging on my arm, urging me to stand up and come to bed. I left a trail of clothing down the hallway and I vaguely remember crawling into bed. I was totally exhausted because I fell back to sleep at once.

After the evening I'd just dealt with, I'd never have thought I could go to sleep so quickly.

I guessed wrong. I did.

HOUSEBOAT

CHAPTER THIRTY-TWO

There were two things I noticed as I woke up. One of them was Sharon's warm body curled around me and the other was a phone next to my head ringing. I reached out to answer it. I still wasn't completely awake, and I moaned something into the mouthpiece. I recognized Sakol's voice, and I heard him say, "Matt?" I grunted affirmatively. "It's Sakol." Again, I grunted. I knew who it was, I wasn't ready to acknowledge anybody yet. "Jeff's at Harborview. He is in the ER and they found him shot in a warehouse down in Auburn, south of Seattle. The person who called in the shooting took off after the medics and police arrived. Do you know anything about any of this?"

Of course, I knew all about it. I would not tell him that, however. I was happy to hear Sakol say he was at the ER. That meant Jeff L. was still alive. My mind raced for the proper response.

After a moment I mumbled, "How's he doing? Will he be all right?"

"They're operating on him as we speak. He was shot twice. One bullet went through his leg, but the other was a front entry, and that's the one they have some concern about.

Without an operation, they don't know how much damage he's sustained."

"Is there anything I can do?" I asked.

Sakol paused a moment, "Jeff called me when he got home last night and told me you were waiting for him at his house. He told me about your conversation, and I want you to know we've been working on the two names you gave us, but we haven't told Frank about anything. If he knew where the names came from, we'd all be toast. I think after we find out what the prognosis is on Jeff, you and I need to talk. Oh… by the way, I'm warning you now, Frank wants me to pick you up and take you down to the station."

"Why?" I was wide awake now and I could feel Sharon stirring beside me.

"Frank thinks you might have had something to do with the shooting this past evening. He doesn't think you did it, but he believes you know who might have. He also thinks you could have prevented it. I don't know what to tell him. When Jeff called me, he told me he was waiting for a phone call, but he didn't tell me from whom. Keep in mind Frank's the boss and I need to do what he says."

I shouted so loud Sharon put her hand on my shoulder and made a shushing sound. "What! How could he think something like that?"

"Matt, you must admit with all that's gone down and with your involvement, Frank's just covering the bases. Be grateful he isn't aware of Price and Hollis. I would have a difficult time covering for you then."

"OK, Sakol," I paused for a moment, "you tell me. What do you think?"

"Matt, we are having this conversation because I don't believe you had anything to do with Jeff, or with Slim or the other shooting. If I did, well, let's just say we would have our little chat at the station. For what it's worth, I'm just warning you Frank's on the warpath. He is getting a lot of heat from above, I mean way above, and he wants to make sure you're not in the way. In addition, the military putting up a stone wall about you and Price and Hollis hasn't helped his attitude, either."

"OK, I understand. Thanks! I really do appreciate it. I will get dressed and head over to Harborview immediately."

"I'm there now. I'll see you in a few…"

When I heard the phone click in my ear, I headed to the bathroom and quickly brushed my teeth and my hair. As I dressed, I explained to Sharon some of what Sakol had told me. I asked her to watch BJ for me and I'd try to call when I got a chance.

I drove across town to Harborview and as I was speeding through the empty early morning streets, it suddenly hit me. I'd just finished a conversation with Sakol and to my surprise, I'd not heard any sign of an accent. In fact, he'd used complete sentences and not once had I heard his familiar broken English. There was no question he had completely fooled me all this time. Evidently having to deal with Jeff's shooting had made him forget his little act. If possible, I was even more impressed with him than before.

~ ~ ~ ~ ~

When I arrived at the hospital, I entered through emergency and I saw Sakol standing in the hall talking to a man dressed in scrubs. As I approached, I overheard Sakol ask, "Anyway you can be more specific?"

I assumed the man in scrubs was the surgeon or Jeff L.'s doctor. The doctor replied, "I think by tomorrow evening, but maybe earlier." The doctor looked down at his wristwatch, "I mean sometime this evening. We'll have a better idea then if there will be any permanent damage. All in all, though, it appears that he is in good health and he's resting as comfortably as we can expect."

Sakol turned as the doctor left, "One bullet went through his leg and the other entered through the right side. There's been some damage, but as you heard, by tonight we should know just how bad, or how good things are."

"What happened?" I asked.

"Jeff called me after he saw you near his house. We do need to talk about that. I know about Hollis and Price and how you got the information. He told me after dinner he had one lead he wanted to follow up because he thought he might know somebody who would know where to find this Hollis person."

"You think Hollis did this?"

"It hard to tell. Look like..." I noticed Sakol was lapsing into his normal, funny way of speaking. I had to mention it.

"What is it with your speech?"

"What mean?"

"What mean bullshit? Sakol, your English is perfect! Why do you talk like someone who just got off the boat?"

"Not understand, explain please." He grinned, looking up at me.

"Let me take a guess. When you talk to people as if you barely understand English, people underestimate you, and that's just what you want?"

His answer was another one of his grins. All I could do was grin back at him. It was a brilliant ruse. When somebody can't speak your language well, there is a tendency to think of them as either a little slow or perhaps stupid. For a time, I have to admit, I too thought he wasn't the brightest light in the harbor. But I'd also seen him figure things out far too quickly for somebody who was stupid. My opinion of him continued to grow by leaps and bounds.

"Can we talk and you and I will be totally honest with each other? Nobody will ever know about this conversation. Is that possible?"

"Possible, we try."

"And can we cool it with the Charlie Chan act for a few minutes?"

"Possible... we try." Sakol responded again, but he grinned at me.

"Since I don't know what Jeff L. told you, I'll tell you what my friend told me about Price and Hollis. I explained to Sakol about Walter and why he knew them so well. Because Sakol knew I had the picture of Price from the morgue I shared with him I'd shown the picture to Walter and he'd identified Price. I mentioned the stripper who was supposed to know Price and Hollis. Finally, I ended my story with the question, "Why is everybody so pissed at me? You know I've done nothing wrong."

Sakol looked at me and I could see in his eyes he was trying to decide just how much he wished to confide in me. After a pause, he started, "First, thank you for sharing what you learned from your friend. That explains a lot. You already know Frank is upset with us, Jeff and I, and with you. He feels you're the reason the military came and took away the body and the records of the shooting behind your place. But with what you told me, I can see why the military would intervene."

I started to speak but Sakol stopped me. "There is something else. Off the street, we've heard a local drug dealer named Jersey hired a mechanic to kill somebody, or at least someone told us this Jersey dude knows something about the affair. Narcotics knows all about this Jersey guy and the story of looking for a hitman going around, so Jeff and I went to see him. Turns out he's from the East coast, and that's why he's called Jersey." Sakol shrugged his shoulders.

"At first, of course, he said he knew nothing. But after a little coaxing," Sakol grinned at me for a moment, "he told us he knew Price from a long time ago. Back East, there had been a problem during one of their drug wars and one side brought Price in to handle a huge problem. Basically, he did a couple of hits. Jersey met Price once during this time and he knew roughly how to go about finding him.

"Jersey told us about this kid who is small timer around here. This kid buys from Jersey from time to time, never a lot, but enough so Jersey would do business with the kid. One time this kid asked Jersey if he knew anybody who could do a hit for him. Jersey said it scared the shit out of him the way the kid asked. Since he didn't want to have a thing to do with the kid, he told him he had no idea what the kid was talking about and for the kid to go away. The kid wouldn't take no for an answer and he kept bugging Jersey, telling him he had heard things had happened where Jersey came from, and the rumor was Jersey knew how to get things done. So, to get rid of the kid, he told him about Price and how to contact him."

"Did this Jersey guy tell you what the kid looked like?"

"Yeah, Jersey kept calling the kid a punk. When I asked him why he kept calling the kid a punk, Jersey said, 'You know, like spiked hair, nose ring and the kid always wore black: black shirt, shoes, pants and sweatshirt'. Jersey said the kid was way overweight for somebody so young and he even had black fingernails."

The hair on the back of my neck stood up. On my God, now it all made sense. I said to Sakol, "Price was the one who killed Slim Rockingham."

Sakol looked at me as if I was crazy. "How you know? 'Sides, you said not possible. Remember right hand, left hand?" He was dropping back into his old cop routine.

"My old war friend, the one who told me about Price, also said Price was amazing with a knife. He told me it didn't matter to Price, either left or right hand, he was just as good with either one. Anyway, I met a kid the other day, and he was like a shirttail relative of Slim's and he sounded exactly like Jersey described. The nose ring, black fingernails and all. The punk was the one who hired Price and Hollis."

"What punk name?"

"Dudley. Just a second," The silence grew as I tried to remember that day in Richard's office. "Shit! I can't remember his last name. Anyway, Rockingham's stepsister's nephew looks just like your description. This Jersey character told you all this?"

"Yes." The way Sakol said that word left me to understand there was more to the story, but I would not hear it. "What Dudley last name?"

"Sorry, it was a very intense morning with all the lawyers and Jennifer. The only reason I even remember the kid's first name is when I heard it, I thought Dudley fit him; the kid really looks like a dud." I paused for a moment and then wondered if Richard would know the kid's name. "Do you know the lawyer Richard Silversmith?"

"Yes, why?"

"He was at the meeting with the kid and I have his cell number. We're friends."

"Please call."

There was a sign on the wall in the hospital asking people to step outside when making cell phone calls. I obliged, stepped outside, and called Richard. I didn't realize how early it was until I heard the sleep in his voice. "Oh God, Richard, I'm so sorry. I didn't realize how early it was."

"What do you want, Matt? What kind of trouble are you in now?

His voice was still sleepy, but I could tell he was listening carefully. This was great, I call him at the wrong time of day, and his very first thought was I'm in trouble.

"Do you remember the kid with Bottomsley the other day?"

"Yeah," Pause, "why?"

"Word on the street is he hired a hit man. I haven't heard for sure who the person was he wanted killed, but I'll give you one free guess."

The sleep was gone from his voice. "Are you kidding me? How sure are you of the information?"

"Someone shot my friend, Lt. Jeff L Davenport this evening." At that moment, I looked at my watch and saw it was now 4:30 AM, so I said, "excuse me, last night. I'm at the hospital now and I was talking to his partner, telling him how I got the information on the John Doe killed in my backyard. A fellow I served with in Nam told me the name of the JD, Dennis Price and his best friend, and sometime lover named Hayward Hollis. The rumor on the street is that someone hired Price to kill someone here in town. A drug dealer described the person who hired Price, and the description fits Bottomsley's nephew perfectly. The police want to have a talk with the kid, and all I can remember is his first name was Dudley. Do you remember his last?"

There was a moment of silence, and then, "Bell. Dudley Bell."

"Yes! That's right, thanks Richard, and I owe you."

"Your payment is telling me how this turns out."

"Deal!" I went back into emergency and found Sakol talking to the same doctor I'd seen him with before. Then both stopped talking when I walked up. "Is everything all right?" I asked.

The doctor responded, "He's doing much better than we could have hoped for. It looks now as if he'll pull through and be okay."

Both Sakol and I breathed a deep sigh of relief. I stuck out my hand to the doctor, and when he took it, I thanked him, several times

Sakol and I walked out into the early morning, pleased with the good news. Sakol turned "Thank you for phoning in and staying there until help had arrived."

"What the hell are you talking about?" I asked.

Sakol winked at me, "I talked to the two officers who showed up at the warehouse. They were pissed that you left, but I squared it. They also saw the tattoo on your shoulder, and when they described it and you, well, you're easy to remember. And I knew who it was. Thank you for sticking around after you called it in. I know you didn't have to do that. That will go a long way with Frank, and with me." He put out his hand.

As I shook it, I had to laugh, "What funny?" He asked, lapsing into his broken English.

"You're a character. Your English is perfect. You almost have an English accent when you speak normally."

"What normally? I speak normally all time. You speak funny." We both laughed.

"I got the name you wanted. The name is Dudley Bell, and I believe he lives with his aunt. Her name is Audrey Bottomsley, I don't know her address, but her lawyer is Don Green and he would know where to find both of them."

Sakol scowled, "Green is asshole. He give lawyers bad name. I make phone call." Sakol pulled his cell phone out and punched in numbers. I heard him instruct whoever was on the phone to go to Green's house and get Bottomsley's address, then call him back. He looked at me and with a grin, "I not supposed to do this, but come with me."

"Are you taking me in?" I asked.

"No, we going hunt drug dealer. Promise me you not get hurt. Frank kill me if find out I take you along.

HOUSEBOAT

CHAPTER THIRTY-THREE

You don't have to think too hard to figure out why cities have varied and different types of neighborhoods. Some are perhaps for economic reasons, or ethnic, or family and social reasons or for all of the aforementioned. Most parts of a city play to the people who make up those parts. Other parts of a city are ritzy, and others not so much. Invariably, there are those parts in large cities that become less desirable and are actually dangerous to live in. Those are places people call the ghettos. Usually, these rundown areas are left over from a well-intentioned government project that's gone awry, and, sad to say, Seattle is no different. Seattle has its own ghetto.

Sakol and I were deep inside The Projects. This area consisted of boarded up old buildings, rundown apartment houses, empty storefronts and filthy streets. We cruised slowly down back streets until Sakol finally turned onto a long, dark alley. This alley was in the heart of what people would define as ghetto territory. I'll admit, I'd never been to this area before, and had I not been with Sakol, I would not be here this morning. Cruising slowly down the alley, Sakol sat with his left hand resting on the steering wheel looking back and forth until we reached the end. Pulling in behind a dumpster, he put the car in park and turned off the motor.

Glancing over, he told me, "Come!" I got out of the car and followed him down the street. "Stay close," he said. I thought for a moment about some smart-assed quip, but I kept my mouth shut.

The morning was cool, and a slight fog hung over the streets, blurring the building outlines. We'd been the only two people in the alley and we were still alone on the street after we left the alley. Walking down a trash-strewn, deserted street, the sounds of our shoes echoed off the buildings brick walls. We came to two sets of stairs in the middle of the block and Sakol stopped and looked both ways. One set of stairs went up towards the building entrance, and another set went down. We took the stairs going down and reached the building's basement. As Sakol opened the door at the bottom of the stairs, he turned, and again he advised me, "Stick close."

His comment almost made me guffaw. Telling me to stick close was not something he needed to say twice. The truth was, he didn't even have to say it the first time. The area at the bottom of the stairs didn't have proper lighting. It appeared to be lit with a 25-watt bulb. There was trash scattered everywhere, and I figured it was just as well I couldn't see much.

Sakol opened a door, and we passed into a room which was almost pitch dark. As my eyes slowly adapted to the diminished light, I could see we were in a very large room with chairs and beds scattered around the perimeter. There were several tables in the middle of the room which had candles burning on them, giving off some very feeble light. I thought I saw forms in some beds, but I didn't want to stare. What I found the most difficult to deal with was the stench of unwashed bodies, urine, and old smoke. It was unbelievable. How anybody could spend more than a few minutes in the room was beyond me. My main thought was how quickly we could do what we had to do and get out of there.

Sakol seemed to know where he was going, so I followed him as he walked directly towards the back of the room. I wanted to ask him if we really needed to be here but thought better of it. I'd lived my entire life in Seattle, and I'd never imagined there was anything like this room in my town. Without a doubt, this was a true drug den. This was like something out of a horror film. As hip as I thought I was, I felt like a naïve kid from the sticks as we walked through the room. Until this point in my life, I'd suffered through the horrors of SE Asia, and I'd witnessed many things I'd just prefer to forget. But this room was something I couldn't understand at all.

If Sakol hadn't reached out to open the door at the back of the room, I never would have known there was a door or even a knob there. Once Sakol's hand touched the doorknob to open it, a massive man stepped out of a shadow and grabbed Sakol's hand. It was so dark all I could see was a large black shadow.

"What do you want?" A deep rumbling voice asked.

In a whisper, Sakol told him, "You have two seconds to remove your hand, or I'll break it off and hand it to you." The giant looked down at Sakol for a moment and then pulled his hand back.

"What do you want back here?" The large man asked again. I stood there trying to make out his features. About the only thing I could tell for sure was he was a black man. The other thing was that considering I am around 6'4", this man had to be well over seven feet tall.

"I'm here to see Mouse."

"Does he expect you?"

"Mouse and I go way back. He always expects me." Sakol paused for a moment, and then continued, "And the longer you keep me out here, the worse it will be for you when I finally see him." The giant thought a moment and then nodded. "Go ahead."

After the depressing room we were leaving, the next room we entered was even more unreal. The room we left was like something from a nightmare, and this room was something from a dream. Concealed soft lighting lit the room which surrounded the edge of the coffered ceiling. The walls were oak-paneled and there was thick, soft carpet underfoot. In addition, one end of the room had an arrangement of expensive leather furniture, while the other side held a large executive table. There was a fireplace with a fire going, surrounded by a large mantelpiece.

Behind the table sat a small man in a well-tailored suit. When he saw Sakol, he jumped up, clapped his hands together, and ran around the table. He extended his right hand, and with a smile, he exclaimed, "Sakol, my old friend, it's wonderful to see you. It has been way too long."

The two of them hugged one another, and then ended up by leaning close and bumping shoulders, similar to how black men tend to greet each other. In order for Sakol's shoulder to touch the small man's shoulder, Sakol had to bend deeply at the waist. As they stepped back, Mouse looked over at me, and exclaimed, "Who is this?"

Sakol motioned me over, as he spoke, "This is Matt Preston. Matt, this is Steve Fox, but you should call him Mouse." The little man extended a well-manicured hand, and, as I shook it, my hand engulfed his. I doubted if the man was five feet tall, but his voice and manners were impeccable.

Mouse said, "Sit, both of you." He waved his hand towards the overstuffed leather chairs. After we both settled down, the diminutive man asked, "Can I offer you a cup of coffee? Tea? A drink perhaps?"

Sakol replied, "Coffee please, lots of cream."

The man looked at me. "Same, please." I replied.

The petite man went to his desk, and I guessed there must be a button there. A second later, an invisible door set into the paneling opened, and a lovely young Asian woman entered the room

"Sir?" she asked.

"Three coffees, please, two with cream and one how I prefer."

"Sir." The young woman bowed slightly and then left.

"Woman still very beautiful."

The tiny man laughed, "Sakol, knock it off. You and I go too far back for you to pull that stupid Charlie Chan crap on me," and they both laughed. The way they spoke to each other I could tell their friendship was deep and lengthy. Mouse gave a small bow as he smiled at me and said, "I'm so pleased to meet you, Mr. Preston. Your poker games are legendary."

Words don't convey how that remark struck me. There was a knock at the door, and Mouse called out, "Come!" The door opened, and the beautiful girl returned with a serving tray. She set the tray down, and when she reached for the coffeepot, Mouse told her to leave and that he'd pour. He poured us each a cup, handed one to Sakol, and one to me. The color of mine was perfect. I noticed Mouse's cup already had something in it.

After Mouse sat down, he turned to Sakol, and asked, "What brings you to my lair so early this morning?"

"We're looking for a dealer named Jersey, and I don't have time to go hunting for him. I think you know where to find him. I need to chat with him in the worst way. Where is he?" I noticed Mouse didn't ask Sakol who Jersey was, or anything about him, concluding that I Mouse already knew who Jersey was.

Mouse held out his hands with the palms up. "Why do you ask me?"

Sakol hung his head for a moment acting dejected. "Mouse, for old times, sake, please, let's not play games. We really need to talk to him, and the sooner the better.

Mouse smiled at Sakol and shook his head. "Okay, I had to try. Let me ask you this, does it have anything to do with the two mechanics who were in town?"

Sakol didn't seem surprised that Mouse would know about Hollis and Price. "Yes. And one, the man named Price, is dead,"

Mouse interrupted, "I knew that. I've also heard he was as good as dead from cancer. I was told he had between 4 and 6 months to live." Again, Sakol showed no sign of surprise Mouse would know something about Price's medical condition.

"And the problem is we need to find Hollis before he murders any more people. I believe he shot my partner last night…"

Mouse interrupted again, "Jeff was shot last night?"

"Yes, he's at Harborview," Sakol informed him.

"This is a surprise. My sources haven't mentioned that piece of information. How is he?"

"He'll recover, and thanks for asking."

Mouse bowed his head for a moment, and then looked back at Sakol, "I interrupted you, please continue."

Sakol went on, "I even think Jersey might be in danger."

Mouse seemed surprised by that. "Really, why?"

"Did you know it was Hollis who killed Price?"

Mouse tented his fingers in front of his face, nodding his head. "For a while, I wondered about that and then I decided it had to be Matt or else Hollis." Mouse smiled at me and continued, "As soon as I wondered if it could have been you, I dismissed the thought." I nodded my head, and he looked at Sakol, "Why do you think Hollis did it?" Mouse stressed the word 'you' and pointed at Sakol.

Sakol nodded his head at me. "If you don't mind, I'll let Matt tell you the story. It concerns things that happened to him when he served in Viet Nam."

Mouse smiled at me and opened his arms, signaling me to talk. However, before I could say a word, Mouse spoke, "I apologize for interrupting you, but I wanted to thank you for your service. I know it was not a popular war, but those who served thought they were doing the right thing. I salute you, Matt."

His words pleased me. Few people will acknowledge those of us who served in Nam. I really didn't know who Mouse was, but his comments made me feel good. I took a sip of the excellent coffee and started. "If I may, like Sakol said, it goes back to Nam where Price and Hollis served together. I was in the same outfit as the both of them, but I was leaving just as they arrived.

"Once when they were out on a mission, a friend of mine overheard the two of them make a pact. The deal was, if a situation came up where one of them was too injured to go on, the other wouldn't leave his partner behind alive. The night Price broke his leg, there was no way Hollis couldn't extract him from the vacant lot. Since Price was dying of cancer anyway, it probably was easier for Hollis to shoot him. My guess was because of the cancer, the treatments had weakened Price's bones to the point when he fell, his leg just snapped."

Mouse asked me, "How do you know all this?"

"Like I said, I was there. I served in the same outfit as they did, and I know how they think. My friend was with them on the mission where they made the pact with each other. My friend heard the conversation where they agreed to never to leave the other behind."

Mouse continued to stare into his tented hands, as he nodded his head, "This is your friend who lives over on the peninsula?"

I noticed my hands were trembling slightly, and I was covered in goosebumps. I wondered exactly who this little man sitting in front of me was, and what other things he knew. I was so stunned by his comment all I could do was nod my head to answer his question.

"Interesting on several levels," he parted his hands, and turned to look at Sakol, "Why do you feel Jersey is in danger?"

"Jersey knows who hired Price and Hollis, and who they killed."

"Will you tell me who hired them and who they killed?" Mouse asked.

"Not today, but I promise to return and tell you. I promise to tell you the whole story. Will that do?"

Mouse turned his hands over and smiled, "Yes, you've never lied to me." Mouse turned. "Did you know I saved Sakol's life one time? When we were young?"

I responded, "I know very little about Sakol. It wasn't until a few hours ago I thought he always spoke in his funny little way."

Mouse laughed so long and hard he had tears in his eyes. "Sakol loved to watch old Charlie Chan movies when he was a kid, and he thought it was great the way Chan talked. He also liked what a great detective he was. He practiced for hours to talk like that. By the time we were in junior high school, he had all the teachers fooled. They even tried to put him in special education classes because they thought he was mentally slow. The problem was he scored in the top percentile on all the tests they gave him." Mouse laughed at his recollections.

"The best thing about it all was the girls seemed to love the way he talked." Until that moment, I'd never thought of Sakol as a sexual person. I looked at Sakol, and he grinned for a moment.

Sakol turned back to Mouse, "Where's Jersey? I need to see him and the sooner the better. It's important and you know I'd never ask you for your help if it wasn't necessary. True?"

Mouse nodded, and I could see he was deep in thought before he responded. Finally, he told Sakol, "Tell me when and where, and I'll have him delivered to you." Sakol gave Mouse an address and asked if it was possible to have him delivered today. Mouse held his arms open with his hands facing outwards. "I will try my best. As always, I can make no promises. I'll call you on your cell when I have him."

Sakol stood, signaling me it was time to go. He walked over to the diminutive man and wrapped him in his arms. They hugged each other for a long time. When Sakol released Mouse I heard him say, "I miss you, little man. I really miss you. I wish we could see one another more."

Mouse nodded his head, "I understand. We all do what we have to. It was great to see you. Even if the circumstances weren't what we would have chosen." Mouse turned "Matt, it was nice to meet you. Please give Sharon my best." Again, I was stunned, too surprised to make any comment regarding his comment about Sharon.

Sakol turned to leave the room, and I followed. My mind was trying frantically to organize what I'd just learned. It would take time to sort through all of this and even longer for it to make any kind of sense.

HOUSEBOAT

CHAPTER THIRTY-FOUR

After we left Mouse's, I found I didn't have the words to describe what I'd seen. Home doesn't seem proper. Place of business doesn't accurately describe it either. Would it be a terrible pun to call it Mouse hole? I wondered for a second if I dared ask Sakol what he would call the place we'd just left.

Sakol and I left the rundown area and headed for a coffee shop where we stopped and ordered breakfast. Both of us sat quietly in the booth; each lost in our own thoughts. Mine bounced between what was going on with Hollis and Price and everything that entailed, and Sharon. It was becoming clear she was a larger part of my life with each passing day, and it pleased me how much the idea excited me.

Another part of my mind kept reviewing my short conversation with Mouse. I didn't know exactly who the little man was, but his knowledge of what was happening in Seattle, and with me, was beyond frightening. I wondered how he knew about Walter and our relationship? And, I also didn't want to forget to ask Sharon what she knew about the fascinating little man I'd just met. Mouse acted as if they were old friends. That conversation would be an interesting one.

Finally, Sakol grunted, pushed away his empty plate and looked at me. "We go. Now," he said and stood up. When I asked him where he told me he wanted to return to the hospital. He wanted to see Jeff.

As we rode towards our destination, I asked him to tell me about Mouse and the story about saving Sakol's life. Sakol told me the story about the two of them growing up together. When they were both six years old, Mouse's family moved in next to Sakol's family, and because there weren't any other kids on the block, the two of them played together. Over time, they became best friends.

Sakol reminisced, telling me stories about their antics during grade school and junior high. Sakol mentioned how several times he'd saved Mouse from various bullies. Finally, when the two of them were in junior high, they signed up for self-defense classes. Sakol looked over at me and grinned, "You might not know this to look at him, but Mouse holds several degrees in various martial arts disciplines. He keeps bodyguards around, but if it came down to it, he could save them faster than they could save him." Sakol laughed aloud at this remark and it was obvious from the warmth in Sakol's voice as he told me the stories, he considered the diminutive man a close and dear friend.

I tried several times to get Sakol to tell me how Mouse had saved him, but he would carefully steer the conversation away from that subject and he never told me exactly what Mouse did. But Sakol confided in me before we got to the hospital even though he was fairly positive he knew what Mouse did as a profession, it would be difficult to bust him. As we drove up in front of the hospital, Sakol ended his story with, "Someday my supervisors will force me to decide. Someday I'll have to either resign from the force or arrest Mouse." Sakol looked at me and shook his head, "I know this, and yet I've no idea what I'll do when the time comes." Sakol parked the car in silence and I remembered how he had dropped the Charlie Chan routine when he talked about his old friend.

The doctors let us see Jeff L. and I was happy to see how well he looked, considering what had happened. At one point he asked Sakol to leave the room. That surprised me. After we were alone, he looked at me and beckoned for me to come closer. Looking me in the eye, Jeff L.'s voice was almost a whisper as he said, "I know what you did last night. I knew you were with me and talking to me. Your words helped me a lot. You are a better friend than I was. I'm sorry. You saved my life and I owe you."

I know there were tears in my eyes, but I didn't care. "Bullshit. You owe me nothing. You'd have done the same thing if the roles were reversed. I'm glad I was there, and I could help."

"But I was so nasty to you." Tears were running down his face. "If you'd done what I told you to do if you'd gone home, I'd be dead now. I'm so sorry for the way I acted."

I was getting embarrassed now. I needed this to stop. Besides, there were other issues which needed we needed to address. "Please, Jeff, please stop this. You're safe and that's all that's important. Sakol and I are working on the rest. And most of all, I need to get out of here before Frank finds me. Don't know if you know this, but he thinks I could have prevented this. And I guess possibly I could have. Maybe I shouldn't have told you about Price and Hollis. Anyway, I need to leave. Now!"

Jeff L. lifted one hand a little, and I took it in mine. I could still see tears in his eyes and his voice was still a whisper. "Thanks for coming to see me. And thanks for last night. Somehow, I'll make it up to you. I promise."

I squeezed his hand gently, laid it back on his chest and with a smile on my face, I told him, "Just get better and don't be such a turd when I call you next time." As I left the room, I could hear him chortling.

~ ~ ~ ~ ~

I headed home where I found a note from Sharon. One nurse had called in sick and they were short staffed. She wrote she didn't know when she'd be back but she would call me when she had a chance. I took BJ out and watched her wander around the vacant lot.

After I returned from the lot with BJ, I was restless. There was nothing I could do except wait for Sakol to call. Sharon called and told me she would be late and I assured her things were just fine. She told me she had looked in on Jeff L. and he was pestering the doctors to go home. His wife Dee and Sharon were trying to get him to see the wisdom of sticking around for a few days to make sure there were no complications. Finally, Frank stepped in and ordered Jeff to stay in the hospital, and more importantly, told him to shut up and deal with it. I laughed, and we hung up.

Around midnight I got the call from Sakol I'd waited for all day. He gave me the address where we were to meet in about an hour. I told him I'd see him there. I took BJ out for another outing and then we went down to the garage to get my truck and go meet Sakol. The address he gave me turned out to be his home, and I parked my truck on the side of his garage. I rolled the window down part way for BJ and noticed she was sacked out. Sakol and I got in his squad car and we were off to find Mouse.

When we finally stopped, it was in a remote area of North Seattle. We stayed in the car, waiting. After about a ten minute wait, a stretch limo came around the corner and stopped next to Sakol's car. Two men who looked like ex-offensive football linemen got out of the limo and stood. Considering Mouse's size, I understood why he'd want to surround himself with large, frightening looking men. It was simple; they offered great protection. However, I now that I knew the truth about Mouse and his ability to protect himself; I realized the bodyguards were more for show than for protection.

Once the bodyguards were sure nobody was waiting to harm Mouse, they opened the back door. Mouse stepped from the back of the limo, his attire still impeccable, you'd have never guessed it was the middle of the night. From the pocket square in his suit coat pocket to his highly polished shoes, he looked like something from an ad in Gentleman's Quarterly.

Sakol got out of the car and stepped over to Mouse. The little man looked up at Sakol, and, as he spoke, he sadly shook his head, "We seem to have a problem." Mouse nodded at one bodyguard who stepped to the trunk of the limo. The key fob was lost in the giant's hand. He pushed the proper button on the fob, and the trunk popped open. Mouse had moved to the end of the limo and pointed at the body curled up in the trunk, "Here he is; as promised."

We all stood looking into the trunk for a moment until finally Sakol asked, "This is Jersey?"

Mouse nodded his head, "Yes, I'm sorry. We found him too late."

"What happened?" Sakol responded.

"We found him dead in his apartment. He had been shot twice in the back of the head, obviously an execution." The five of us all stood for a moment looking at Jersey's dead body tucked into the large trunk. It would seem Hollis was quickly cleaning up loose ends. Finally, Mouse turned to Sakol, and asked, "What do you want me to do with him?"

Sakol pondered the situation for a moment, "Well, I really wish you hadn't disturbed the crime scene, but it's too late now. How about you take him back to where you found him? When you're finished, call me and give me the address and I'll call it in. Please be careful and leave no evidence to indicate you or your people were involved."

Mouse nodded his head in understanding. "Will you still come and tell me what this is all about sometime?" Mouse asked.

"It's a promise." Sakol paused for a moment, and continued, "Is there any way Hollis could know about you?" Mouse seemed surprised at Sakol's question. "I don't see how; it was Jersey who contacted Price, not me. I'd never heard about Price and Hollis until they got to town. Why do you ask?"

"It would appear Hollis is making sure there's nobody left to talk. I'd hate to see you swept up in this somehow." Mouse smiled warmly at his old friend. "Thanks for caring, but I feel safe, at least for now." Mouse extended his hand to Sakol, and they shook hands. Mouse looked at me and bowed his head. "I hope to see you again, Mr. Preston. Please come visit me anytime."

I thanked Mouse for his generosity, but I knew in my heart I doubted if I'd ever go back to the place Sakol had taken me. Sakol and I got into his car, and we found an all-night restaurant and had a cup of coffee.

~ ~ ~ ~ ~

I pondered that lately Sakol, and I were spending a lot of time sitting in restaurant booths when Sakol's cell phone went off in his pocket. He grunted into the phone. "You talk. I listen." I heard buzzing on the other end of the phone, and then Sakol turned "Write down, please." We were back to 'Sakol the cop'.

"8909 Freemont," he said aloud. I wrote it on a piece of paper I found in my pocket.

Sakol spoke a few more words into his phone, thanked the person he was speaking to and then hung up. As he slid out of the booth Sakol told me, "We go. Come!"

Once we were in his car, he reached down to the floor, picked up his blue light, and placed it on the roof. Sakol flipped on the siren, and we went careening out of the restaurant parking lot. As we sped down deserted streets, I asked Sakol who was at the address. He told me one of his detectives had found Green and the lawyer had provided an address for Bottomsley and for Dudley. Sakol finished up, "I hope we're there in time. I'm afraid Hollis may have already gotten there and silenced them."

When we were about two blocks from our destination, Sakol reached over and turned off the siren and then pulled the light down off the roof. After he turned onto Freemont, we drove slowly down the block looking at addresses. Once we were across from 8909, we parked on the street. Even though it was dark, I could see the front door of the house was standing wide open. When I pointed it out to Sakol he muttered, "Not good."

Sakol picked up the microphone off the dashboard and called in the address, explained what was happening and then requested backup.

"Do we wait?" I asked.

"You wait. I go," he replied. Sakol looked at me and pointed his finger at his chest. "Alone!" he added.

"But I want to…" I never got the chance to complete my sentence.

Before I could say any more, "You wait! I go! I go, alone." This time he sounded slightly angry with me. "No argue. Understand?"

I nodded my head. I wasn't happy with this idea, but I knew better than to argue.

Sakol quickly crossed the street drawing his weapon. Before he stepped through the open front door, I heard him call out, "Police. Anybody here?" He waited a moment and then stepped inside. In a few minutes, he returned to the car. For me, it seemed like hours. When he leaned over and looked into the car, even under the streetlights I noticed his normally tanned face was drawn and pale. I didn't think he looked good. Sakol continued to lean against the car taking deep breaths. Shaking his head, he told me, "Fat lady dead in kitchen, punk dead in bedroom; both shot in head, twice. Punk also had throat slashed."

It definitely appeared as if Hollis was cleaning up all the loose ends. I thought slitting Dudley's throat had been Hollis' way of paying him back because of what happened to Price. I pondered the gruesome question whether Hollis had slit Dudley's throat first or shot him and then slit his throat. Anyway, it showed a lot of hatred stored up. And then, as I was sitting in the car, I wondered if perhaps I should start looking behind me.

~ ~ ~ ~ ~

I went back to my place and caught up on some sleep. When I woke up, it was early evening. I took BJ out and stood in the vacant lot with rain beating down on my head. Waiting for BJ to finish her business, I realized how close it was to Christmas. Bright colored lights sparkled on some houses surrounding the lot and I remembered I'd done nothing to prepare for the holidays. I hadn't even purchased a gift for Sharon. I promised myself tomorrow I'd rectify that situation.

The previous evening when Sakol sent me away after his gruesome discovery, before I even realized where I was, I'd driven from where the taxi had dropped me to pick up my truck, drove all the way home, parked the truck, came upstairs and released BJ, and the frightening thing was I couldn't remember any of it. My mind was still dealing with all the deaths Hollis had committed and in Jeff L.'s case, tried to commit. It disturbed me I was driving too often without realizing what I was doing. In my defense, there was a lot going on in my life.

When Sakol had walked out of the house after he'd discovered Bottomsley and Dudley, his face had been ashen. I knew this wasn't the first murder Sakol had investigated, but whatever he'd witnessed in the house had really left an impact. When I asked to go into the house, Sakol had told me I couldn't because of the possibility of accidentally contaminating the scene. Sakol concluded, "Even if I could allow you to, trust me, you do not want to go in there." Over the years, I've seen more than my share of dead bodies, and I guess Sakol was correct; I didn't need to see two more. In addition, looking at Sakol, whatever else had happened in that house, I was fairly positive it wasn't something I needed to see.

I could also tell he wanted me gone as quickly as possible. There was the off chance Captain Frank might show because of this being a double murder and both of us were certain I was still on Frank's shit list. The last thing he'd said to Sakol was he wanted my fat ass in jail. We decided I needed to go, now! Sakol summoned a taxi for me and it whisked me away before anybody else arrived at the scene.

I was still standing out in the vacant lot with BJ when my cell played its little song. It was Sakol, I answered, "Sakol, what's up?"

"I still at murder. Two thing. Neighbor report dark blue car, like police drive, and Frank been and went. Got to go." The cell phone was silent in my hand.

My assumption was Sakol was describing the same Crown Vic I'd seen the night when Jeff L. was shot. It was obvious the person driving the car was Hollis. I knew the car I saw that night when Jeff was shot had been a dark color, and it was the same Ford popular with police. If Bottomsley's neighbor had said it looked like a police car, it sure seemed like I was correct. This was more proof Hollis had shot and killed the nephew, the aunt, and shot Jeff. The problem for the police was a Ford Crown Vic isn't that rare. The police liked that model and so did many other drivers. Stopping every dark blue Ford that looked like a cop car was asking the impossible. As much as I didn't like it, it seemed like Hollis was reasonably safe for now.

Finally, BJ scampered back to me, and we wandered down to see if Sharon was home. I summoned the elevator and took it down one flight to her place. As soon as the door slid open, BJ took off towards the back of her apartment. Once she entered the bedroom, BJ barked. I've had BJ long enough to recognize what her different barks mean, and this sounded a lot like the time she found Slim strapped in his chair. I could tell she was frantic.

Moving as quickly as I could, I shoved the bedroom door open the rest of the way. Once I was in the room, I could see legs sticking out on the far side of the bed, and after I crossed the room, I found Sharon lying in a pool of blood. A sob burst from my chest. I felt her neck on the underside of her chin using my fingers. I could just faintly make out a very soft pulse. I fished my cell phone out of my pocket, called 911, reported what I had found and ended the conversation by telling them to hurry.

When I heard the signal alerting me the EMT drivers were downstairs at the front entrance, I went to the elevator to send it down for them. Passing through the kitchen to return to Sharon, I found the note on the counter. It read, "Leave me alone or YOU are next!" I knew who'd left it for me. Hollis had thrown down the gauntlet. If I didn't stop, he would kill me.

The medics were already working on her when one of them recognized her from the ER at the hospital. It seemed from that moment on, their efforts to save her stepped up a couple of notches. One of them had an earpiece which also served as a microphone, and I could tell he was in contact with the ER personnel at the hospital.

As they wheeled Sharon to the elevator, the medics continued talking back and forth with the ER room, getting them ready for her arrival. When the elevator door began shutting, the EMT who knew Sharon from the hospital looked at me, and said, "I think she'll be okay. The wound isn't too bad, and we got here in time. She is stable and they're ready for her at the hospital. Sharon's gonna be fine, trust us." The elevator door closed.

I stood there with tears running down my face. I couldn't deal with the thought of losing her.

Not now.

HOUSEBOAT

CHAPTER THIRTY-FIVE

I have no idea how long I stood there staring at the closed elevator doors. My mind was a fuse box after too much power had been pulled through it. All my fuses were tripped; the lights were out and there was nobody home.

Eventually, my brain functioned, and I realized I needed to take action, I had to do something. I pulled out my cell phone and dialed Sakol. He answered on the second ring, just as he always does. I heard his familiar greeting, "You talk, I listen."

There was no reason to mince words, and I told him straight out, "I found Sharon in her bedroom and she's been shot. The EMT people have been here, and she's on her way to the ER at Harborview Hospital. She was still alive when they took her away and they felt they had got to her in time. I also found a note on my kitchen counter telling us to back off. It's Hollis."

Sakol abruptly told me, "I go. Call later." The phone went dead in my ear.

I headed down to the garage and got in my truck to head for the hospital. As always, BJ followed along. From my car phone, I called the cleaning service who take care of my apartment and explained to them there was a problem in one of my units. I told them where to find the pool of blood, but I left out how it came to be there. I asked them to do the best they could, but I wanted the place cleaned up as soon as possible.

Driving to the hospital, I saw all the Christmas lights decorating people's homes, and it hit me, this was Christmas Eve. It was not how I'd planned to spend the evening. I'm not a religious man, but I asked God for a Christmas present for myself; I asked him to spare Sharon's life. I know it seems selfish, but I wanted her back, alive and well.

When I walked into the emergency receiving area, Nancy, one of Sharon's nurse buddies noticed me. She came over and greeted me and even though all I wanted was to ask how Sharon was doing; I was afraid to speak. I didn't want to break down in front of her. Nancy seemed to know exactly what I would ask, and she told me even though Sharon had lost a lot of blood, she would make it. The bullet had nicked a vein, but she'd made it to the ER in time.

The next thing I knew I was sitting in a chair crying and Nancy had her arms wrapped around me, holding and comforting me. I mean, I loved Sharon, but until that moment, I hadn't realized how deep my feelings had grown. I was discovering the idea of losing her was way too much for me to even comprehend. There were no words to describe how I felt; I was so grateful for Nancy's words that Sharon would pull through. I'd made an important discovery; the importance of Sharon to me.

I heard the doors to the ER waiting room swoosh open and when I looked up, there were two uniformed officers standing directly in front of me with Captain Frank standing between them.

"Oh, shit!" I thought to myself, "Here I go. I'm off to jail." I looked around the room to see if there was a way to escape. My heart was pounding, and I was positive the two officers with Frank would take me into custody. Instead, much to my surprise, Frank gave me a small nod and then came and sat down next to me.

Placing a hand on my knee, he asked, "Evening Matt, how is Sharon doing?"

I told him about going to Sharon's place and finding her on the floor. He asked me how I was doing. His concern was alarming to me. This was not the hard-boiled Police Captain I thought I knew. I wanted to ask, "Where's the old Captain Frank? What've you done to him?" However, I wisely kept my mouth shut. I told him I was doing as well as could be expected considering everything that was going on.

Frank pointed at the two officers still standing in front of us. "These two officers will guard Sharon. I'm assigning officers, twenty-four hours a day until we catch that son of a bitch."

"How did you know about this?" I swept my hand towards the emergency area.

"Sakol called me. He told me about Price and Hollis and everything they suspect them of doing. Sakol also told me you were the one who called in Jeff getting shot last night."

I sat and looked at him for a while and finally I replied, "Frank, I've no idea what you're talking about. I'd heard someone shot Jeff, but you ordered me to stay away from him and Sakol. How could I be the one who called in about somebody shooting him?"

Frank's dark face lit up, as he smiled at me, "Yeah! Right! I forgot I told you that. Then it must've been somebody else who called it in. You always do what I tell you to do. Right?"

I could feel my face breaking into a big grin. "Yes, sir. It couldn't have been me." That was my story, and I would stick to it, at least as long as I could.

"Well," Frank winked at me, "if you ever see the person who stuck around and then called 911, please tell that person thanks." He stood and gave instructions to the waiting officers.

As he started out the door, I called to him, "Thanks for having some of your people watching over Sharon."

Frank took a step back towards me and with a rueful smile said, "I forgot to tell you, I know Sharon. I mean professionally. There is no way you could know this, but I ended up in the ER one night pretty messed up. It was touch and go and she sat with me the entire night," Frank's face looked kind and gentle with his memories, "She's really very special. I feel I owe her. There's no other way Matt but to take good care of her."

Frank turned to leave and then turned back around. He smiled at me and said, "Hey, Merry Christmas." I nodded my head. As he stepped through the door, Frank called back over his shoulder, "See ya around." I'd always had a soft spot for Frank, and now I realized why. Beneath that gruff exterior, there really was a heart of gold. No wonder everybody who serves under him thinks the world of him.

~ ~ ~ ~ ~

I knew Sharon's doctor and when he finally came out to see me; we were able to discuss how long they expected to keep her at the hospital. I thanked him for his time. Now I had a few moments so I stepped outside to call Sakol. "You talk, I listen."

"It's Matt."

"Not now. Call later." As I hung up, I remembered I had BJ out in the truck, and she needed to be let out. I opened the door, and she came barreling out. She proceeded to go around and sniff the different bushes. While I stood there waiting for her, I suddenly remembered Lan, the stripper. Two things came to mind regarding her. The first, how safe was she since she knew all about Hollis killing Price. I also wondered if she could, or even would, tell me about Hollis. Second, I hoped she was still alive, and for some reason, I thought she knew where he was hiding. The more I thought about it, the more it appeared that killing Price had snapped something inside of Hollis. He was probably already a little crazy, and the thing with Price must have completely unhinged him. He was taking out anybody and everybody out he thought was involved with them. I knew Walter was safe, but I wondered just how safe I was.

I got BJ back in the car and pulled out of the hospital parking lot, heading for the strip club. The chances Lan would be there were poor since she preferred working days, but I needed to try. If nothing else, I was hoping I could convince the bouncer to call her to see if she'd meet me somewhere. At this point, I was desperate. Just as I pulled into the parking lot of the club my cell went off, it was Sakol. "What's up?" I asked him.

"Bodies gone. Long day. Many problems. Sorry I not talk to you. Why call?" Sakol was back to Charlie Chan again.

"Sakol, my friend over on the peninsula told me about a stripper named Lan who works at Robby's. She knew Price, and I believe she knows Hollis too, I think she might know where to find Hollis right now."

"Wait. I come. Where you?" I told him where I was, and he again told me to stay where I was. The club was decorated with holiday lights and it seemed rather tacky for a strip club to have Christmas lights. I know it's small of me, but that was what I was feeling. Sakol must've run every red light and busted every speed limit there was. It seemed I'd hardly hung up the phone and locked the truck when he came wheeling into the parking lot with his blue light flashing on top of his dashboard. He didn't bother to park his car properly; instead, he left it sitting in front of the entrance, the light still flashing on his dash. "She here?" he asked.

"I haven't been inside yet. Remember, you told me to wait."

"First time obey; nice." I laughed.

Once again, the wall of noise assailed us as we stepped into the lobby. The same bouncer was standing at the front by the velvet-covered chain. The one I had a problem with the last time I was there. As he stepped forward to collect our money, he recognized me. He then pointed to the door, and I could make out his lips saying, "Get out!"

Sakol whipped out his badge and showed it to the bouncer. He crooked one of his fingers, signaling the bouncer to step outside the door. Once he shut the door, the noise dropped enough so we could talk.

The bouncer started the conversation, "What the hell do you guys want?" I didn't think being so aggressive with Sakol was a wise move on his part.

For the longest time, Sakol just stood there staring at the bouncer. Finally, the bouncer snarled, "What?"

"Give drivers license."

"Why?" The bouncer's voice was still threatening.

I guess Sakol felt this dude needed to see "The Sakol" without the dumb cop routine. In perfect English, Sakol spoke in an intimidating tone, "Did you just ask me why?" The bouncer nodded his head. "Because I said so." Sakol took a step towards the man. "Because I can have you in lockup within an hour. Because I can smell the stink of fear on you. Because, I see in your eyes you have a record, maybe even an outstanding warrant?"

I watched in disbelief as the bouncer dropped his head. Sakol tapped his finger on the man's chest, "If you have any hope of walking back into that den of noise, you'll cooperate with us. Do you understand?"

It looked like somebody had pulled the plug on the bouncer; he seemed to shrink before my eyes. Reaching for his wallet, the bouncer asked, "What do you need to know sir?" The big man was actually civil.

I spoke, "The other day I was here talking to Lan. We believe she's in danger. She might have known two men from back home. We believe they came to see her a few days ago. One man is dead and the other man killed him. Since the man we're looking for has been killing everybody who knew they were in town, we think she might be in danger. Do you know where to find her?"

The bouncer stood for a moment, and then his face brightened. "Wait here, I think I can find her address."

After he left, I asked Sakol why he'd dropped his Charlie Chan routine with the bouncer. "He balloon, need popped." And his comment made perfect sense.

The bouncer returned faster than I expected. "One of the other girls here is good friends with Suzie Wong. Excuse me, that's her stage name. She knows where Lan lives. Here's the address." The bouncer paused, and then added, "On the back of the paper is my cell phone, please call me and let me know if she's OK?"

Sakol smiled at the man, "Concern is good. We make call." The old Sakol cop was back.

After the bouncer had gone back in the building, Sakol looked at me, told me to leave my truck in the back of the parking lot and to come with him. I moved my truck and left the windows down just a crack so BJ could have some fresh air. I told her to behave herself, and I'd be right back. She licked my hand and then curled up on the passenger seat. I got in the car with Sakol. As we pulled out of the parking lot, he flipped on his siren, and we headed off to the address the bouncer had given us.

The apartments where Lan lived were attractive: surrounded by large trees with lots of green areas and a swimming pool in the middle of the compound. We found her building. Her apartment was on the third floor and when we got there, we found the door to her apartment slightly ajar. I was really tired of finding front doors left open. I shuddered to think what we would find inside.

With a sinking feeling, I watched Sakol carefully push the door open. When I stepped into the place, I noticed someone had trashed the apartment. The living room was in a state of total disarray with not one piece of furniture upright.

Somebody had broken off two dining room table legs, along with tipping the highboy on its side, leaving broken dishes scattered everywhere. A small Christmas tree was crushed under an overturned couch. To reach the hallway at the rear of the apartment, we had to climb over all sorts of stuff; at the end of the hallway, we found the bedrooms.

Lan was on her back on the bed, stripped naked with her feet and hands bound. Someone had given her a whipping with something that left marks all over her body and the bottoms of her feet were raw and bleeding. Besides the beating, she had an ugly wound in her right side which was bleeding freely. There was blood all over the bed

Sakol stepped up to her and put his finger on the side of her throat. He looked at me and said, "Call 911."

I was already a step ahead of him and I had my phone in my hand. Waiting for the emergency number to go through, I saw Lan's eyes fluttered open. When she saw Sakol, fear covered her face.

Once Sakol saw her eyes open, he immediately spoke softly to her, saying something to her in a language I didn't understand.

Lan closed her eyes and took a deep shuddering breath. While I was giving the 911 operator instructions, I went to the kitchen looking for a sharp knife. I found one, and I returned to the bedroom and cut away the nylons which were used to tie her up. While I was working on her feet, in a voice so soft

I almost couldn't hear her, she talked to Sakol. She spoke to Sakol for a long time, and he kept his ear just in front of her lips. Sakol kept nodding his head as she spoke until finally, she stopped.

Lan lay there for a moment and then Sakol gently gathered her in his arms and spoke to her again as he rocked her body. Both had tears in their eyes and once more, she whispered in his ear. Suddenly she let out a sharp cry, her body stiffened and then relaxed. I watched Sakol gently move his hand over her eyes, closing them. Lan was dead.

Sakol held her for a long time, and I heard a couple of sobs and I saw tears running down his cheeks. Something was exchanged between them, and I could tell it had affected him. I was concerned, and I asked, "Sakol, are you okay?" He looked at me with tears flooding his eyes and nodded his head. "Yes, I'll be okay. She was from my village. I knew her father. She recognized me, and she asked that I be the one to go to tell her mother and father she's dead. I told her I would."

"I'm sorry." I didn't know what else I could say to him. This was getting to be a very difficult day. Hollis' body count was climbing fast.

Sakol's voice was soft as he reminisced. "I didn't really know her. The last time I saw her she was a little girl, but her father was a friend. I had no idea they were in America. Her parents live up in British Columbia. She told me her father had helped Hollis and Price back home. The two men had helped in getting all the family out of the country when things fell apart back at the end of the war. Her father was positive the invading forces would kill him and his family since they had helped Hollis and Price.

"Hollis had been to her apartment several times and after he killed Price, he returned and told Lan about it. She said it upset him and swore he would extract as much vengeance on you as possible. He holds you responsible for Denny's death." I began to speak and then realized saying anything to Sakol about it was pointless.

Sakol continued, "Lan said Hollis discovered she was listening in on a conversation where he was telling somebody on the phone he would not let anybody catch him and he said he was going to 'the lighthouse on the island', or 'the lighthouse island', and when he caught her, he flipped out.

"Even though she hadn't heard him very well while he was talking, he went wild and whipped her. She tried to get him to stop, and she told him you had come by the club and talked to her, but she swore to him she had told you nothing. That was when he stabbed her. She told me she had no idea what he meant about any island or lighthouse. Do you have any idea?"

I thought for a moment, "No, it means nothing to me. Was she able to tell you who Hollis was talking to?"

"No. However, Lan confirmed he was the one who killed the Bottomsley woman and her nephew. The nephew hired Price and Hollis to kill Rockingham because he thought his aunt would inherit all of Slim's money. After the nephew found out about Jennifer, the nephew hired the two of them to murder the daughter too, but they never even had a chance to carry it out. Price was at your place looking for information about where to find the daughter was staying. When you got home, Price was afraid you'd recognize him, so he ran."

I still had a problem with the explanation, but perhaps time had eroded his nerve. Perhaps the cancer treatment has sapped his strength to the point he was afraid to confront me. For him, it was just easier to run. Being honest, I didn't know if I'd have stuck around, or if I was in his shoes, I'd have run.

CHAPTER THIRTY-SIX

The coroner had a few snide comments to make about coming out on a Christmas Eve, along with a comment regarding the growing number of bodies Sakol seemed to be finding. Finally, from the look on Sakol's face and a comment he made; the coroner figured out Sakol wasn't any happier to be involved than the coroner. It took the coroner several hours to deal with Lan's body before he finally ordered his men to take her away. It took about the same time before the police had finished with the two of us.

They finished with me before Sakol and I wanted to get back to the strip club and my truck, so I called a cab instead. The taxi dropped me off in front of the club and I headed back to where I was parked. When I was close to the truck, I whistled, and I was surprised when I didn't see BJ peering out the window at me. When I got to the truck, I saw her curled up in the passenger seat and after I opened the door, I saw why she wasn't moving. I saw the zip tie somebody had slipped over her neck and pulled tight; a zip tie which had made it impossible for her to breathe. Somebody had killed my dog, and I was positive who'd done it.

Time stopped. I stared down at the little body lying on the seat and I kept thinking she was going to wake up and be happy to see me. This was so sickening I finally turned away and threw up in the bushes. All I remembered after that was slamming the truck passenger door, putting down the tailgate, and just sitting there. I wanted to cry. The thing I knew I had to do was keep my mind away from the loss of Blackjack. I've no idea how long I sat there until finally I heard my cell phone ringing and I looked at the number displayed on the caller ID screen. Since I didn't recognize the number, I answered it. "Hello. Matt here."

The laughter on the other end was cold. His voice was taunting as he asked, "Did you find your pooch yet? How'd ya like my Christmas present?" The sound of his voice gave me goosebumps. Hollis continued, "Now listen buddy boy, this is the last time I'm telling you to back off. I can do anything I want, and you can't stop me. Do you hear me? Back off. Your bitch may still be alive, but I know how to get to her. And tell your little slope buddy how much I love sticking slant-eyed gooks. Both of you better leave me alone. Do you hear me? Do you hear me, Preston? I'm ready to kill you next."

His voice had risen to a hysterical scream by the end of his tirade.

How he'd gotten my cell phone number I did not understand?

I growled in my phone, "Listen you bastard, you've gone too far now. You killed my..." The last thing I heard was his laughter and then the click of him hanging up on me. The light in the phone hadn't even gone out when it rang again. I thought Hollis might call me back, but it was Sakol. "Matt?"

I went straight to the point. "BJ is dead; Hollis killed her." I couldn't help it and I gave an involuntary sob.

"Where are you?" Sakol asked.

"At the strip club."

"Stay there. I'm on my way."

I considered staying, but now the thing with Hollis was just between the two of us.

First Sharon and now BJ.

No.

This was now personal. Very personal!

If it were possible, I wanted to be the one who found Hollis.

~ ~ ~ ~ ~

Slowly I returned to my senses. I cut the zip tie off BJ, but I left her lying on the passenger seat. Memories kept trying to creep in, but I'd push them away as quickly as possible. I had to. Not only did I want my anger to stay cold, but I also wanted to hate Hollis as much as I could. There was plenty of time to remember my little Blackjack later.

So much for a Merry Christmas. Sharon was in the hospital. Jeff was in the hospital. BJ was dead, and I had no idea how to find Hollis.

I drove around for a while, trying to come up with a plan to find Hollis. I racked my brain, trying to come up with a clue. There must be a way to figure out where he might be hiding.

Finally, a thought came to mind to try and find out where he was born, or perhaps where he'd entered the service. That might be of some help; that might be a starting point.

As I rolled that idea around, I remembered a friend from the old days, and I wondered what happened to him. I drove back to my apartment and searched through my desk for an old address book I knew I had. I was positive it was somewhere in my office. Eventually, I found it and his phone number. I dialed it and to my surprise, someone answered it right away.

"Bruce, Bruce Frost?" I asked.

"Yes, who's this?"

"Good evening… er, I guess it actually is good morning. This is Matt… Matt Preston. I apologize for calling so late. And by the way, Merry Christmas."

The voice on the other end of the phone sounded happy to hear from me. "Matt? Is it really you?"

"Yep!"

"Well, Merry Christmas to you too. How long has it been? It's great to hear your voice."

"I know it's been a long time, and I apologize for not keeping in touch."

"Hey, I didn't do much better," said Bruce, laughing as he made the comment. "To what do I owe the honor of this phone call?"

"I need information." I told Bruce about Hollis and Price and all the issues involved in the case. I ended up with, "Do you have any way of getting into Hollis' file and seeing where he was from?"

"Sorry buddy, I can see you're not having the best of holidays. Give me a number to call you back and I'll see what I can find out." I gave him my cell number, and he told me he'd try to be back within the next few hours. Until then I'd just have to cool my heels.

BJ was still down in my truck, and I knew I needed to do something with her soon. I didn't care it was dark outside, actually, the darkness fit my mood better than if it had been sunny. After a lot of thought, I decided to bury BJ in the vacant lot behind the apartment. It made sense since it had been such a favorite place for her. I settled on putting her under a specific bush because I thought she'd always liked to sniff that one a little more than any of the other bushes.

I'd taken a large towel and wrapped it around her with a couple of her favorite toys before I dug the hole. As I was digging, tears streamed down my face. When I finished digging, I got down on my hands and knees and picked up her small body and held it against my body. Then I gently placed her in the hole, and I told her goodbye. Using my hands, I tenderly covered her up. There was no doubt I would really miss her. When I'd spread the last of the dirt over her, Sakol pulled up next to the vacant lot.

As Sakol walked up he said, "I thought I told you to stay at the club."

"Sorry, I wanted to get her buried, and it was something I wanted to do by myself. I hope you understand."

I could see the sorrow on Sakol's face. It was obvious he was grieving too. "I'm sorry Matt. I do understand. I know how much she meant to you."

"Thanks. Right now, I'm not letting myself think too much about her. I'll mourn her after I deal with Hollis. By the way, I called an old friend I served with back in Nam and I think he might dig up some info on Hollis. I hoped something from his past might tip us off about the lighthouse thing."

"Good idea, when friend call back?" Sakol asked.

I noticed Sakol was having a hard time keeping up the Charlie Chan routine with all that was going on. He seemed to keep slipping between the two. What with his partner shot, and then finding Bottomsley and the nephew along with Lan, my guess was that Sakol was having his own demons to deal with.

When I asked Sakol if he wanted to come in for a cup of coffee while we waited, he agreed. We sat in the front room drinking coffee waiting for the phone to ring. I noticed it was growing lighter outside when the phone finally rang, startling both of us. It was my friend, Bruce.

"Matt, Bruce here."

"What did you find out?"

"I could see some initial information from when Hollis first joined. Did you know he was from Washington State?"

"No kidding? Where?" That stunned me. I wondered if Walter knew Hollis was from around here.

"It lists his hometown as Ross Island. I didn't know you could have an island as your hometown. Do you have any idea where that's at?"

I'd written down Ross Island on a piece of paper, and then turned it, so Sakol could read it. Sakol looked at the piece of paper, looked at me and then mouthed, "Bye!" With that, he headed out the back door. I called after him to wait, but before I could end the call with Bruce, I heard his squad car start and then take off.

When I finished my call with Bruce, I tried to call Sakol twice, but he wasn't picking up. I wondered what it was about Ross Island that made him leave so quickly. I thought one way to figure it out was to find out more information on the island. I went over to my computer and searched for Ross Island. I was curious to see if there was any information which might be of use. I looked up the island, and under its history, I found my answer.

Shortly after the Civil War, the government had built a fort on the north end of the island. The government already owned the entire north end of the island because of the lighthouse; so the fort became just an extension of and including the lighthouse.

When they built the fort, the government thought they located it in a very strategic place. From the fort, they could guard all the straits out to the Pacific Ocean. Any invading ship had to come up the straights and the fort could then subject the invading ships to heavy cannon fire from the large cannons placed inside of the walls of the fort.

Once they built large battleships during WWI, the ships made stationary forts obsolete. They abandoned the fort just after the first world war. Shortly after that, they decommissioned the lighthouse. Since Hollis had grown up on the island, I was sure he knew all the best hiding places around the fort and inside the lighthouse. I wondered how much Sakol knew about the old fort and the abandoned lighthouse.

I drove to the ferry dock where I could catch a ferry to take me over to the island. While I was driving, I kept trying to call Sakol, but the calls were forwarded to voicemail.

When I pulled up to the ticket counter the attendant told me I'd lucked out, and I would catch the next ferry just before it pulled out. The ferry ride was difficult since this was the first time I was going anywhere without BJ. I kept reaching over to pet her, but she wasn't there.

At the other side, as I was pulling off the ferry, I tried one more time to call Sakol with no luck. I was getting frantic. I was worried. Finally, in desperation, I called Frank. By the way, he answered the phone I could tell he was wondering who was calling him on Christmas morning.

"Frank Morgan here."

"Frank, it's Matt, Matt Preston."

"Hey, Merry Christmas. What's up, Matt?" I hesitated, "It's about Sakol."

Frank's voice had an edge when he spoke again, "What about Sakol?"

"There was a stripper named Lan, and she worked at Robbys. Sakol knew her parents from the village where he came from too."

"And," Frank was pushing me to go faster.

"Well, someone killed her last night, or early this morning. She identified Hollis just before she passed away. It turns out Hollis was from Ross Island, and Sakol learned that Hollis might be headed over there. As Lan was dying, she said something about an old abandoned lighthouse and an old fort. I keep trying to call Sakol, but he isn't answering."

"Where are you?"

I decided Frank wouldn't be happy if he knew I was already on the island, so I told him a white lie. "I'm at the apartment burying BJ. Hollis killed her last night."

I sure hoped BJ would forgive me for using her like that. Frank was still for a moment, "Oh shit, Matt, I'm so sorry. I know how much that dog meant to you. Look, we're on our way to catch the next ferry, and I'll alert the island police, as well. I'll call you later and tell you how things turn out. Is that okay?"

"Thanks, Frank." I hung up. I knew exactly what I would do next.

CHAPTER THIRTY-SEVEN

After I got off the ferry, I drove as fast as possible up the island. I feared Sakol had caught the ferry before me and may have tried to go after Hollis by himself. I had a pretty good idea what Hollis would do to him. I was grateful it was Christmas morning and the traffic was light. A few times I think my truck went faster than it ever had in its life. I know I took some corners way too fast, and as I drifted through them, I was grateful there was no oncoming traffic. This morning Ol' Faithful earned her name.

The lighthouse is located at the rear of the old fort and when I arrived, I drove through the old gates heading towards the back. Once I reached the old fort's deserted upper parking area, I slipped the transmission out of gear and turned off the motor. My truck slowly coasted across the sloped and weed-choked parking lot. By the deplorable condition of the lot, it was obvious no one had used the area in a long time.

I let the truck continue to roll across the lot while I kept alert for any movements. It had been a long time since I'd been in Nam and had to rely on my instincts for survival. I could feel the adrenaline rush surging through my body and I carefully inspected every bush surrounding the back lot of the park.

When the truck started to go too slowly, I slipped the gearshift into second and let out the clutch to start the motor. Slowly circling the parking lot, I continued heading towards the back of the park. Even though no one had used this parking lot for several decades, I still thought it was quiet - too quiet for my taste.

Off in the distance stood the old abandoned lighthouse, looming over the landscape. Its once white tower was now grimy, weather-beaten and rust stained while most of the lower portion of the tower, and the old lighthouse tender's cabin was covered in ivy and moss.

I turned off the motor again and coasted to a stop. Hollis' old dark blue former state patrol Ford, the same one I'd seen a few nights ago when he had shot Jeff, stood abandoned. The driver's door was open, and it stood next to a pathway leading towards the old lighthouse. It appeared someone had left the car standing where it stopped near the path.

Towards the far end of the lot, sitting on four flat tires, was an old derelict truck with both its doors and hood missing. Vandals had busted out every piece of glass. I noticed a Seattle Police undercover car, also vacated, next to the old truck. It was Sakol's squad car. Since the trunk was open, I assumed he'd removed his shotgun from the trunk before he went after... after whom? From what I was seeing in the parking lot, it had to be Hollis. I had tried to call Sakol on his cell phone as I drove up the island with no luck. I didn't hold out much hope, but I'd left a message on his voicemail anyway asking him to please call me.

I hoped Sakol wouldn't put himself in a position where Hollis felt he'd have to defend himself. By now, we both knew Hollis would stop at nothing. At this stage of the game, shooting another person meant nothing to him, even another cop. Sakol probably had his shotgun with him, but that did little to ease my fears for his safety.

I pulled out the pistol I keep hidden under the passenger's seat and checked to see it was loaded and then chambered a bullet. I grabbed a handful of bullets out of the glove box and stuck them in my pocket. Taking a last look around, I bailed out of my truck at the back of the lower parking lot.

Moving as quickly as I could through the bushes up towards the derelict lighthouse, I tried to remain hidden from sight. I found even though the years had put a few pounds on my frame, a lot of the old training was coming back, and I advanced briskly towards the lighthouse.

After years of hooligans shooting out every piece of glass, none of the windows remained intact throughout the entire structure. I'd read online the lighthouse was on some list for restoration someday, they considered it a historic landmark, but as far as I could see, they had done nothing.

I carefully moved to my left as I continued to use the bushes and sand dunes to shield my approach. I didn't want to give Hollis any opportunity to catch sight of me from the lighthouse if possible. In all probability, he must have heard the motor from my truck, but I didn't need to advertise my location.

When I reached the last bunch of bushes, I'd be able to use as cover, I stopped for a moment, waiting for my heart to stop trying to jump out of my chest. It had been a long time since I'd stalked anyone. Some old training was coming back, but the fear of failure was new. I'd always had some fear in the past when I was on patrol back in country, but I'd always believed I had the upper hand. The attitude came from what I perceived as the better training if you will, which I realized was arrogant, but it was how we were trained and how I felt all during my time in SE Asia. Now years have passed, and I didn't know if the old training would help me stay alive.

I peeked around the last bush. What I saw lying on the sand in front of me realized my worst fears. There was a man on the ground, and from the size and the dark hair on top of his head, and a shotgun lying a few feet from an outstretched hand, I was afraid it was Sakol. I knew I had to extinguish those thoughts, quickly. I needed to keep a calm head, but things were becoming difficult. Try as hard as I could I found my mind awash with all the fond memories I had of Sakol. I knew I didn't have time to reminisce, and I forced myself to wrap up those thoughts. I consoled myself with the knowledge I'd have time to deal with those feelings later, however; it was becoming increasingly more difficult to stay focused. With the loss of BJ and seeing so many others who meant anything to me getting hurt, it was making it almost impossible to keep my mind clear and focused.

I realized the longer I delayed behind the bushes, the more time I was giving Hollis to become entrenched wherever he was hiding up in the lighthouse. I knew I had to make a move, and I had to make it now.

After I took a quick breath, as quickly and quietly as possible, I ran zigzag to an opening which I assumed must have been the main entrance to the lighthouse at the side of the tower. Any moment I expected to hear a gunshot, or even worse, feel the hot searing pain of a bullet tearing into my flesh.

By the time I reached the shadow of the tower, my heart was pounding in my chest again, and once more I had to force myself to take slower breaths and calm down. As I tried to settle down, I glanced back and from this new angle, I could tell it was definitely Sakol lying on the ground.

He moved slightly, groaned, and then settled down again. My heart soared to see he was still alive, for now anyway. I wanted to go to him and tell him to stay quiet. If he could just do that, then everything would be all right, but I didn't want to give Hollis any idea of how many people were here, or of my location. Since Hollis must have heard my truck drive into the parking lot, he knew there was at least one more person at the lighthouse. I found it impossible to believe he wasn't aware someone new was on site.

Several plans flipped through my mind and as I thought each one through, I discarded each in turn. It seemed the only way I could reach him was to go up the stairs wrapping around the walls of the lighthouse.

I knew the correct thing to do was to wait for help. Frank was on his way, the island police were on their way, but that wasn't good enough for me. No, this was something I wanted to do for myself. Hollis had called the tune, and he had made this a personal matter. I wasn't sure what I would do to him; I just knew I had to be the first one to see Hollis.

I quickly peeked inside the tower and then pulled my head back. What I could see of the tower was empty. The concrete steps circling around the inside of the tower were tiled and the center cavity of the lighthouse was empty from the bottom to the top. I warily slipped inside the tower and then stepped onto the first step, keeping my back tight against the wall. I could feel the cold dampness through my shirt from the tower wall as I tried to keep my body as close to the wall as possible.

Although there was a great temptation, I resisted the urge to lean forward and try to look up through the center of the tower to see if I could spot Hollis. For a brief moment, I wondered if I looked up the hollow shaft I might spot him, or better yet, be able to get a shot at him. Just as quickly though I realized there was one big flaw in my thinking. I knew if he saw me first, any advantage I might have would be lost, and in addition, he'd have a direct and easier shot down at me.

I'd just taken the next step up the stairs when a deafening noise filled the tower as Hollis fired his gun. It startled me and I thought what an idiot I was for even trying to climb up the steps. The noise trapped inside of the tower was earsplitting, and my ears rang from the loud report. I heard gunfire being returned from outside the tower, telling me someone else with a weapon had shown up, and Hollis was shooting at them. Hollis fired two more times, the noise filling the tower again with the loud bark of his gun. I didn't know what sort of gun, but from the sounds of it, it must be a large-caliber gun. I tried to take comfort in knowing he had three bullets fewer than before, but it did little to calm my nerves.

During the exchange of gunfire which masked any noise of my movement, I'd moved up several steps. I had the measure of the height of the steps down and I no longer felt the need to look down at my feet. I tentatively moved up the inside of the tower. Finally, I'd climbed up far enough and now I was in a position where I could see a little of the top floor. I'd reached a point where the next time I moved around the spiral stairs; I'd be able to see across the entire top floor. The downside was anyone on the top level would then have a clear view of me as well. Standing there wondering what to do next, Hollis stepped into my view. Instantly I pointed and fired twice using all the training Uncle Sam had provided me so long ago.

Hayward screamed and fell to the floor. As he fell, I saw him grab at one of his knees and he rolled away from the opening. Keeping my eyes on the opening above me, I moved around the stairs again until I was in full view if anyone glanced over the ridge of the top floor. With my gun held in front of me, I knew I had to take my advantage now. Without looking at my feet, I continued moving up the stairs, as quickly as possible.

Hollis was quiet now, too quiet. I continued to keep my eyes trained on the rim of the top floor where I'd seen him fall, ready to take another shot if I had an opportunity. My focus was only on watching what was above me and suddenly one stair was just different enough which caused me to trip and fall forward onto the remaining stairs. When my body hit the steps, the pain in my ribs made me gasp, and I let out a loud groan. I quickly glanced down to see what had tripped me. When I looked up, I saw Hollis looking down at me with a grin on his face, aiming his gun at me. Lucky for me I'd fallen forward with my gun hand in front and above me. Immediately I lifted my pistol and as fast as I could, I snapped off two more shots. As I fired, I saw the flash from his pistol. The roar of the two guns rang in my ears and suddenly my upper right leg went numb. I could feel it was hot and wet. I had no idea if I'd hit Hollis with my wild shots, but he'd wounded me.

I lay there waiting several minutes to see if Hollis would look again over the edge. After seeing no Hollis peering over the rim, I tried to move upward. My right leg would no longer move on its own. I knew I couldn't stay where I was; I had to move. I found by using my arms and left leg, I could crawl upward one step at a time.

Finally, I reached a point where the next stair would give me a completely unobstructed view across the top floor. I pushed myself up for a quick look, expecting to feel another hot pain strike my body again. I saw Hollis sitting with his back propped up against the tower wall. When he saw me, he lifted his gun from his lap to take a shot at me and I dropped back down as far as I could. I heard his pistol click on an empty chamber, and then a second later I felt his pistol bounce off the top of my shoulders. He'd thrown his empty gun at me. The pain caused by the dull blow made me involuntarily grunt. I wanted to look again, but I thought he might have another weapon.

The stalemate continued for a few more moments and I became aware if I didn't move soon; I would have problems from the loss of blood. It already felt as if the tower was moving on its own, and my leg was throbbing. I saw the growing pool of blood on the stone step. Reaching deep inside me, I screwed up all the strength I had left and peeked again over the rim. Hayward was holding his left arm against his body, trying to keep his shoulder from moving and losing any more blood. I was pleased to see I'd managed to hit him with one of my wild shots. There was another pistol on the ground, and I could see he was trying to load it, but doing so with great difficulty. His lower left leg was lying in a pool of blood from my bullet which had hit his knee.

I motioned for him to toss the pistol to the side and as I pulled myself up the last few stairs; he did. I never took my pistol off him. Finally, I was on the top step, resting on the concrete at the top of the lighthouse. Hollis was now leaning against the wall of the turret, his head resting on the rusted railing, while I was prone with my gun trained on him.

As I lay there, my thoughts turned to Sakol lying outside on the sand, and not knowing if he was still alive started a slow burn inside of me. Then I thought of when Hollis had shot Jeff L., and how close it had been for him. My thoughts then went to Sharon and when he shot her, how close I'd come to losing her. I knew I had to keep my thoughts away from her. Finally, I remembered BJ and all the wonderful memories of her flooded through my mind.

The anger welled up inside of me at the man lying in front of me. What his issues were with me were still unknown. But what angered me the most was why he would think he had the right to put those I cared for in harm's way? In my anger, I cocked my gun. Hollis looked at me, and then he laughed.

Eventually, his laughter faded, and he whispered, "You can't just shoot me. I'm unarmed. It's been too long since Nam. You can't just kill anyone in cold blood anymore. You're not scaring me in the least."

I kept my pistol cocked and aimed at him. "Why!" I asked. "Why did you come after me? What did I do to you?"

Hollis hissed at me, "You took away the last few weeks I should have had with Denny."

I snarled back at him, "Bullshit. You were the one who shot him."

"It was your goddamn dog that shit in that yard, and then Denny slipped and fell. His bones were so brittle from all the cancer medication he never had a fair chance. But I got even for Denny, didn't I?"

"But it was still you who shot Denny. You killed him; not me."

Hollis screamed, "I had to, there was no way I could carry him, and we promised to never leave the other behind. But it was your damn dog's fault, and that makes it yours."

"You will not put that on me, you shot your fudge packin' buddy. There was no reason to do what you did; you're just fucking crazy!"

"Shut up. Just shut up," he screamed at me.

All the pain this asshole had caused me over the past few weeks continued to wash over me. I thought about how close I'd been to losing Sharon and the pain of those thoughts brought tears to my eyes. My thoughts went to Jeff, and now I wondered if Sakol was still alive. I knew better, and I carefully stayed away from any thoughts about BJ.

Hollis looked at me and laughed harder than before. "See what I mean? See how pissed you are, but you can't do a thing. You have become quite the pussy. Too long since you had to do this…" He waved his hand at my outstretched gun, "Well, pussy, what are you going to do now?"

I tried. Honest, I tried as hard as I could to just turn and crawl back down the stairs. For some strange reason, I found I was willing to let the law deal with him.

I was fairly certain what he was trying to do to me. I figured he didn't want to spend the rest of his life in prison, and he wanted to goad me into pulling the trigger. Hollis knew once the prison population learned of his sexual orientation, he was in for a difficult time. He would spend the rest of his life in hell. He wanted me to end it right there. In his mind he felt since Price was gone there was nobody left, nobody left to take care of him and make sure he wasn't left behind alive. He would keep pushing until he pushed me to shoot him, and the problem was I really wanted to. Every fiber inside me wanted to even the score, for everything he'd done to me, and everything he'd done to everyone I cared for.

If he hadn't called me a fucking pussy again, I probably would have crawled away. He called me a pussy again, and I wanted him to shut up! I wanted him to leave me alone. "Pussy. Pussy. Pussy." He chanted, and that's when I shot him. Shot him right in the arch of his right foot. I watched as his body jumped and he screamed in pain.

I hate to admit it, but I got a lot of satisfaction from causing him so much pain. He reached down as best he could to grab the foot, and with the blood oozing through his fingers he swore at me again, screaming now how he'd enjoyed shooting Jeff.

He leaned towards me, screaming, "My only regret is your cop buddy didn't die." And I shot him in the arch of his left foot. That was for Jeff L. Now he was screaming at the top of his lungs. I knew this wasn't what he wanted. He wanted one bullet; he wanted everything to end quickly. He wasn't supposed to feel the pain. It was supposed to end as it had for Price, a bullet and then the eternal sleep.

I could feel my world tilting and I knew I probably would pass out shortly. Hollis continued screaming at me. In the distance, I heard more sirens, and I knew it was over. It was time for me to see if I could crawl down the stairs. There was no way Hollis would crawl down the tower and make an escape. His time had run out.

I would have made it this time, except now Hollis was screaming at me about Blackjack. Hearing her name released the flood. No longer could I keep the memories at bay. His tirade brought back all the memories of my sweet wonderful dog, and I no longer tried to stop them, I allowed them to flow through my mind. I remembered all the times we rode together in the car, all the walks at night, the nights with her sitting in my lap as I looked across the lake and up the canal. I remembered everything I could about her, and I allowed myself to wallow in my grief for her I'd worked so hard up to that point to put aside. Of course, what hurt the most was the thought I'd never see her again, never hold her again. I thought about how this pig had stolen her away from me.

His voice intruded on my thoughts. As I focused on his voice, I could hear him telling me how he'd enjoyed killing BJ. He told me about how he had paid her back for causing Denny to fall and break his leg. Hollis described in careful detail how much he'd enjoyed slipping the zip tie over her head and then watching her struggle for breath.

The sirens had stopped, and I could hear people running across the parking lot. I could hear people shouting just outside the bottom of the tower. But it didn't matter anymore. His last comment about BJ was the final straw. I aimed my pistol between his eyes and slowly pulled back the hammer. Hollis could see the decision I'd made in my eyes. He realized he'd gone too far, and now I would grant him his wish. I was ready to pull the trigger.

However, now that he realized he really would die, he was having a change of heart. His mouth formed the word "no" as he comprehended I was really going to pull the trigger. I was going to grant him his wish and he would die. It was time he paid for what he'd done to BJ and I was the one who got to settle up.

I squeezed the trigger and the last bullet in my gun nailed him directly between his beady little eyes, stopping the short scream coming from his lips. As if in slow motion, I saw the hole appear in his forehead, and then his head snapped back and I watched as the back of his head exploded, and he fell on his side. I can't describe the feelings the surged through my body, but my mind was positive of one thing. The asshole was dead.

My gun slipped from my hand and fell onto the stone floor. My tears flowed, but I found killing Hollis didn't help ease the pain of losing BJ. The pain of her loss was still there. However, what I found satisfying was the way things were. Hollis was dead, and no trick lawyer would persuade a jury he was not guilty. There might have been poetic justice if Hollis had spent the rest of his life in prison, but I'd ended it. As far as I was concerned, I'd served out the proper justice.

I felt everything slipping away, and in the background, I heard people shouting. There was the sound of people coming up the steps, and as I laid my head on the top stair, I felt the cold stone against my wet cheek.

As the lights faded, my last thoughts were, "BJ, sweetheart, that was for you! I love you, and I miss you. Sleep well little one! I will see you over the rainbow."

EPILOGUE

It was May 2000, and January had passed without the world ending. Elevators didn't plunge downwards, stoplights kept working, ATM machines kept spitting out money and all the computers kept things on track. The world had been saved and all the doomsayers had been proven wrong. And the best part of it was I still had an extra pound of coffee in the freezer.

I'd been in the hospital when January 1st happened, but when I finally woke up, the world was still spinning, Sharon was recovering, Sakol was recovering, Jeff L. was recuperating, however, the police wanted to discuss with me what happened on Ross Island on Christmas Day. At least most of the things going on were good.

On this beautiful May morning, Sharon and I were sitting in the sun's warmth on the ferry deck, and the heat felt good on my thigh. Other than a slight limp, I'd recovered from my gunshot wound. I was still doing therapy, but the outlook was good, and the pain was infrequent. With Sharon's head resting on my shoulder, the two of us stood there holding hands, watching the ferry dock fade off into the distance.

I glanced to my left, "Wanna cup of coffee?" I asked Sharon.

Her smile warmed my soul. "Sure, you buying?" Sharon slipped her arm around my waist and gave me a hug.

"For you, anything, Doll." And she knew I was telling her the truth, and she hugged me once more.

After we got our hot drinks, we made our way back down to my new truck. Ol' Faithful had finally given up the ghost, and I felt obligated to buy a different truck. The new one had a lot more bells and whistles than Faithful, but for some reason, I missed Ol' Faithful. I'll admit one thing. I don't do well with change.

As I unlocked the truck, it occurred to me I hadn't come up with a name for this truck. For now, it was just "the new truck." Not a lot of zip I'll admit, but I was having a problem coming up with a fitting name. Sharon suggested perhaps I was growing up, and no longer needed to name my cars. Guess what, what I said to her and what I thought were two different things.

When I opened the door for Sharon for her to step into the truck, she had to fight for her seat. The two puppies we'd bought a few weeks ago were settled in and it seems they felt since we had left them in the truck, it entitled them to the front seat. It was theirs.

And you ask, "How did we end up with two dogs?" Well, that's a story by itself. A few days after the hospital released us, Sharon took me for a ride to a farm way out in the sticks. The farm was also a kennel, and they specialized in breeding Cocker Spaniels.

Sharon had called ahead and found out one of their show females had just had a litter of nine and they were ready for adoption. They informed Sharon all of them were available.

When we got there, the owner, a pleasant woman named Alice greeted us. Alice was a large round woman with rosy cheeks and curly white hair who was all smiles, and she just looked like a dog-breeding person. She explained how I would not pick out a puppy, instead, we'd sit on the floor, interact with them, and one of them would pick me. That was the only way she would allow me to adopt one of her dogs. Since I knew what she was telling us was true, I agreed.

When she opened the cage, a pile of wiggling puppies greeted us. Seeing all those beautiful puppies made my eyes water. To avoid any embarrassment, I had to look away quickly. Sharon seemed to sense how I was feeling, and she slipped her arms around me and hugged me. As I've said before, there's a reason she's such a damn good nurse.

Alice, Sharon, and I were down on the floor when the puppies came bounding out of their cage. There were black dogs, chocolate colored dogs, and two of them were blond, which I was told is called buff colored. One of the blond male puppies went at once to Sharon, and pawed at her leg, wanting her to pick him up. Sharon picked him up and held him in front of her face. Once the puppy was close to her face, he kept lunging forward, trying to lick her, and when she finally tucked the puppy under her chin, you could hear the grunts of happiness across the room. I couldn't tell who was happier, Sharon or the puppy.

I noticed one little female chocolate-colored puppy with pale tan eyebrows waiting off to one side. The other puppies seem to have pushed her off and when I stuck my finger out towards the female, she carefully licked the tip. As I pulled my hand back towards me, she followed my hand. Once she was beside my leg, she put her paws on my thigh and tried to pull herself up. I helped her out, picked her up, and sat her in my lap. I looked over at Sharon and saw the puppy she'd picked up was now fast asleep in her arms.

Finally, the one in my lap grew restless and tried to stand on my legs, wanting to gain access to my chest. I lifted her up, and once she was close enough to my face, she reached up and chewed on my mustache. This was exactly what BJ had done when she was happy and content with me. A sob escaped and I could feel the tears flowing down my face. The puppy stopped chewing on my mustache and licked away the tears running down my cheeks. Her rough little tongue lapped at the tears, bringing even more tears to my eyes. There was still a big hole in my heart left from losing BJ, but this little critter in my arms was trying her best to fill the void. As I sat there, holding the puppy, I felt I'd found my new dog, or more correctly, my new dog had found me.

I asked Alice if she'd consider letting us purchase two dogs since it was plain to see two of her puppies had adopted Sharon and I. Alice seemed touched by my display of emotion at the new puppy and remembering BJ. Alice smiled at me, and replied, "I think these two might have the best homes out of the entire litter. I'd love for the two of you to have them. I've never seen a puppy go to a new owner more quickly than those two went for the two of you. It just proves the puppy will pick the new owner, not the other way around."

Now as we tried to step into the truck, we had to force our two puppies to move from Sharon's seat to mine. Then I had to fight with them and coax them to move, so I could get inside the vehicle. Once we were all settled in, Sharon and I endured licks and kisses from the two. They needed to show us they were happy we were back. After all, we must've been gone at least ten minutes. Since mine was the color of a coffee bean, I'd taken to calling her Beanie. Her full registered name was something like Cinnamon Miss the Sixth, or some such thing, which I knew I'd never call her. She was now Beanie or Bean for short.

As I sat in the truck petting my puppy and looking at Sharon, I realized how happy I was with my life right now. I don't know what I did to deserve such a good life, but I was at peace. Moreover, the main reasons I was so at peace were sitting next to me and curled up in my lap.

~ ~ ~ ~ ~

When I pulled up to the gravel parking place, I saw Walter coming out of the woods. After I got out, he came up to me, and I extended my hand. He pushed my hand away and wrapped his arms around me. "God am I glad to see you. When I heard what happened, I was so worried." As he pulled back, I saw tears in the corners of his eyes.

"You know by now, I'm indestructible." I joked.

Walter grinned at me, "Bullshit, remember I was the one who loaded your sorry ass on the chopper back in Nam." And we both laughed. When I introduced him to Sharon, I felt stunned at the way he held out his arms to her. I'd never considered Walter as a touchy-feely kind of person, but he wanted to hug both of us. Sharon seemed to think nothing about hugging him back, either. She tipped her head back and looked up at Walter. In his gruff voice, I heard him tell her, "Looks like both of us have saved this bum."

Sharon smiled up at Walter, and murmured, "Yes, but it would seem he also has saved both of us as well. You seem happy here Walter, and I know I've never been happier since Matt and I've been together."

Walter by now had noticed the two little dogs pawing at his legs, and he reached down to pick one up. We introduced him to the two new members of our family, as he hugged and scratched both of them behind their ears. When he finished becoming acquainted with our new puppies, we headed off for his cabin. Because the dogs' legs were so short, Sharon and I didn't have a problem carrying the two most of the way to the cabin. But I was so happy to have Beanie in my life and it didn't matter.

Thien was standing on the deck when we arrived. She went to Sharon first and the two of them hugged each other for a long time, and then finally stepped back. Both of them were a little misty eyed

Thien spoke first, "I'm so glad to see Matt has somebody in his life. The last time he was here, I could tell he wanted you but was afraid to do anything about it. For all he's done for Walter and me, I love him just about as much as I love Walter. However, I've been so sad for him. He has such a large heart, and he really needs somebody in his life."

Sharon smiled and hugged Thien again, "Matt told me he'd talked to you about me the last time he was here. I thank you for helping him understand how I feel about him, and how he feels about me."

Just then, we heard a baby crying inside the cabin. Thien walked over to the door and picked up the small infant. Without giving it a second thought, Thien opened her blouse and moved a breast to the baby's mouth. The baby stopped crying at once. Thien brought the child back to where we were all standing. Without removing her breast from the feeding infant, she turned, so Sharon could look at the baby's face. Looking up at me, Thien said, "This is Matthew. Matthew Chan McLaughlin."

I felt stunned. "Why did you name him Matthew?"

Thien smiled, "Because, without you, there would be no baby or cabin. Walter would probably be dead from a drug overdose. I'd be living back in Seattle, sad because Water was dead. Everything that's here is because of you. What other name could we call our son? This is the son you helped create!"

It seemed my eyes were leaking again. Ever since the afternoon in the lighthouse tower, my emotions had become very difficult to keep in check. The baby had released Thien's nipple, and she handed the baby to Sharon. Thien stepped up and wrapped her arms around me and softly told me, "I want to thank you. Thank you for what you did for Walter. Thank you for bringing Sharon here to meet us and thank you for being such a wonderful person."

With tears brimming in my eyes, I looked down at her. "I don't know if you'll ever understand, but helping Walter was something I needed to do. More than just saving my fat ass, he allowed me to help a person do something. I expected nothing in return, I just wanted to help Walter. Who knew it would turn out this way? You with the baby, the cabin, and you helping me see I needed Sharon in my life. I'm the one who is grateful and who owes you."

Thien's eyes were now brimming as well, and she reached up and pulled my head down. Her lips were soft and gentle on mine. The kiss had passion, but not of a sexual kind. I could feel in her kiss how she felt about me. It was a strange kiss, but I understood why she kissed me, and what it meant. Her voice was just a whisper, "I love you, Matt. For everything you have done for us, I love you." I am happy I have them as friends.

~ ~ ~ ~ ~

With his great talent in woodworking, Walter had built two large oversized chairs which were sitting on the deck. The chairs were amazingly comfortable and now the two of us were sitting with our legs stretched out, watching the sun slip behind the far mountain peak while turning the clouds various shades of pink and orange. Far in the distance, we could hear the soft soothing sounds of the pounding surf. A lone eagle had just soared overhead for a few moments, given a mighty screech, and then headed off to its nest some-where. The evening was one of great beauty and comfort. I'd brought a bottle of excellent Scotch with me, and Walter and I were working on making a serious dent in it. He leaned over and handed me the pipe packed with some of his special homegrown, and asked me, "Do you mind if I ask you a few questions about how things ended?"

I knew this would happen eventually, and I felt prepared as much as I ever would be. "I think I know where you want to go, and being honest with you, this will be the first time I've talked about it with anyone. Anyway, I think I'm ready to talk about what happened."

"Well, I see Sharon recovered." Walter commented.

"Yes, and you've no idea how worried I was." I replied.

"I know Hollis shot your two police buddies. How did that turn out?"

I took a long pull on the pipe and handed it back to Walter. I let the smoke slowly release from my lungs, feeling the high spreading through my body. "Jeff has recovered, and he's up for Captain." Walter looked over at me and grinned, giving me a thumbs-up. "They're considering Frank for the Chief of Police position since the old one has retired, and I think he'd be an excellent Chief." Walter took a big puff and handed the pipe back to me.

"Sakol recovered, then took time off and went to find Lan's father. I heard from Jeff L. that Sakol had found the father up in Canada. I believe he said somewhere in Vancouver, British Columbia. The last I heard was that Sakol was considering retiring from the force. I hope not 'cause he really is a great cop.

"Jeff L. said Sakol was having problems reconciling in his mind his relationships with people like Mouse. Sakol's problem is he's not really a black and white type of person. He sees shades of grey, and if you're a cop, you need to keep your perspective more black and white."

I paused a moment, as I lit the pipe. A long pull ensued, and then I continued, "Speaking of perspectives, I've had to do a lot of soul searching."

"About what?" Walter asked.

"Revenge. About what I did up in the tower. Is revenge always wrong? Did I have a right to become Hollis' judge, jury, and executioner?"

Walter held out his hand for the pipe and I handed it to him. Pausing before he lit it, he remarked, "I think you're asking the wrong person, Matt. Why would you ask me?"

"You knew them both, what they were like, and you understand how Hollis could do the things he did. I just wonder if you can condone righting an injustice outside of the law. I want to think Hollis drove me to the point where I shot him. But now I've thought it through, I know I went up into the lighthouse with the specific intent of making sure I got revenge. I've admitted to myself I wanted him dead, and it was what I set out to do. And that bothers me. I thought I left those attitudes and feelings back in Nam.

"I believe if Hollis had been returned back to Seattle alive, the Feds would have snatched him away, probably set him up someplace new to keep him quiet about the past, and he'd have just died peacefully. Maybe. Anyway, the bottom line was I wanted my revenge, and well, as I said, it bothers me. A lot."

Walter grunted, and I could tell he would say something. I reached over, took his arm, and told him, "It's okay. You're the only one I can think of I could tell this to, and who might understand. After some of the shit we did in Nam, well, it seems strange how much Hollis got to me. But I had to tell you."

"Thanks, Matt. And I really understand how you feel. Anyway, finish your story."

"By the time they got Hollis' body back to the morgue in Seattle," I interrupted my story, "Hey! I almost forgot. You should have seen how fat Hollis was. I bet he was pushing a good 300 plus, and I heard it was a real bitch bringing his body down from the tower." Walter laughed at the image of them moving Hollis's body.

"Any idea what happened, I mean for him to become so heavy?" Walter asked.

"No, I've no idea, and I guess we'll never know either. It wasn't from overeating because Denny boy was dead. This was fat put on over a long time."

"Sounds like if you hadn't ended things when you did, a heart attack would have taken care of him, eventually."

"Anyway, I was right about one thing. There were several government agencies there to take possession of the body. Surprise!" We both laughed. "This didn't surprise me in the least." I said with a bitter tone in my voice. "Frank knew it would happen and had resigned himself to that fact.

"Since it was just Hollis and me on top of the tower, and Hollis wasn't in any condition to say my story wasn't true, I lied and told them I shot him in self-defense. No one ever said anything about Hollis' empty pistol next to his leg, or that another empty pistol was on the stairs behind me.

"When I was in the hospital, Sakol came to my room to ask me how it ended up in the tower. I carefully let him know I was aware I shouldn't have gone up there, and I knew what was happening when I pulled the trigger. I told him I knew I had a choice when I shot him. Sakol nodded his head, told me the conversation never took place, and I haven't seen him since."

I fiddled with the pipe some more and handed it off. "Turns out Slim was going to become a silent partner with Wheeler. Slim had a new S Corporation all set up to fund the deal. When Slim heard there could be problems with the city, he told Wheeler he wanted to back out of the arrangement. Wheeler had been on the phone all day trying to keep Slim from backing out on the day they killed him. When Wheel found out about Slim's demise, because he was so involved with that business deal with Slim, he was sure he would become a suspect in Slim's death. All he was trying to do was distance himself from the entire mess. Wheel was lying through his teeth. I think he'll have to pay a fine to keep out of jail, but the upside of it all is things have worked out with the city, and Wheel gets to keep his marina.

"Wheel has sold me a space, and because of that, I now have permanent moorage. Scott thinks he has a buyer, or maybe even two, for the houseboat. In addition, it also turns out one night when one of the other tenants was coming home late, he actually saw Dudley Bell sneaking away from the houseboat after he'd ransacked the place looking for a will.

"I don't know how Hollis found out that Slim had a daughter, but once he had that knowledge, he told Dudley about Jennifer. At that point, Dudley was desperately trying to see if he could find a will to see what it said. He hoped that if possible, he could destroy it before Jennifer could do anything about it.

"As for Jennifer, she's back in Europe with her two lovers, and she ended up with all of Slim's money. Well, not all of it. Turns out, she felt she owed me something, for all I did. I tried to tell her I wanted none of Slim's money. Since she had planned on giving Bottomsley part of the estate, she ended up creating a trust fund which puts a vulgar amount of money every month in my bank account."

I was still trying to find a way to tell Walter I would split the monthly checks and give half to him. Call it a start on a college fund for Walter's son or something like that. I just knew I wanted to share the money with Walter and Thien.

The sun was now gone, and the two of us sat in the dark on the deck in silence. We could hear Sharon and Thien in the cabin talking and taking care of little Matt. Bean was lying there curled up in my lap asleep, and the other puppy, Max, was asleep in Walter's lap.

Walter leaned over and placed his hand on my arm again. "By the way, I don't know if I've ever really told you how grateful I am?"

"About what?" I asked.

"I know you were under pressure to tell the police how you learned about Price and Hollis. For doing that for me, I'll always be grateful. You already know how thankful I'm about the rest of everything. "You've no idea how happy I am things have turned out so well for you. Matt, you deserve it. I still have the bad dreams, but when I wake up Thien is there. As she holds me between those silken thighs of hers and she makes things all better. Now I have new memories to replace the old bad ones." Walter leaned over, we touched glasses, and we both took a deep sip of the excellent Scotch we were drinking. Walter continued, "I hope Sharon does the same for you."

I wasn't ready to share this with Walter, but Sharon had already done that for me, and best of all, I knew she'd do it again. It was after my episode in the lighthouse with Hollis, when I'd killed him and after they had released Sharon and me from the hospital. A few nights later, I had a bad dream. One of my worst. The dream involved Hollis and Price, and even Walter was part of the dream. We were all back in the jungle, and when I woke up, I was screaming, shaking and bathed in sweat.

I don't really know how Sharon did it so quickly, but suddenly I was aware she was on top of me and had her arms and legs wrapped around me. She was kissing my face, whispering in my ear telling me it was okay, and she was there for me. At first, it was her soft voice which helped calm me. Then I noticed her sweet nakedness wrapped around me. She kept whispering in my ear, "Remember this, this is now, this is real. The past is gone, and you are okay. Think about me. I love you. I love you."

Sharon was right, the dreams are slowly going away, and instead, the most erotic dreams about her have replaced them. Sharon seems to know when one of the bad dreams is about to happen, so she'll wake me, and wrap her body around me.

I still don't know what I did in a past life to deserve such a great life this time around, but I'm grateful. That's what is the most important, being grateful. Share your joy with the Universe and it comes back stronger and better.

Even though I might carp about a lot about things, I am appreciative.

Truly, I'm very grateful.

And if this is what the new century will be like, I'm all for it.

THE END

Well, maybe not, but it's a good place to leave the story now.

LIST OF CHARACTERS

Albert Bradson, Lawyer, Matt's attorney

Art, Works for Matt, Repairs Matt's cars

Audrey Bottomsley, Slim's Half-sister

Blackjack, BJ, Matt's dog

Bob Silversmith, Lawyer, Matt's Attorney

David Wheeler, Poker Player

Denny Price, Bad guy, Vietnam Veteran

Don Green, Lawyer, Bottomsley's Lawyer

Dudley Bell, Bottomsley's Nephew

Elmo Rockingham, Slim, Houseboat owner

Frank Morgan, Police chief

Heyward Hollis, Bad guy, Vietnam Veteran

Jeff L. Davenport, Police detective, Childhood friend of Matts

Jennifer Rockingham, Slim's daughter

Julius Epstein, Lawyer, Slim's attorney

Lan, Suzi Wong, Stripper works at Robbies

Marvin Galante, Lawyer, Slim's attorney

Sakol Hasaphonhse, Police detective, Jeff's partner

Scott, Poker Player, Matt's friend, real estate broker

Sharon Crowell, Matt's love interest

Steve Fox, Mouse, Friend of Sakol

Thein McLaughlin, Walter's wife

Walter McLaughlin, Matt's buddy from Viet Nam

ACKNOWLEDGMENTS

I would like to thank Kevin G Summers for his expertise in formatting this book and his preparation of the manuscript. Thank God for people who understand our computer world. I'd also like to thank him for a great cover. Don't know where he found the picture, but those are the exact houseboats I had in mind when I started this novel. In addition, in the distance is Lake Union and as you can see from the bare limbs of the trees, it is fall or winter.

I'd like to thank the various residents of Admiralty Yacht Club where who read the original *Houseboat* and still encouraged me to keep writing. I've toned down some of the passages from the original text to keep the story more acceptable for a wider audience. Thank you for all of those who encouraged me to keep writing. Without your reassurance, I would never have allowed any of my books to be published.

I wish to acknowledge my little black Cocker Spaniel, Buttons who sadly is no longer with us. She gave me the idea for BJ, and I miss them both.

Finally, I want to express my gratitude to my wife, Sandy, who always had been urging me to finish *Houseboat* and then do something with it. Without her support, this story would still be lurking the depths of my computer, never to see the light of day. I also thank her for her encouragement to keep me writing. Actually, I thank all of you who have inspired me to keep writing. Every one of my novels is a testament to your faith and confidence in me.

I would like to invite all of you to read the next adventures of Matt Preston. *Code Name; Crescent,* which is available as well as the rest of my novels.

Please enjoy…

Until next time... good night.
Okay, that ends this adventure.
Pull back the covers darling, I am on my way...

ABOUT THE AUTHOR

Paul lives in North Fort Myers Florida with his wife, Sandy, his biggest fan and their American Cocker Spaniel, (Samantha) who is known as 'Our little girl'.

Born and raised in Seattle and now transplanted to Florida Paul keeps busy being involved with community events and working on an HO scale model train layout besides his writing.

A graduate of Western Washington University in education, Paul taught for 4 years and became self-employed when he left teaching. Over the years Paul has owned and operated several businesses where he met many interesting people who always seem to confide the most astounding things to him hence the varied knowledge of people that he uses to create his fascinating characters.

The dog in this novel actually existed and spent every day going to his various accounts during his business day, however, luckily her life didn't end like BJ's. There are many stories that can be told about Buttons, the real dog, and ones of her adventures too.

Houseboat grew out of a story idea Paul had many years ago while driving from one business appointment to another. Over the years he would work on the story in bits and pieces until retiring, in 2010, when he focused more of his time and energies toward finishing the novel.

THANK YOU FOR READING

Thank you for reading this book. If you enjoyed it, please post a review on one or more of the websites or pages listed below. Also please tell your friends about my novel. (If you didn't like it just let Matt Preston know... just kidding! An author lives for feedback of all kinds.) By the way, word of mouth and reviews are an independent author's lifeblood and best allies.

Amazon:
www.amazon.com/author/paulshadinger

Goodreads:
www.goodreads.com/pshadingerauthor

Readers Favorite:
www.readersfavorite.com/book-review/Houseboat

To contact Paul Shadinger:
pshadingerauthor@outlook.com

Follow Paul Shadinger on:
www.facebook.com/pshadingerauthor
Twitter: @paulshadinger

Also Check for Events and Announcements on:
www.paulshadingerauthor.com

43914033R00197